BOOZE, BROADS, & BULLETS

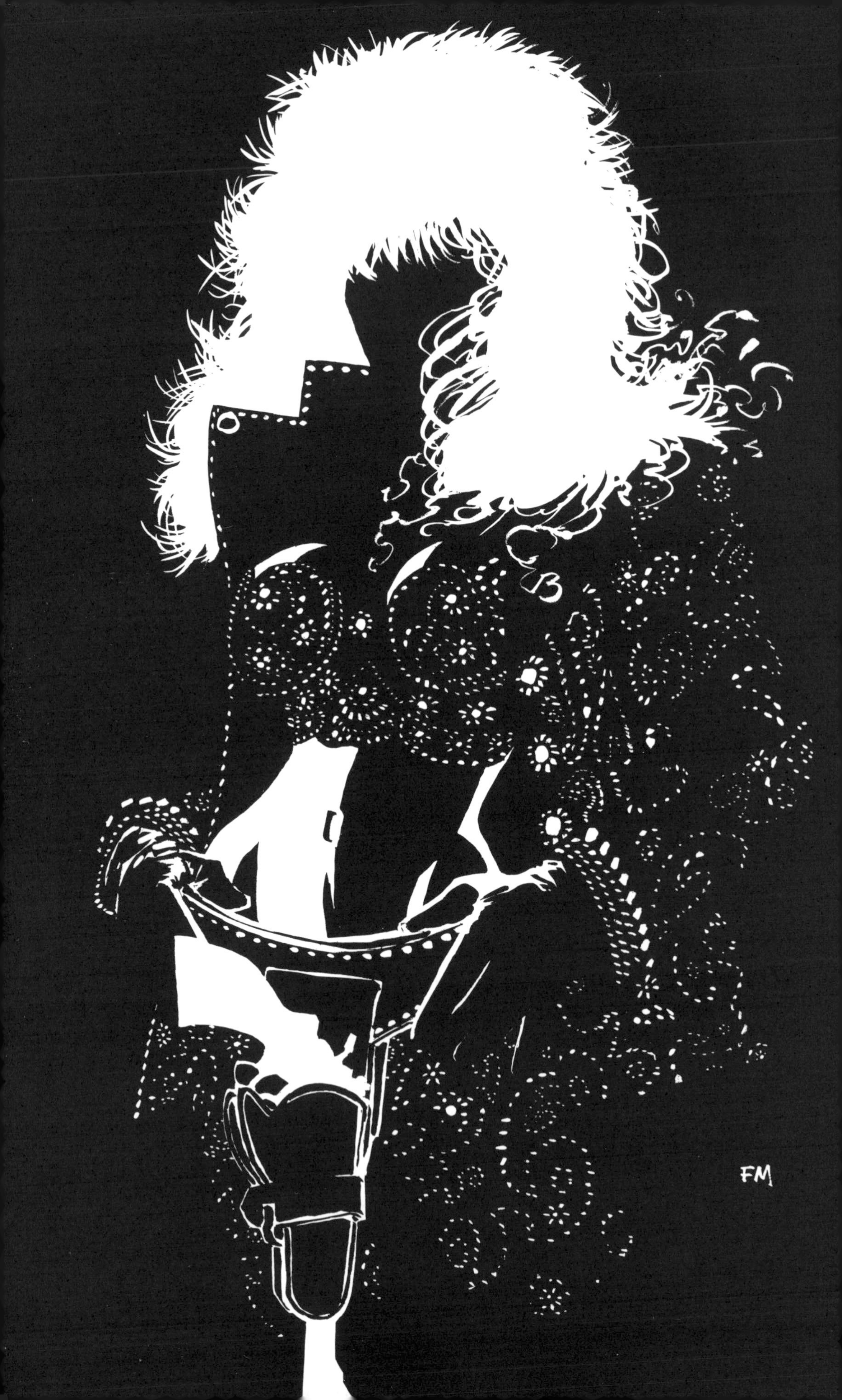
FM

FRANK MILLER

BOOZE, BROADS, & BULLETS

ELEVEN *SIN CITY* YARNS

DIANA SCHUTZ editor

MARK COX book design

MIKE RICHARDSON publisher

DARK HORSE
MAVERICK™

This book collects Sin City *stories from* The Babe Wore Red and Other Stories; Silent Night; A Decade of Dark Horse; Lost, Lonely, & Lethal; Sex & Violence, *and* Just Another Saturday Night.

Published by Dark Horse Comics, Inc.
10956 SE Main Street
Milwaukie, Oregon 97222

www.darkhorse.com

First edition: December 1998
ISBN: 1-56971-366-9

10 9 8 7 6 5 4
Printed in China

SIN CITY®: BOOZE, BROADS, & BULLETS

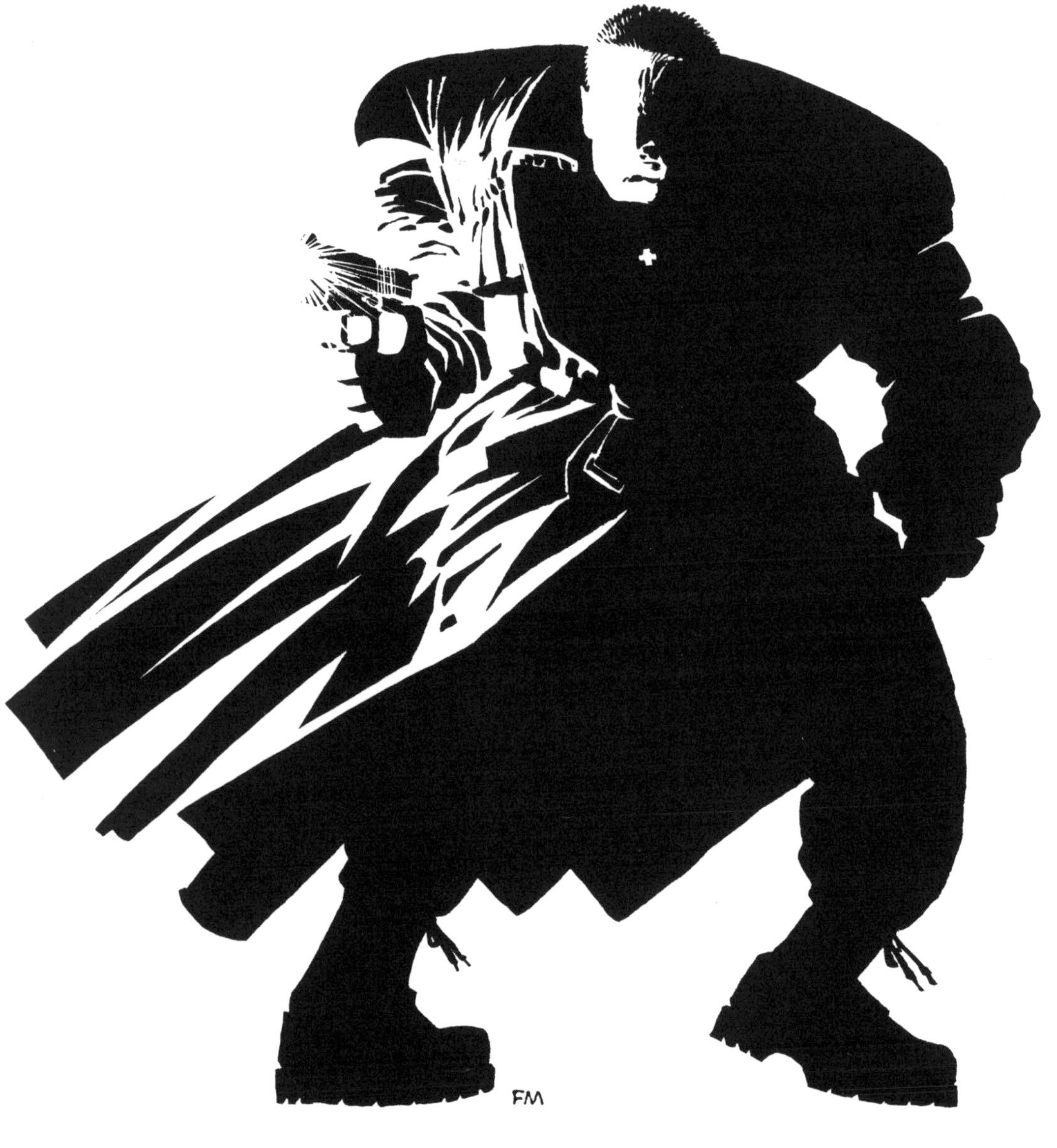
FM

CONTENTS

All stories written and illustrated by
FRANK MILLER

Cover color for **Sin City: Silent Night** and **A Decade of Dark Horse** by **Lynn Varley**

Original stories edited by **Bob Schreck, Randy Stradley, Peet Janes, Kris Young, Barbara Kesel,** and **Diana Schutz**

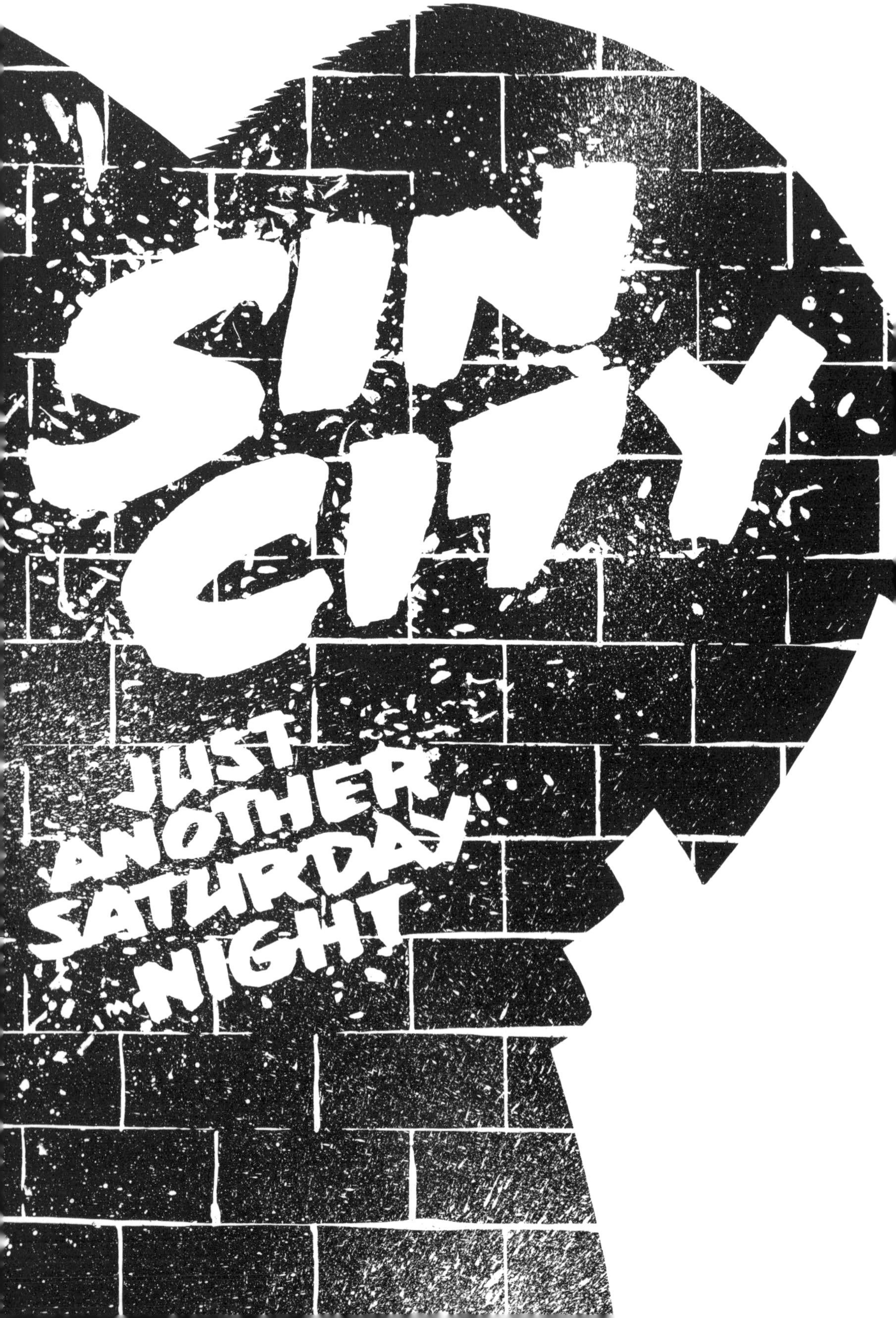
SIN CITY
JUST ANOTHER SATURDAY NIGHT

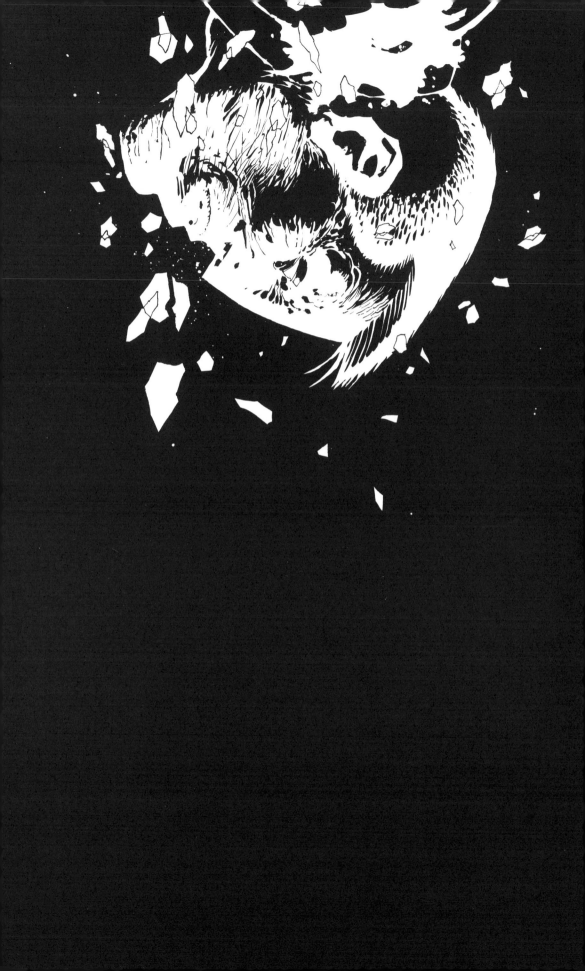

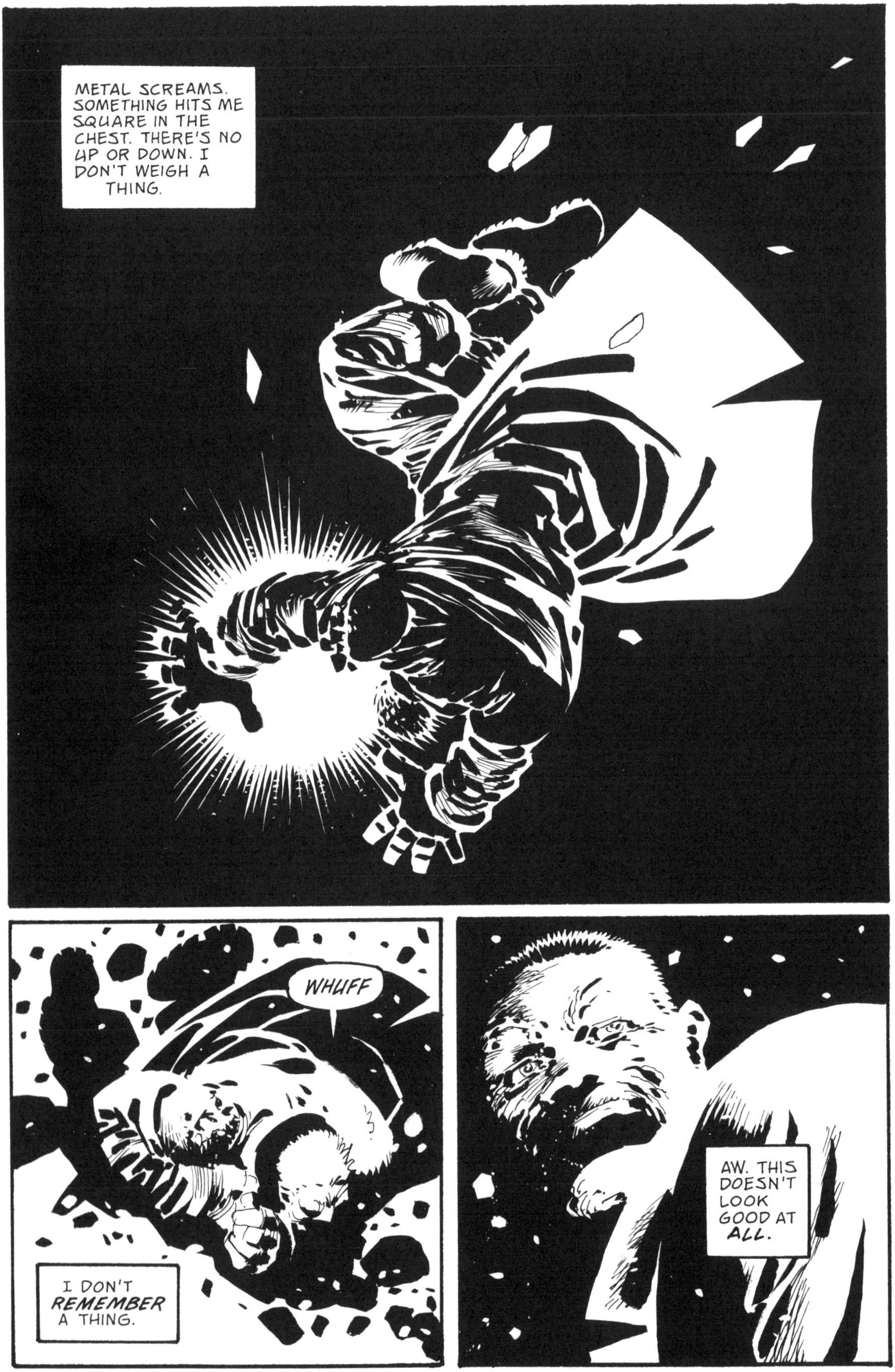
METAL SCREAMS. SOMETHING HITS ME SQUARE IN THE CHEST. THERE'S NO UP OR DOWN. I DON'T WEIGH A THING.
WHUFF
I DON'T *REMEMBER* A THING.
AW. THIS DOESN'T LOOK GOOD AT *ALL*.

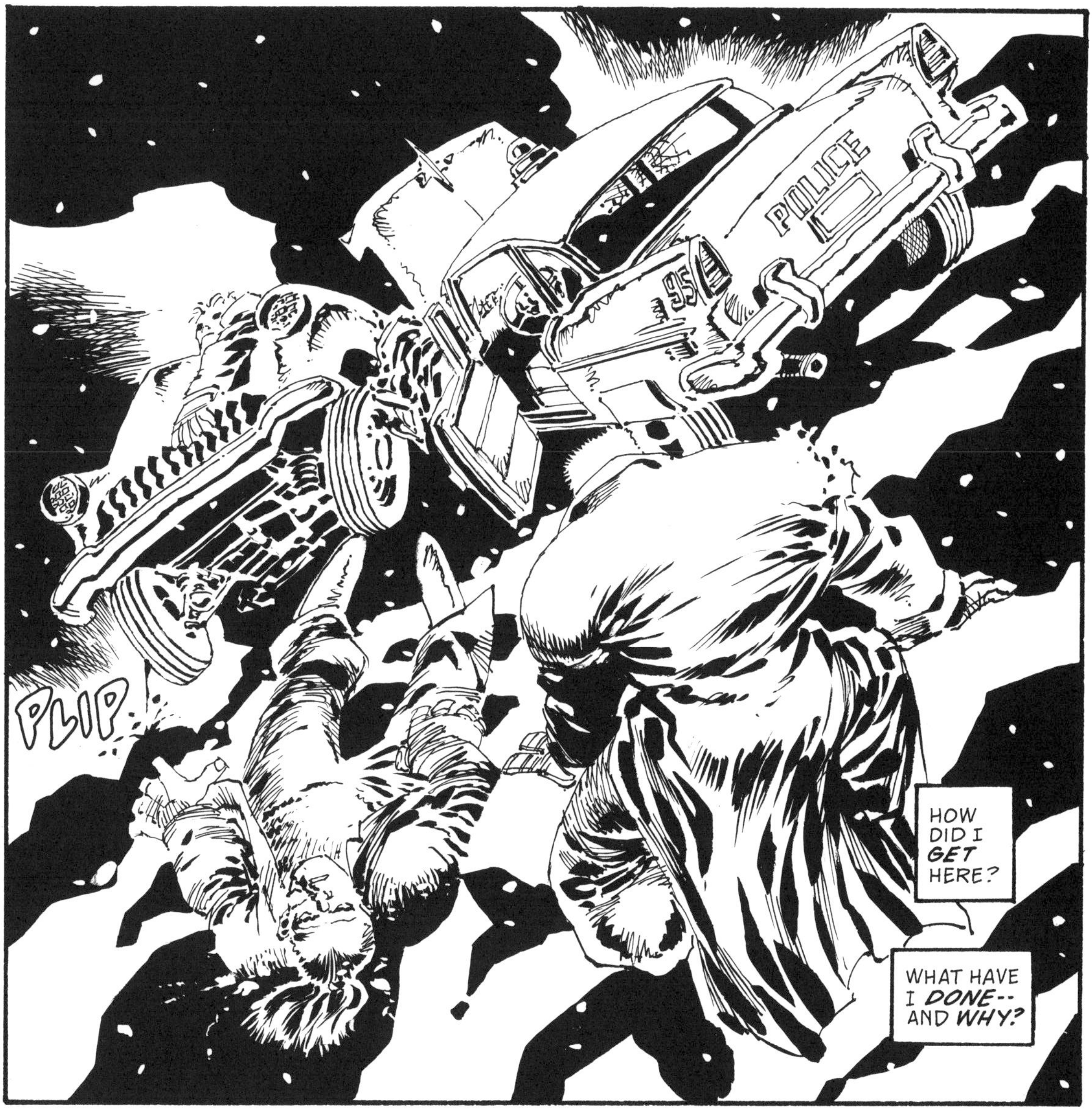
POLICE
95
PLIP
HOW DID I GET HERE?
WHAT HAVE I DONE-- AND WHY?

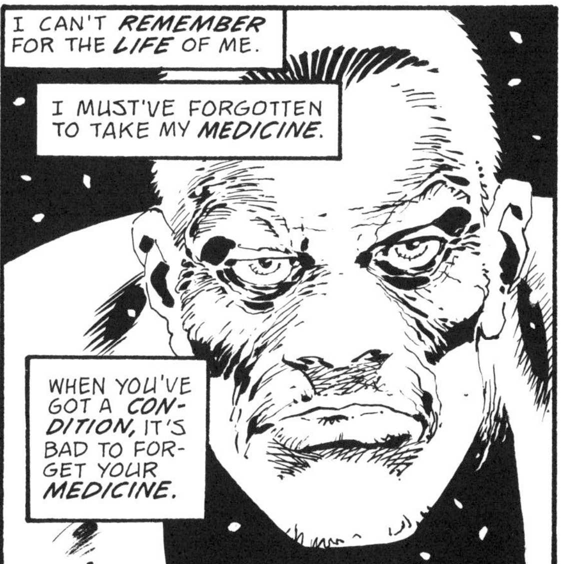
I CAN'T REMEMBER FOR THE LIFE OF ME.
I MUST'VE FORGOTTEN TO TAKE MY MEDICINE.
WHEN YOU'VE GOT A CON-DITION, IT'S BAD TO FOR-GET YOUR MEDICINE.

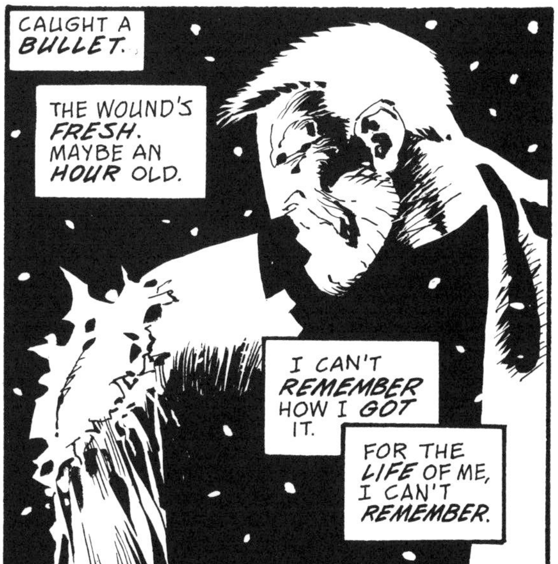
CAUGHT A BULLET.
THE WOUND'S FRESH. MAYBE AN HOUR OLD.
I CAN'T REMEMBER HOW I GOT IT.
FOR THE LIFE OF ME, I CAN'T REMEMBER.

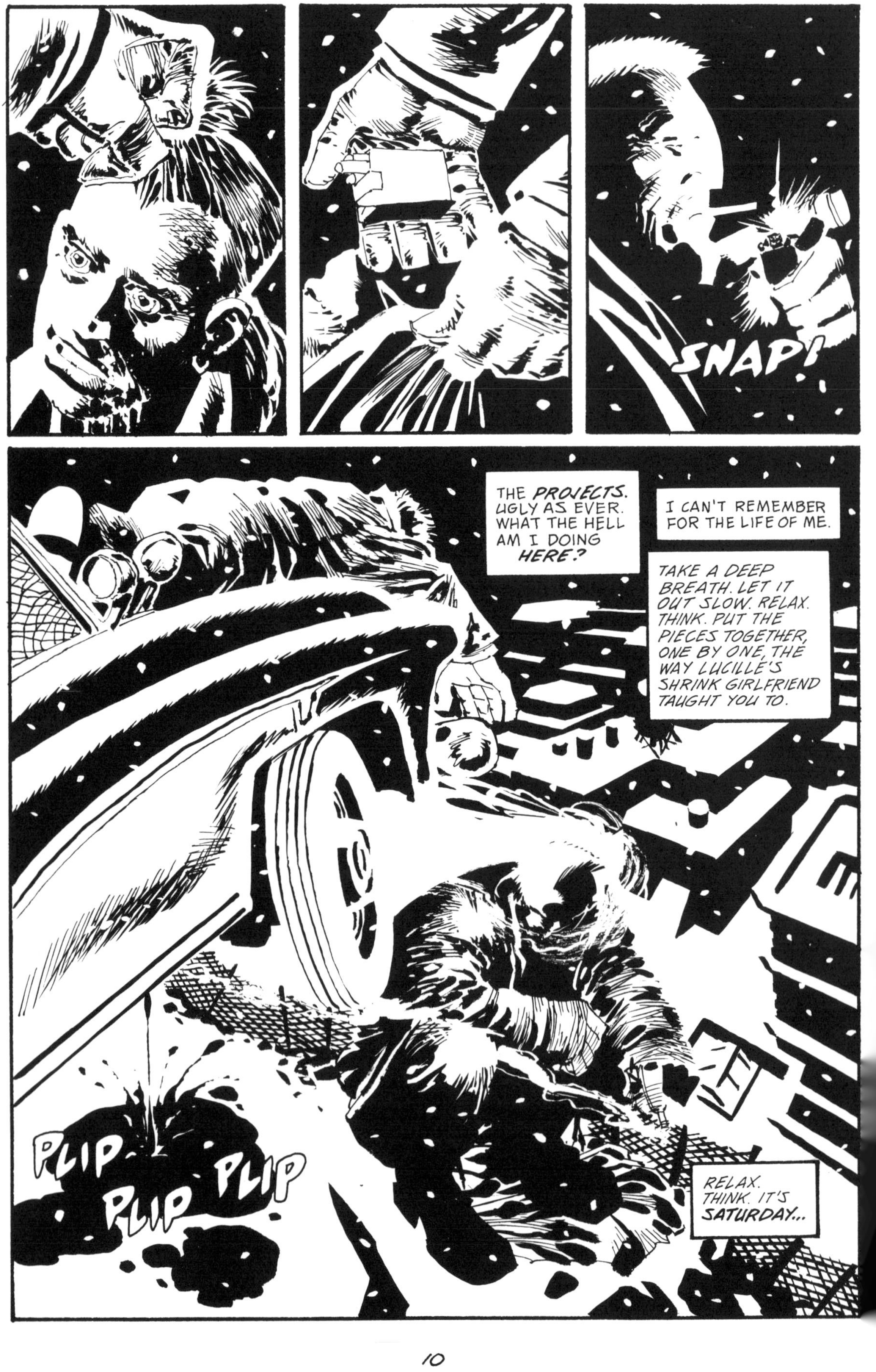
SNAP!
THE PROJECTS. UGLY AS EVER. WHAT THE HELL AM I DOING HERE?
I CAN'T REMEMBER FOR THE LIFE OF ME.
TAKE A DEEP BREATH. LET IT OUT SLOW. RELAX. THINK. PUT THE PIECES TOGETHER, ONE BY ONE, THE WAY LUCILLE'S SHRINK GIRLFRIEND TAUGHT YOU TO.
PLIP PLIP PLIP
RELAX. THINK. IT'S SATURDAY...

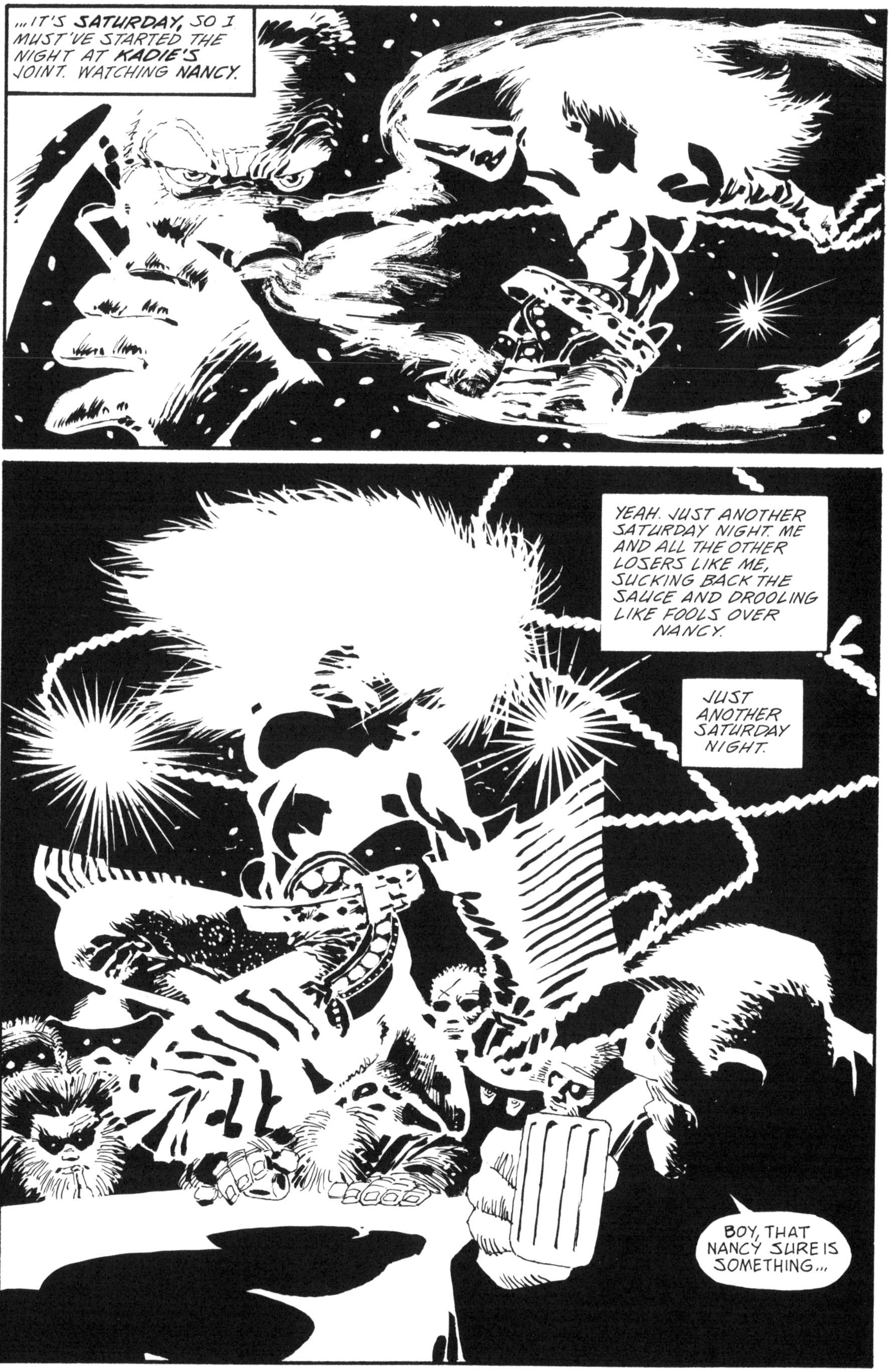
...IT'S SATURDAY, SO I MUST'VE STARTED THE NIGHT AT KADIE'S JOINT. WATCHING NANCY.
YEAH. JUST ANOTHER SATURDAY NIGHT. ME AND ALL THE OTHER LOSERS LIKE ME, SUCKING BACK THE SAUCE AND DROOLING LIKE FOOLS OVER NANCY.
JUST ANOTHER SATURDAY NIGHT.
BOY, THAT NANCY SURE IS SOMETHING...

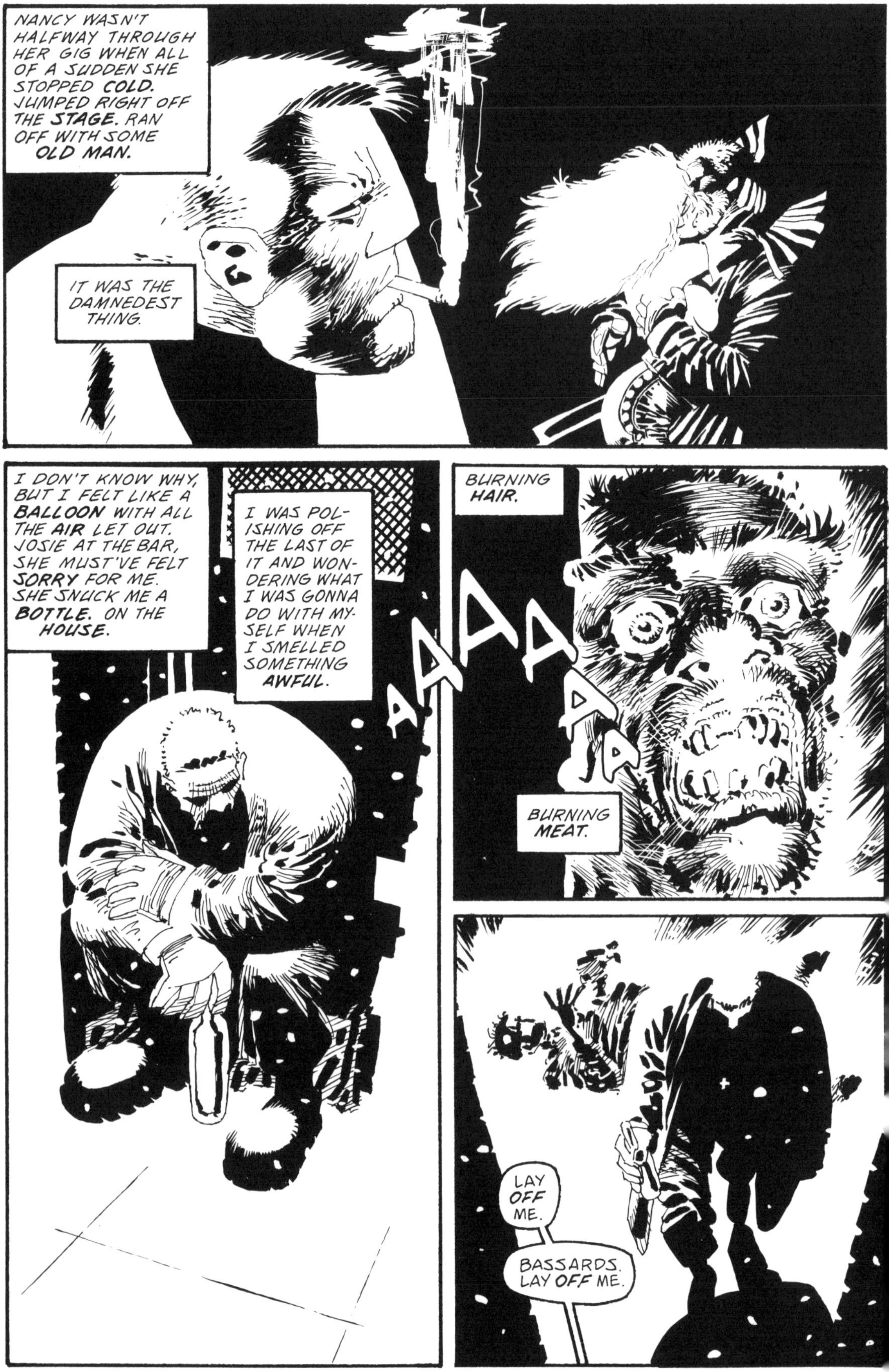
NANCY WASN'T HALFWAY THROUGH HER GIG WHEN ALL OF A SUDDEN SHE STOPPED COLD. JUMPED RIGHT OFF THE STAGE. RAN OFF WITH SOME OLD MAN.
IT WAS THE DAMNEDEST THING.
I DON'T KNOW WHY, BUT I FELT LIKE A BALLOON WITH ALL THE AIR LET OUT. JOSIE AT THE BAR, SHE MUST'VE FELT SORRY FOR ME. SHE SNUCK ME A BOTTLE. ON THE HOUSE.
I WAS POLISHING OFF THE LAST OF IT AND WONDERING WHAT I WAS GONNA DO WITH MYSELF WHEN I SMELLED SOMETHING AWFUL.
BURNING HAIR.
AAAAAAAA
BURNING MEAT.
LAY OFF ME.
BASSARDS. LAY OFF ME.

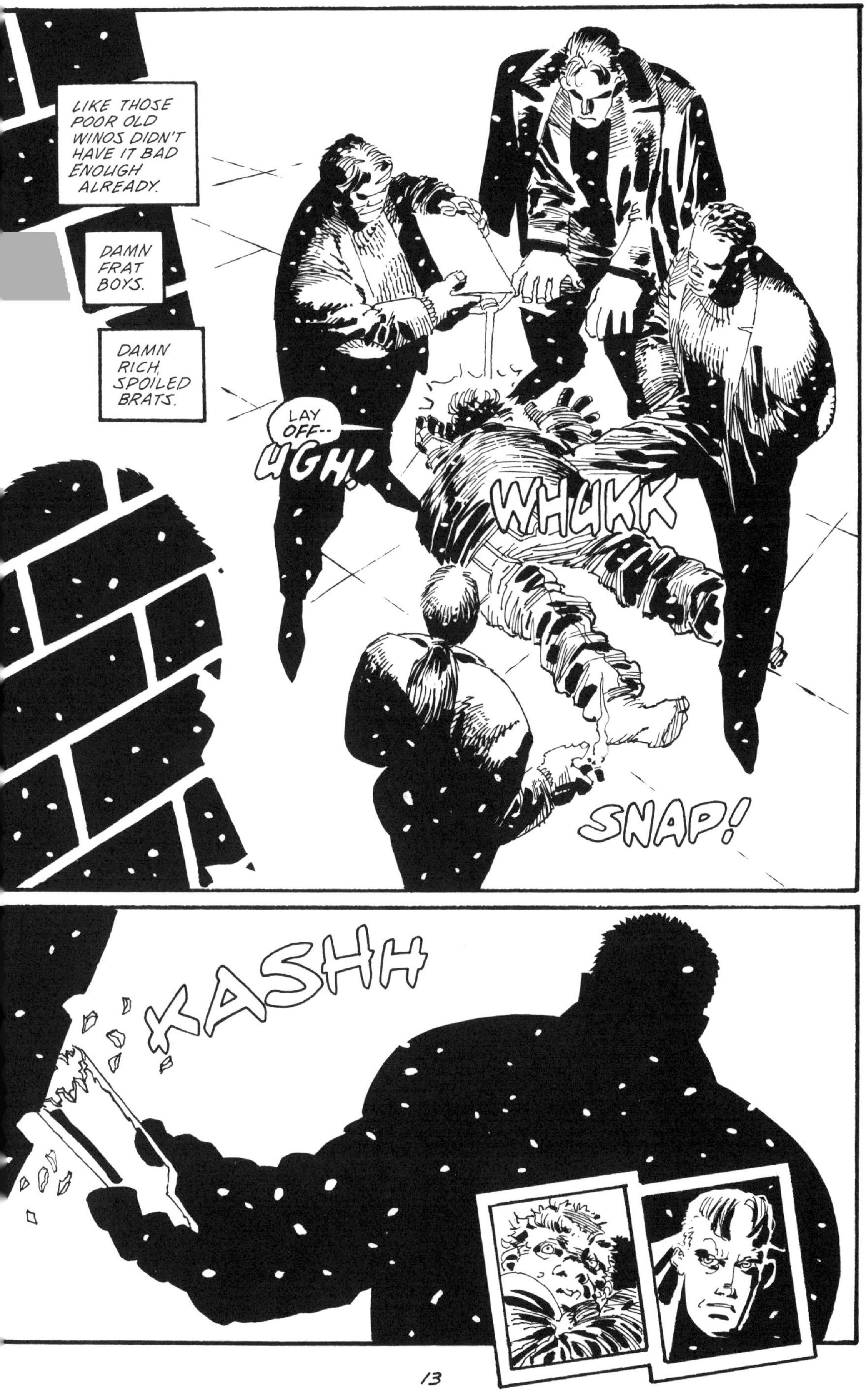
LIKE THOSE POOR OLD WINOS DIDN'T HAVE IT BAD ENOUGH ALREADY.
DAMN FRAT BOYS.
DAMN RICH, SPOILED BRATS.
LAY OFF-- UGH!
WHUKK
SNAP!
KASHH

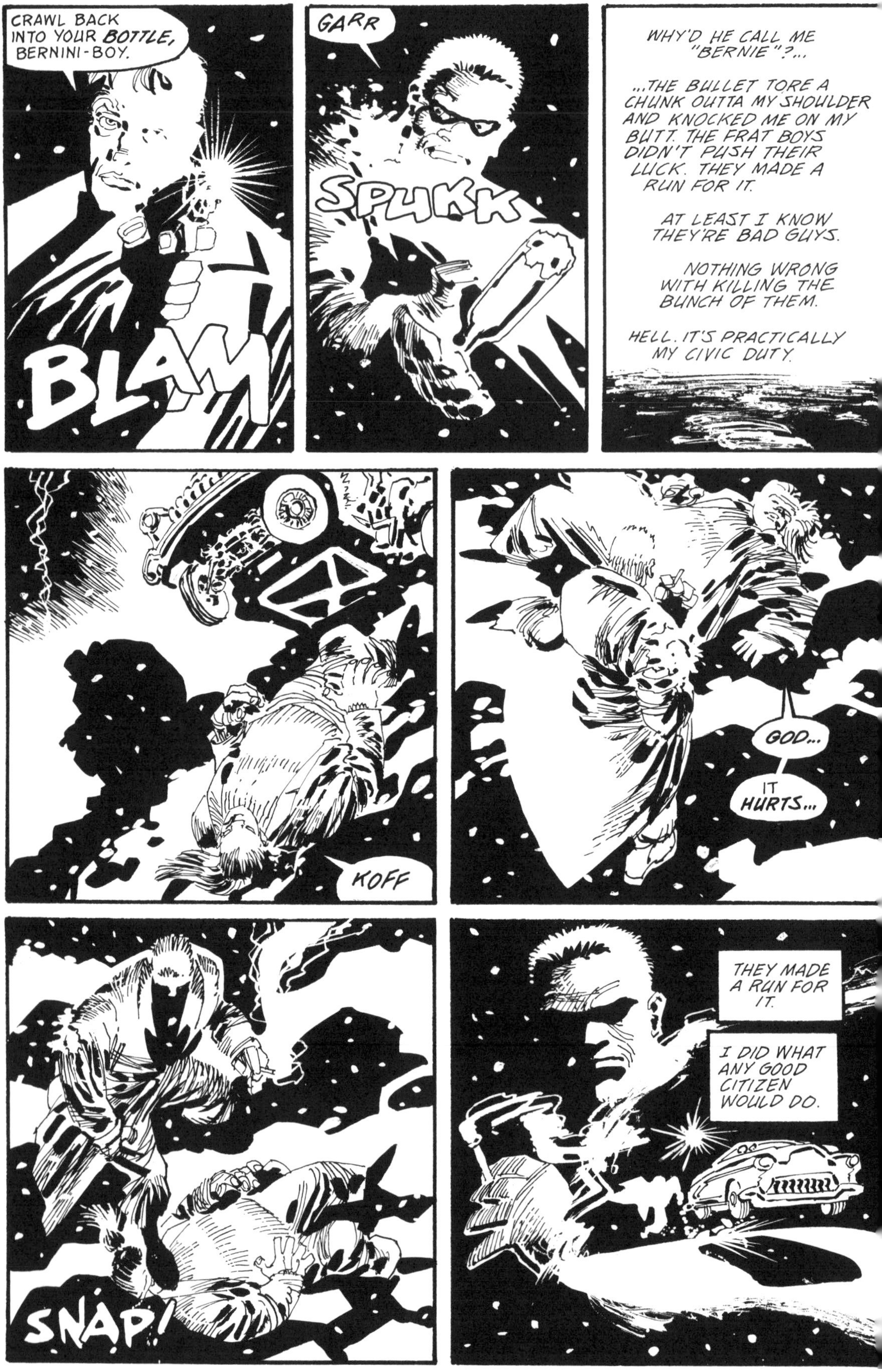
CRAWL BACK INTO YOUR BOTTLE, BERNINI-BOY.
BLAM
GARR
SPUKK
WHY'D HE CALL ME "BERNIE"?...
...THE BULLET TORE A CHUNK OUTTA MY SHOULDER AND KNOCKED ME ON MY BUTT. THE FRAT BOYS DIDN'T PUSH THEIR LUCK. THEY MADE A RUN FOR IT.
AT LEAST I KNOW THEY'RE BAD GUYS.
NOTHING WRONG WITH KILLING THE BUNCH OF THEM.
HELL. IT'S PRACTICALLY MY CIVIC DUTY.
KOFF
GOD...
IT HURTS...
SNAP!
THEY MADE A RUN FOR IT.
I DID WHAT ANY GOOD CITIZEN WOULD DO.

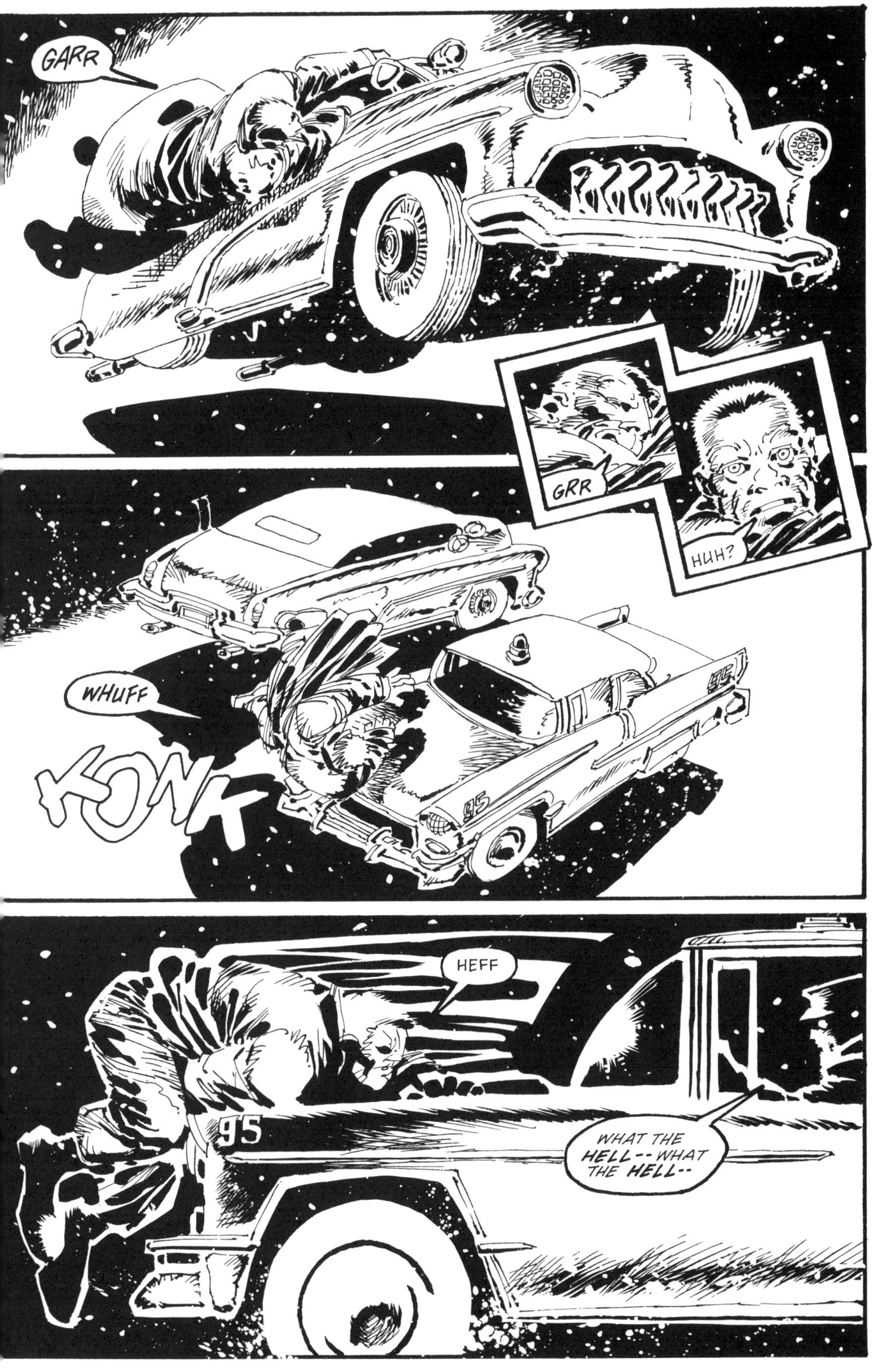
GARR
GRR
HUH?
WHUFF
KONK
HEFF
WHAT THE HELL--WHAT THE HELL--

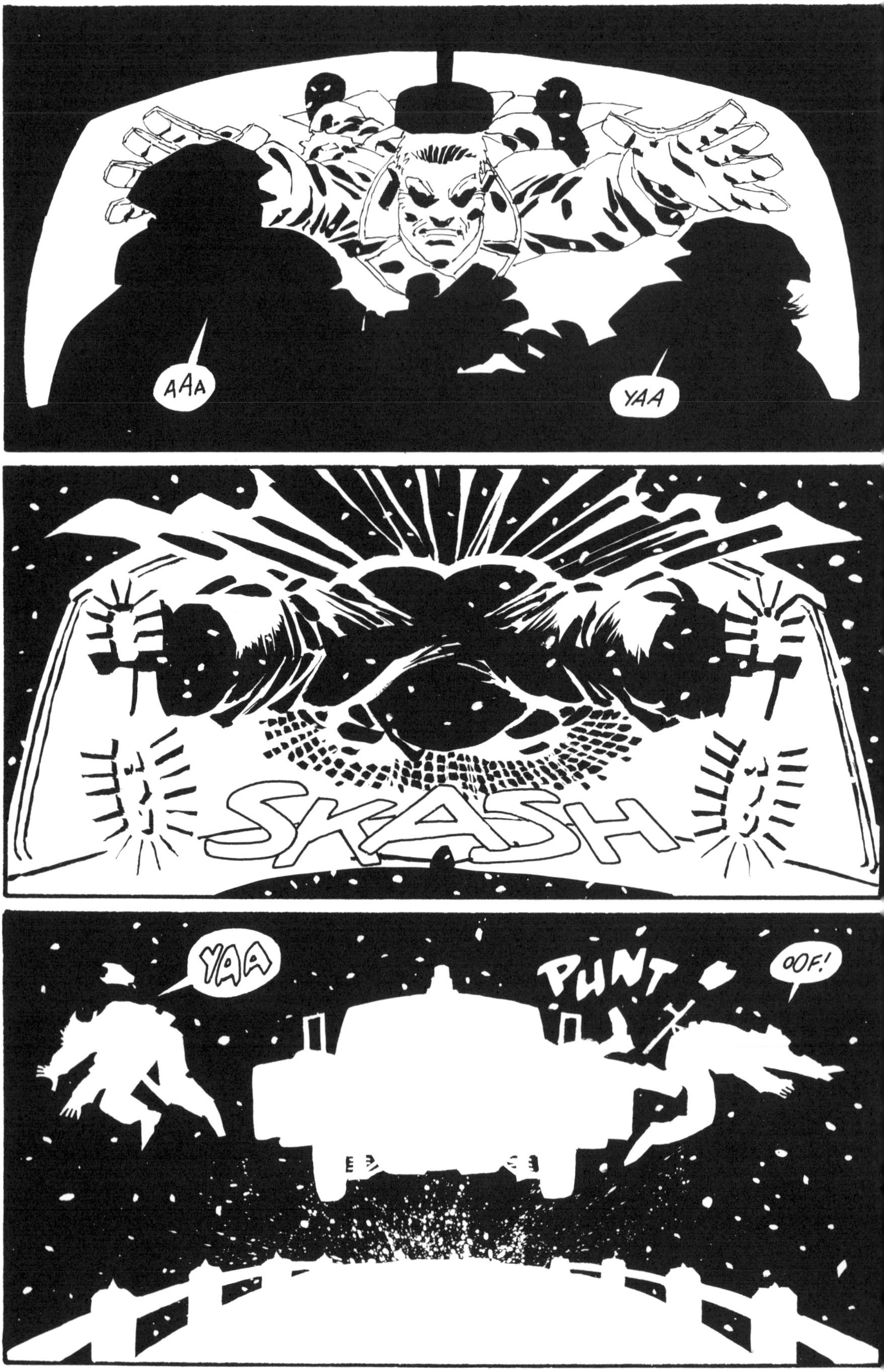
AAA
YAA
SKASH
YAA
PUNT
OOF!

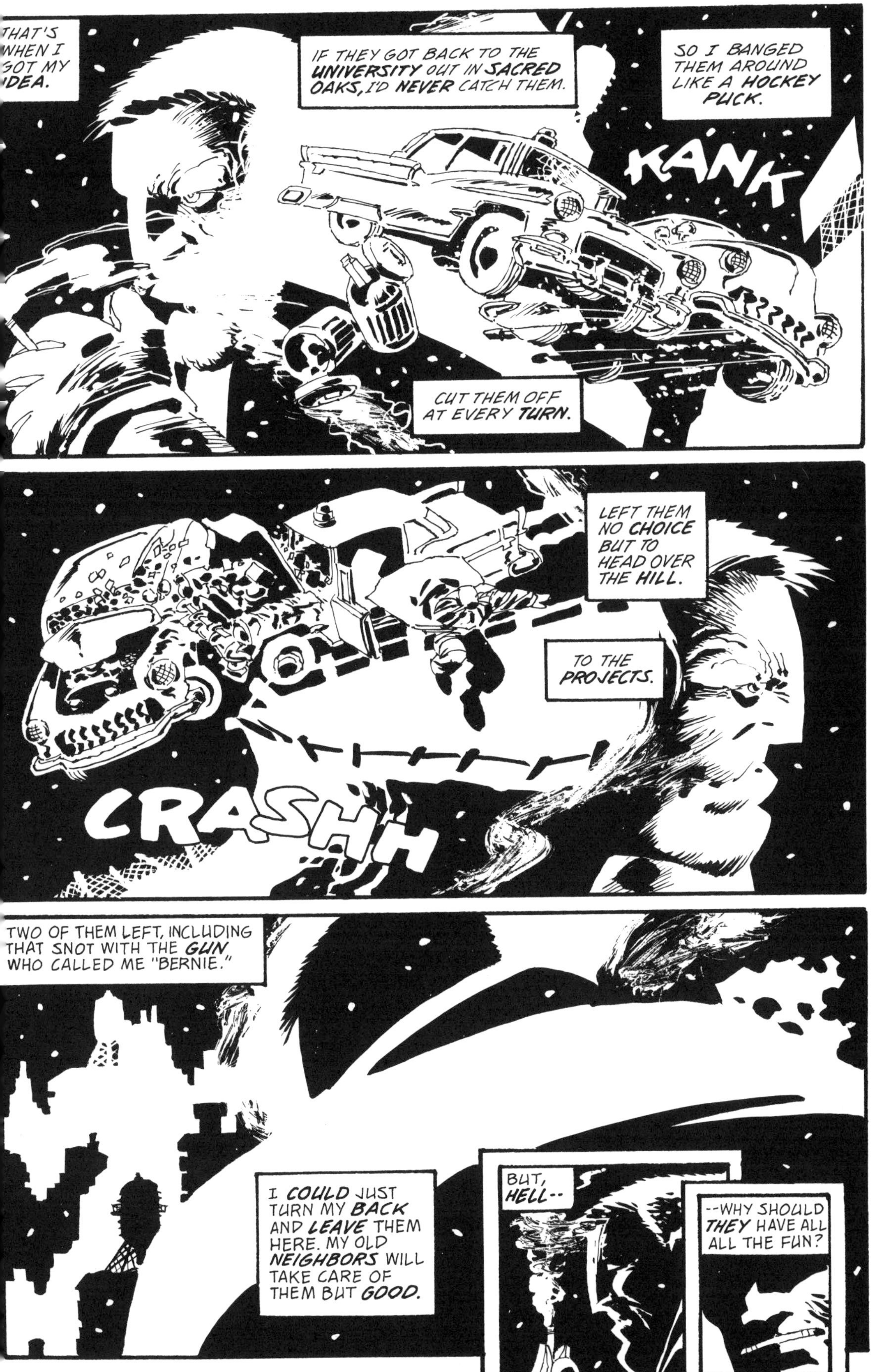
THAT'S WHEN I GOT MY IDEA.
IF THEY GOT BACK TO THE UNIVERSITY OUT IN SACRED OAKS, I'D NEVER CATCH THEM.
SO I BANGED THEM AROUND LIKE A HOCKEY PUCK.
KANK
CUT THEM OFF AT EVERY TURN.
LEFT THEM NO CHOICE BUT TO HEAD OVER THE HILL.
TO THE PROJECTS.
CRASHH
TWO OF THEM LEFT, INCLUDING THAT SNOT WITH THE GUN WHO CALLED ME "BERNIE."
I COULD JUST TURN MY BACK AND LEAVE THEM HERE. MY OLD NEIGHBORS WILL TAKE CARE OF THEM BUT GOOD.
BUT, HELL--
--WHY SHOULD THEY HAVE ALL ALL THE FUN?

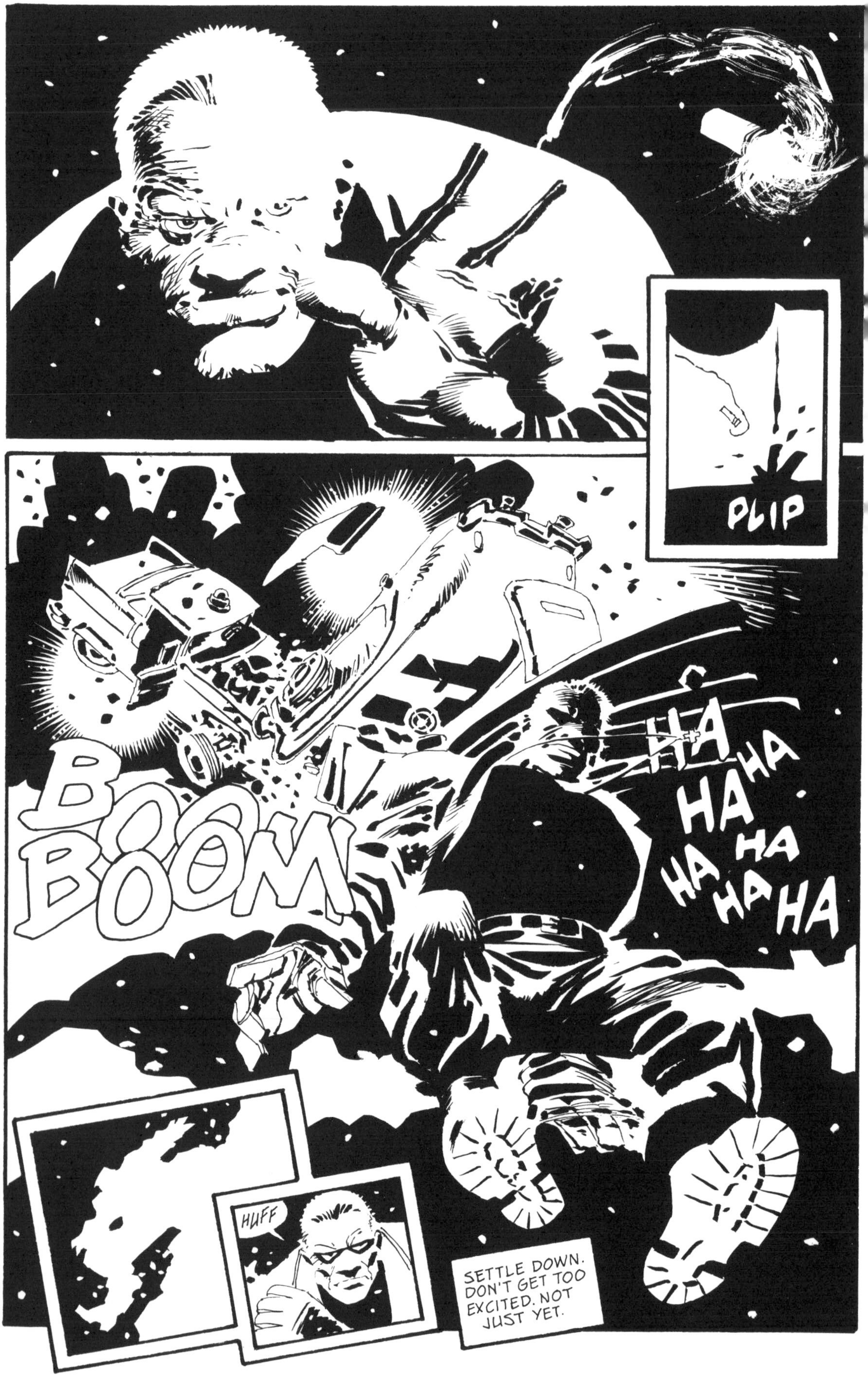
PLIP
BOOOM
BOOOM
HA HA HA HA HA HA HA HA
HUFF
SETTLE DOWN. DON'T GET TOO EXCITED. NOT JUST YET.

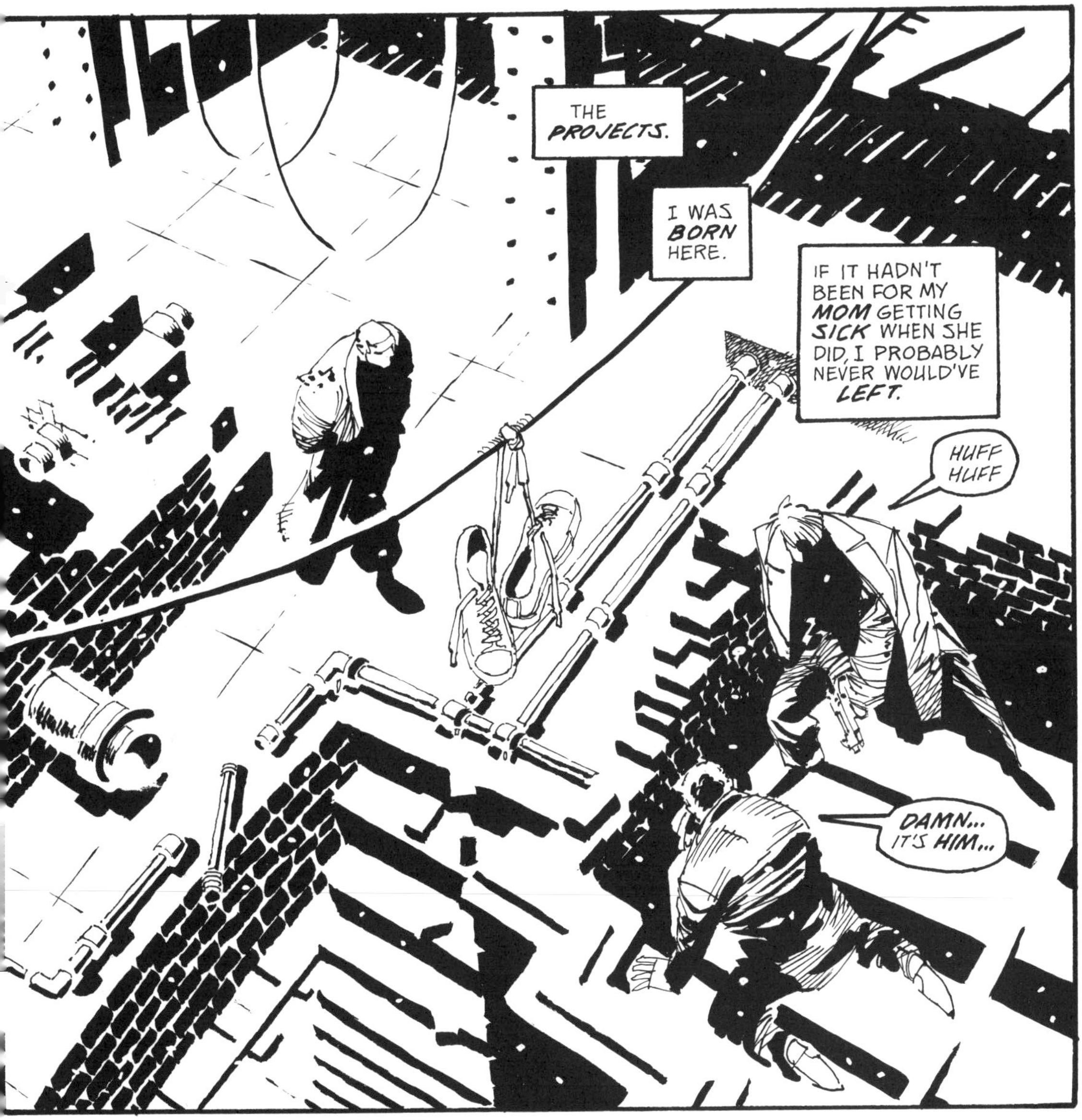
THE PROJECTS.
I WAS BORN HERE.
IF IT HADN'T BEEN FOR MY MOM GETTING SICK WHEN SHE DID, I PROBABLY NEVER WOULD'VE LEFT.
HUFF HUFF
DAMN... IT'S HIM...

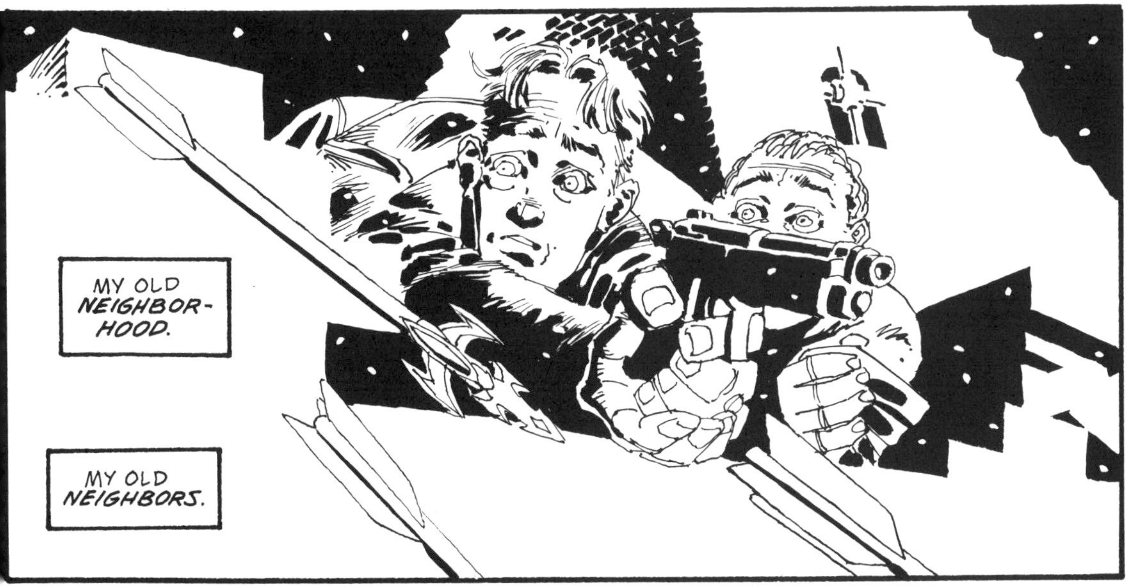
MY OLD NEIGHBOR-HOOD.
MY OLD NEIGHBORS.

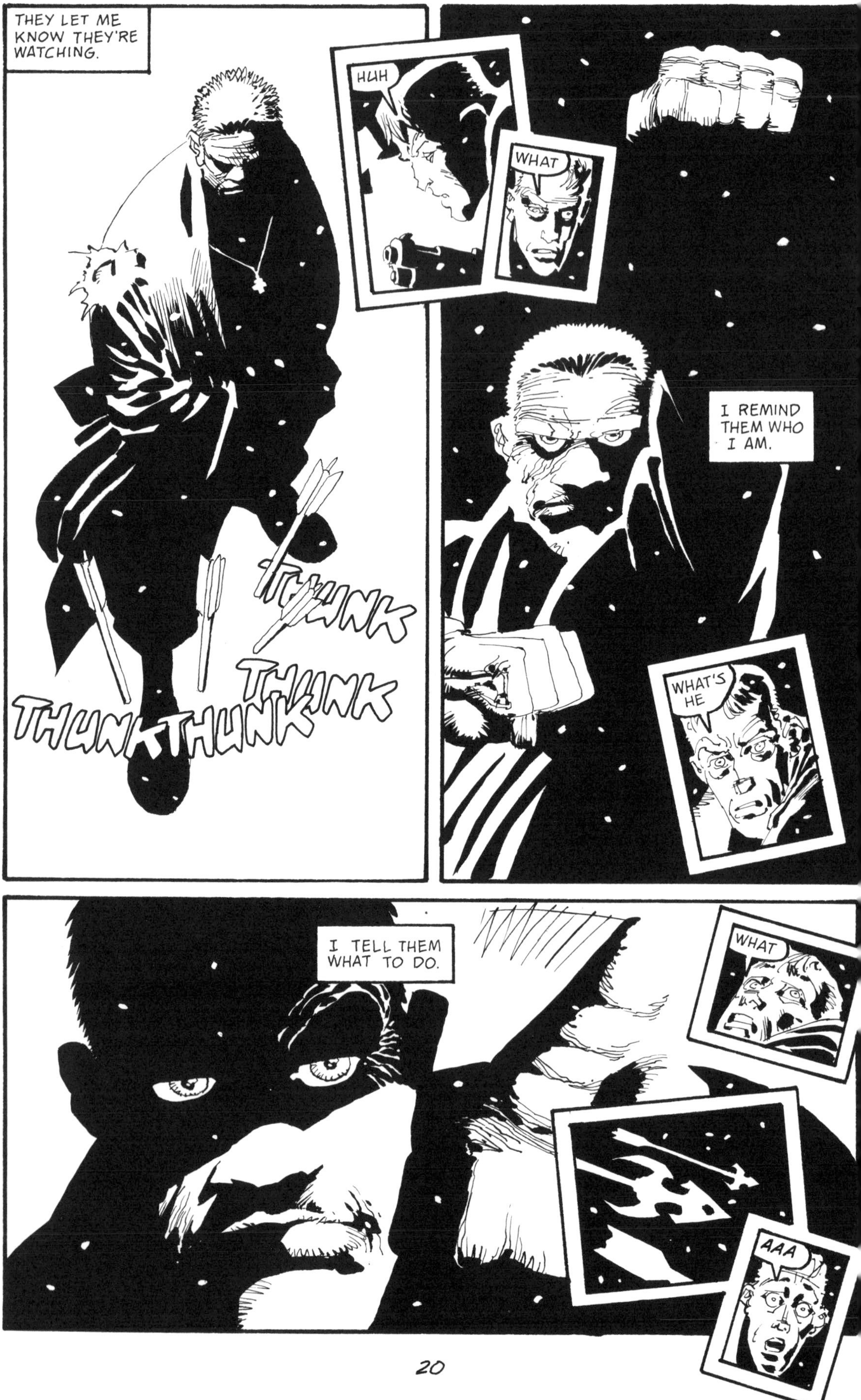
THEY LET ME KNOW THEY'RE WATCHING.
HUH
WHAT
THUNK
THUNK
THUNKTHUNK
I REMIND THEM WHO I AM.
WHAT'S HE
I TELL THEM WHAT TO DO.
WHAT
AAA

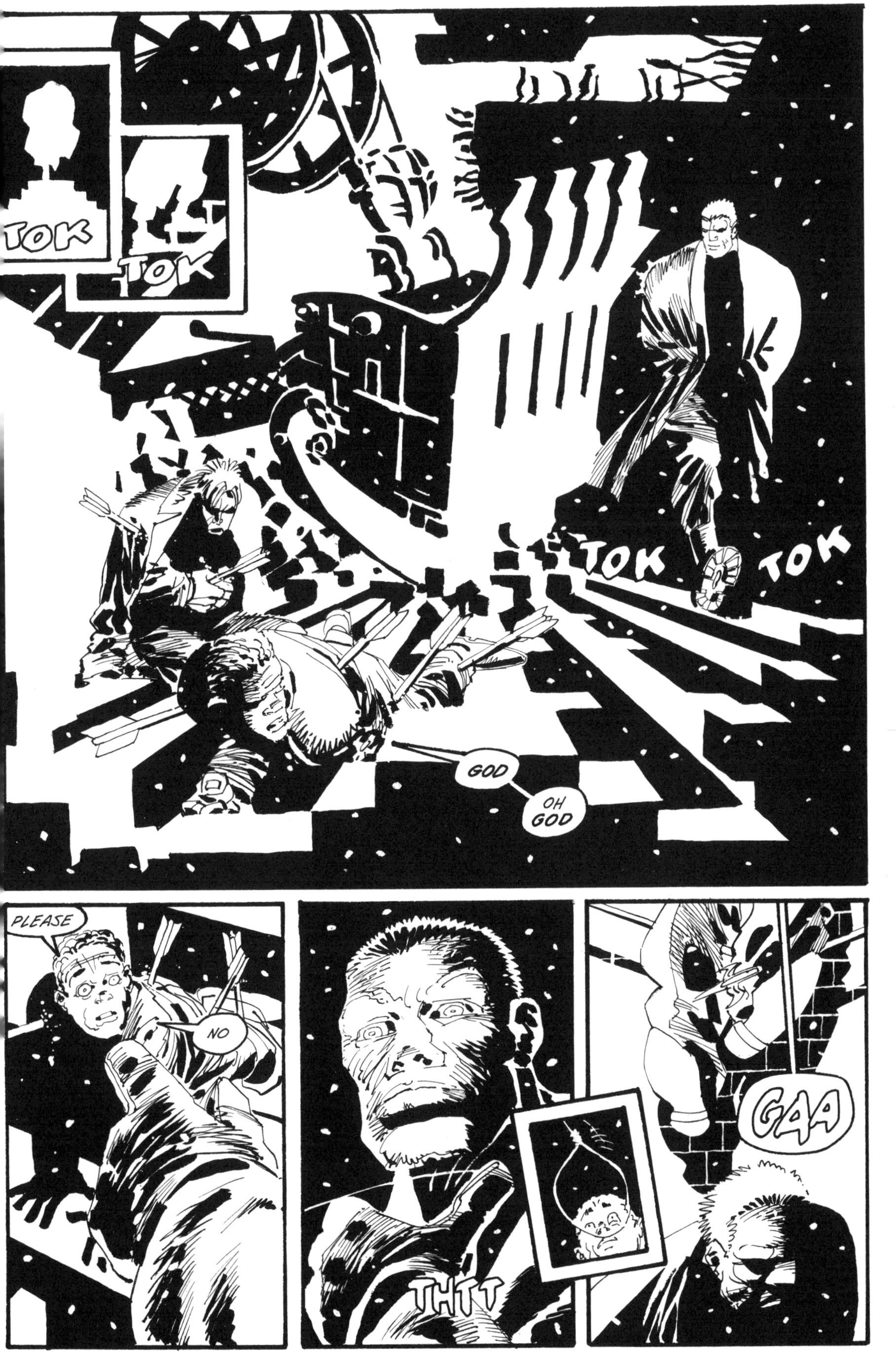
TOK
TOK
TOK
TOK
GOD
OH GOD
PLEASE
NO
THTT
GAA

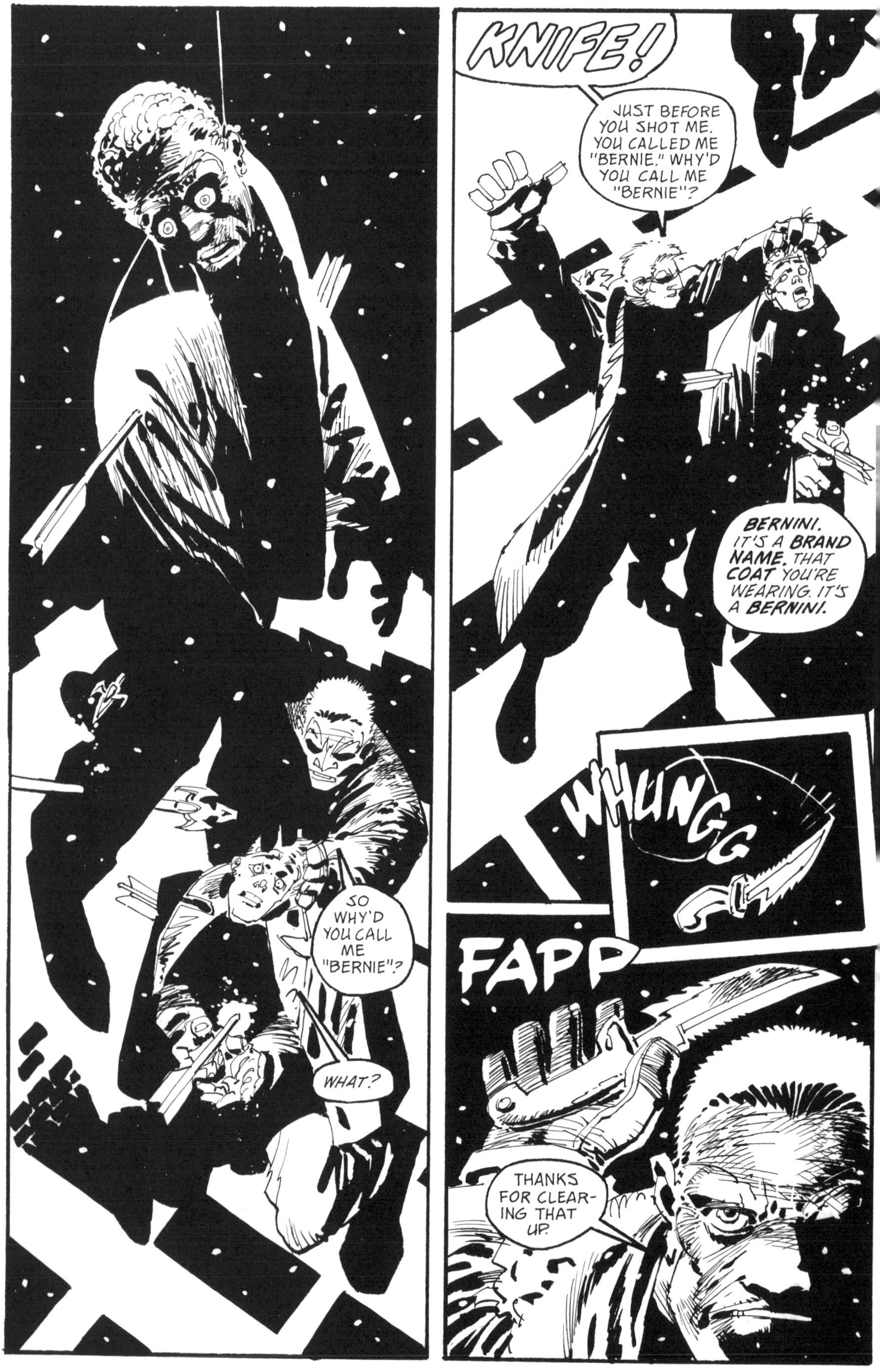
SO WHY'D YOU CALL ME "BERNIE"?
WHAT?
KNIFE!
JUST BEFORE YOU SHOT ME. YOU CALLED ME "BERNIE." WHY'D YOU CALL ME "BERNIE"?
BERNINI. IT'S A BRAND NAME. THAT COAT YOU'RE WEARING. IT'S A BERNINI.
WHUNGG
FAPP
THANKS FOR CLEAR-ING THAT UP.

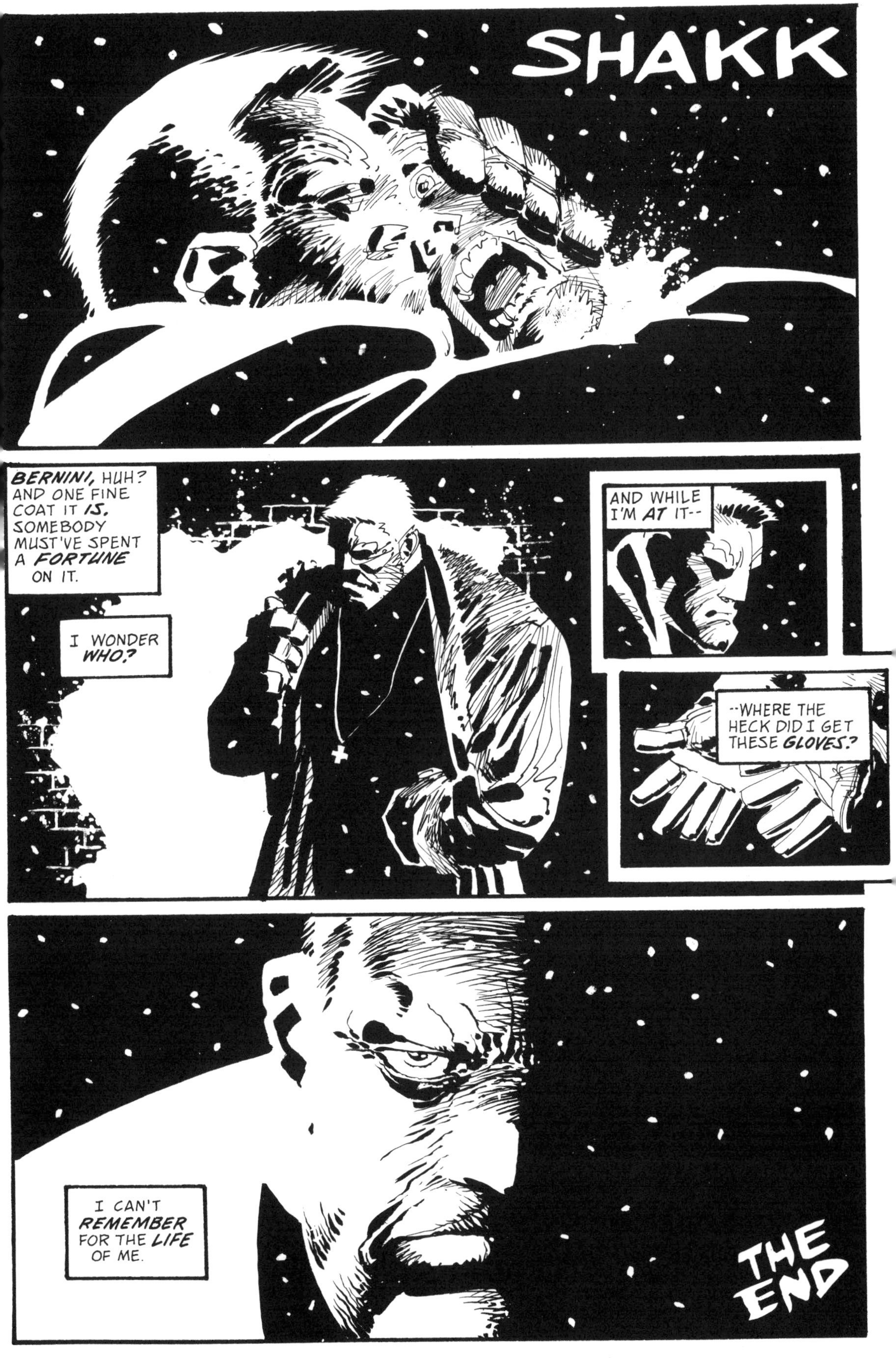
SHAKK
BERNINI, HUH? AND ONE FINE COAT IT IS. SOMEBODY MUST'VE SPENT A FORTUNE ON IT.
I WONDER WHO?
AND WHILE I'M AT IT--
--WHERE THE HECK DID I GET THESE GLOVES?
I CAN'T REMEMBER FOR THE LIFE OF ME.
THE END

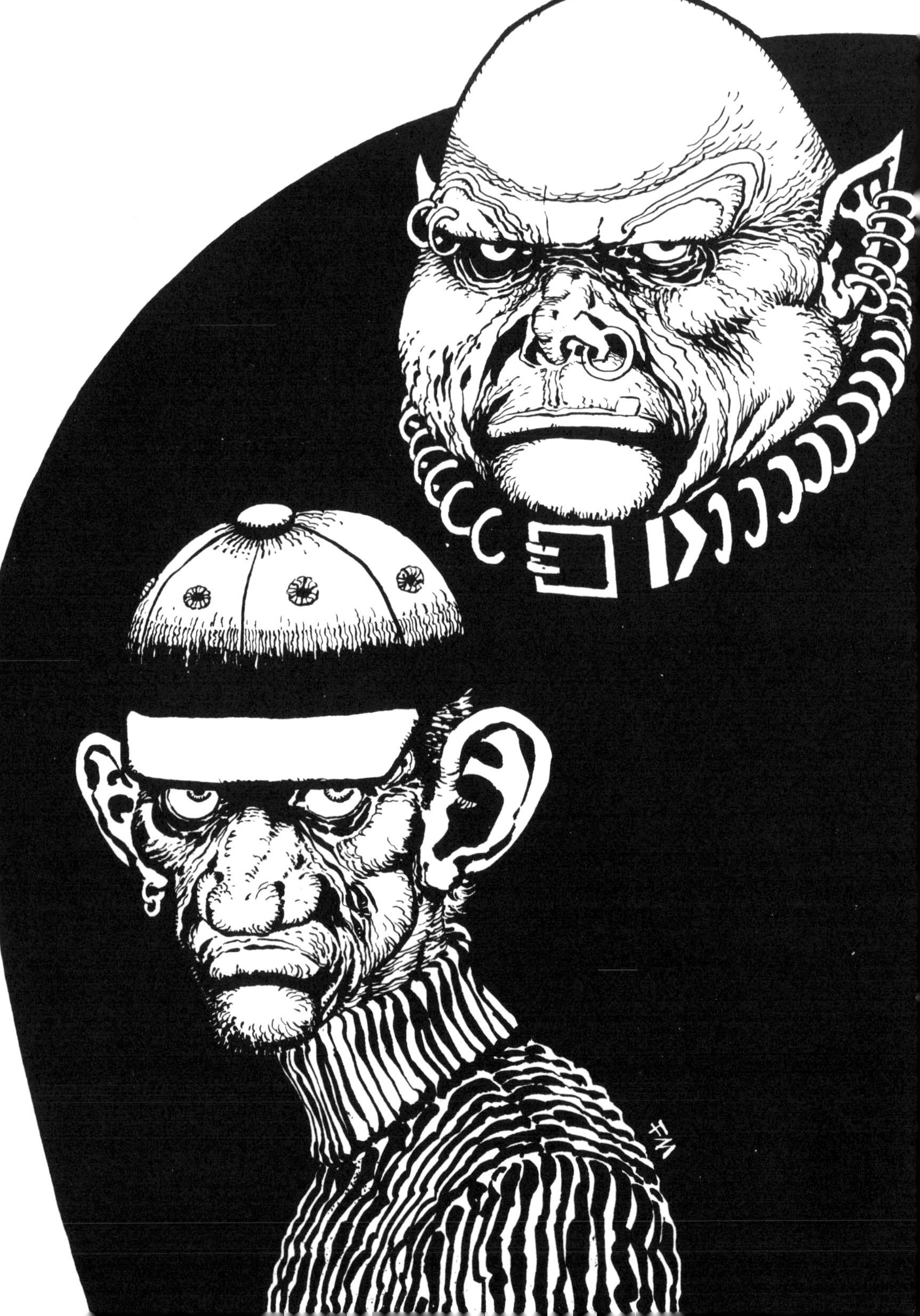

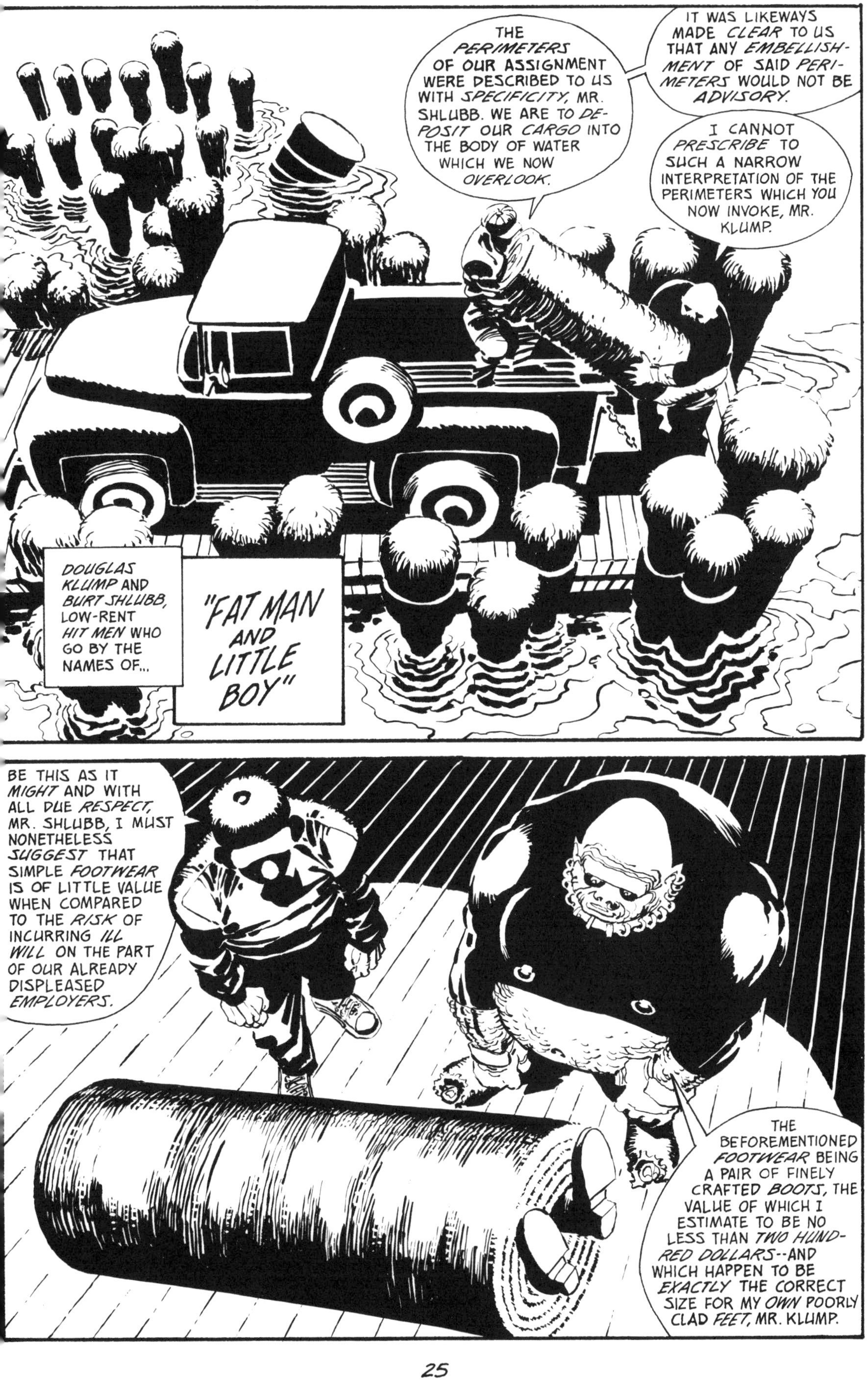

THE PERIMETERS OF OUR ASSIGNMENT WERE DESCRIBED TO US WITH SPECIFICITY, MR. SHLUBB. WE ARE TO DEPOSIT OUR CARGO INTO THE BODY OF WATER WHICH WE NOW OVERLOOK.
IT WAS LIKEWAYS MADE CLEAR TO US THAT ANY EMBELLISHMENT OF SAID PERIMETERS WOULD NOT BE ADVISORY.
I CANNOT PRESCRIBE TO SUCH A NARROW INTERPRETATION OF THE PERIMETERS WHICH YOU NOW INVOKE, MR. KLUMP.
DOUGLAS KLUMP AND BURT SHLUBB, LOW-RENT HIT MEN WHO GO BY THE NAMES OF...
"FAT MAN AND LITTLE BOY"
BE THIS AS IT MIGHT AND WITH ALL DUE RESPECT, MR. SHLUBB, I MUST NONETHELESS SUGGEST THAT SIMPLE FOOTWEAR IS OF LITTLE VALUE WHEN COMPARED TO THE RISK OF INCURRING ILL WILL ON THE PART OF OUR ALREADY DISPLEASED EMPLOYERS.
THE BEFOREMENTIONED FOOTWEAR BEING A PAIR OF FINELY CRAFTED BOOTS, THE VALUE OF WHICH I ESTIMATE TO BE NO LESS THAN TWO HUNDRED DOLLARS--AND WHICH HAPPEN TO BE EXACTLY THE CORRECT SIZE FOR MY OWN POORLY CLAD FEET, MR. KLUMP.

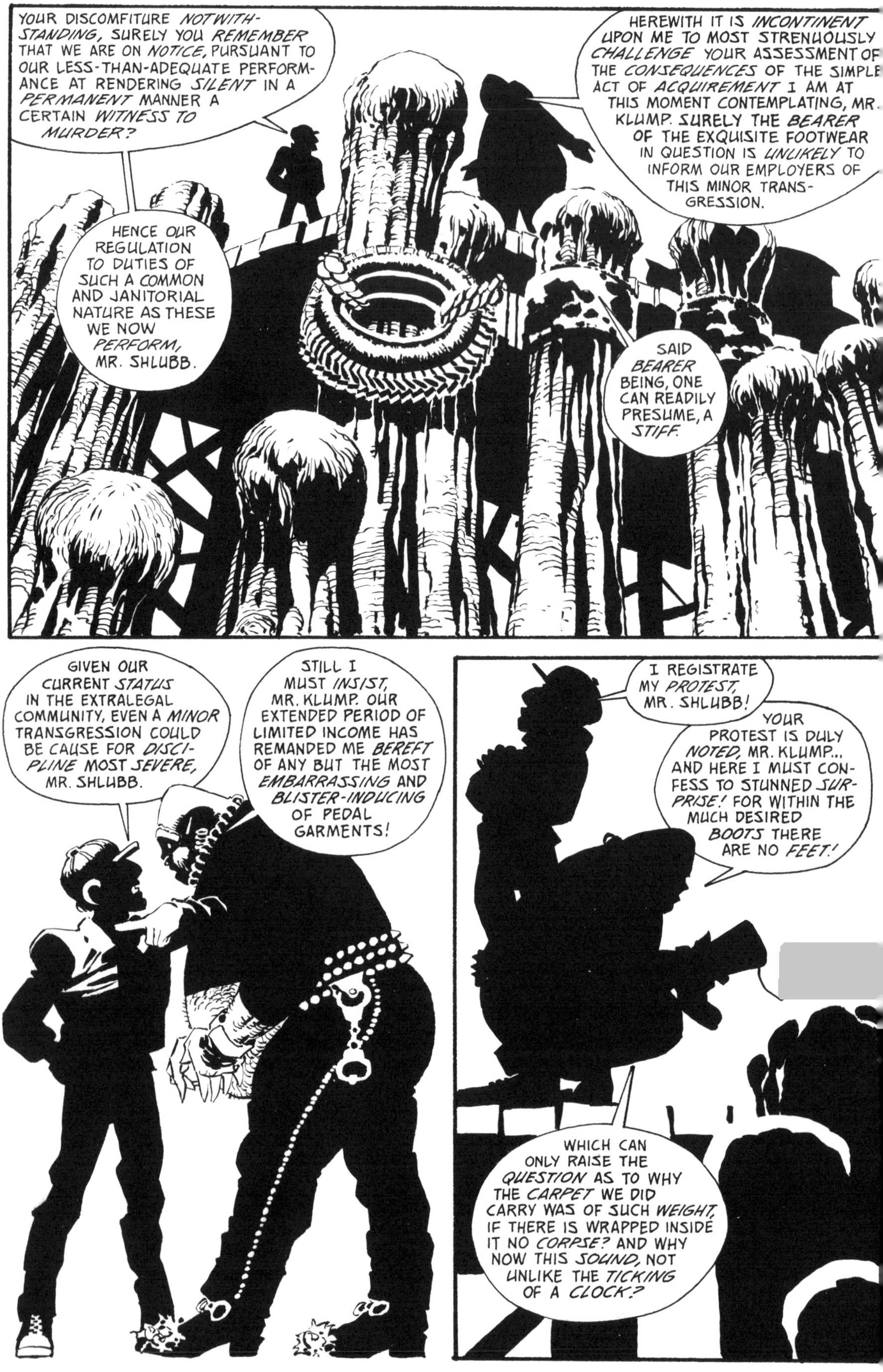
YOUR DISCOMFITURE NOTWITHSTANDING, SURELY YOU REMEMBER THAT WE ARE ON NOTICE, PURSUANT TO OUR LESS-THAN-ADEQUATE PERFORMANCE AT RENDERING SILENT IN A PERMANENT MANNER A CERTAIN WITNESS TO MURDER?
HENCE OUR REGULATION TO DUTIES OF SUCH A COMMON AND JANITORIAL NATURE AS THESE WE NOW PERFORM, MR. SHLUBB.
HEREWITH IT IS INCONTINENT UPON ME TO MOST STRENUOUSLY CHALLENGE YOUR ASSESSMENT OF THE CONSEQUENCES OF THE SIMPLE ACT OF ACQUIREMENT I AM AT THIS MOMENT CONTEMPLATING, MR. KLUMP. SURELY THE BEARER OF THE EXQUISITE FOOTWEAR IN QUESTION IS UNLIKELY TO INFORM OUR EMPLOYERS OF THIS MINOR TRANSGRESSION.
SAID BEARER BEING, ONE CAN READILY PRESUME, A STIFF.
GIVEN OUR CURRENT STATUS IN THE EXTRALEGAL COMMUNITY, EVEN A MINOR TRANSGRESSION COULD BE CAUSE FOR DISCIPLINE MOST SEVERE, MR. SHLUBB.
STILL I MUST INSIST, MR. KLUMP. OUR EXTENDED PERIOD OF LIMITED INCOME HAS REMANDED ME BEREFT OF ANY BUT THE MOST EMBARRASSING AND BLISTER-INDUCING OF PEDAL GARMENTS!
I REGISTRATE MY PROTEST, MR. SHLUBB!
YOUR PROTEST IS DULY NOTED, MR. KLUMP... AND HERE I MUST CONFESS TO STUNNED SURPRISE! FOR WITHIN THE MUCH DESIRED BOOTS THERE ARE NO FEET!
WHICH CAN ONLY RAISE THE QUESTION AS TO WHY THE CARPET WE DID CARRY WAS OF SUCH WEIGHT, IF THERE IS WRAPPED INSIDE IT NO CORPSE? AND WHY NOW THIS SOUND, NOT UNLIKE THE TICKING OF A CLOCK?

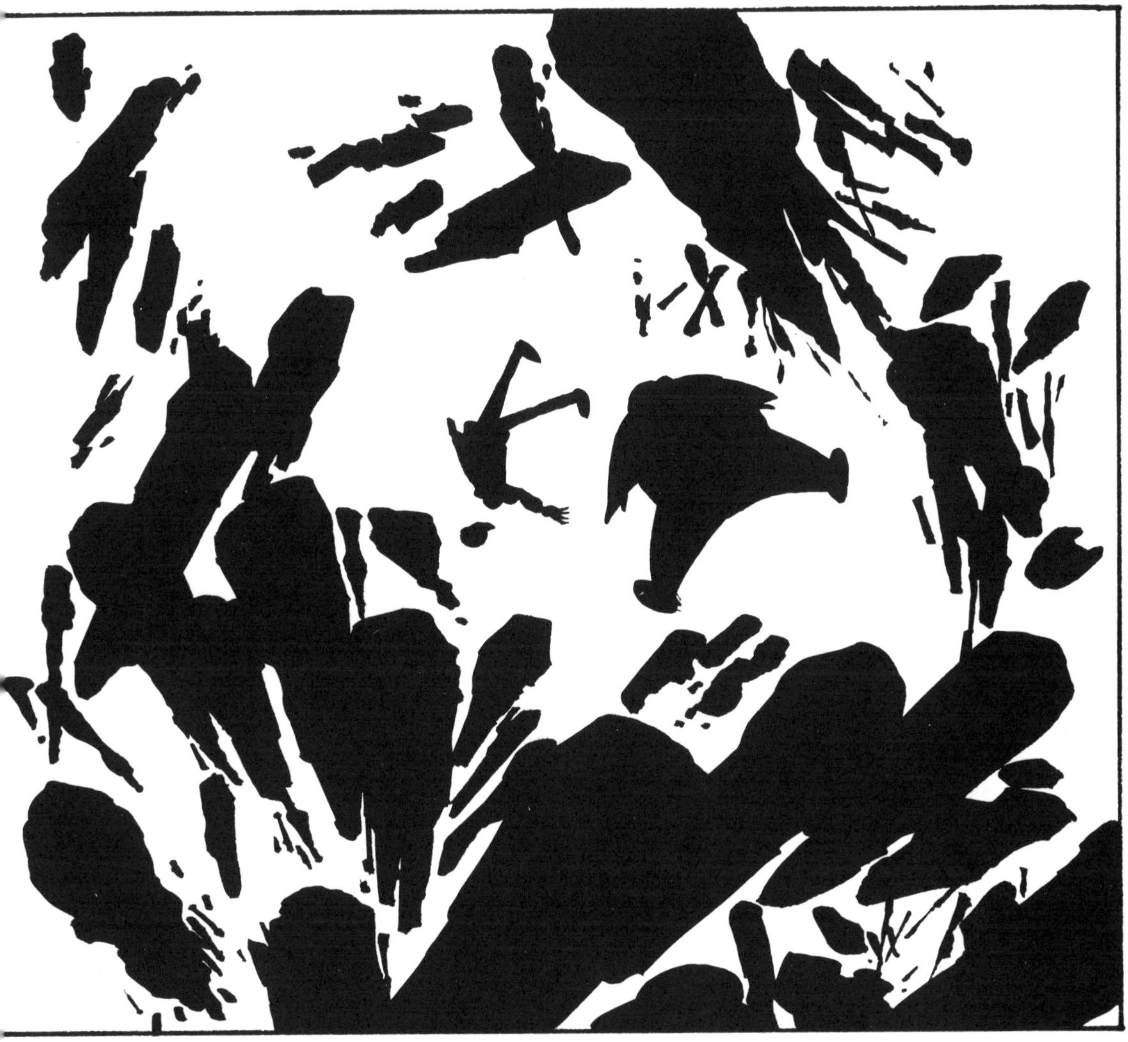

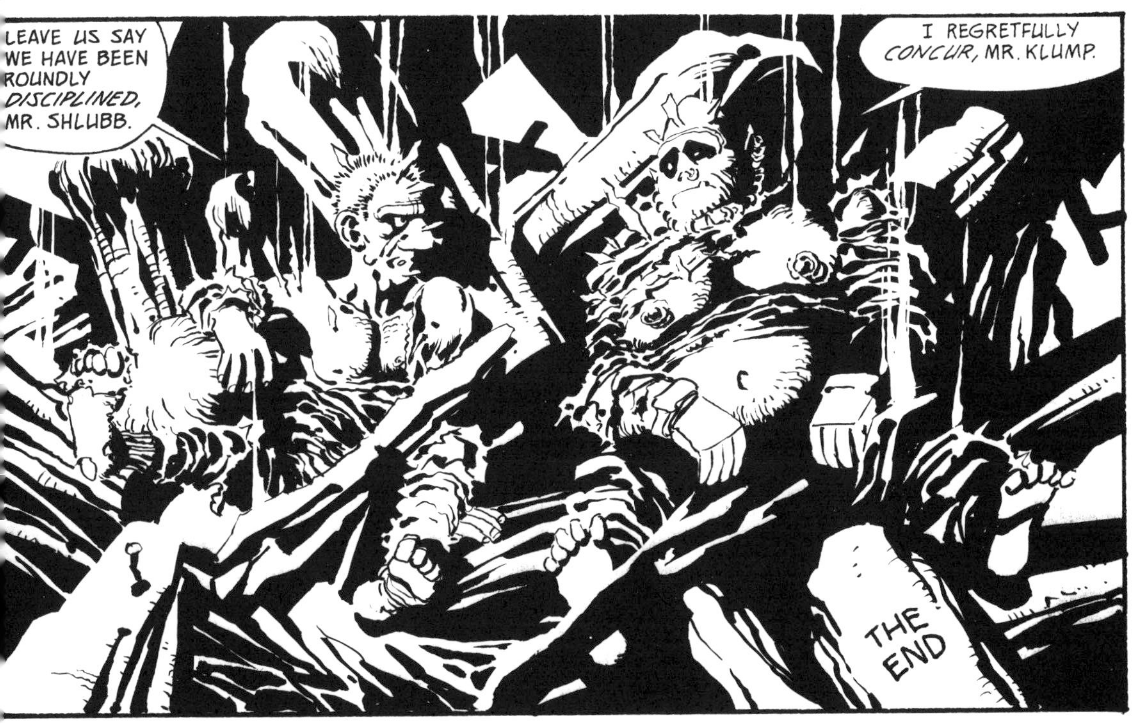
LEAVE US SAY WE HAVE BEEN ROUNDLY *DISCIPLINED,* MR. SHLUBB.
I REGRETFULLY *CONCUR,* MR. KLUMP.
THE END

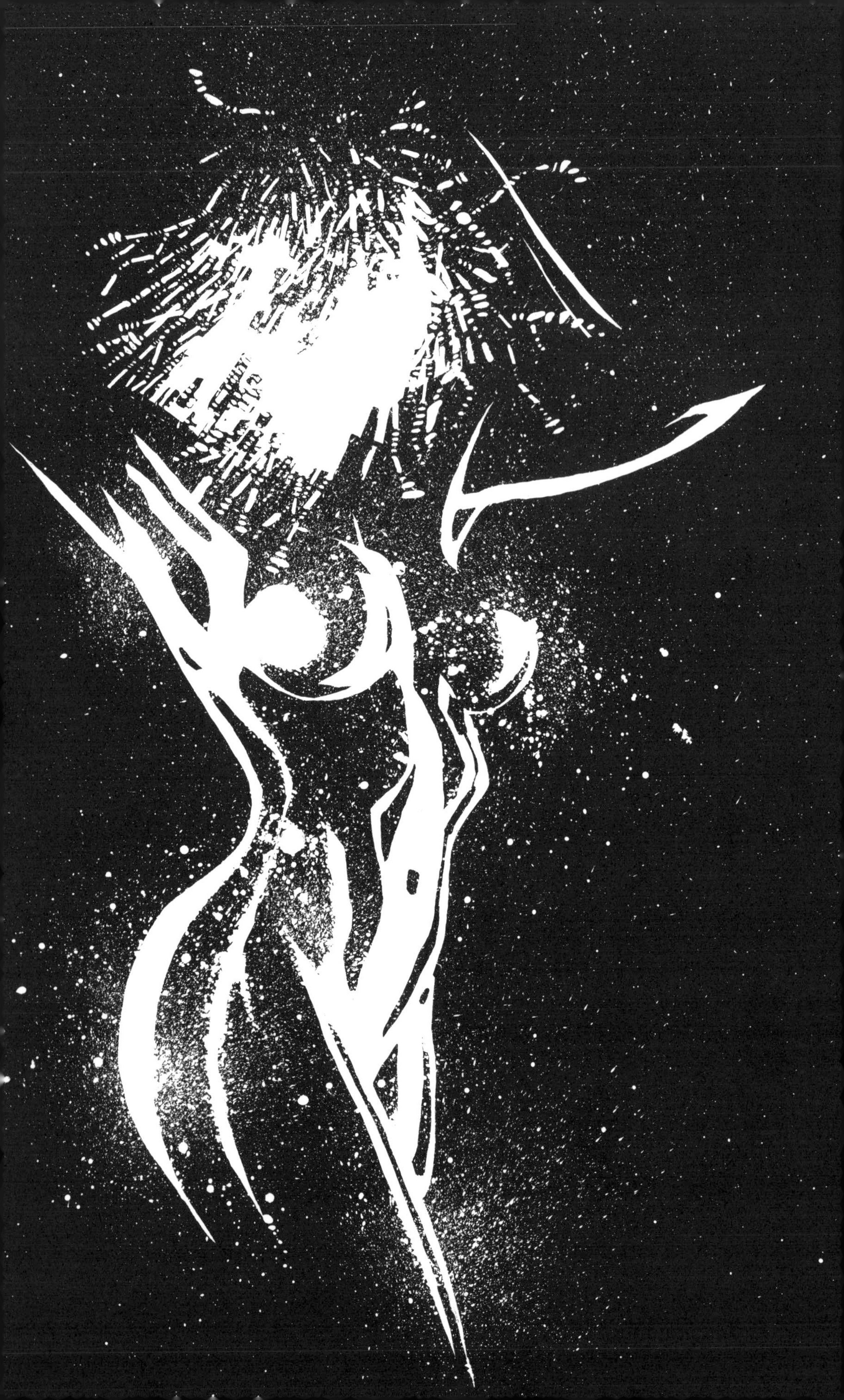

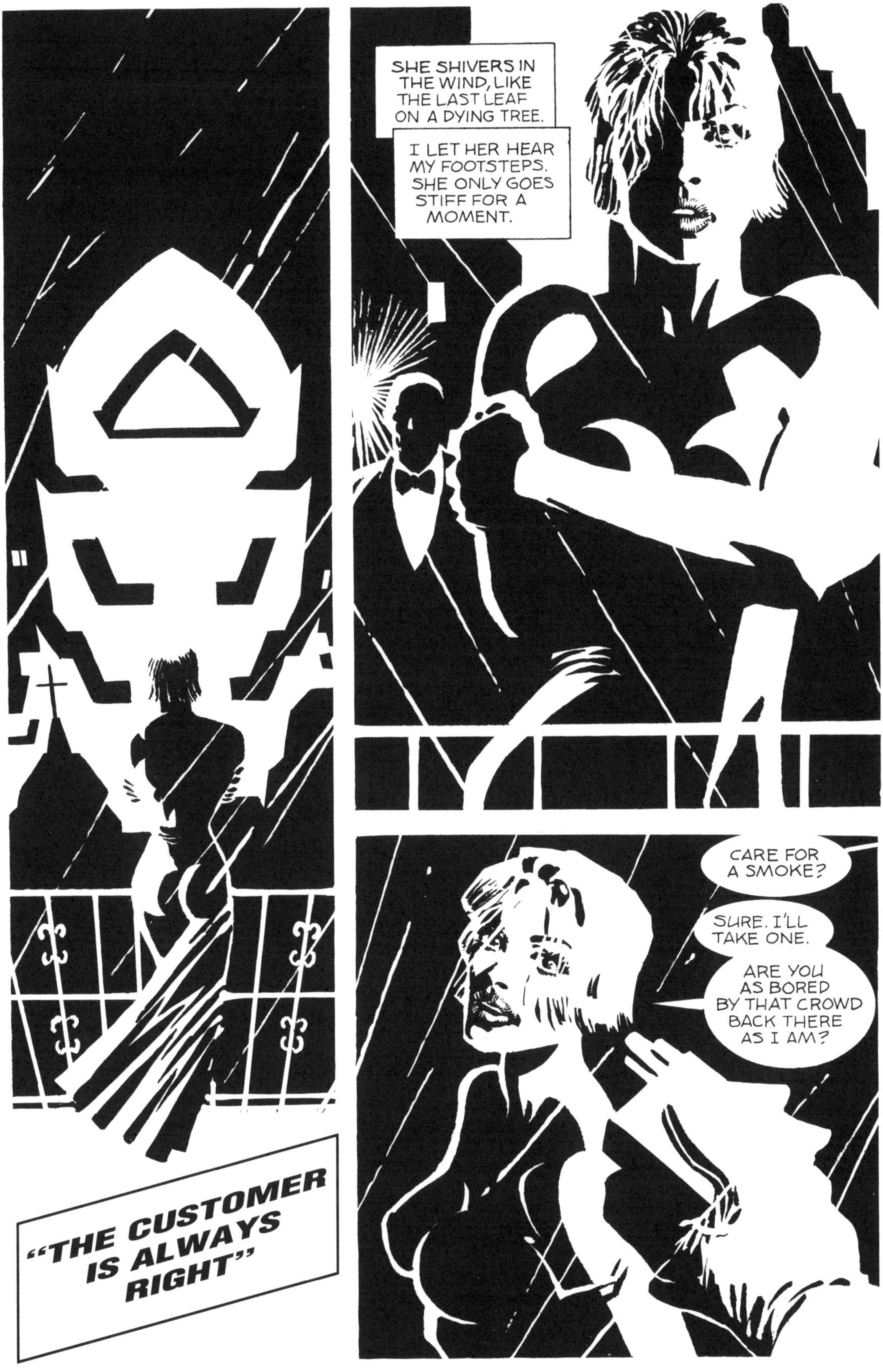

"THE CUSTOMER IS ALWAYS RIGHT"
SHE SHIVERS IN THE WIND, LIKE THE LAST LEAF ON A DYING TREE.
I LET HER HEAR MY FOOTSTEPS. SHE ONLY GOES STIFF FOR A MOMENT.
CARE FOR A SMOKE?
SURE. I'LL TAKE ONE.
ARE YOU AS BORED BY THAT CROWD BACK THERE AS I AM?

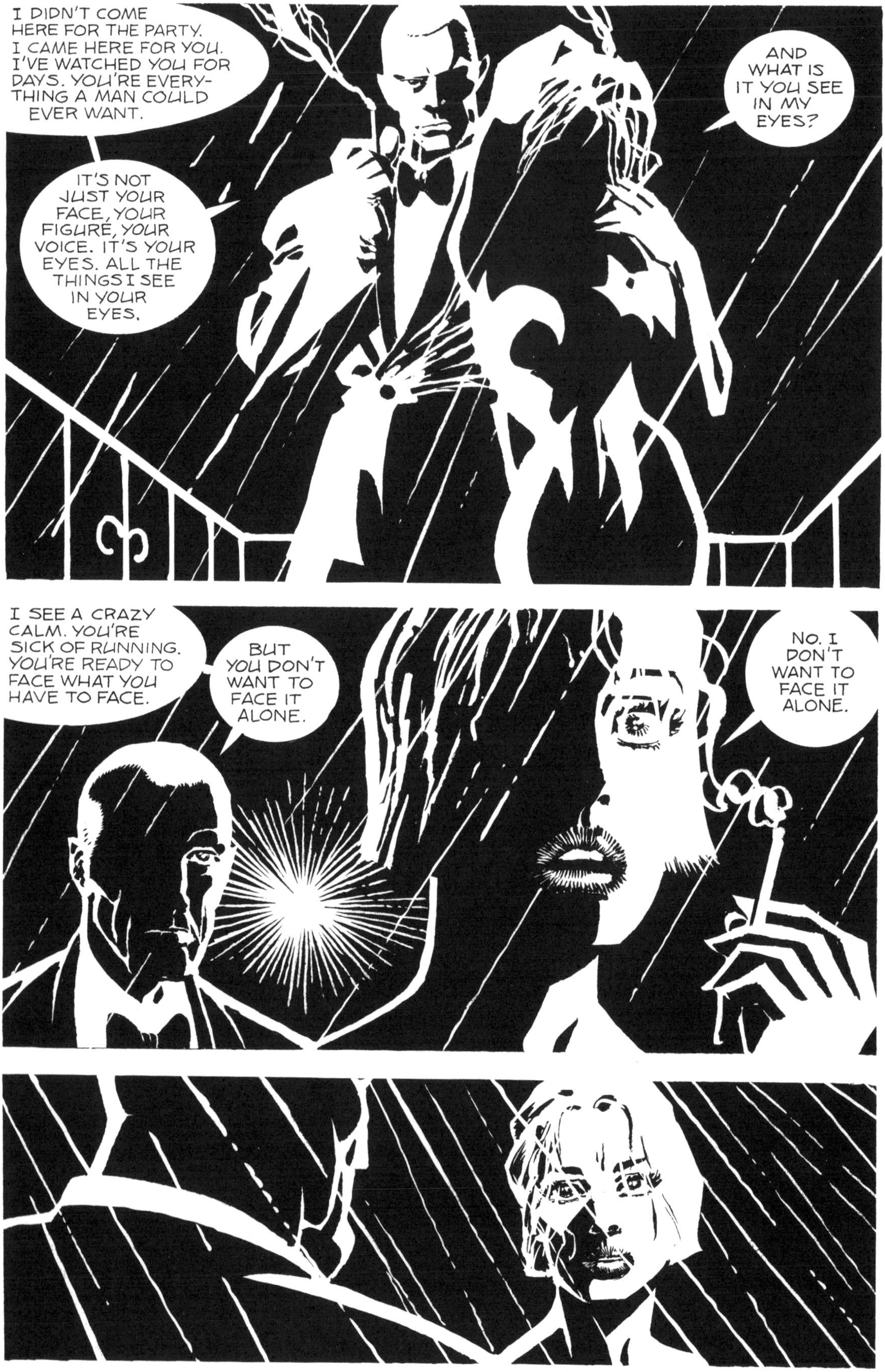
I DIDN'T COME HERE FOR THE PARTY. I CAME HERE FOR YOU. I'VE WATCHED YOU FOR DAYS. YOU'RE EVERY-THING A MAN COULD EVER WANT.
IT'S NOT JUST YOUR FACE, YOUR FIGURE, YOUR VOICE. IT'S YOUR EYES. ALL THE THINGS I SEE IN YOUR EYES.
AND WHAT IS IT YOU SEE IN MY EYES?
I SEE A CRAZY CALM. YOU'RE SICK OF RUNNING. YOU'RE READY TO FACE WHAT YOU HAVE TO FACE.
BUT YOU DON'T WANT TO FACE IT ALONE.
NO. I DON'T WANT TO FACE IT ALONE.

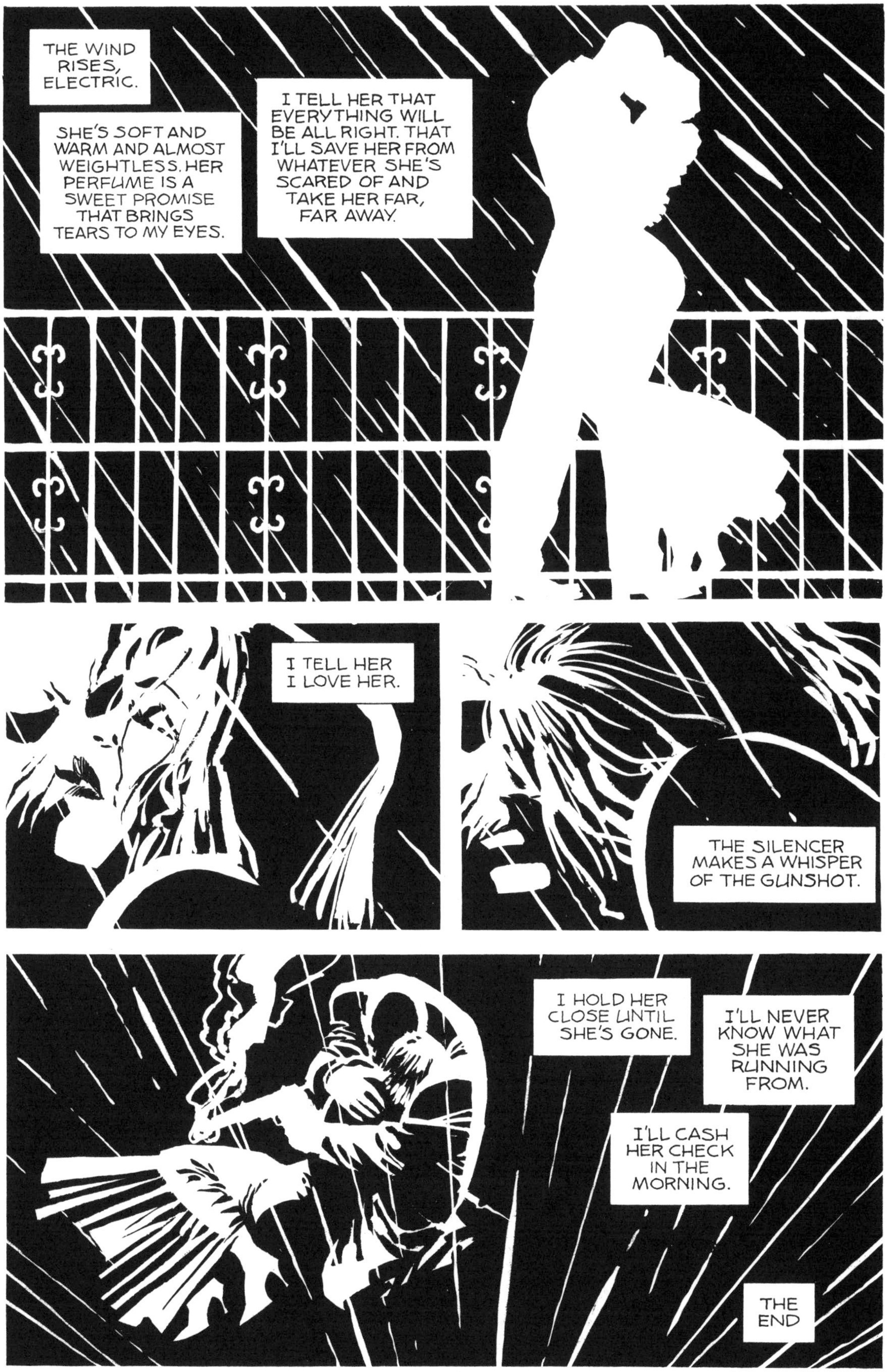
THE WIND RISES, ELECTRIC.
SHE'S SOFT AND WARM AND ALMOST WEIGHTLESS. HER PERFUME IS A SWEET PROMISE THAT BRINGS TEARS TO MY EYES.
I TELL HER THAT EVERYTHING WILL BE ALL RIGHT. THAT I'LL SAVE HER FROM WHATEVER SHE'S SCARED OF AND TAKE HER FAR, FAR AWAY.
I TELL HER I LOVE HER.
THE SILENCER MAKES A WHISPER OF THE GUNSHOT.
I HOLD HER CLOSE UNTIL SHE'S GONE.
I'LL NEVER KNOW WHAT SHE WAS RUNNING FROM.
I'LL CASH HER CHECK IN THE MORNING.
THE END

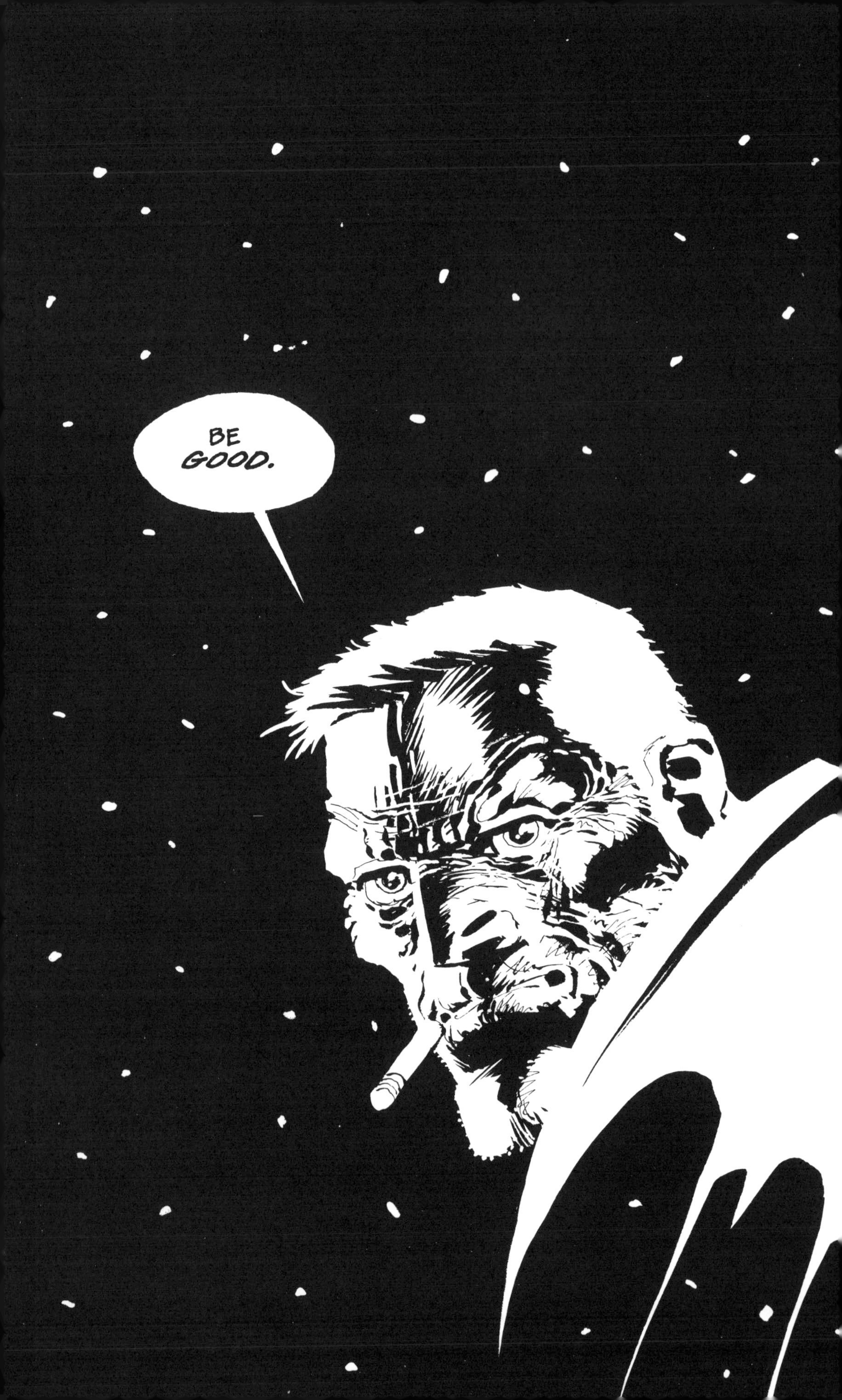
BE GOOD.

silent night

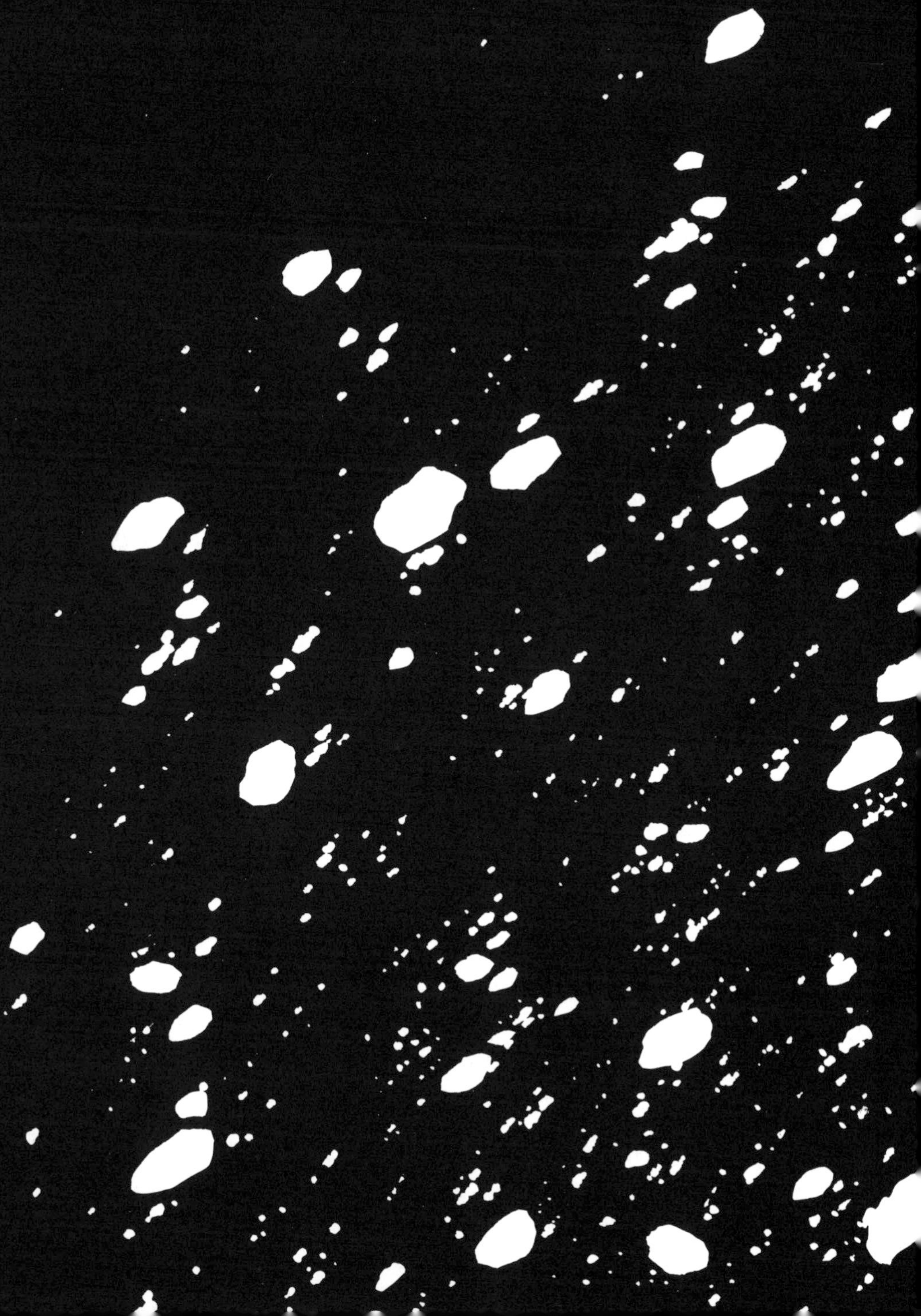

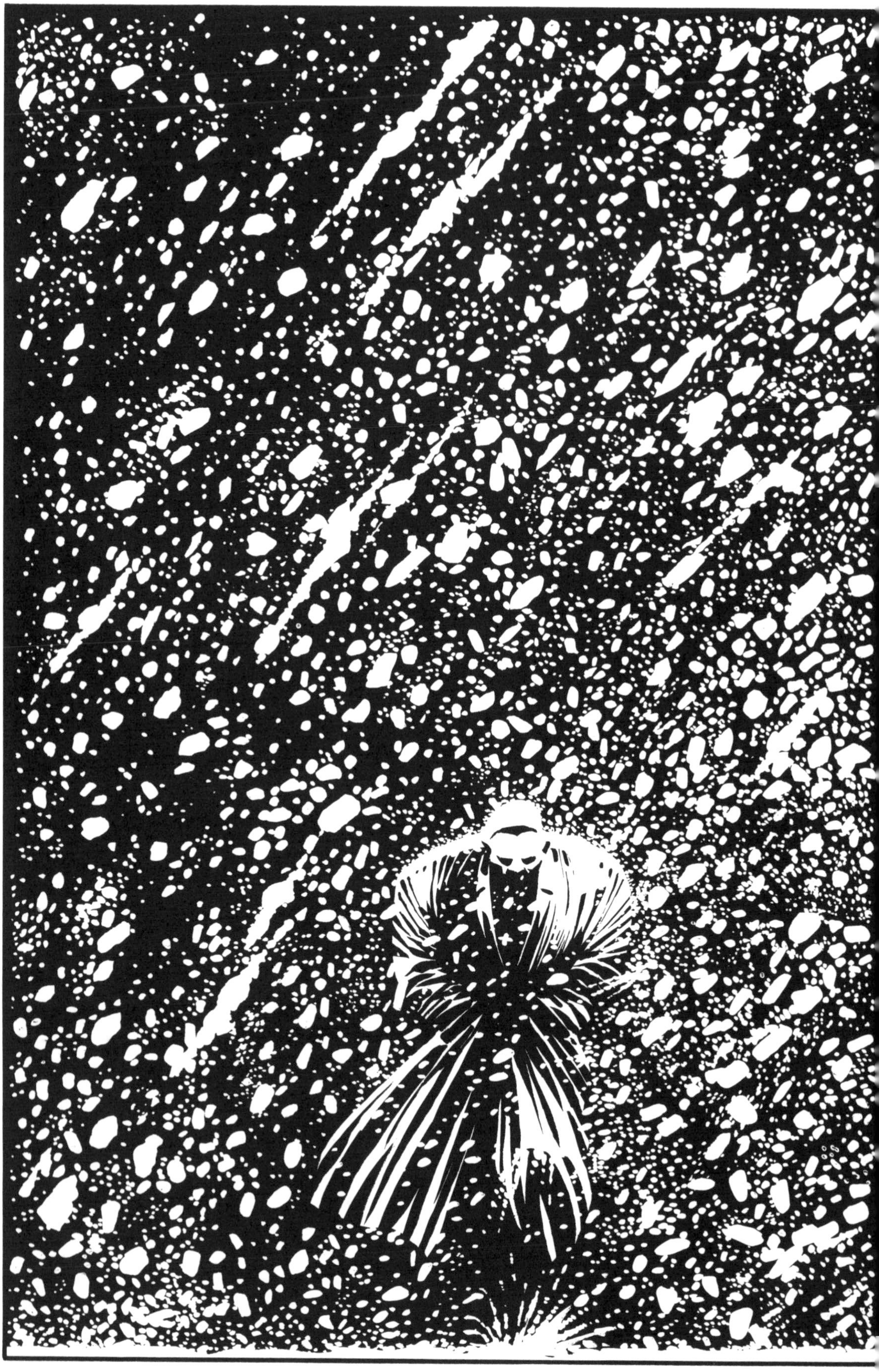

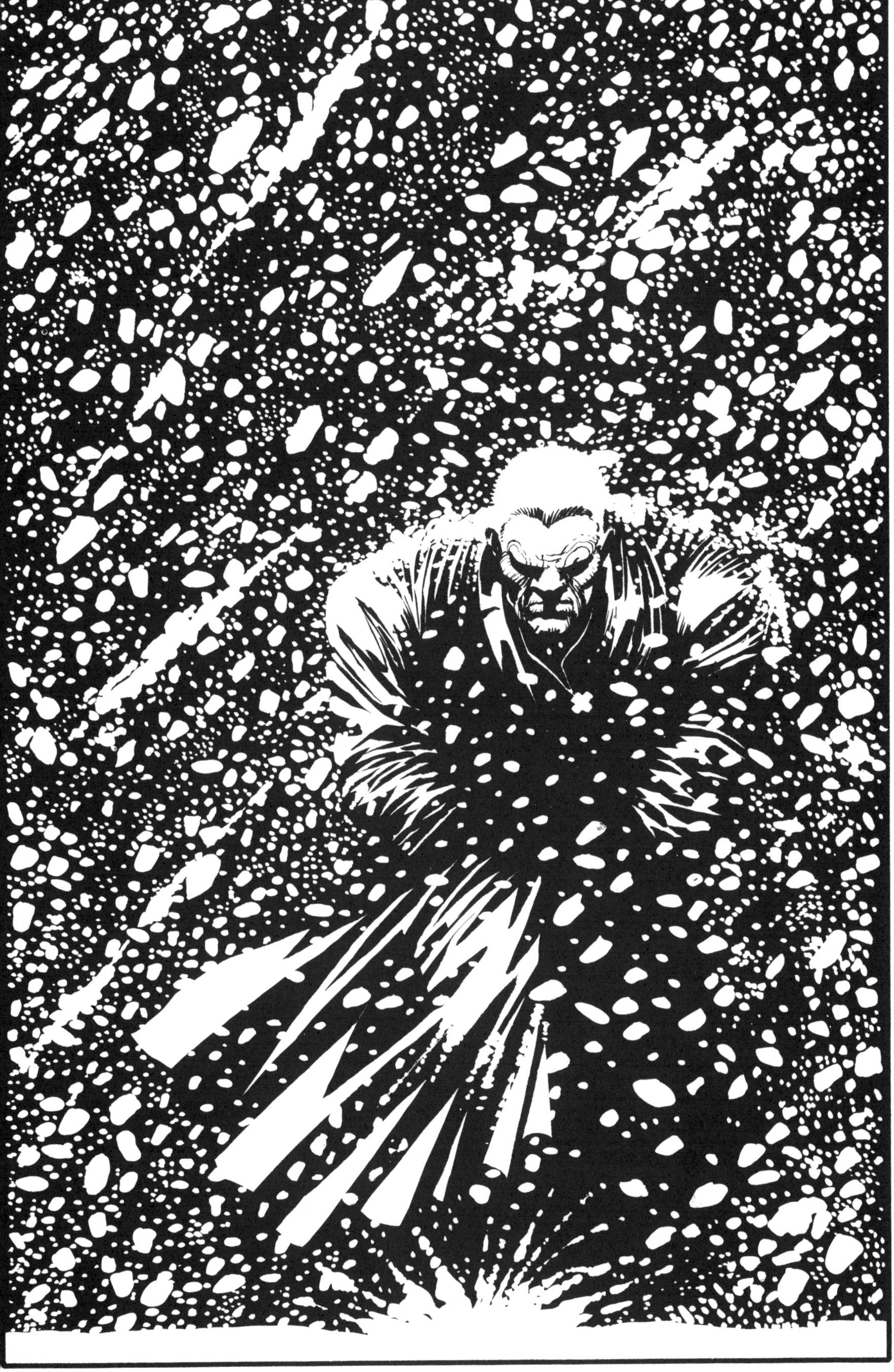

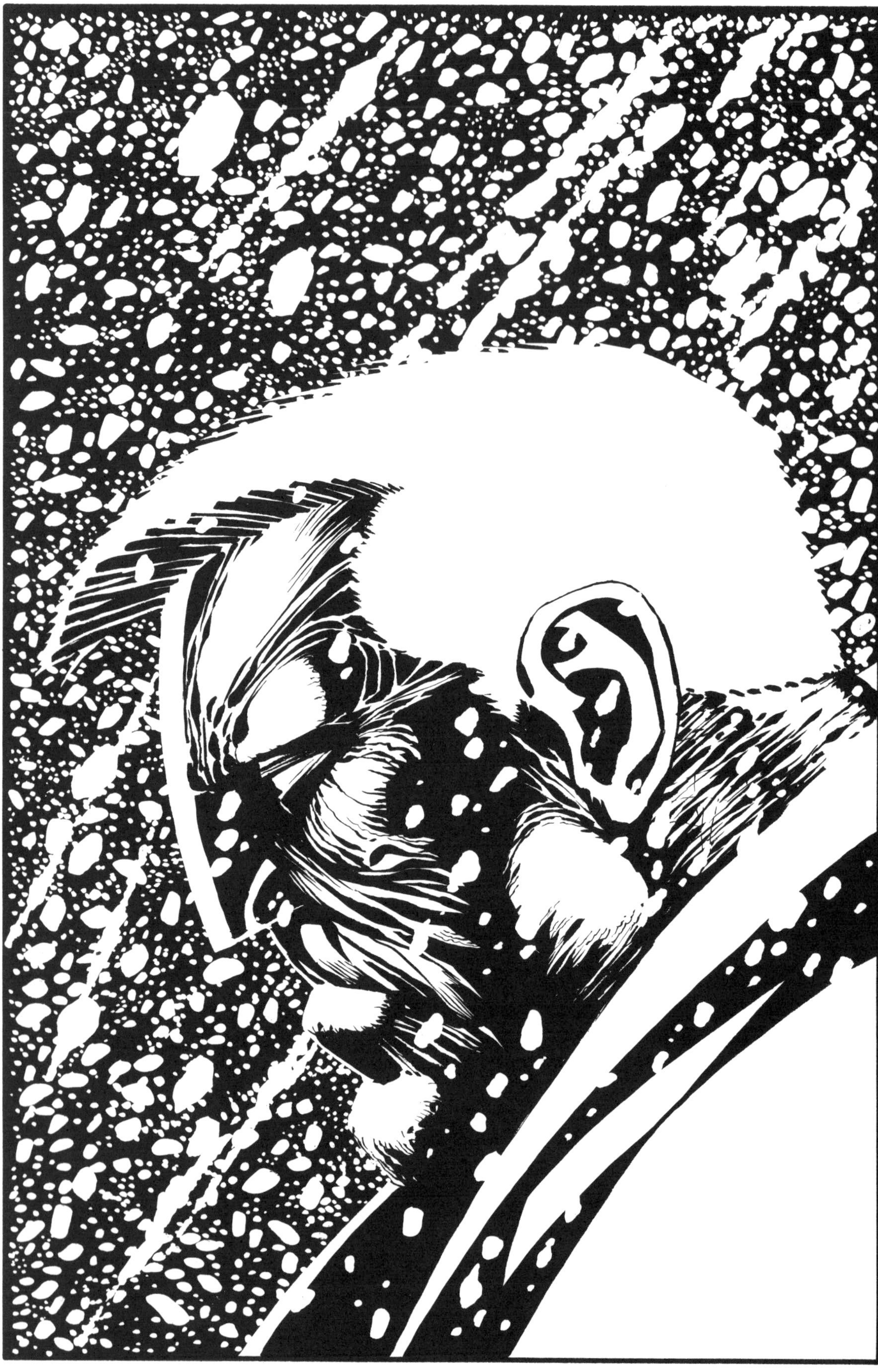

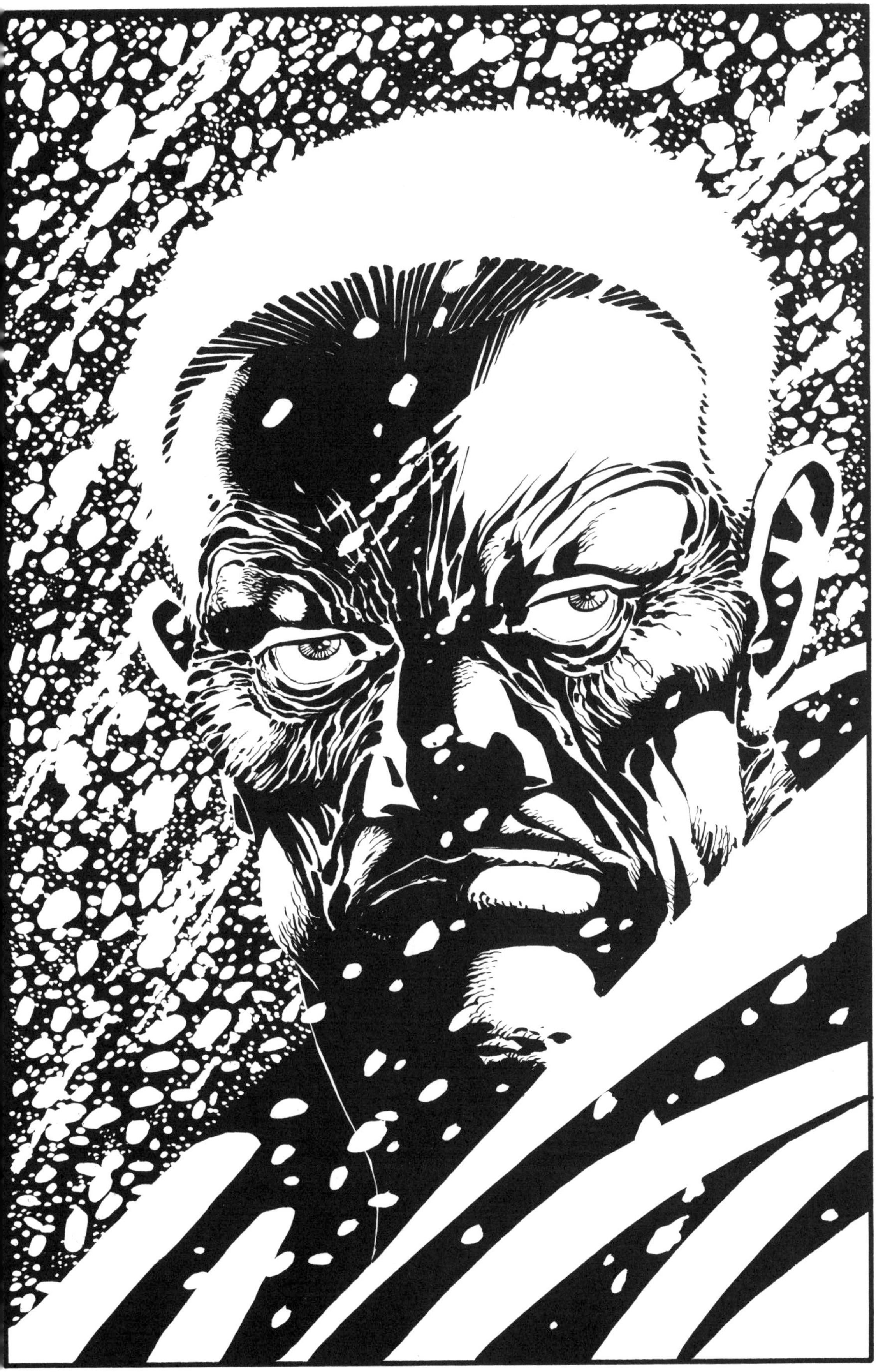

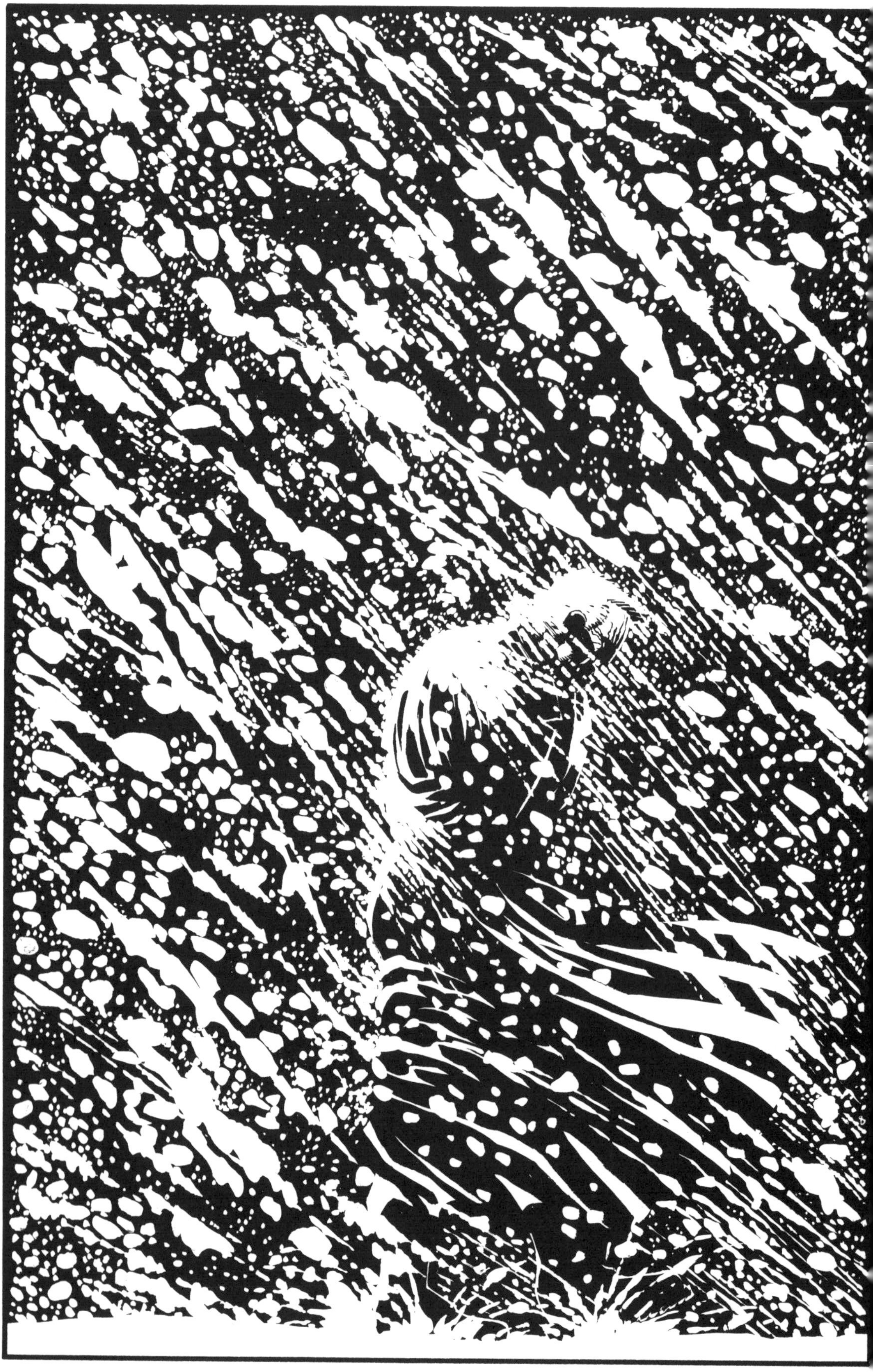

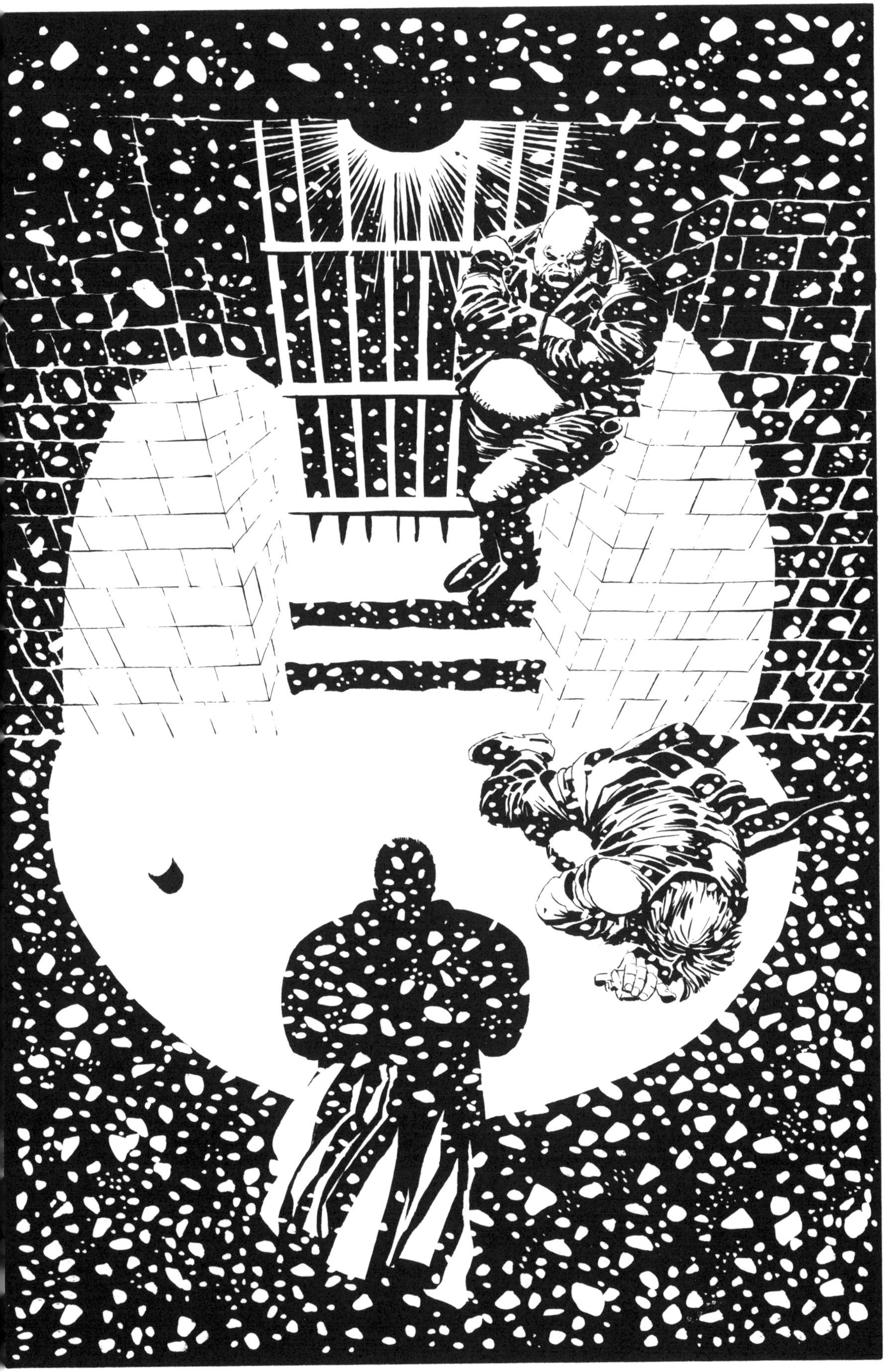

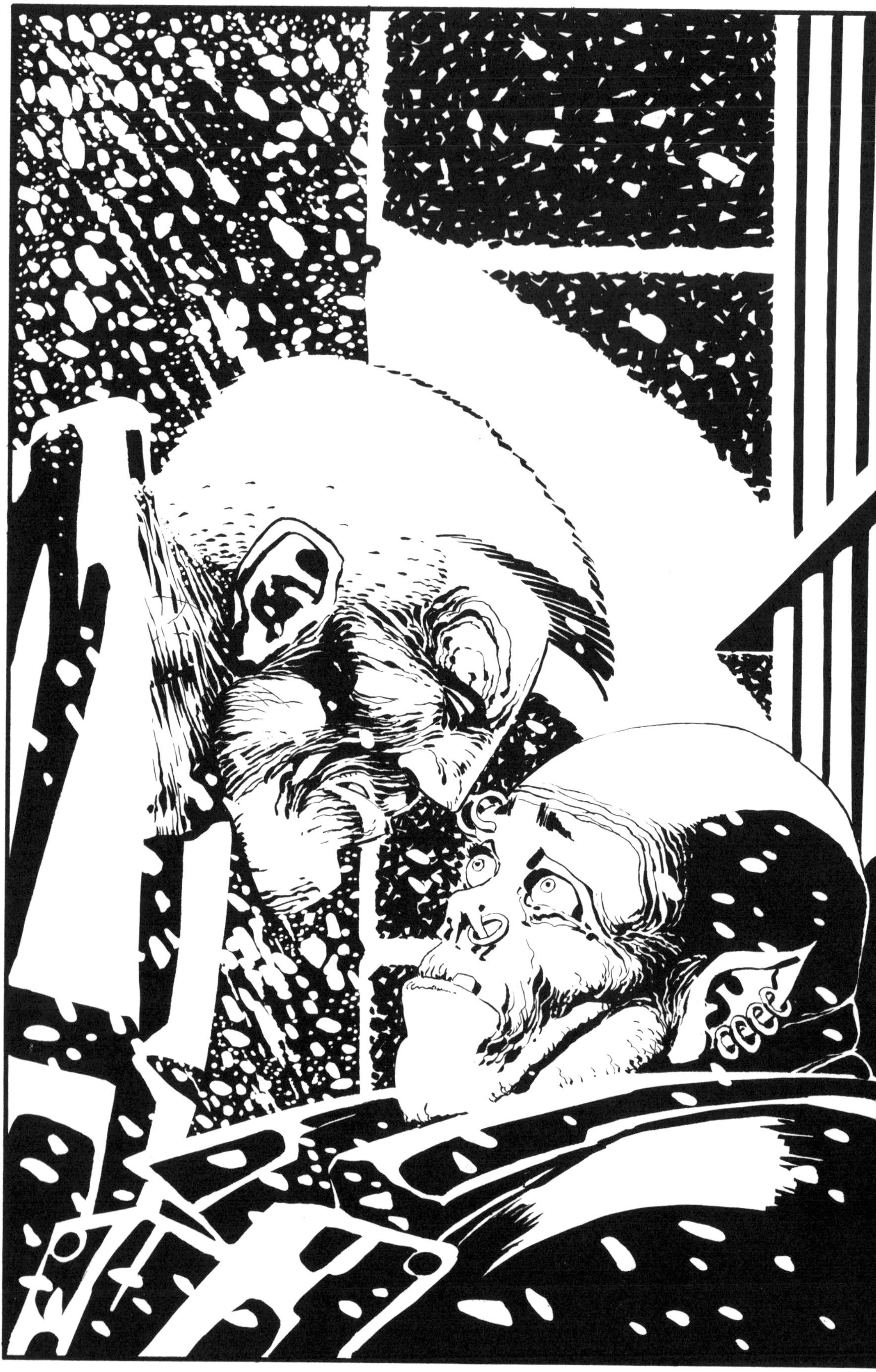

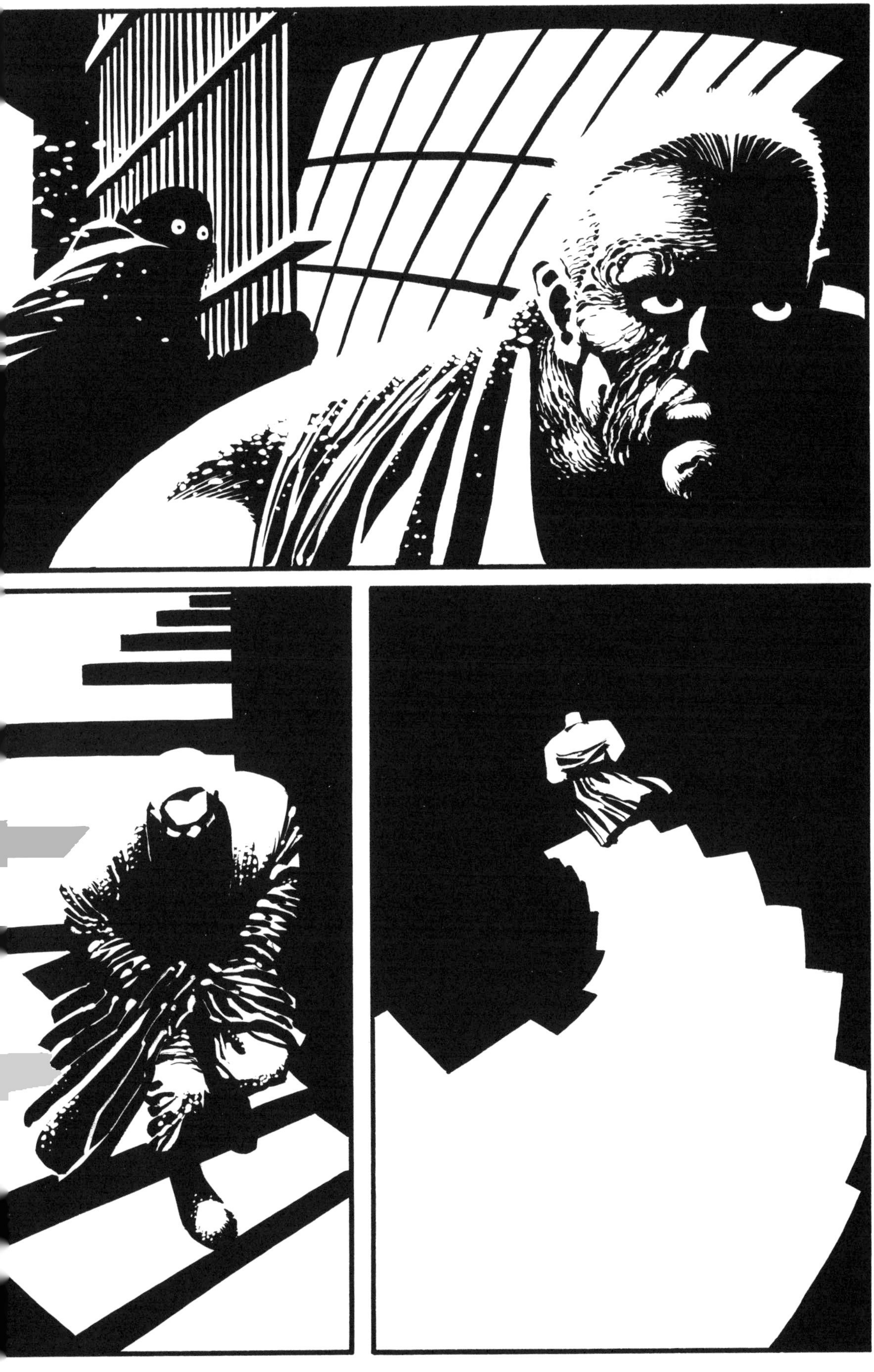

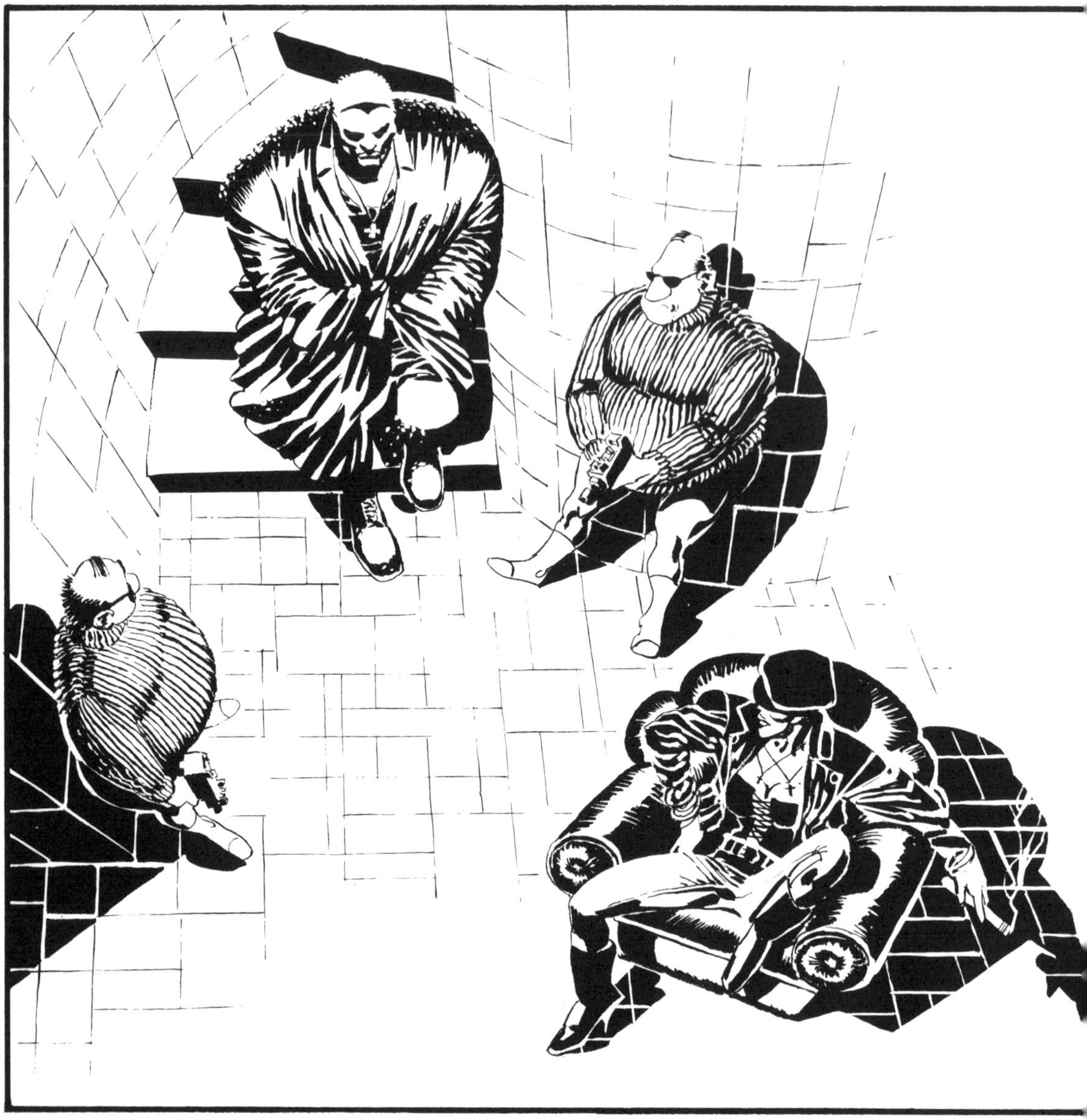

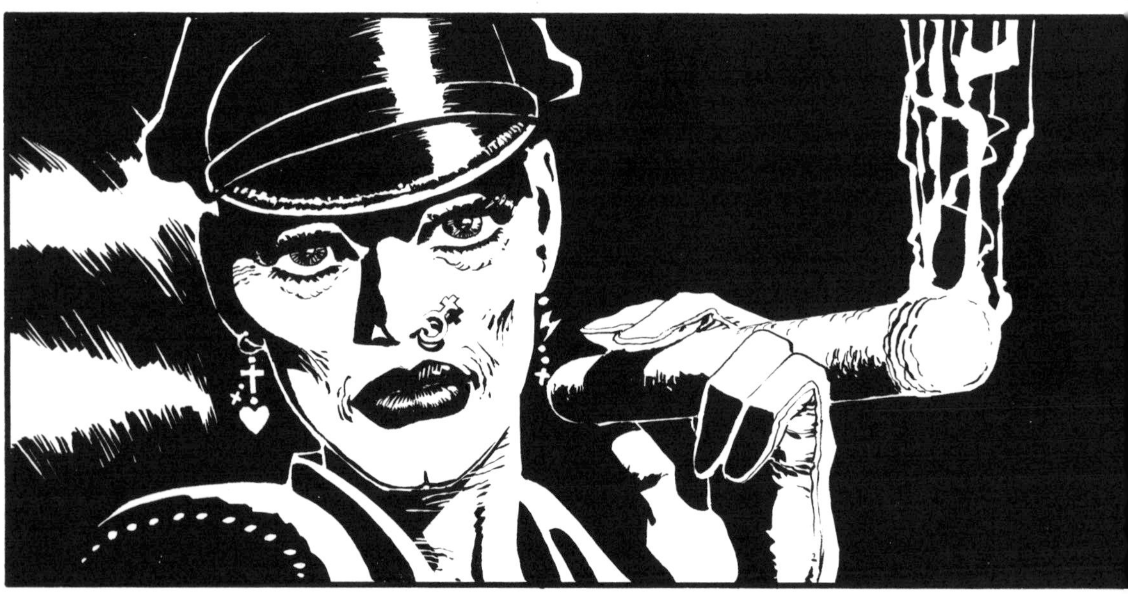

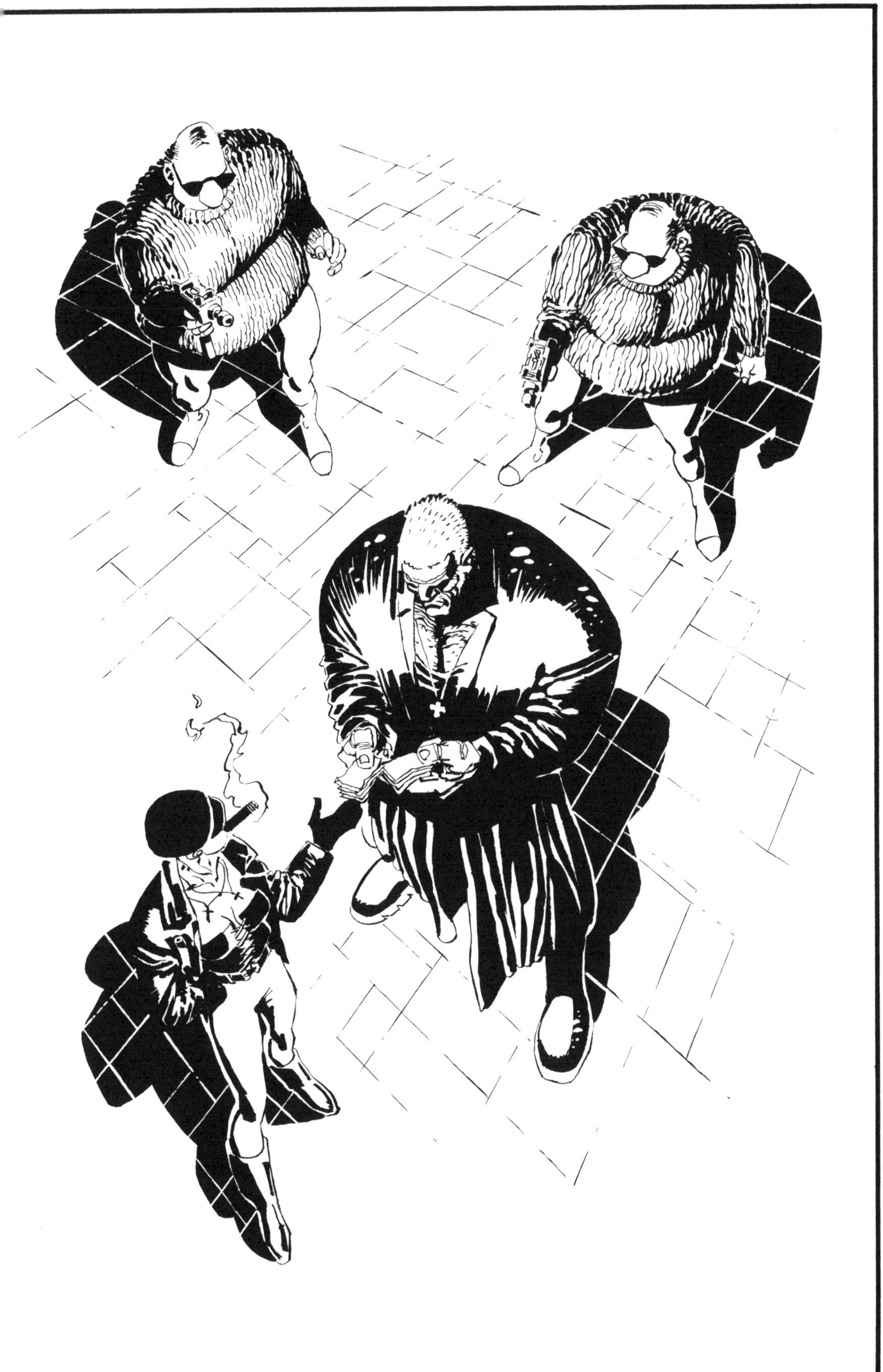

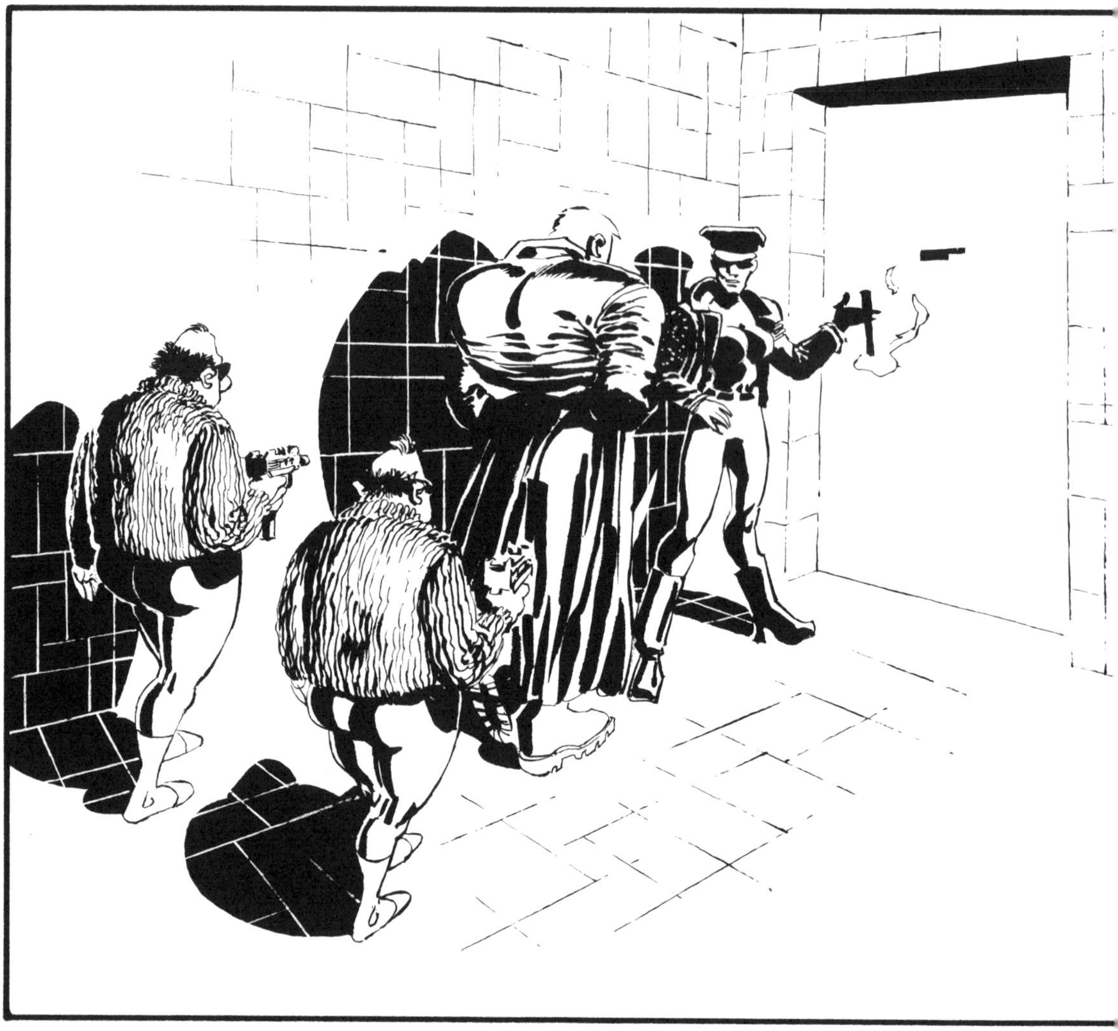

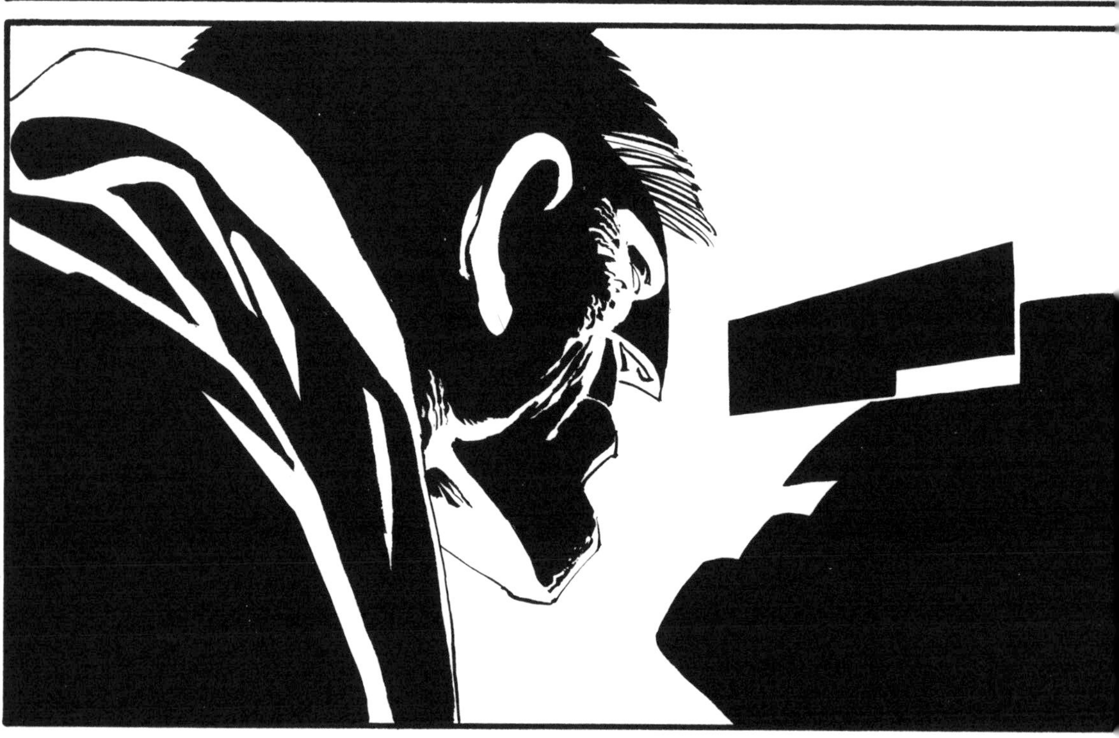

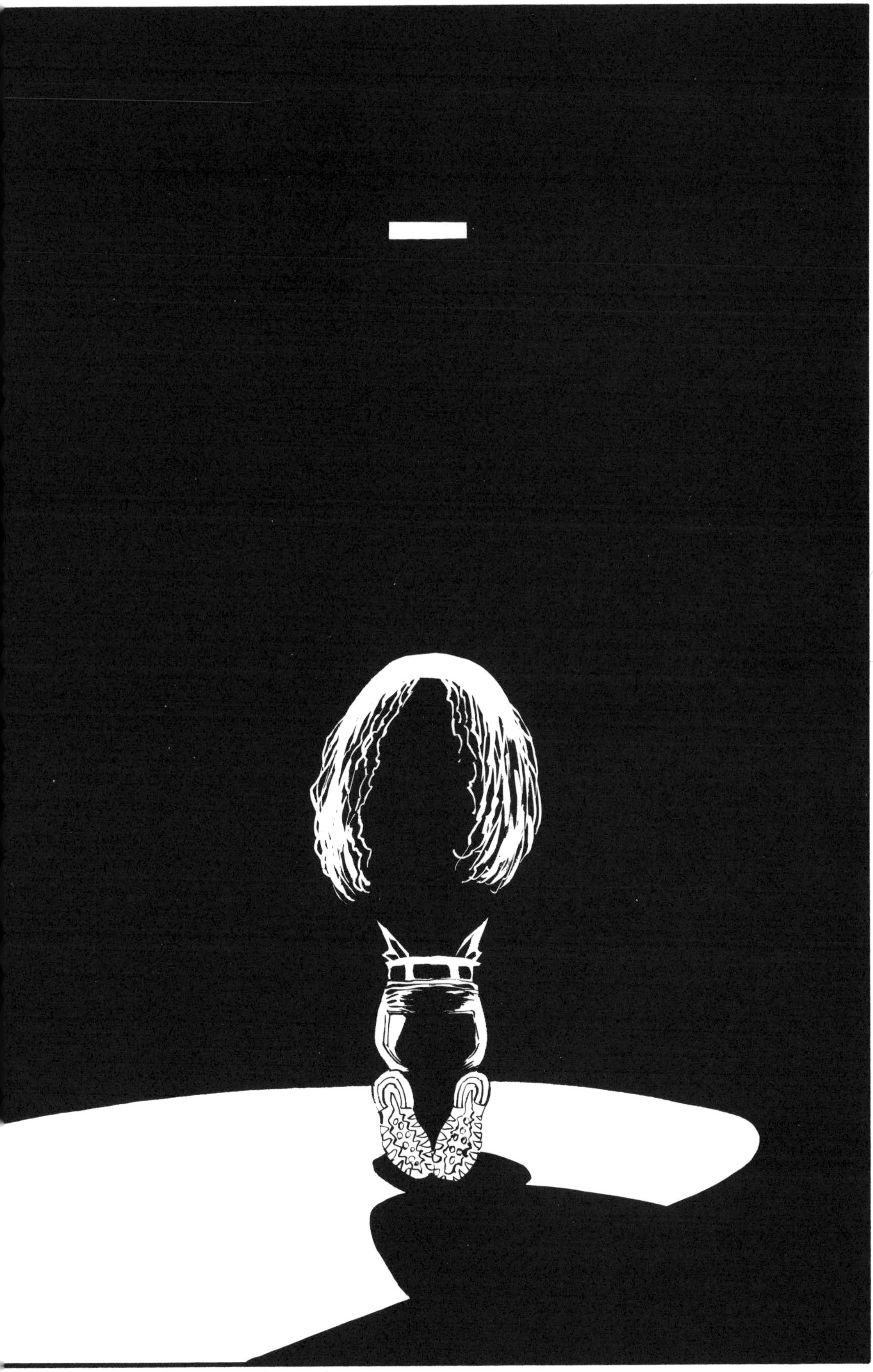

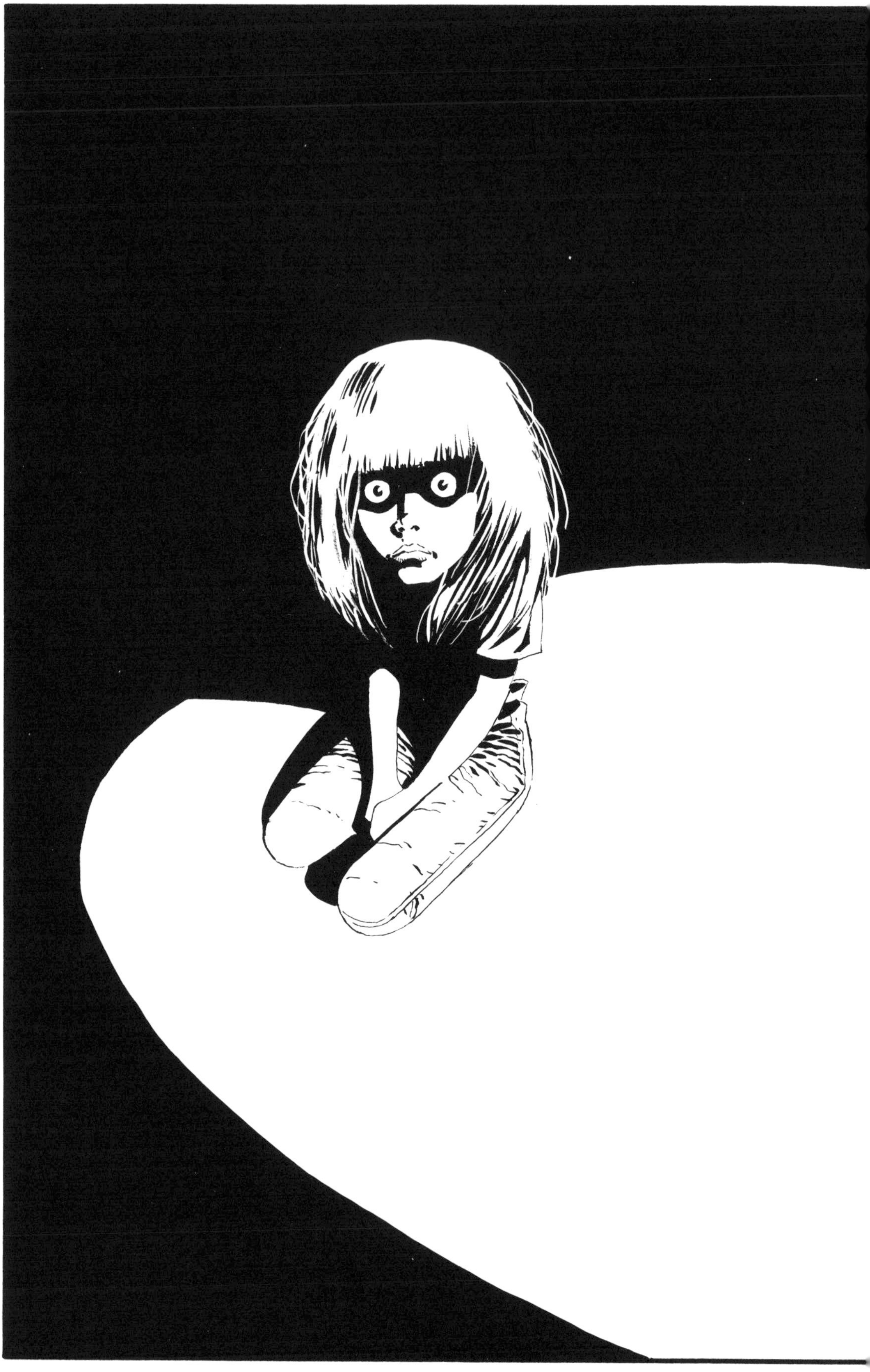

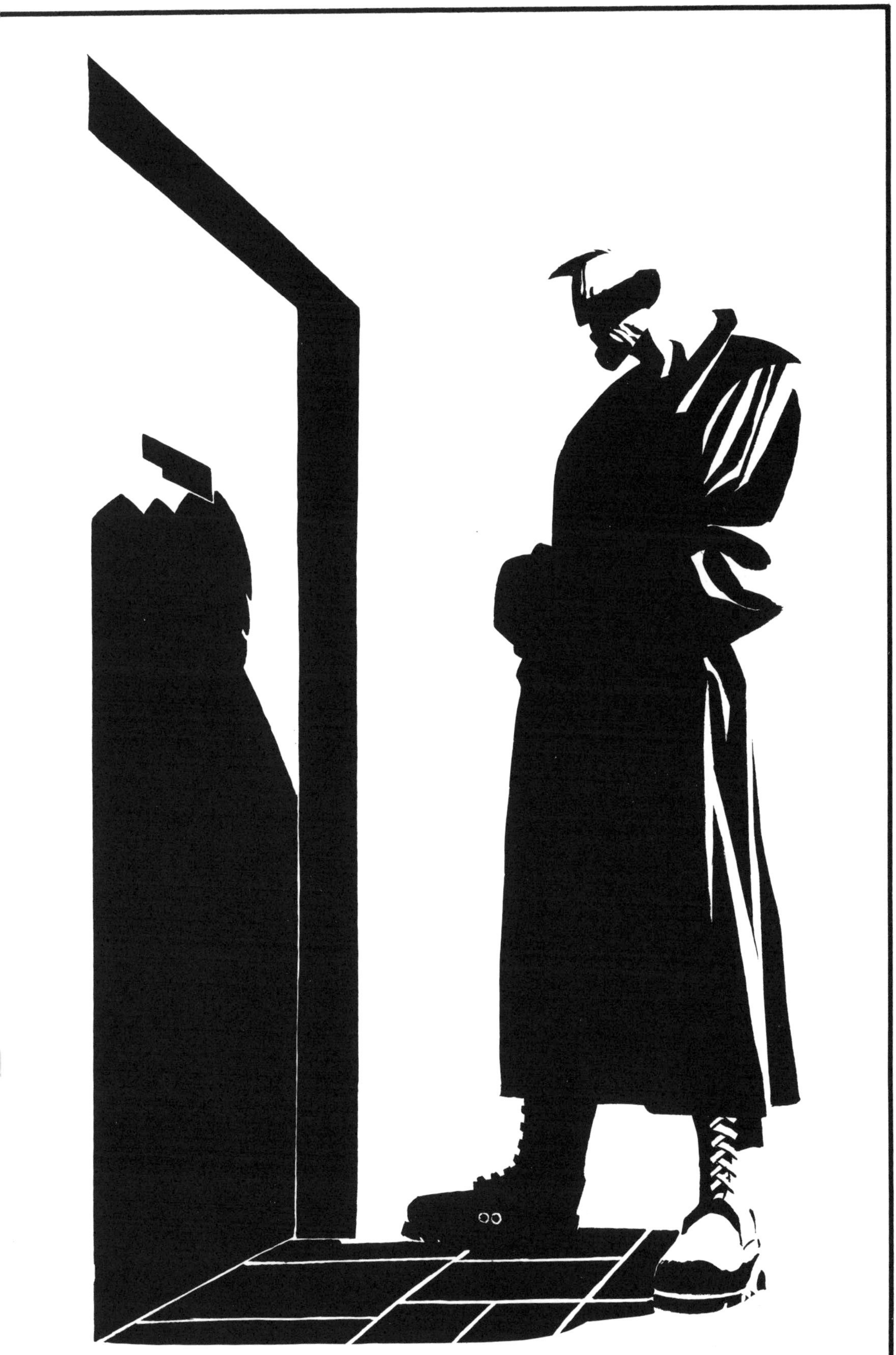

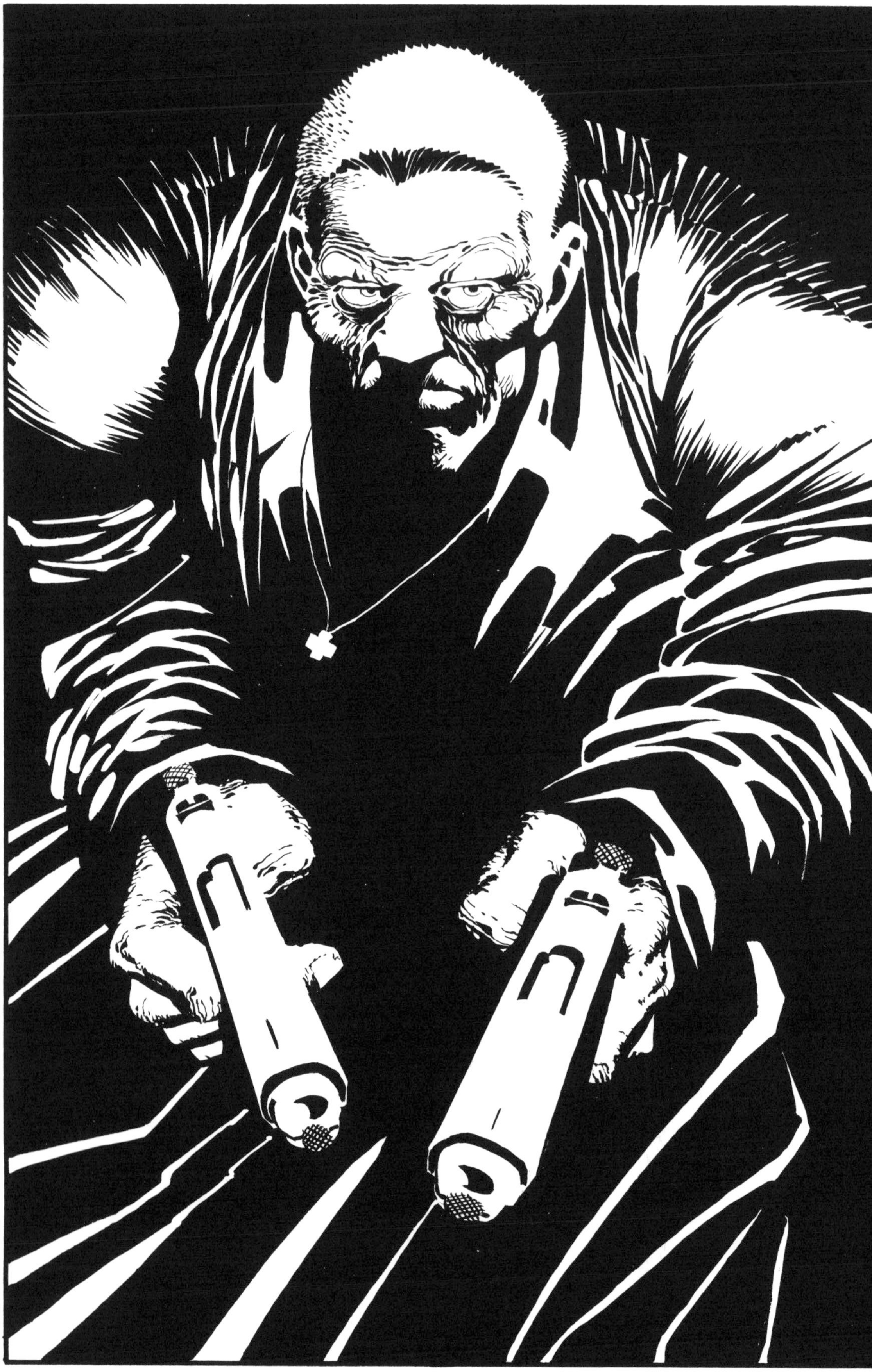

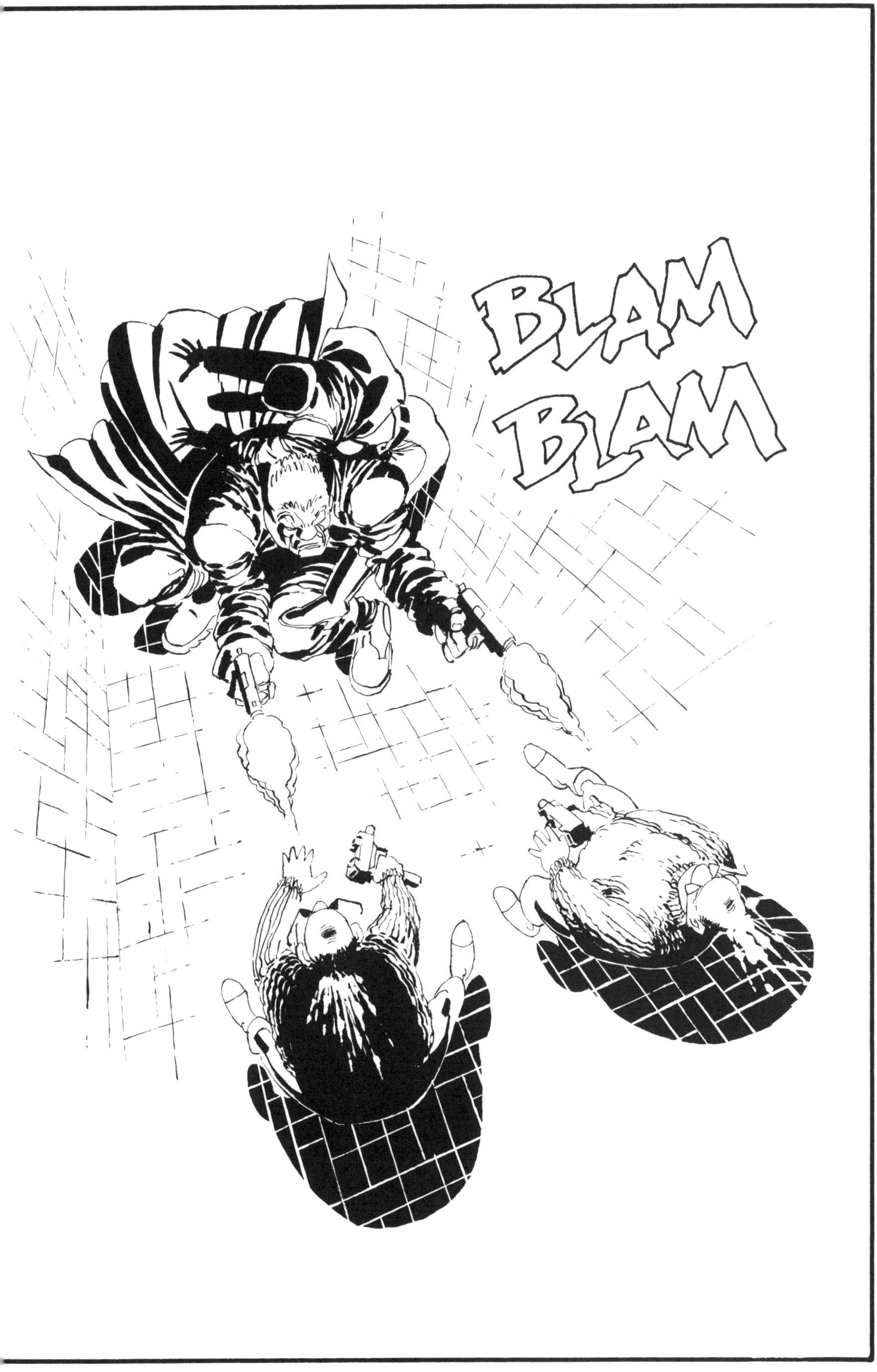
BLAM
BLAM

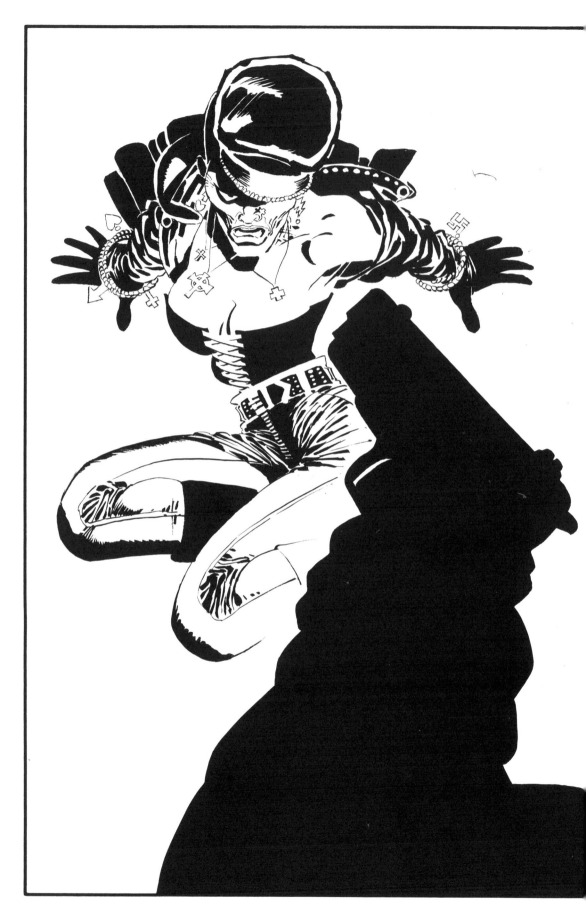

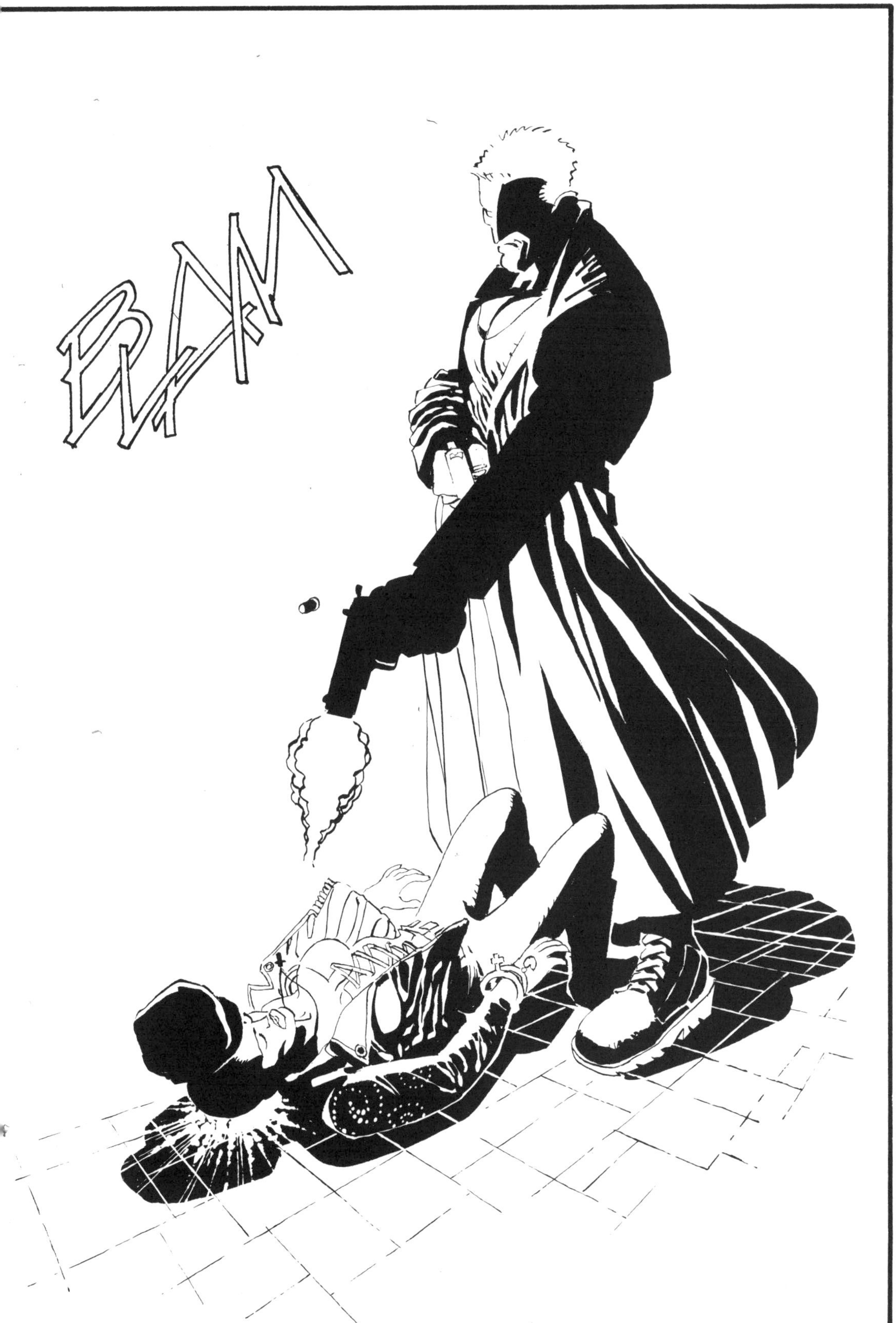
BLAM

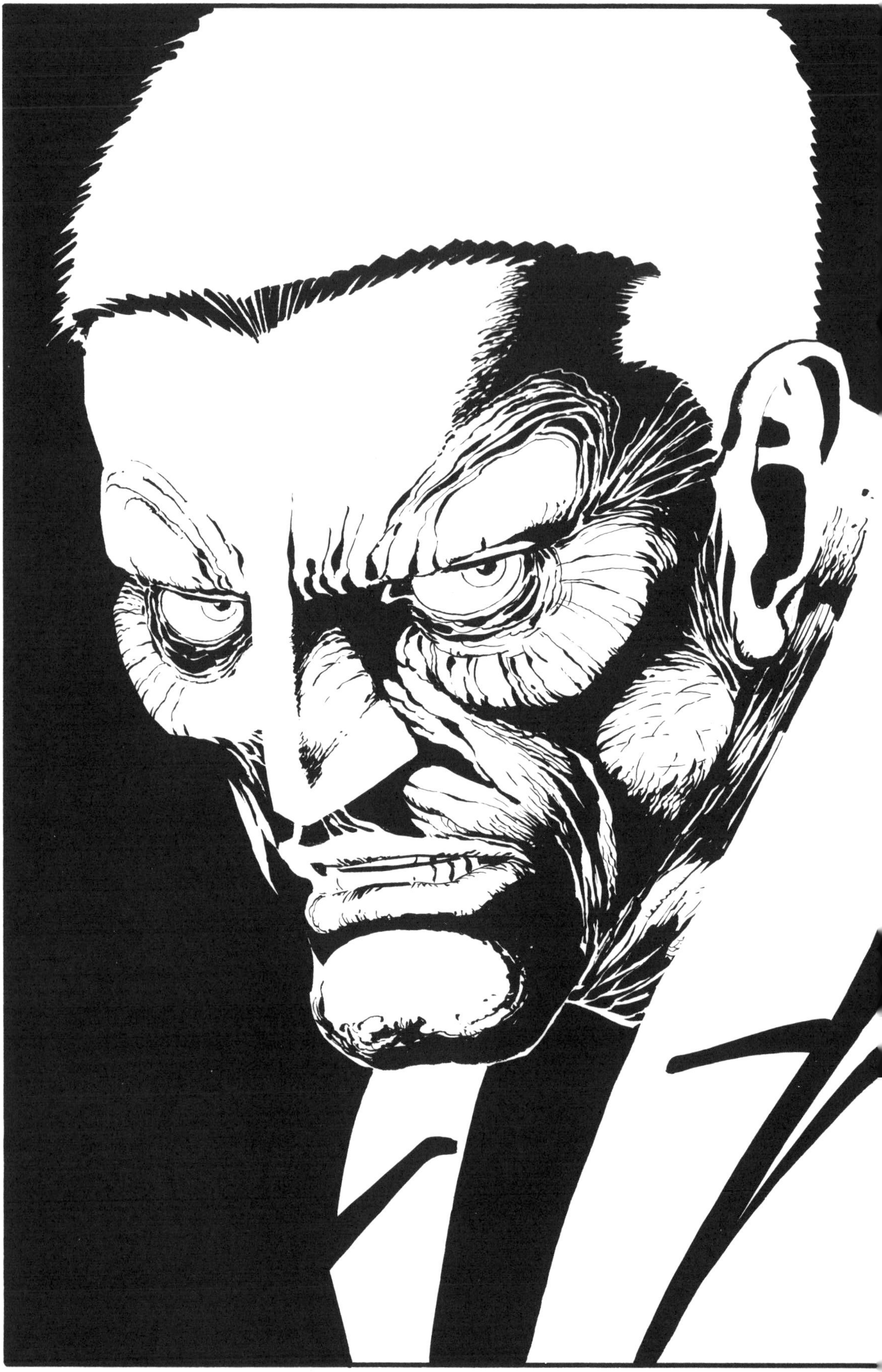

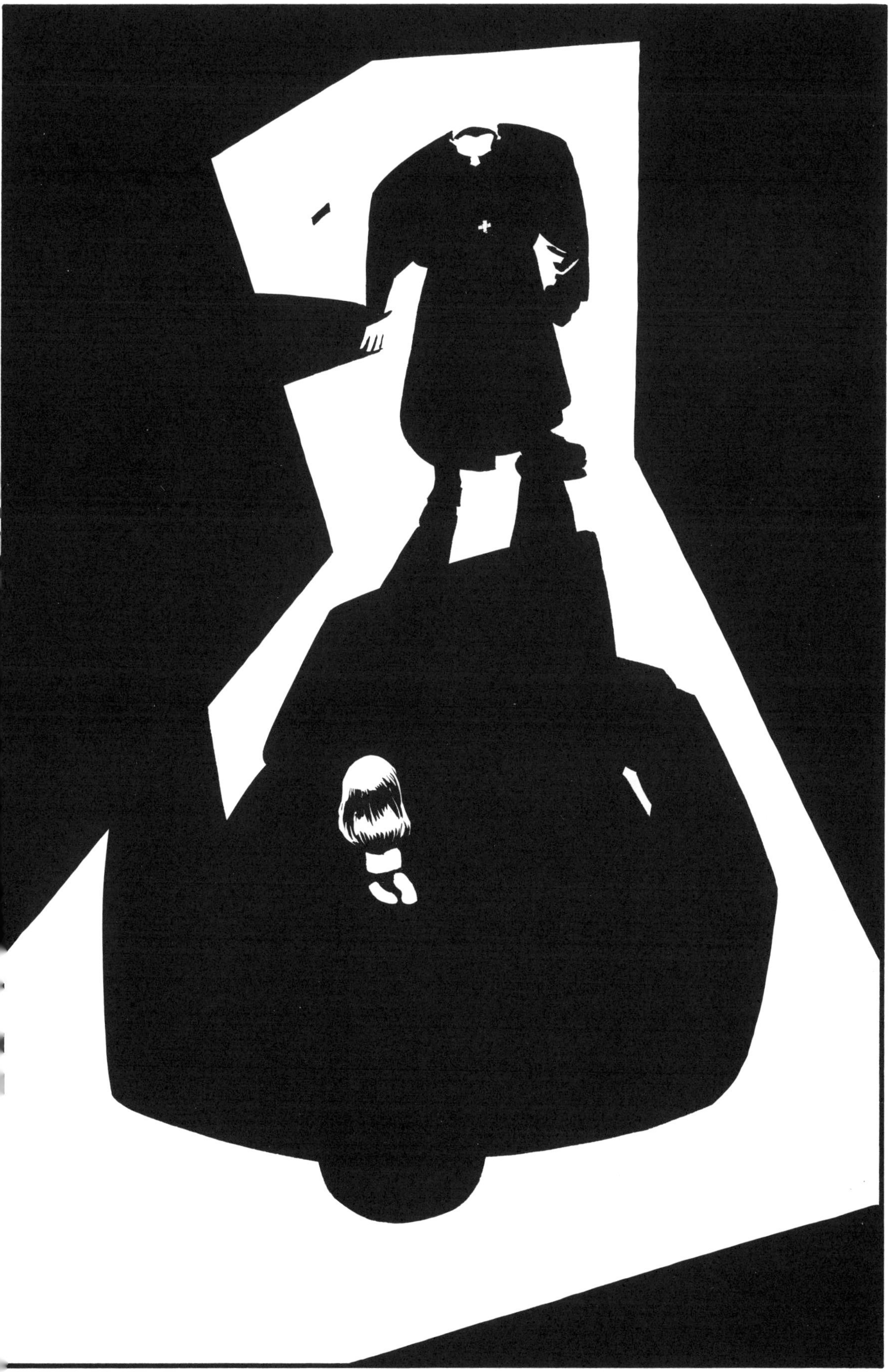

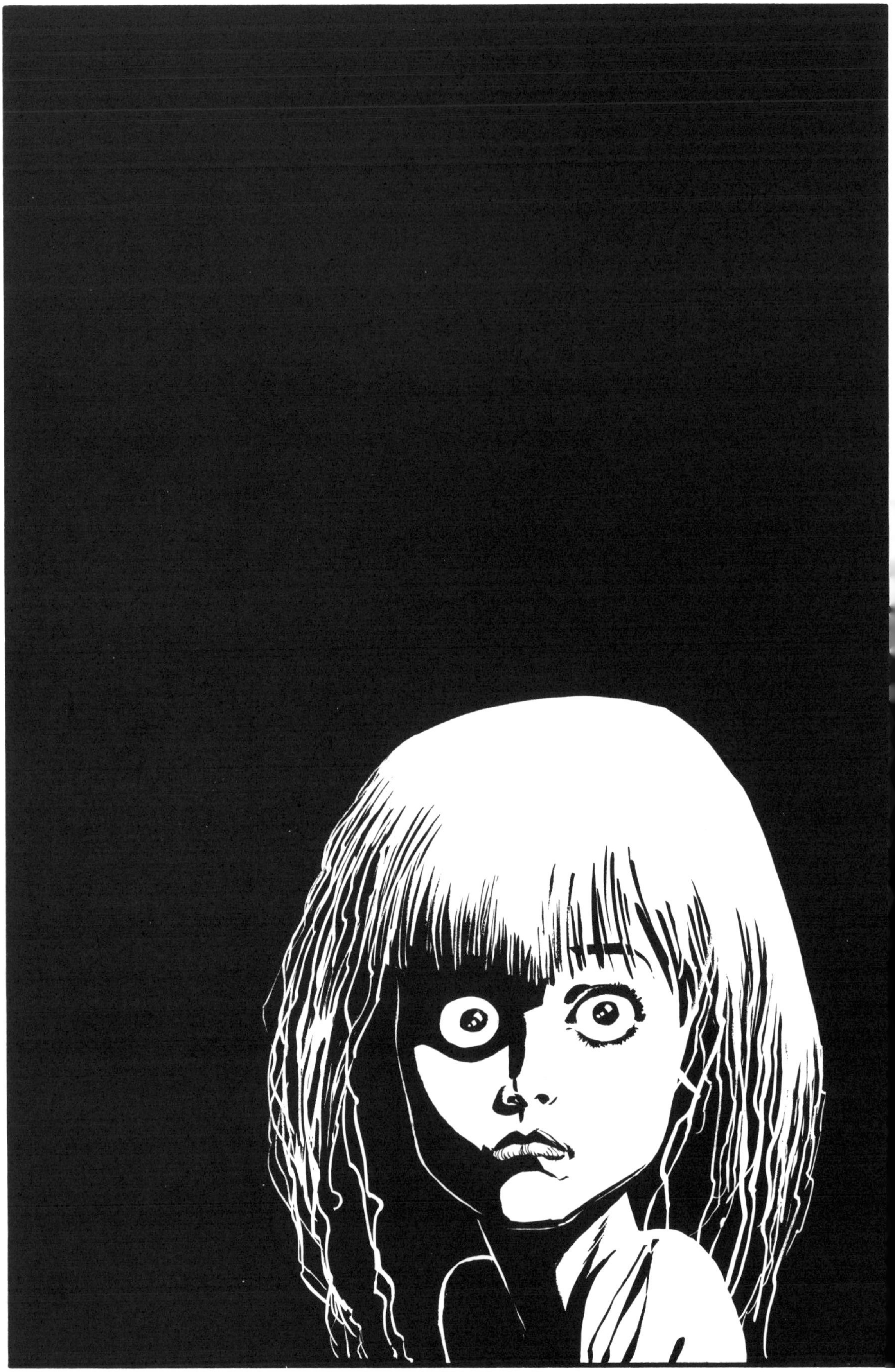

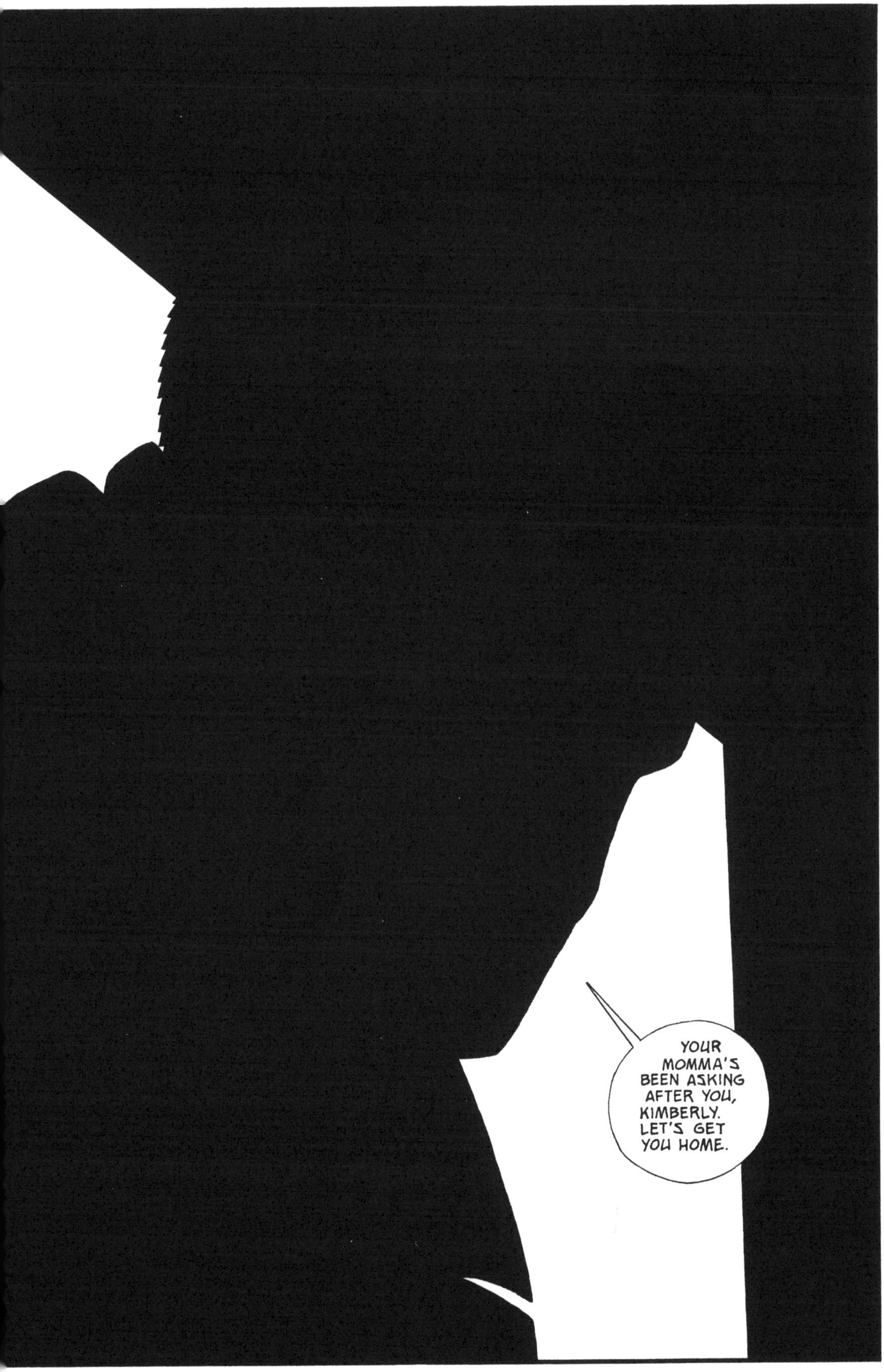
YOUR MOMMA'S BEEN ASKING AFTER YOU, KIMBERLY. LET'S GET YOU HOME.

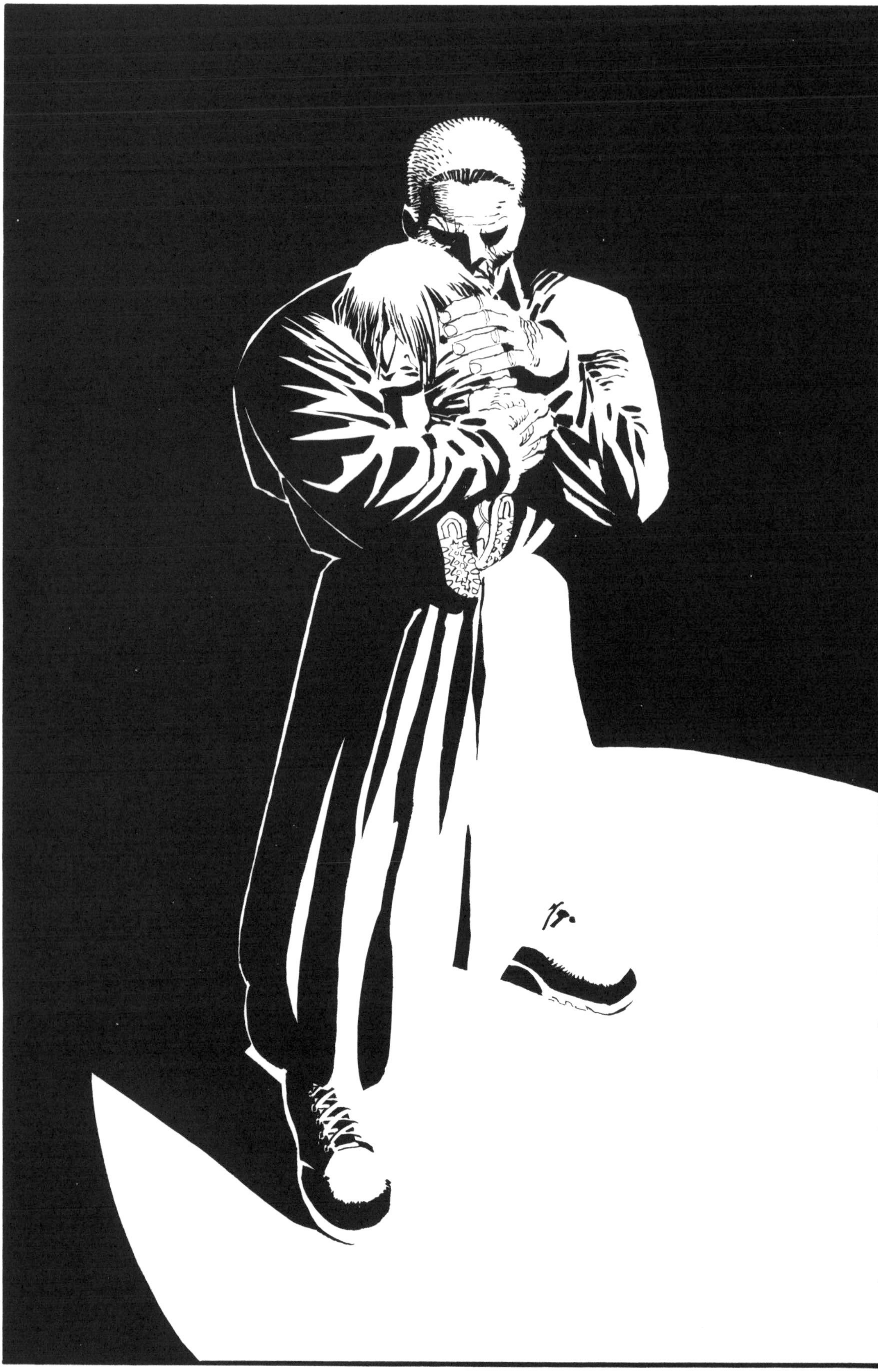

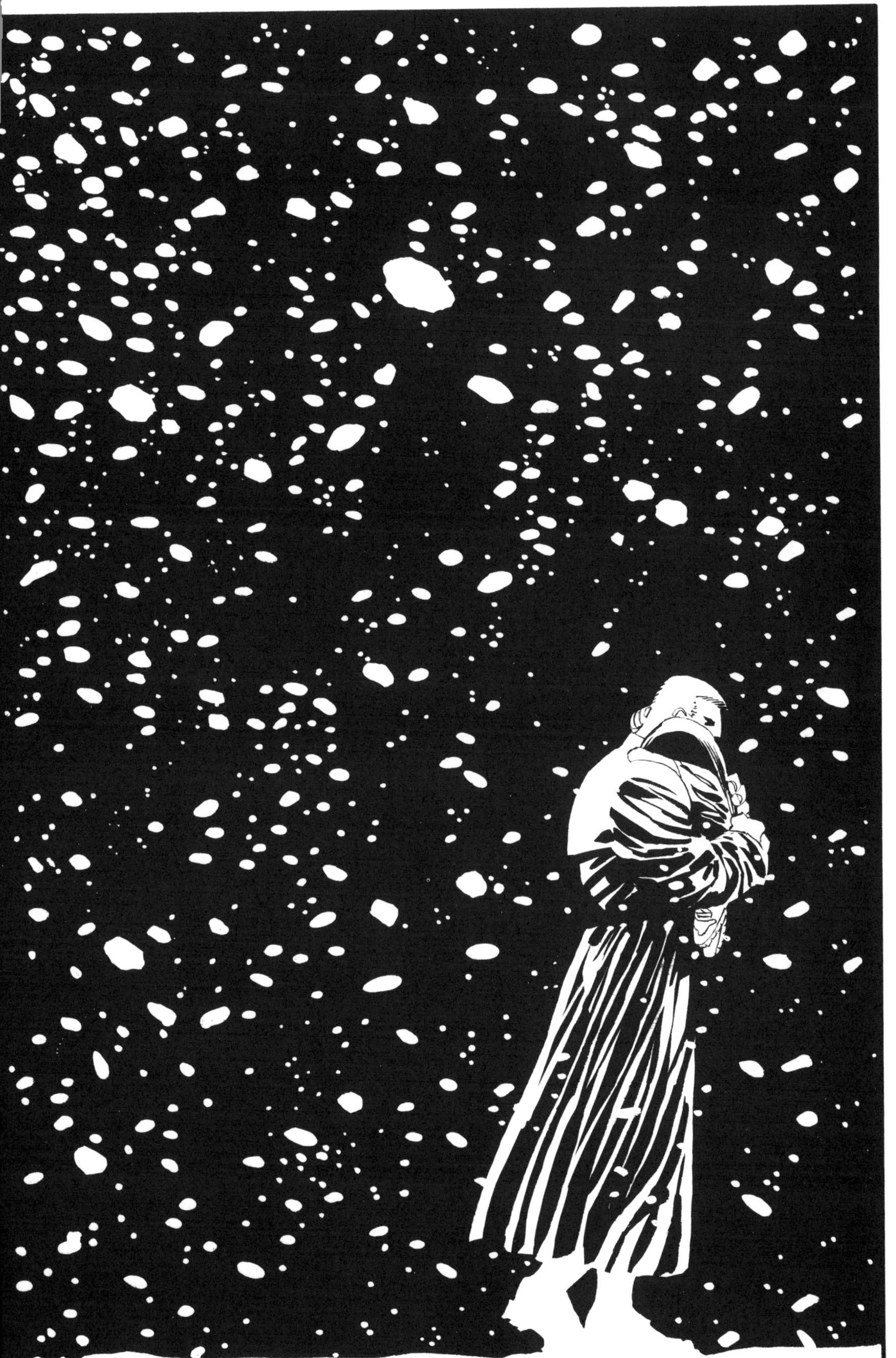

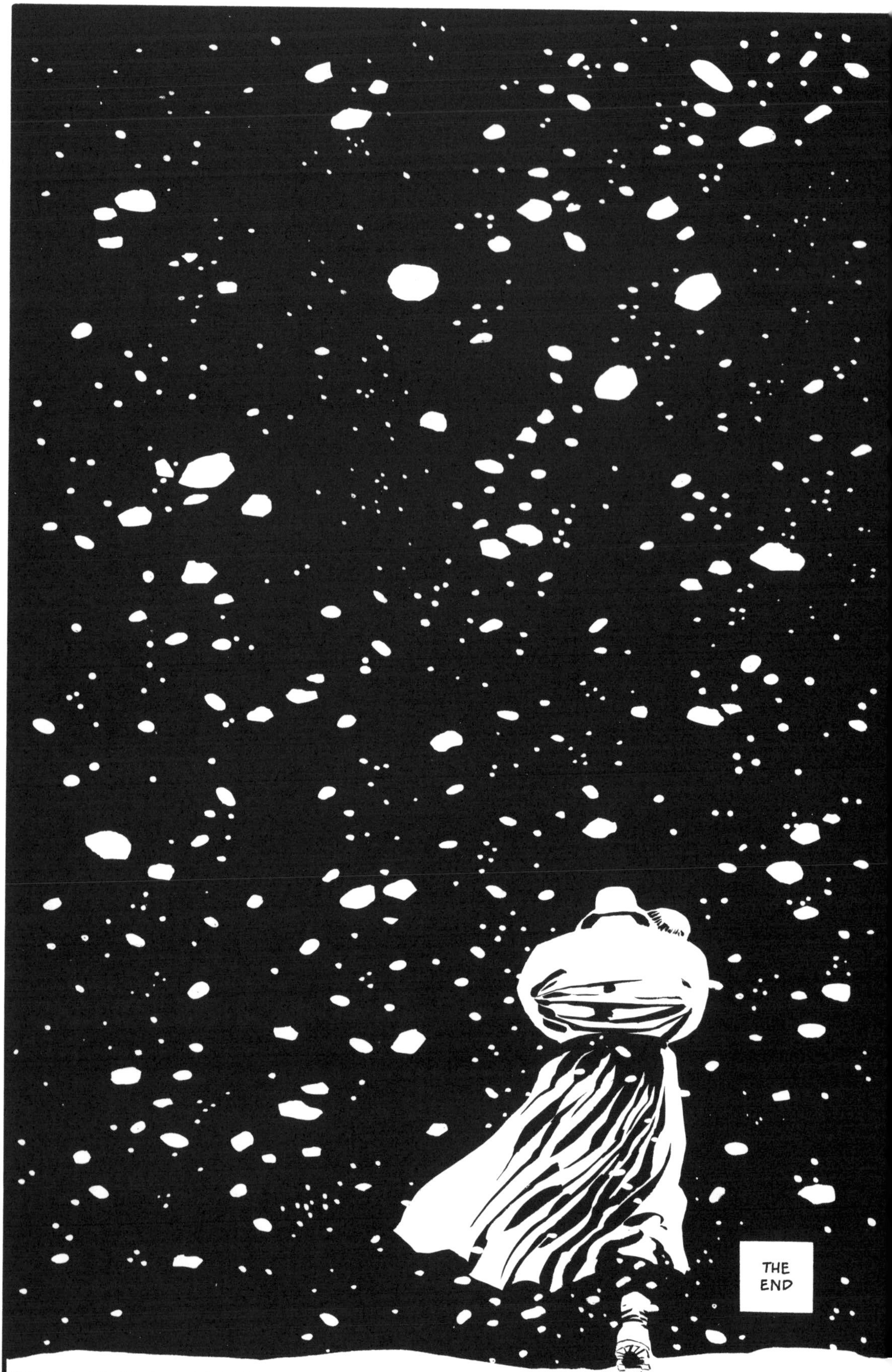
THE
END

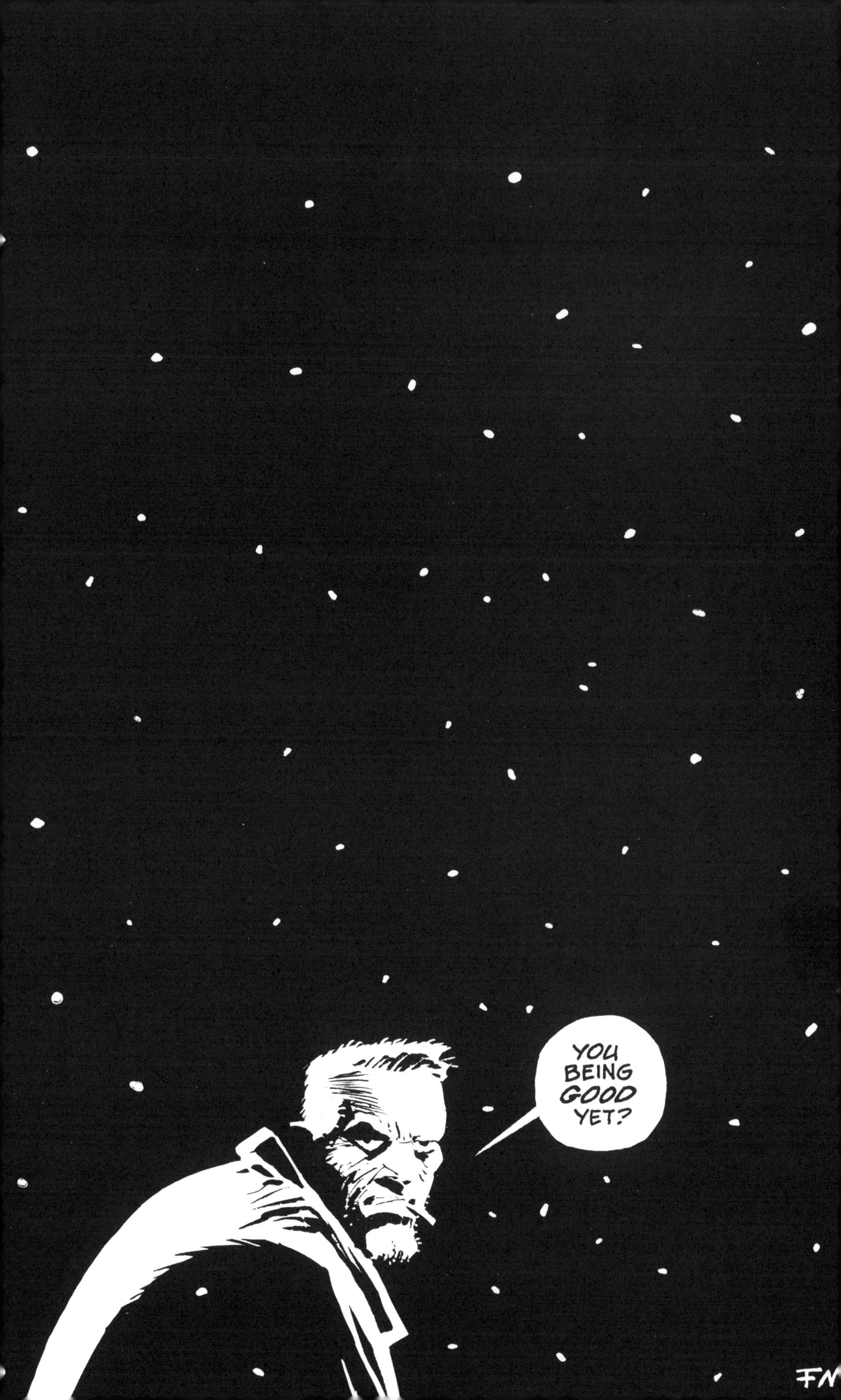
YOU BEING GOOD YET?
FM

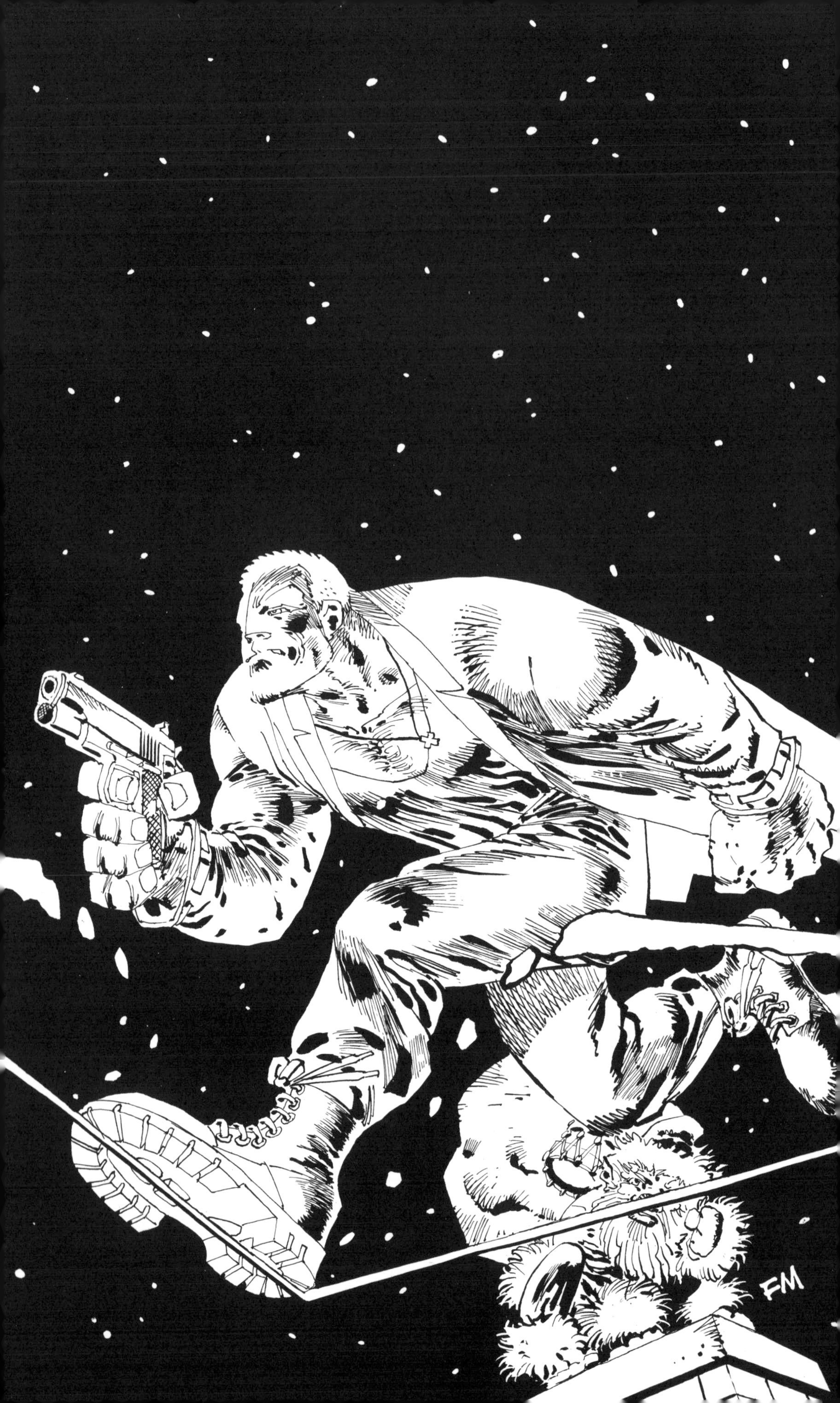
FM

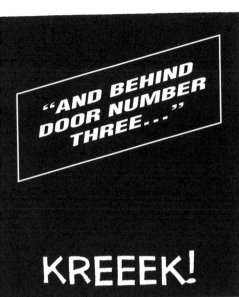

"AND BEHIND DOOR NUMBER THREE..."

KREEEK!

YOU SURE ARE A PRETTY ONE. I GUESS EVERYTHING I HEARD ABOUT YOU SIN CITY GALS IS TRUE.

THAT'S A BIG KNIFE YOU'VE GOT THERE, COWBOY. GOING HUNTING?

THE SWEATY NEIGHBORHOOD THEY CALL "OLD TOWN," WHERE ALL YOUR DREAMS CAN COME TRUE.

AS LONG AS YOU'VE GOT THE CASH--AND AS LONG AS YOU PLAY BY THE *RULES.*

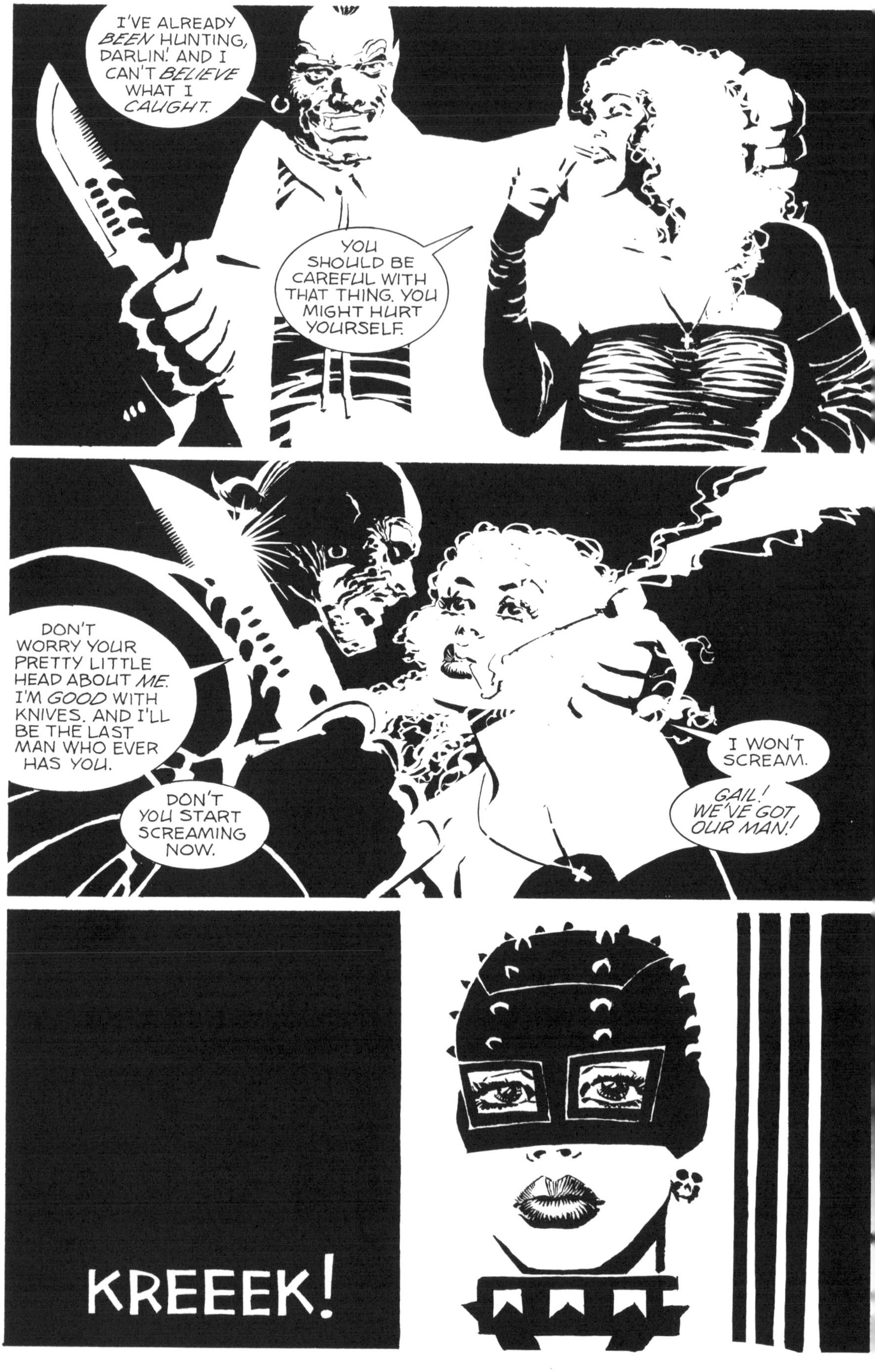

I'VE ALREADY BEEN HUNTING, DARLIN'. AND I CAN'T BELIEVE WHAT I CAUGHT.
YOU SHOULD BE CAREFUL WITH THAT THING. YOU MIGHT HURT YOURSELF.
DON'T WORRY YOUR PRETTY LITTLE HEAD ABOUT ME. I'M GOOD WITH KNIVES. AND I'LL BE THE LAST MAN WHO EVER HAS YOU.
DON'T YOU START SCREAMING NOW.
I WON'T SCREAM.
GAIL! WE'VE GOT OUR MAN!
KREEEK!

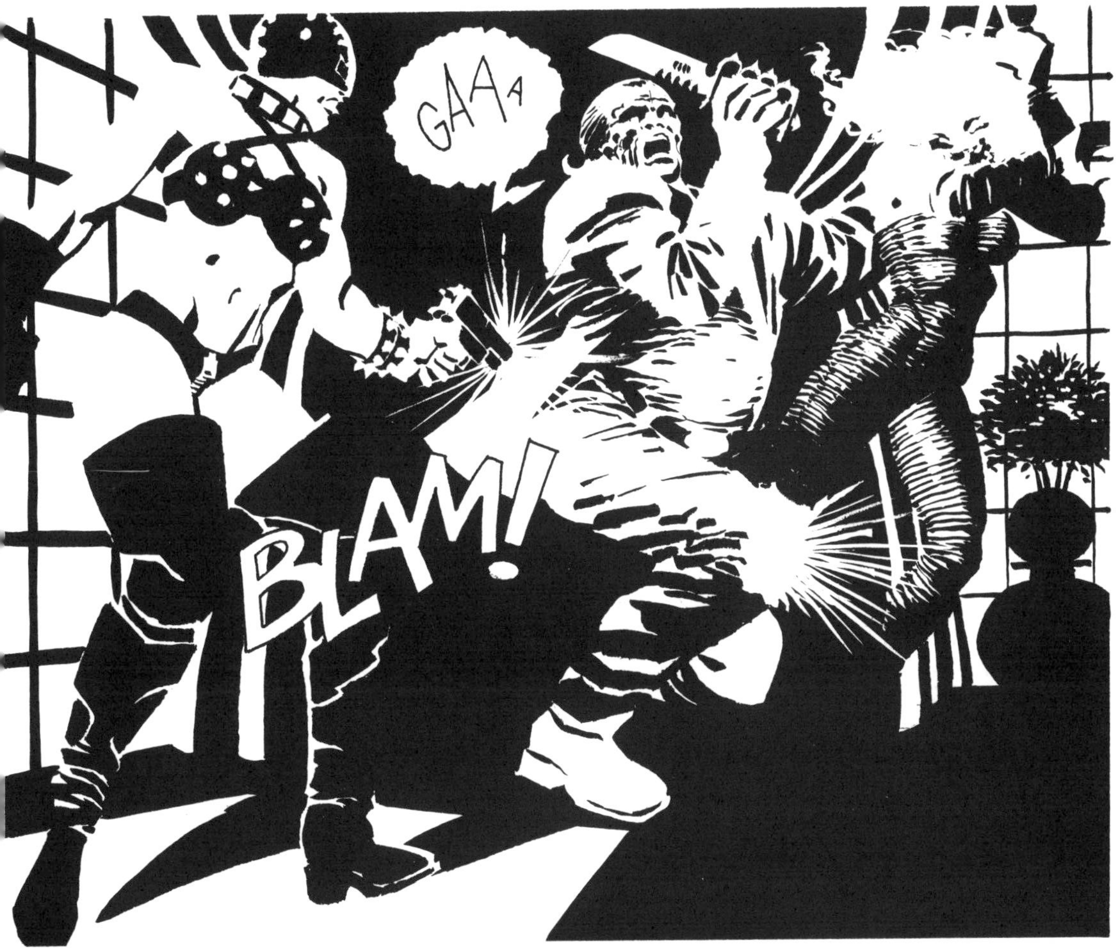
GAAa
BLAM!

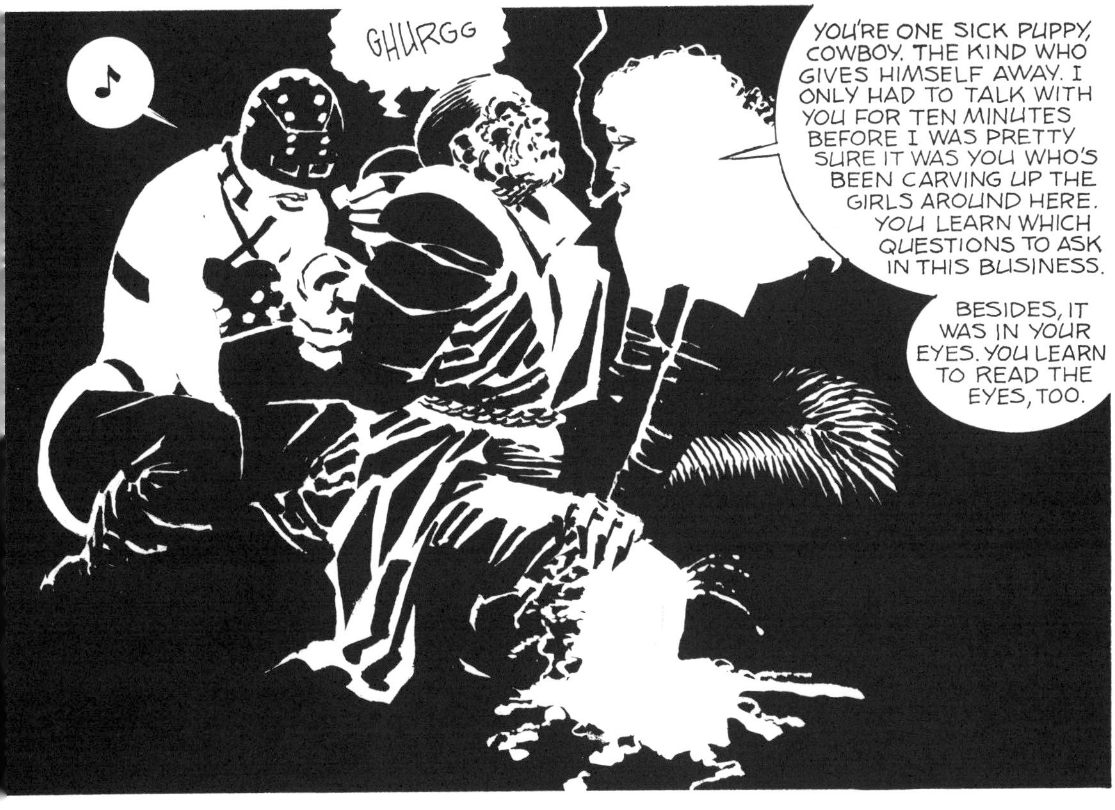
♪
GHURGG
YOU'RE ONE SICK PUPPY, COWBOY. THE KIND WHO GIVES HIMSELF AWAY. I ONLY HAD TO TALK WITH YOU FOR TEN MINUTES BEFORE I WAS PRETTY SURE IT WAS YOU WHO'S BEEN CARVING UP THE GIRLS AROUND HERE. YOU LEARN WHICH QUESTIONS TO ASK IN THIS BUSINESS.
BESIDES, IT WAS IN YOUR EYES. YOU LEARN TO READ THE EYES, TOO.

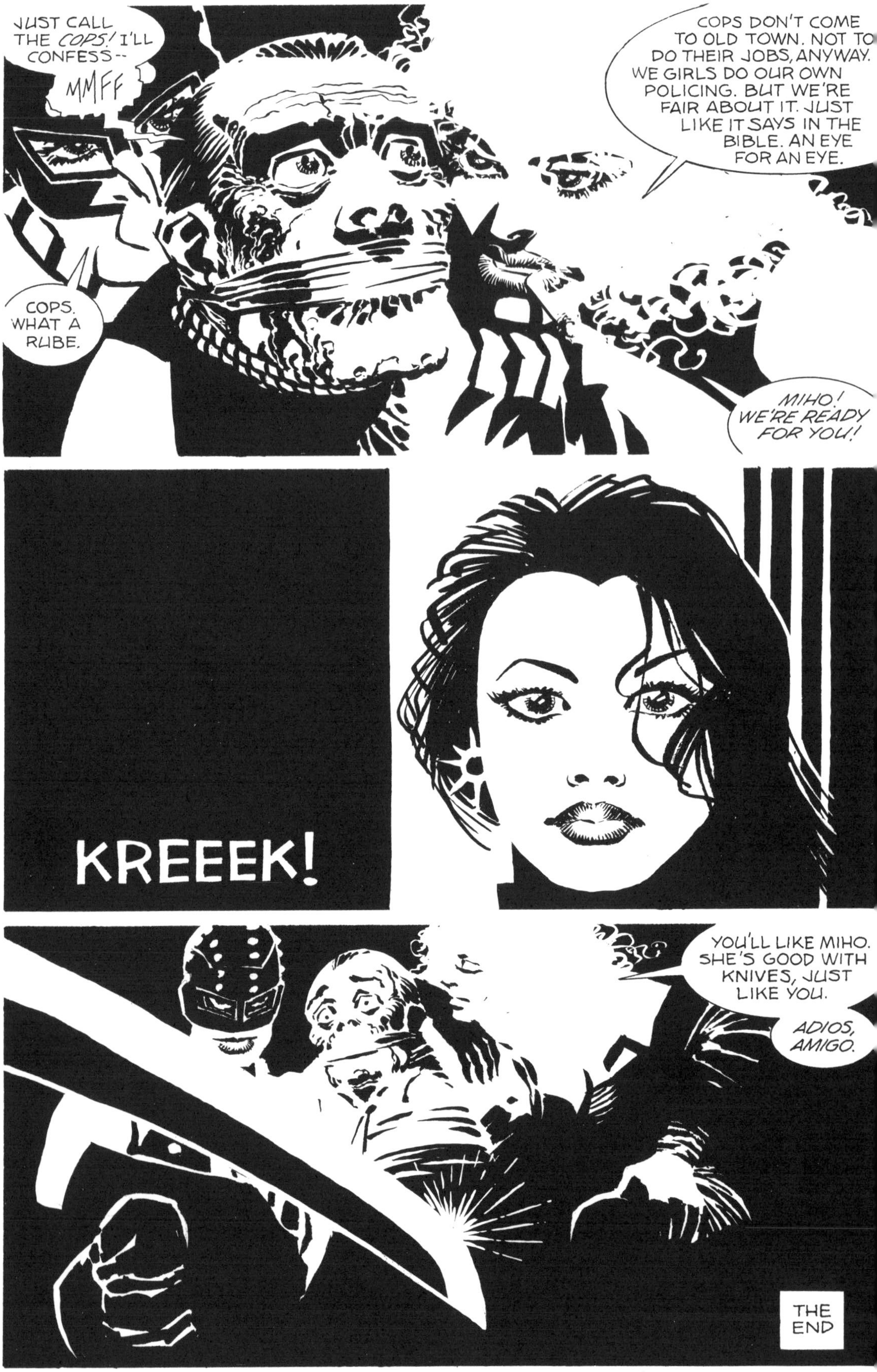
JUST CALL THE COPS! I'LL CONFESS--
MMFF
COPS DON'T COME TO OLD TOWN. NOT TO DO THEIR JOBS, ANYWAY. WE GIRLS DO OUR OWN POLICING. BUT WE'RE FAIR ABOUT IT. JUST LIKE IT SAYS IN THE BIBLE. AN EYE FOR AN EYE.
COPS. WHAT A RUBE.
MIHO! WE'RE READY FOR YOU!
KREEEK!
YOU'LL LIKE MIHO. SHE'S GOOD WITH KNIVES, JUST LIKE YOU.
ADIOS, AMIGO.
THE END

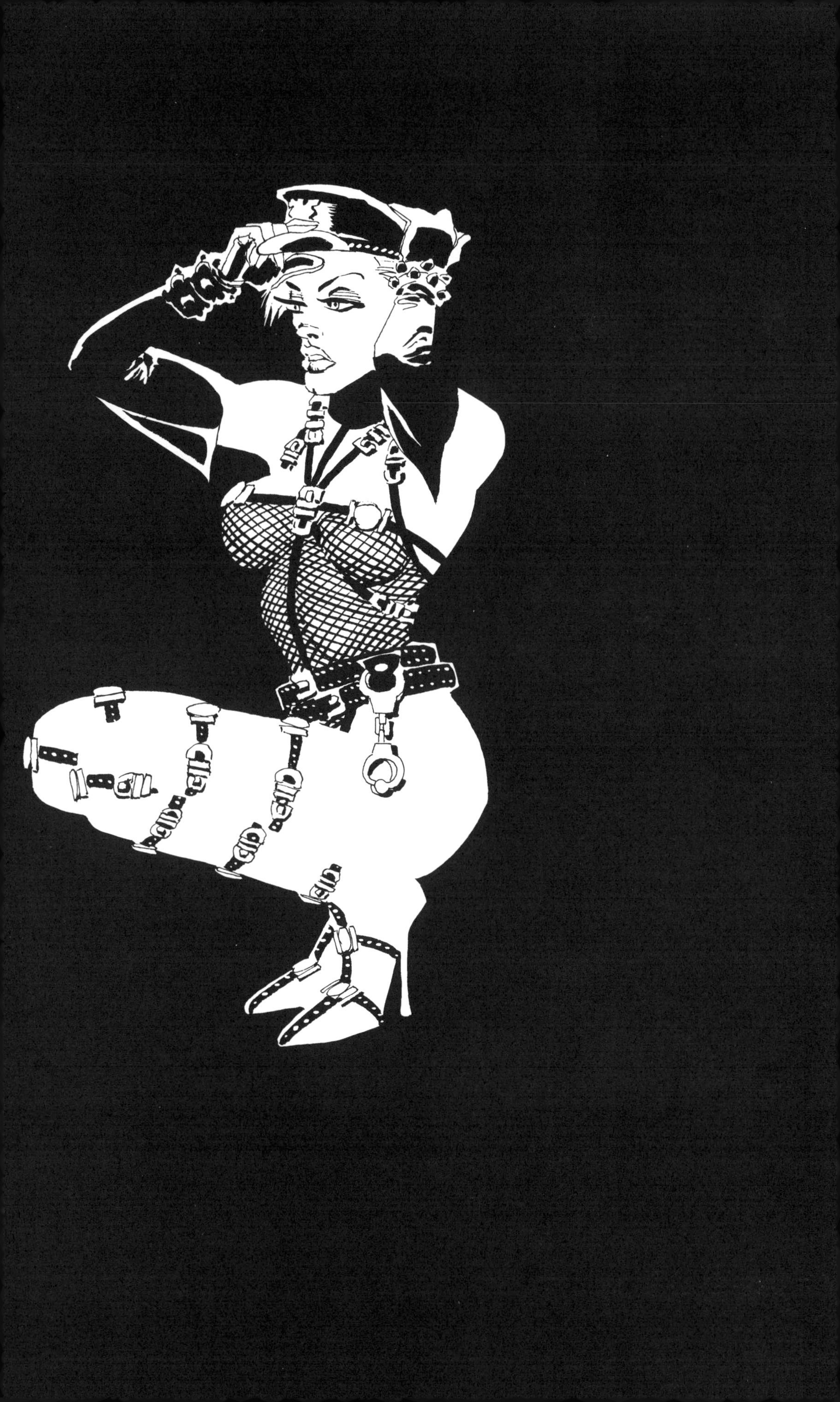

BLUE EYES

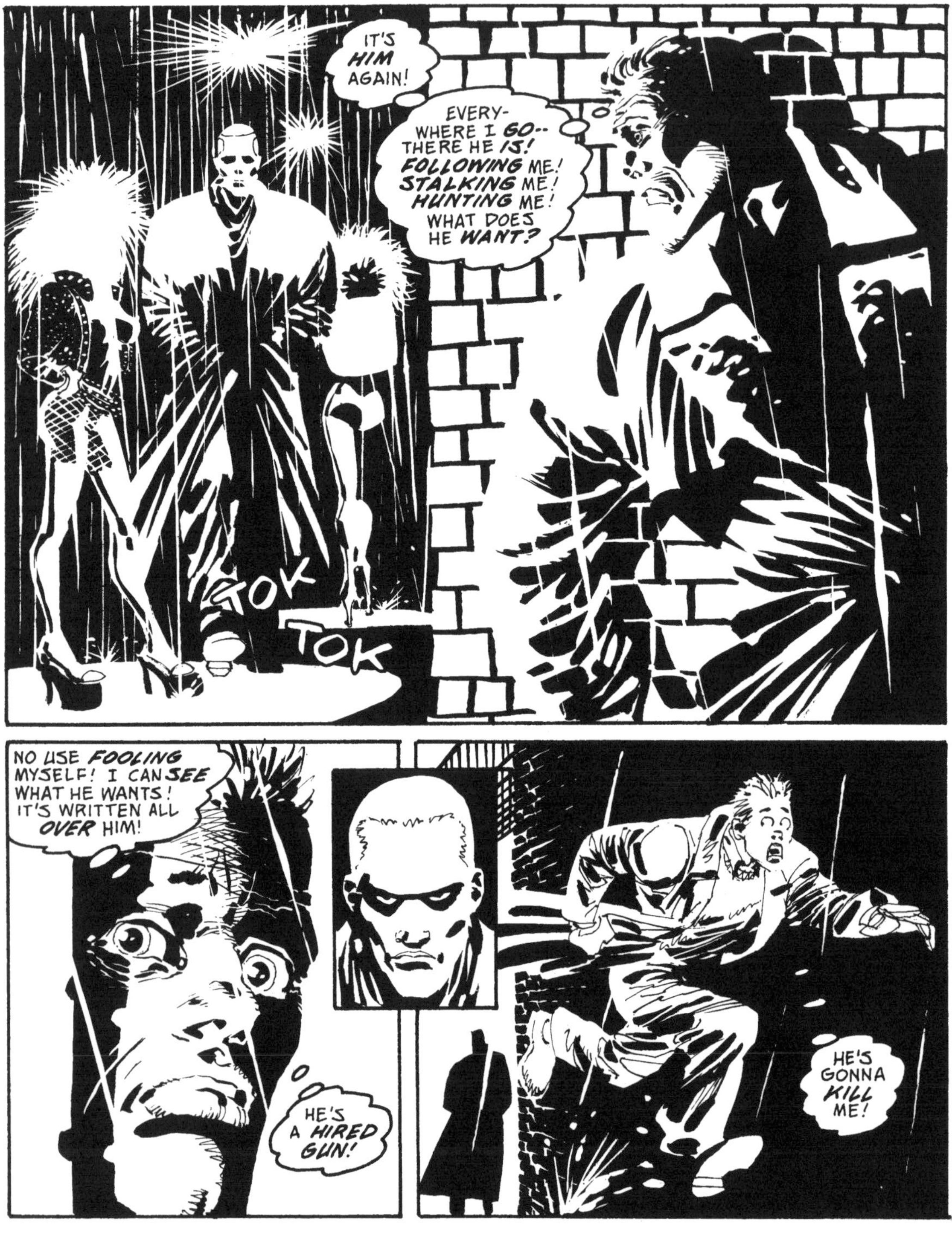

IT'S HIM AGAIN!
EVERY-WHERE I GO-- THERE HE IS! FOLLOWING ME! STALKING ME! HUNTING ME! WHAT DOES HE WANT?
GOK
TOK
NO USE FOOLING MYSELF! I CAN SEE WHAT HE WANTS! IT'S WRITTEN ALL OVER HIM!
HE'S A HIRED GUN!
HE'S GONNA KILL ME!

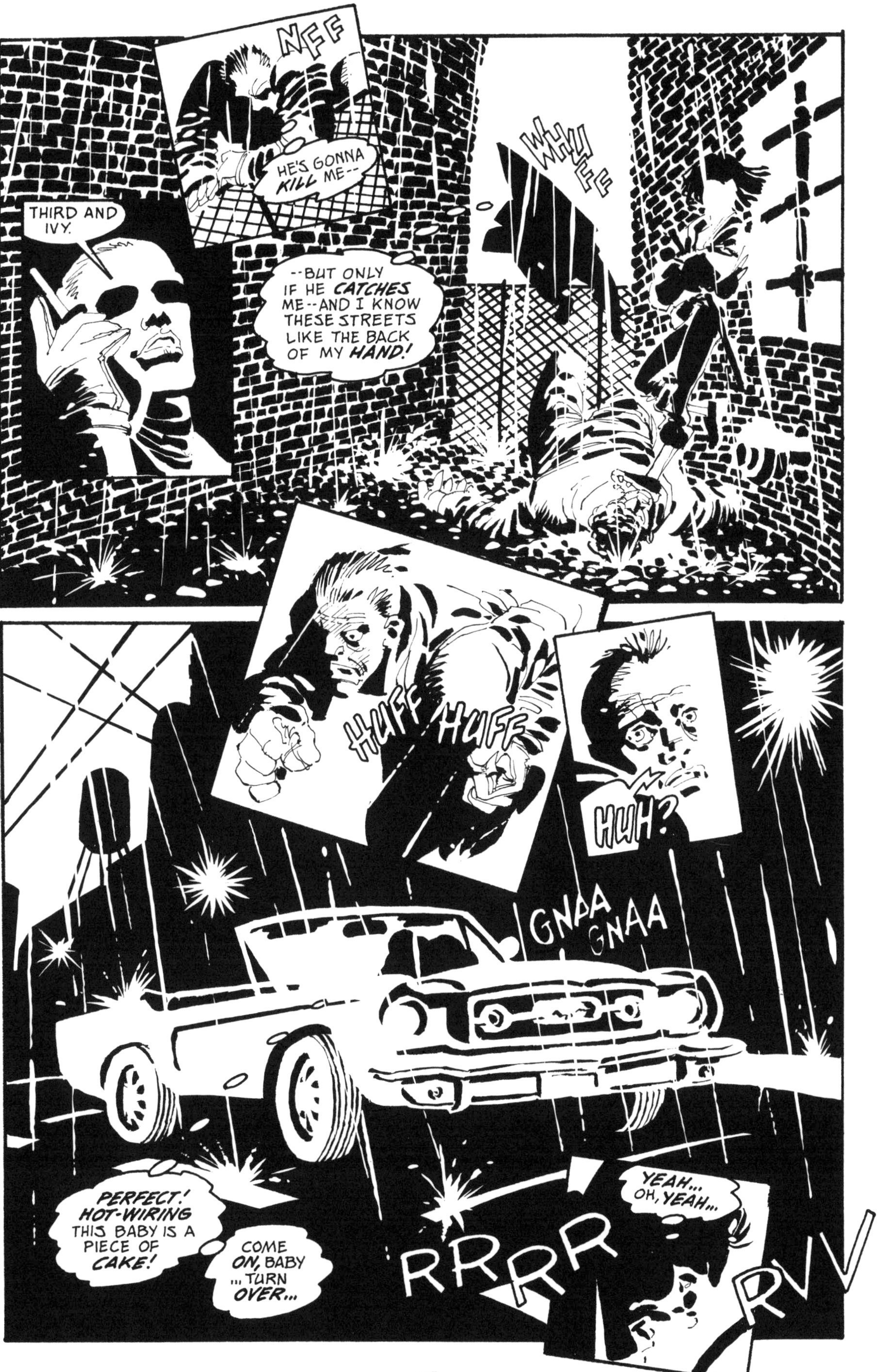
NFF
HE'S GONNA KILL ME--
THIRD AND IVY.
--BUT ONLY IF HE CATCHES ME--AND I KNOW THESE STREETS LIKE THE BACK OF MY HAND!
WHUFF
HUFF HUFF
HUH?
GNAA GNAA
PERFECT! HOT-WIRING THIS BABY IS A PIECE OF CAKE!
COME ON, BABY ...TURN OVER...
YEAH... OH, YEAH...
RRRRR
RVV

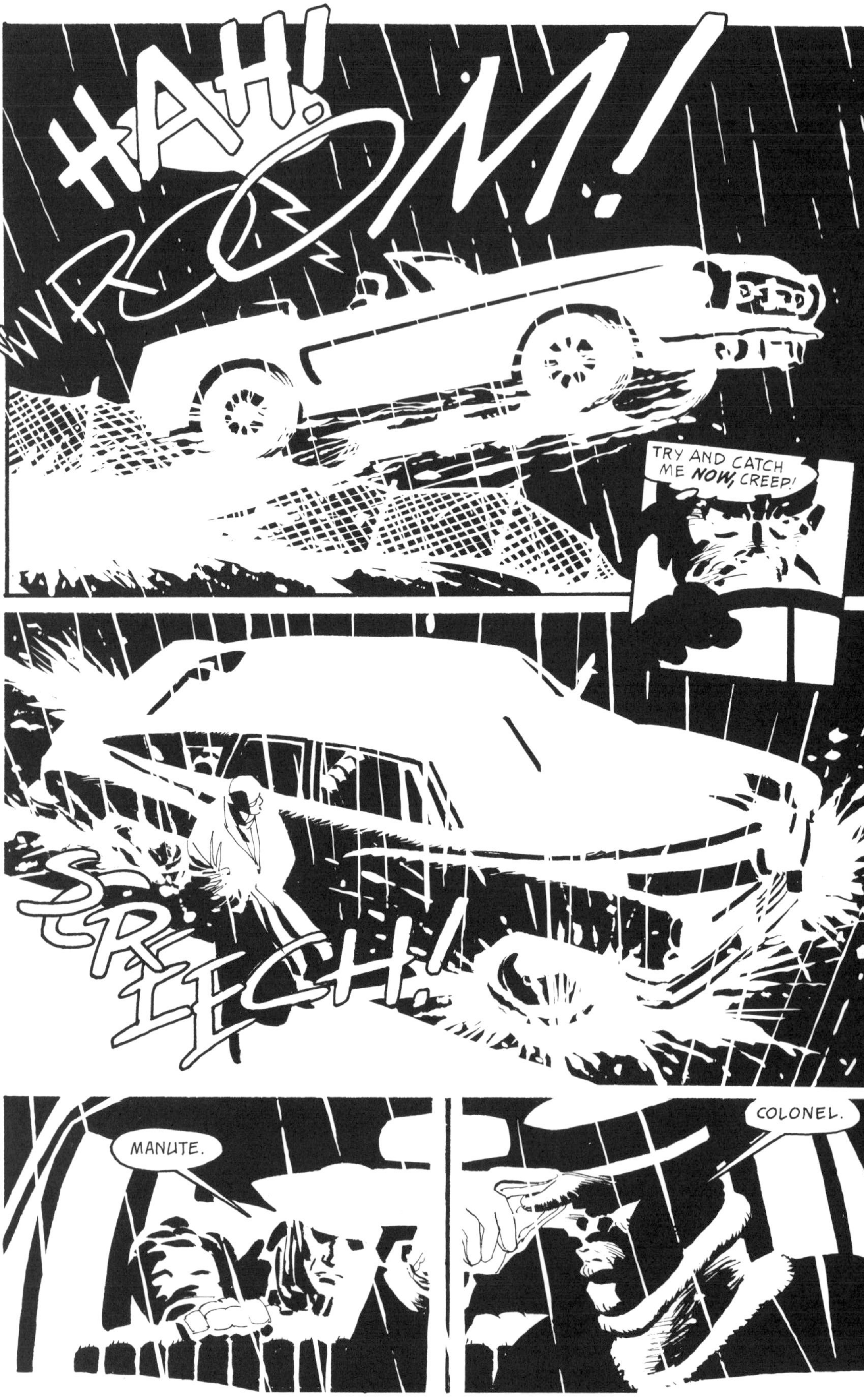
HAH!
WRROOM!
TRY AND CATCH ME NOW, CREEP!
SCREECH!
MANUTE.
COLONEL.

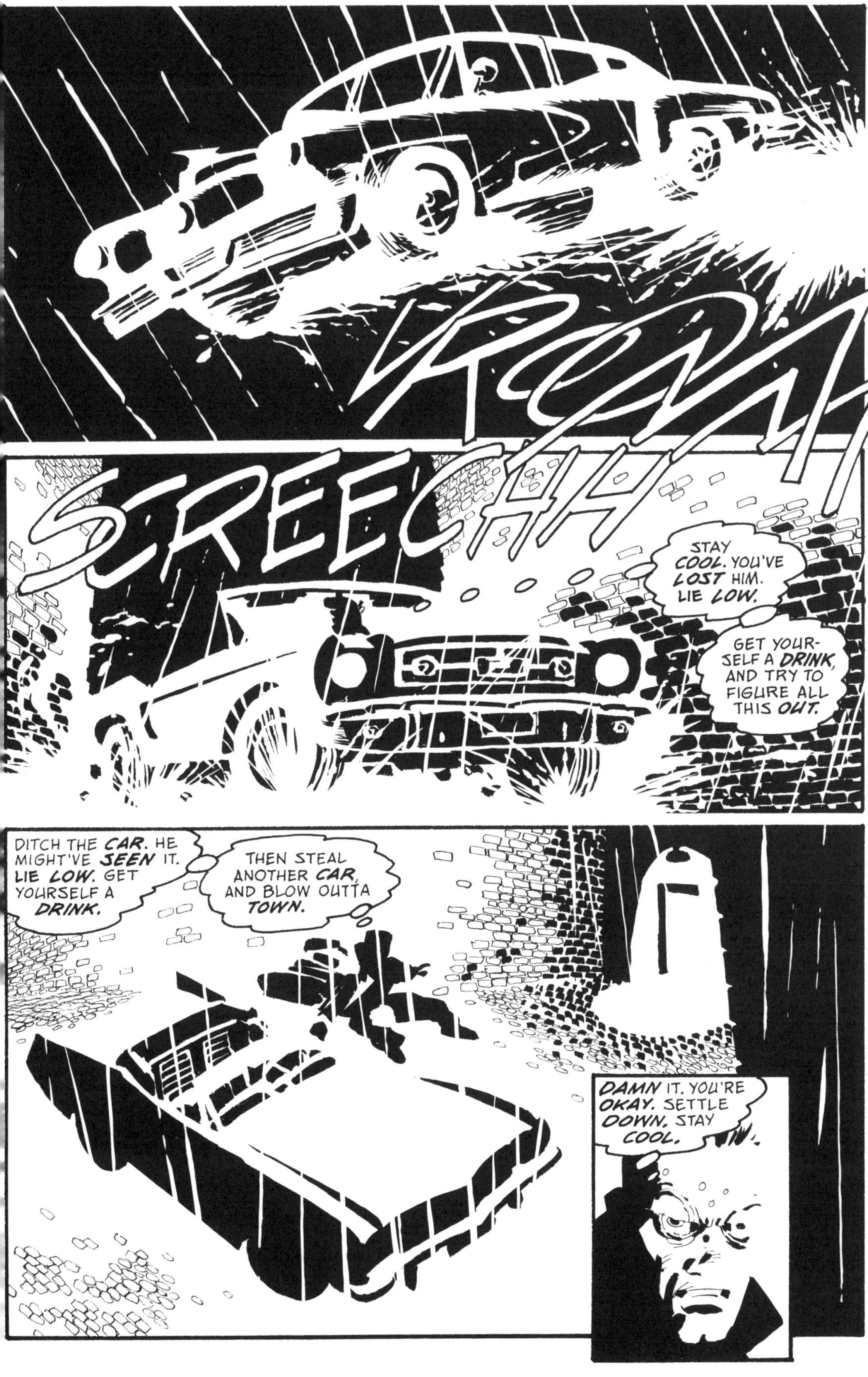
VROOM
SCREECHHH
STAY COOL. YOU'VE LOST HIM. LIE LOW.
GET YOURSELF A DRINK, AND TRY TO FIGURE ALL THIS OUT.
DITCH THE CAR. HE MIGHT'VE SEEN IT. LIE LOW. GET YOURSELF A DRINK.
THEN STEAL ANOTHER CAR, AND BLOW OUTTA TOWN.
DAMN IT. YOU'RE OKAY. SETTLE DOWN. STAY COOL.

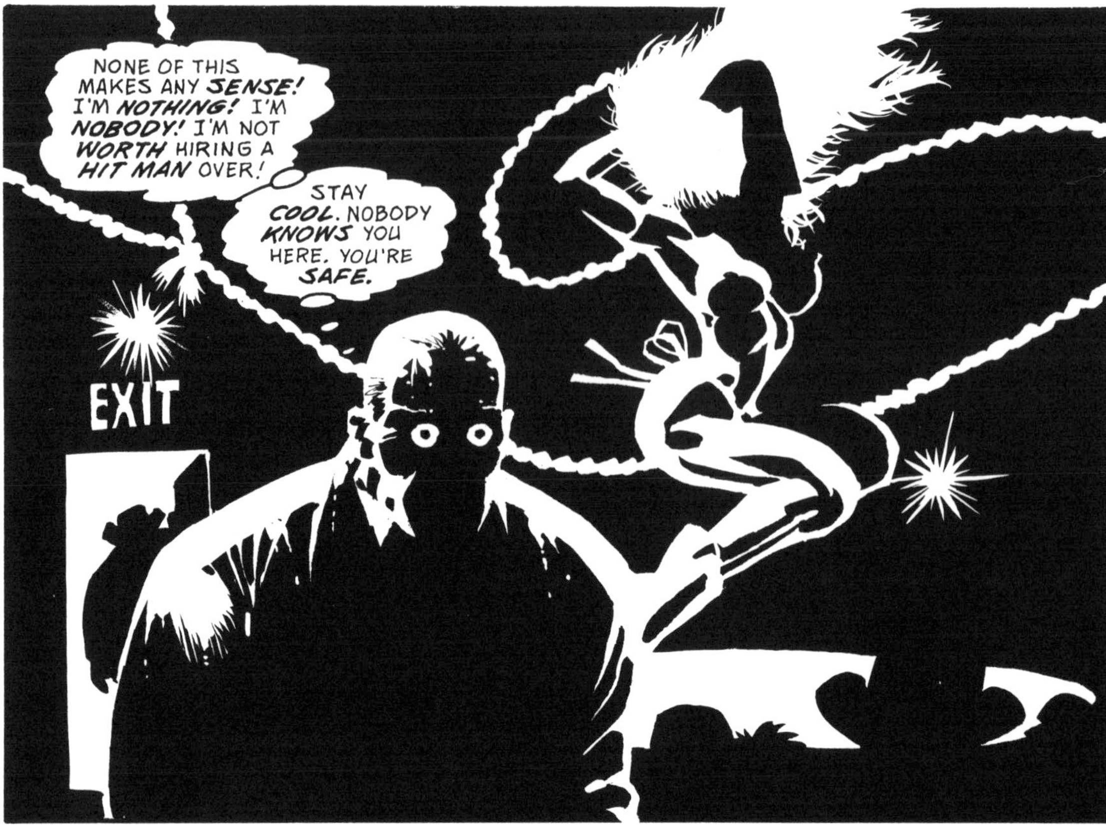
NONE OF THIS MAKES ANY SENSE! I'M NOTHING! I'M NOBODY! I'M NOT WORTH HIRING A HIT MAN OVER!
STAY COOL. NOBODY KNOWS YOU HERE. YOU'RE SAFE.
EXIT

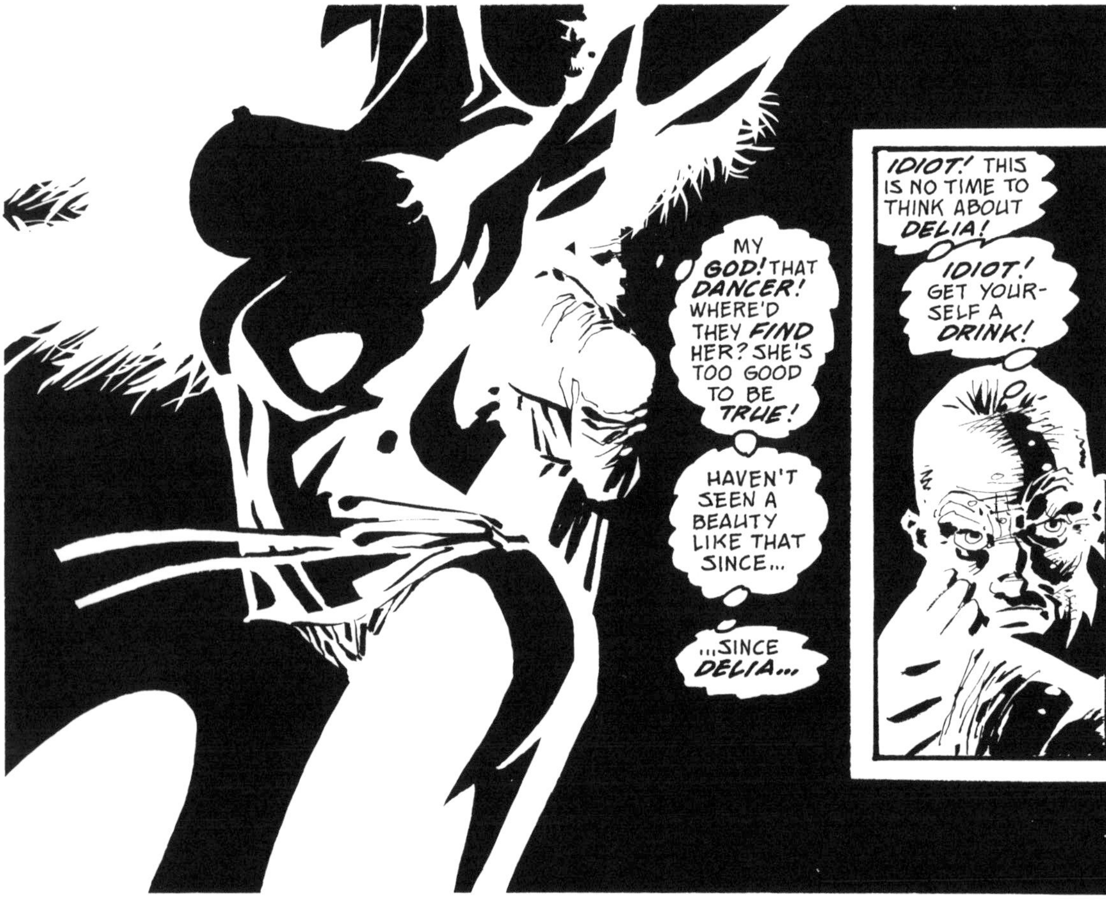
MY GOD! THAT DANCER! WHERE'D THEY FIND HER? SHE'S TOO GOOD TO BE TRUE!
HAVEN'T SEEN A BEAUTY LIKE THAT SINCE...
...SINCE DELIA...
IDIOT! THIS IS NO TIME TO THINK ABOUT DELIA!
IDIOT! GET YOURSELF A DRINK!

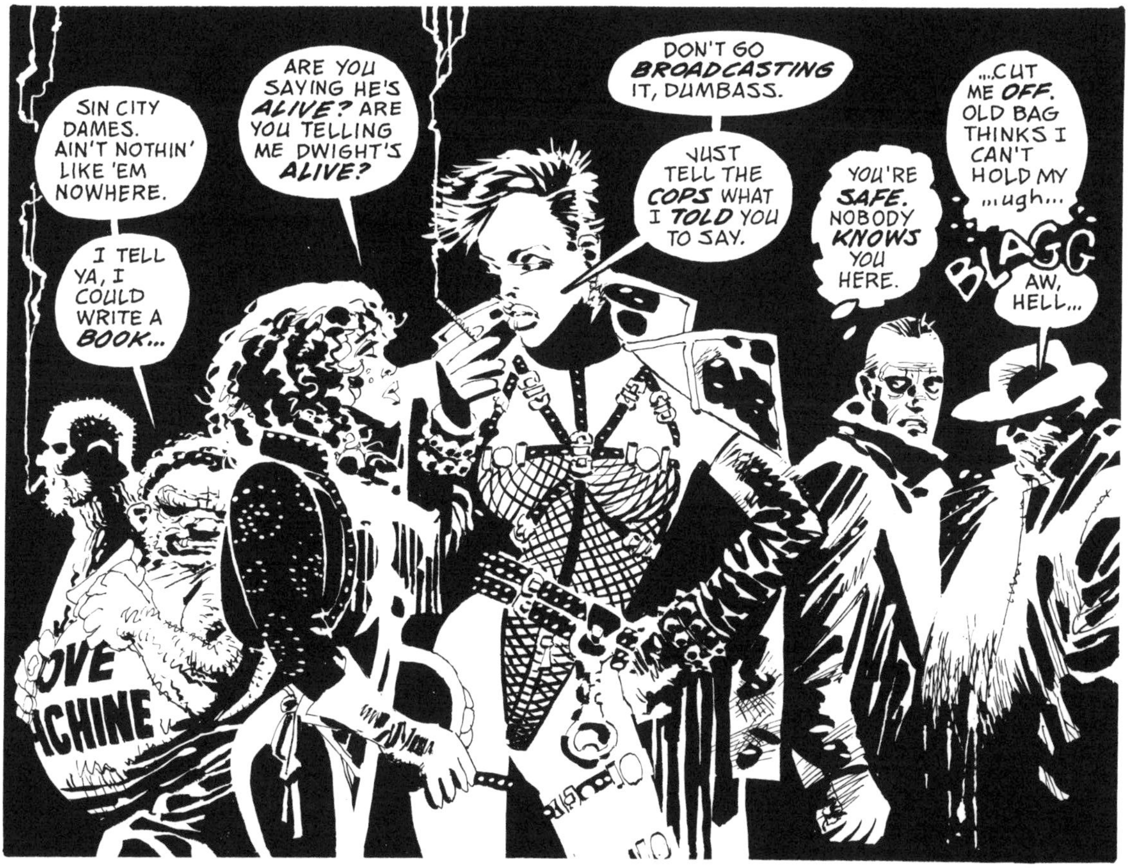
SIN CITY DAMES. AIN'T NOTHIN' LIKE 'EM NOWHERE.
I TELL YA, I COULD WRITE A BOOK...
ARE YOU SAYING HE'S ALIVE? ARE YOU TELLING ME DWIGHT'S ALIVE?
DON'T GO BROADCASTING IT, DUMBASS.
JUST TELL THE COPS WHAT I TOLD YOU TO SAY.
YOU'RE SAFE. NOBODY KNOWS YOU HERE.
...CUT ME OFF. OLD BAG THINKS I CAN'T HOLD MY ...ugh...
BLAGG
AW, HELL...
OVE
CHINE

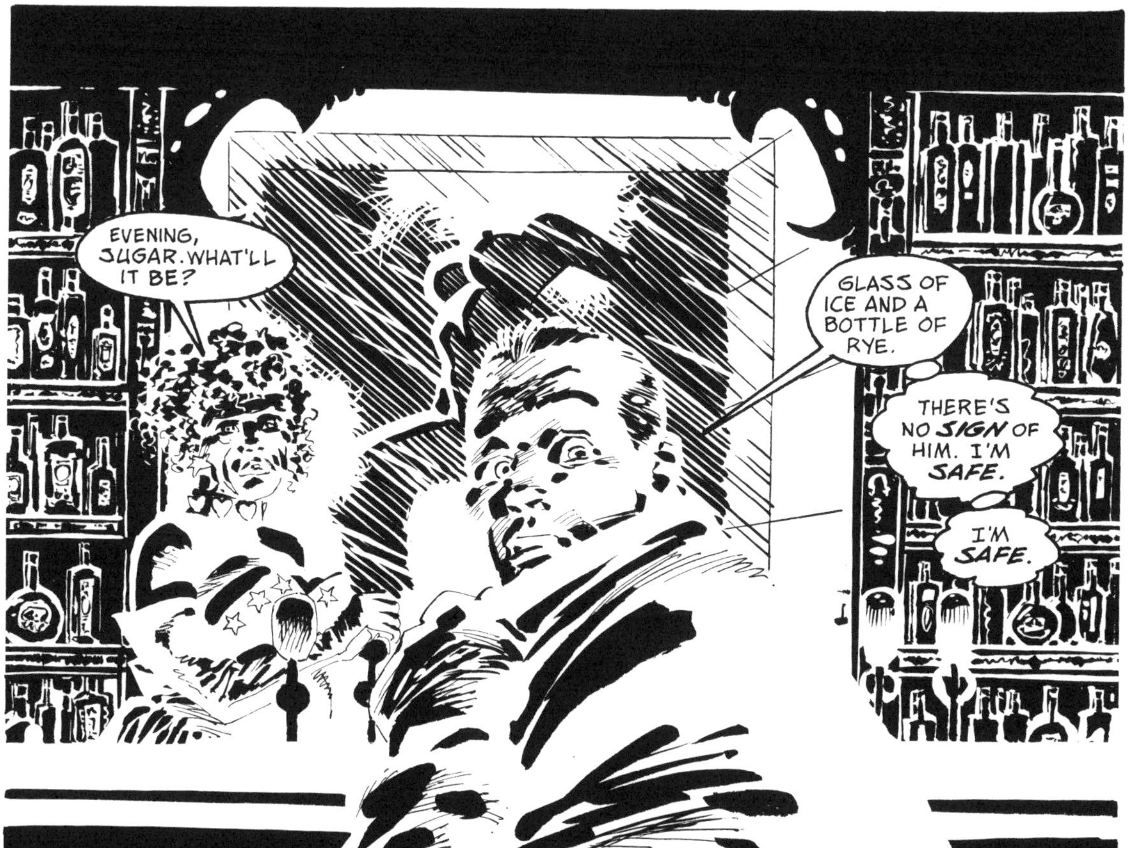
EVENING, SUGAR. WHAT'LL IT BE?
GLASS OF ICE AND A BOTTLE OF RYE.
THERE'S NO SIGN OF HIM. I'M SAFE.
I'M SAFE.

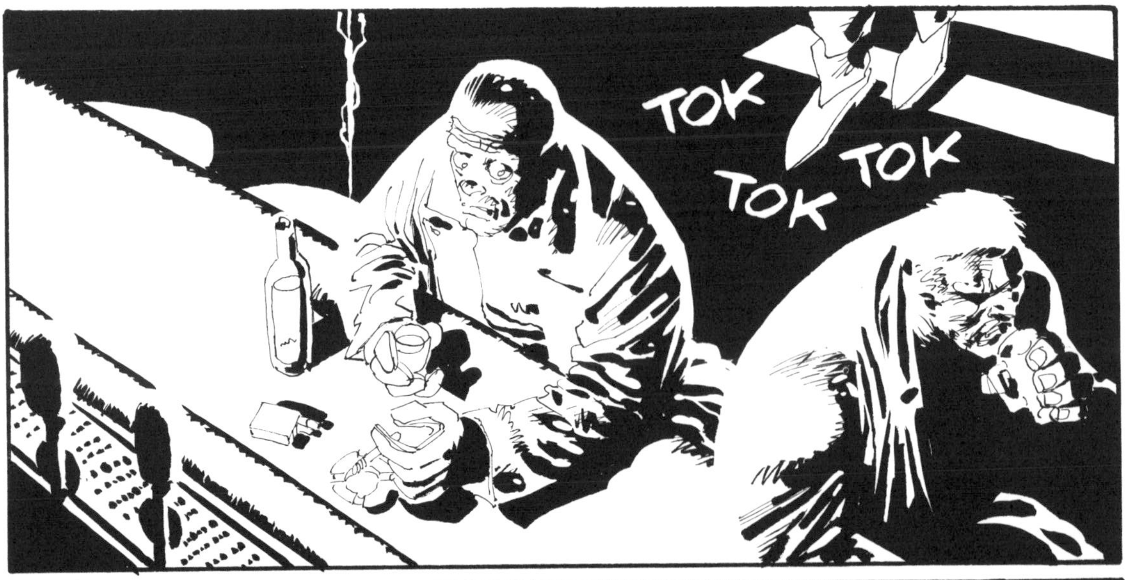
TOK
TOK TOK
TOK
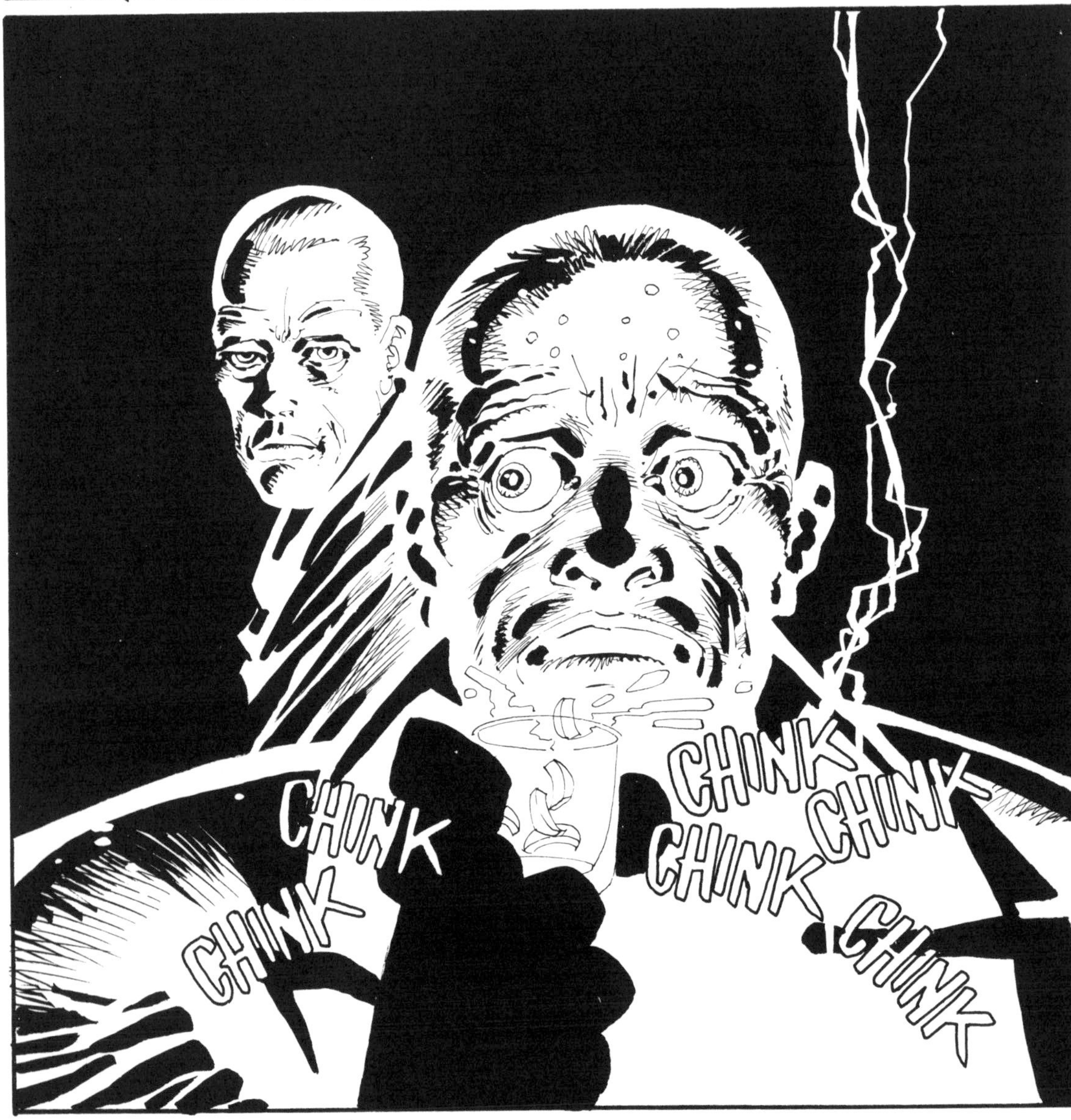
CHINK
CHINK
CHINK
CHINK
CHINK
CHINK

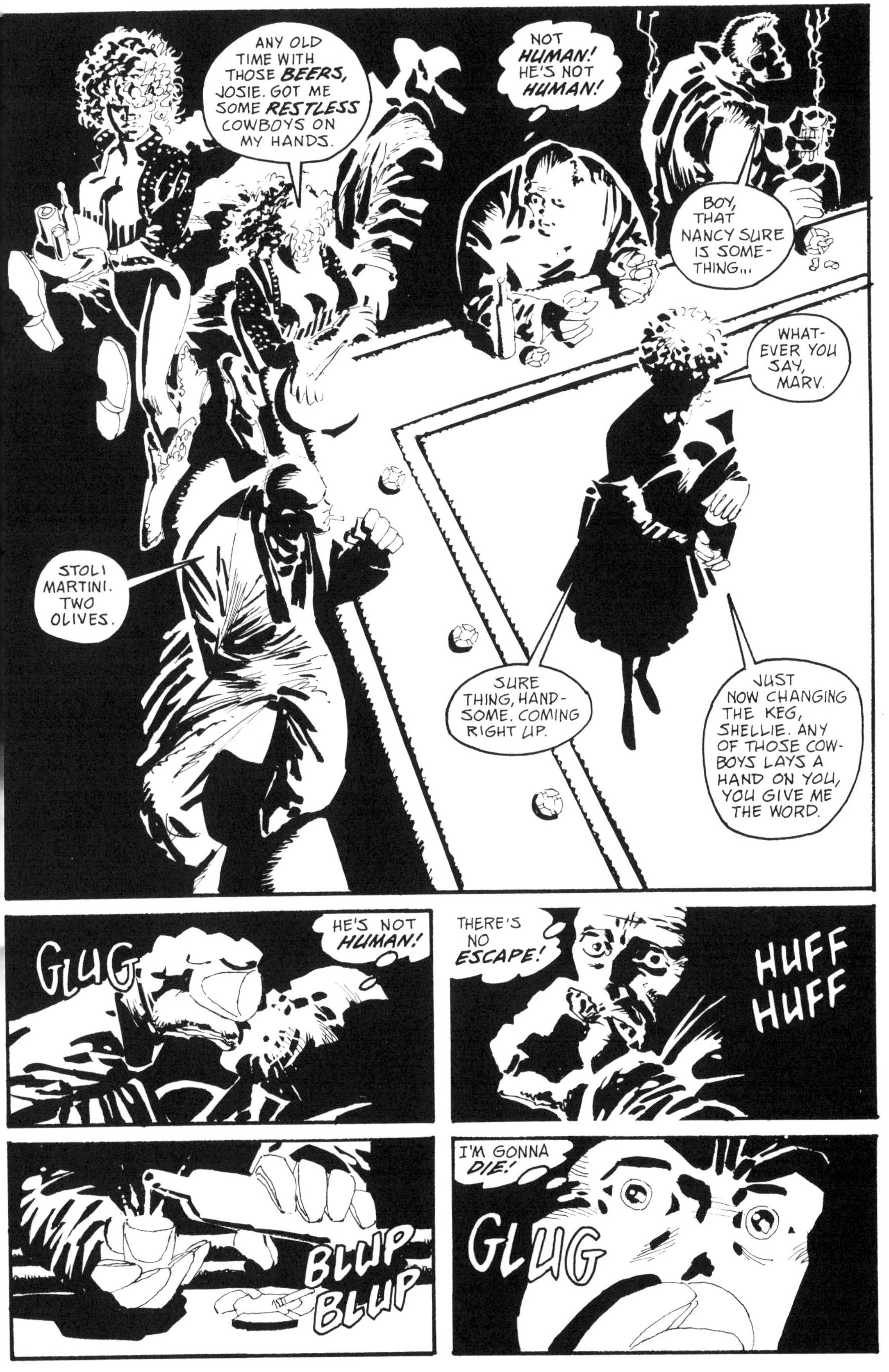
ANY OLD TIME WITH THOSE BEERS, JOSIE. GOT ME SOME RESTLESS COWBOYS ON MY HANDS.
NOT HUMAN! HE'S NOT HUMAN!
BOY, THAT NANCY SURE IS SOME-THING...
WHAT-EVER YOU SAY, MARV.
STOLI MARTINI. TWO OLIVES.
SURE THING, HAND-SOME. COMING RIGHT UP.
JUST NOW CHANGING THE KEG, SHELLIE. ANY OF THOSE COW-BOYS LAYS A HAND ON YOU, YOU GIVE ME THE WORD.
GLUG
HE'S NOT HUMAN!
THERE'S NO ESCAPE!
HUFF HUFF
BLUP BLUP
I'M GONNA DIE!
GLUG

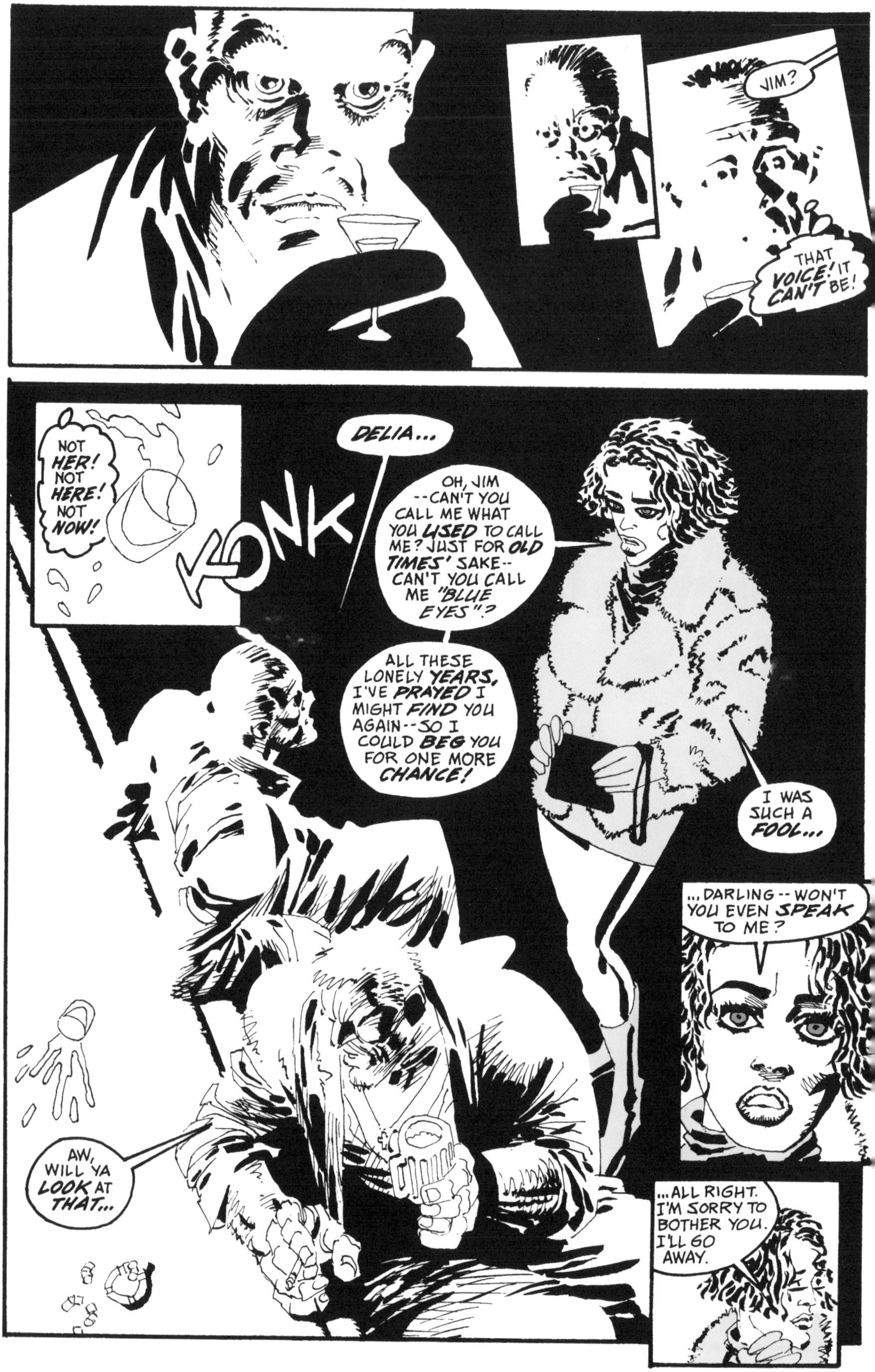
JIM?
THAT VOICE! IT CAN'T BE!
NOT HER! NOT HERE! NOT NOW!
KONK
DELIA...
OH, JIM --CAN'T YOU CALL ME WHAT YOU USED TO CALL ME? JUST FOR OLD TIMES' SAKE-- CAN'T YOU CALL ME "BLUE EYES"?
ALL THESE LONELY YEARS, I'VE PRAYED I MIGHT FIND YOU AGAIN--SO I COULD BEG YOU FOR ONE MORE CHANCE!
I WAS SUCH A FOOL...
...DARLING--WON'T YOU EVEN SPEAK TO ME?
AW, WILL YA LOOK AT THAT...
...ALL RIGHT. I'M SORRY TO BOTHER YOU. I'LL GO AWAY.

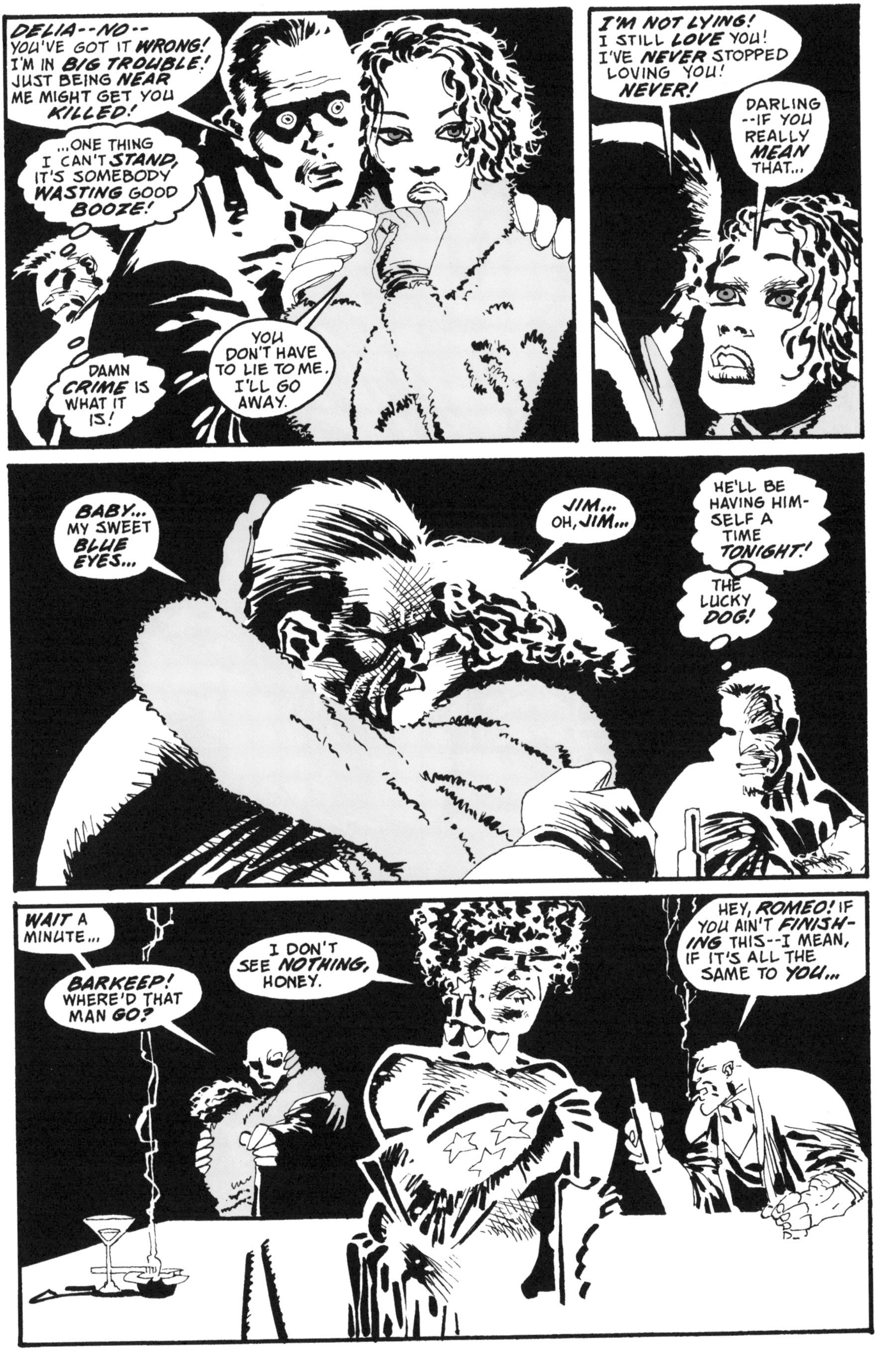
DELIA--NO-- YOU'VE GOT IT WRONG! I'M IN BIG TROUBLE! JUST BEING NEAR ME MIGHT GET YOU KILLED!
...ONE THING I CAN'T STAND, IT'S SOMEBODY WASTING GOOD BOOZE!
DAMN CRIME IS WHAT IT IS!
YOU DON'T HAVE TO LIE TO ME. I'LL GO AWAY.
I'M NOT LYING! I STILL LOVE YOU! I'VE NEVER STOPPED LOVING YOU! NEVER!
DARLING --IF YOU REALLY MEAN THAT...
BABY... MY SWEET BLUE EYES...
JIM... OH, JIM...
HE'LL BE HAVING HIM-SELF A TIME TONIGHT!
THE LUCKY DOG!
WAIT A MINUTE...
BARKEEP! WHERE'D THAT MAN GO?
I DON'T SEE NOTHING, HONEY.
HEY, ROMEO! IF YOU AIN'T FINISH-ING THIS--I MEAN, IF IT'S ALL THE SAME TO YOU...

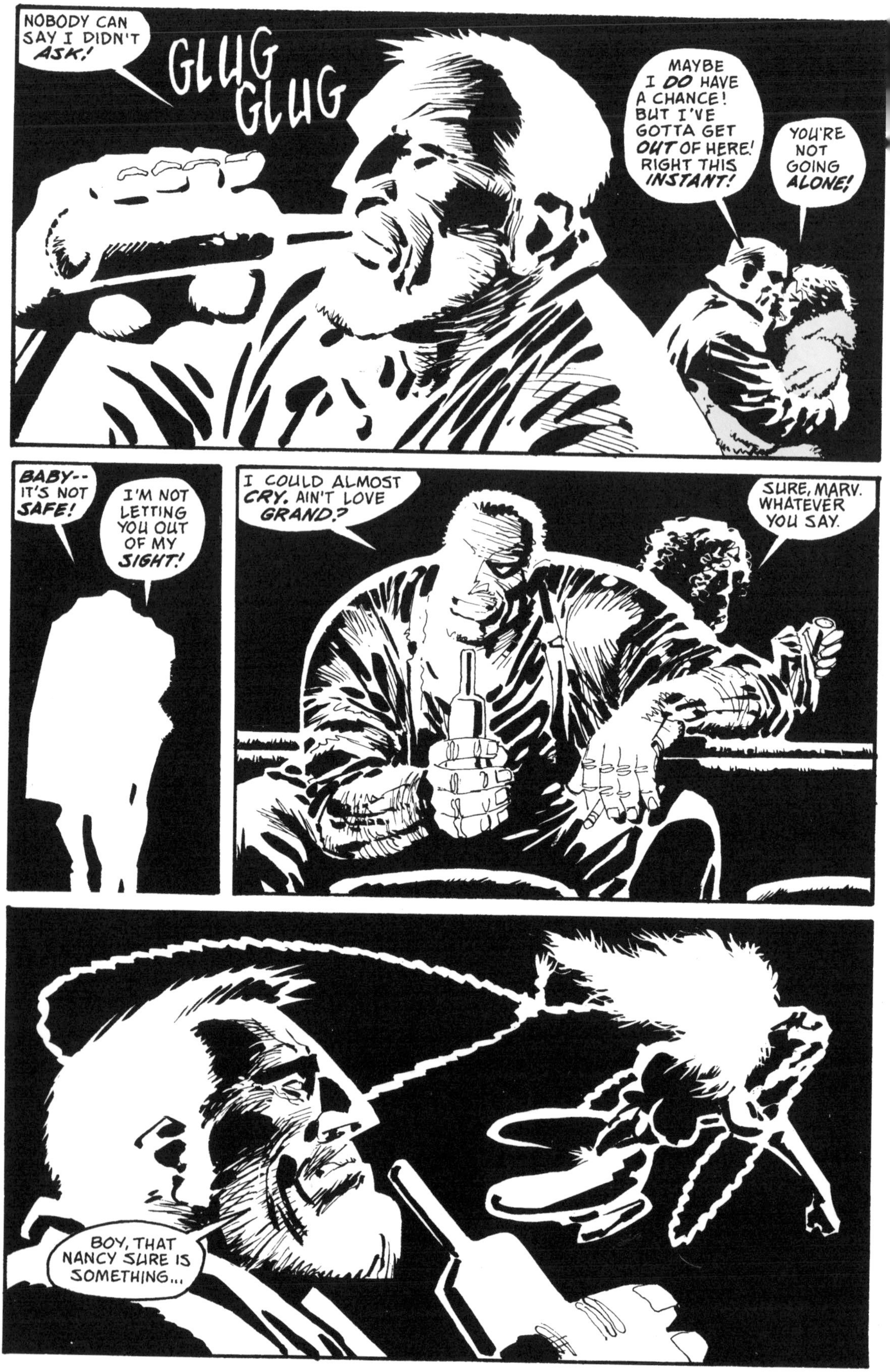
NOBODY CAN SAY I DIDN'T ASK!
GLUG GLUG
MAYBE I DO HAVE A CHANCE! BUT I'VE GOTTA GET OUT OF HERE! RIGHT THIS INSTANT!
YOU'RE NOT GOING ALONE!
BABY-- IT'S NOT SAFE!
I'M NOT LETTING YOU OUT OF MY SIGHT!
I COULD ALMOST CRY. AIN'T LOVE GRAND?
SURE, MARV. WHATEVER YOU SAY.
BOY, THAT NANCY SURE IS SOMETHING...

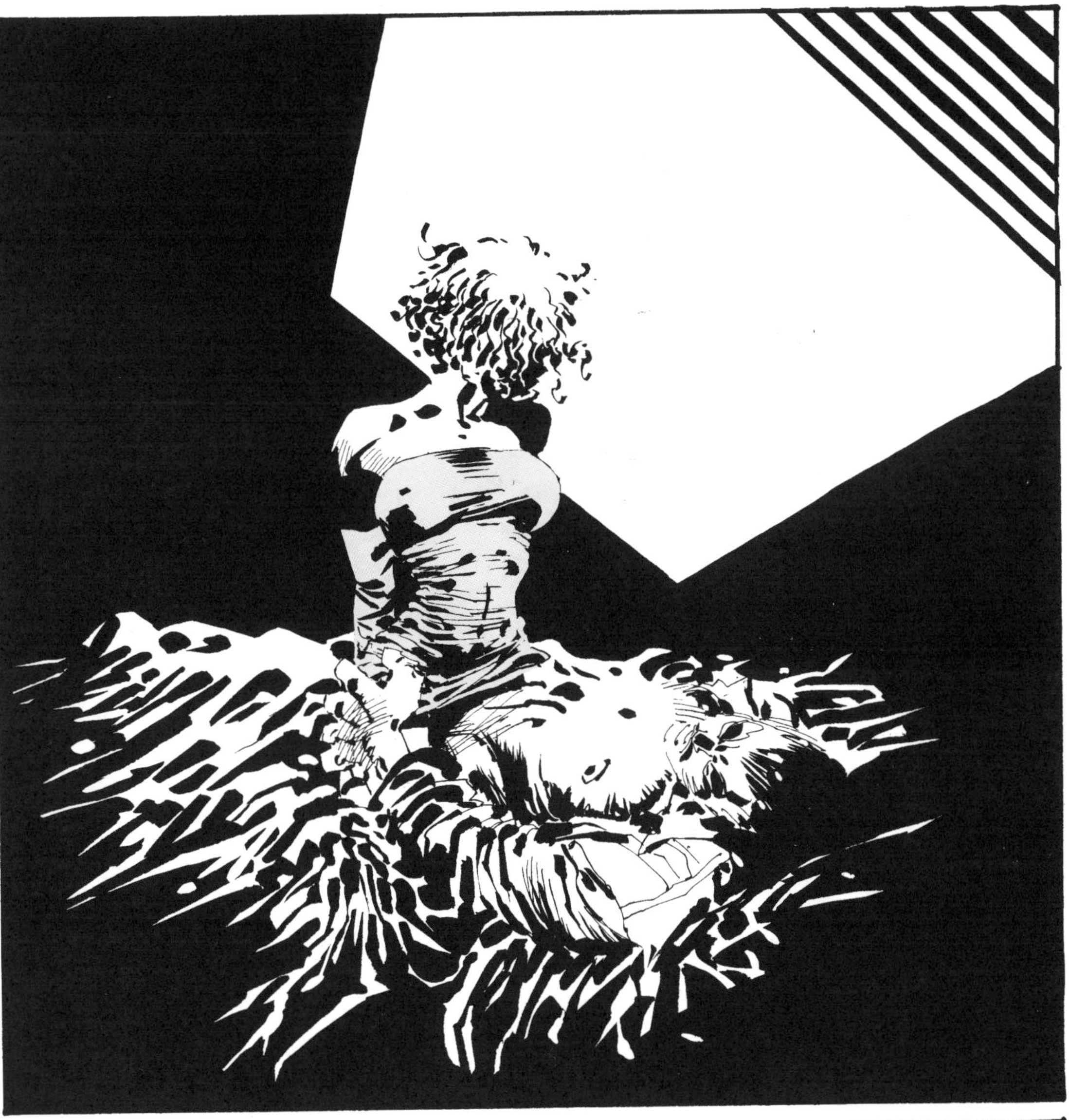

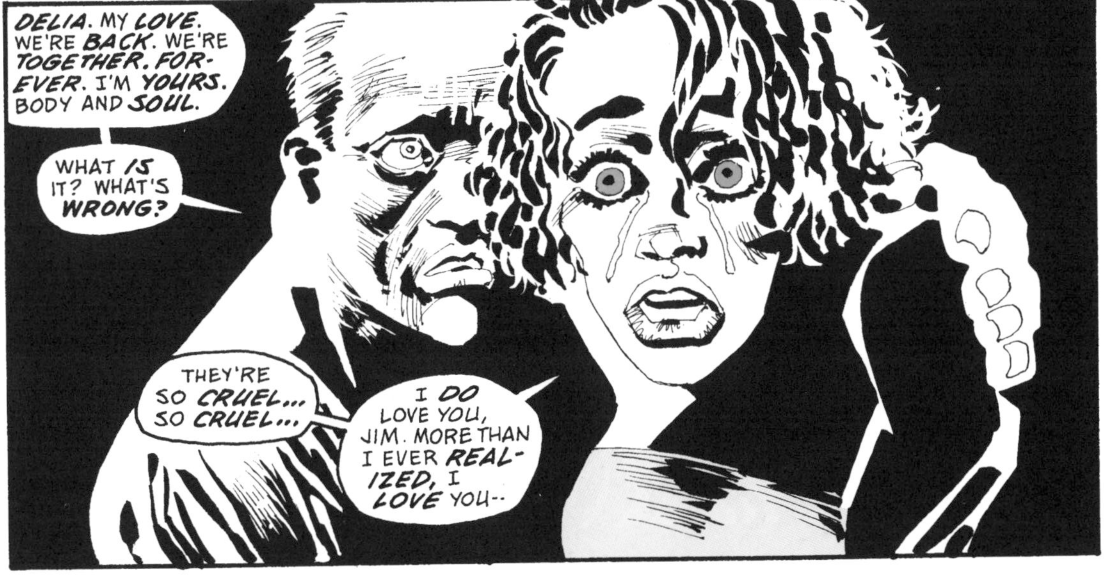
DELIA. MY LOVE. WE'RE BACK. WE'RE TOGETHER. FOR-EVER. I'M YOURS. BODY AND SOUL.
WHAT IS IT? WHAT'S WRONG?
THEY'RE SO CRUEL... SO CRUEL...
I DO LOVE YOU, JIM. MORE THAN I EVER REAL-IZED, I LOVE YOU--

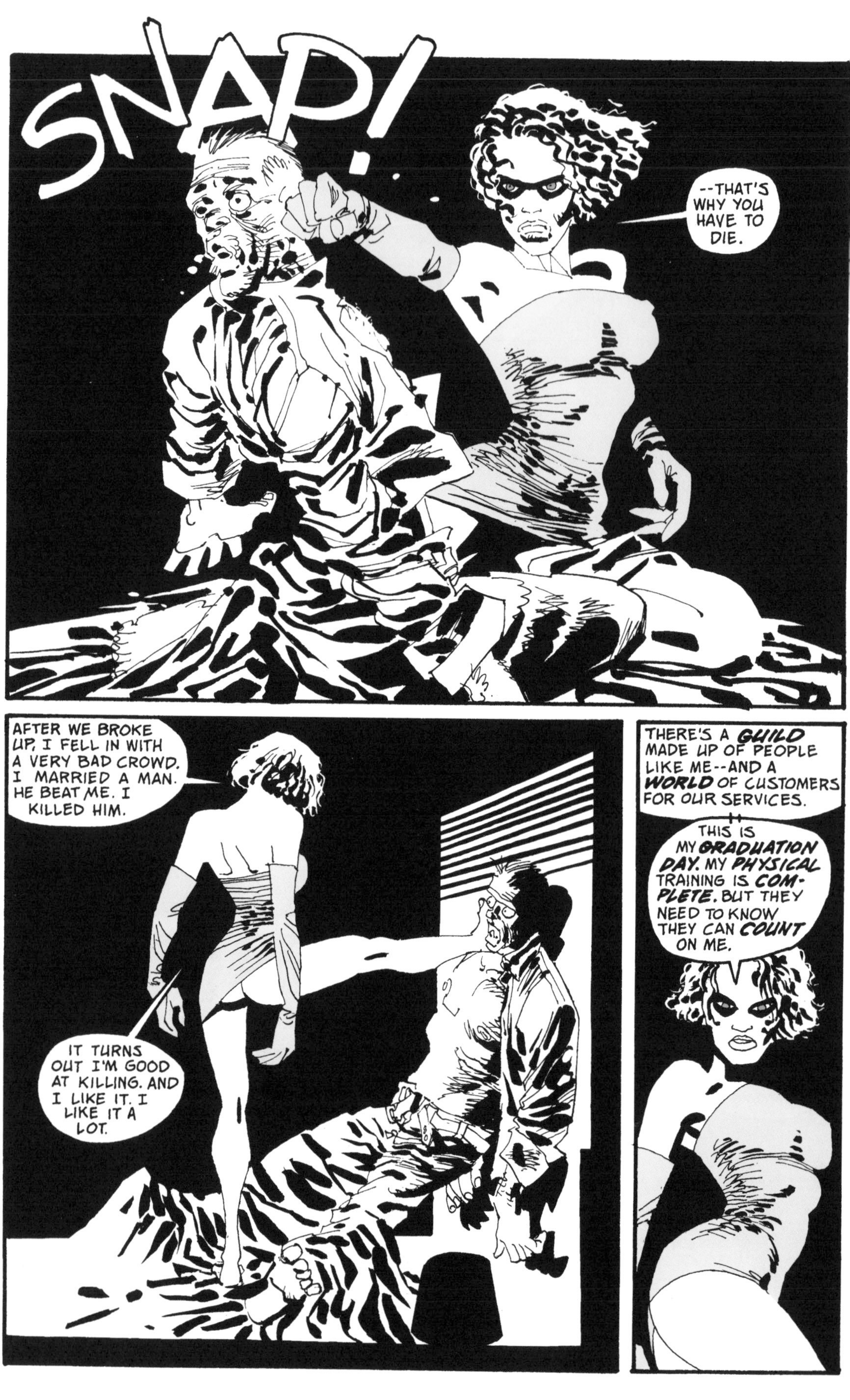
SNAP!
--THAT'S WHY YOU HAVE TO DIE.
AFTER WE BROKE UP, I FELL IN WITH A VERY BAD CROWD. I MARRIED A MAN. HE BEAT ME. I KILLED HIM.
IT TURNS OUT I'M GOOD AT KILLING. AND I LIKE IT. I LIKE IT A LOT.
THERE'S A GUILD MADE UP OF PEOPLE LIKE ME--AND A WORLD OF CUSTOMERS FOR OUR SERVICES.
THIS IS MY GRADUATION DAY. MY PHYSICAL TRAINING IS COMPLETE. BUT THEY NEED TO KNOW THEY CAN COUNT ON ME.

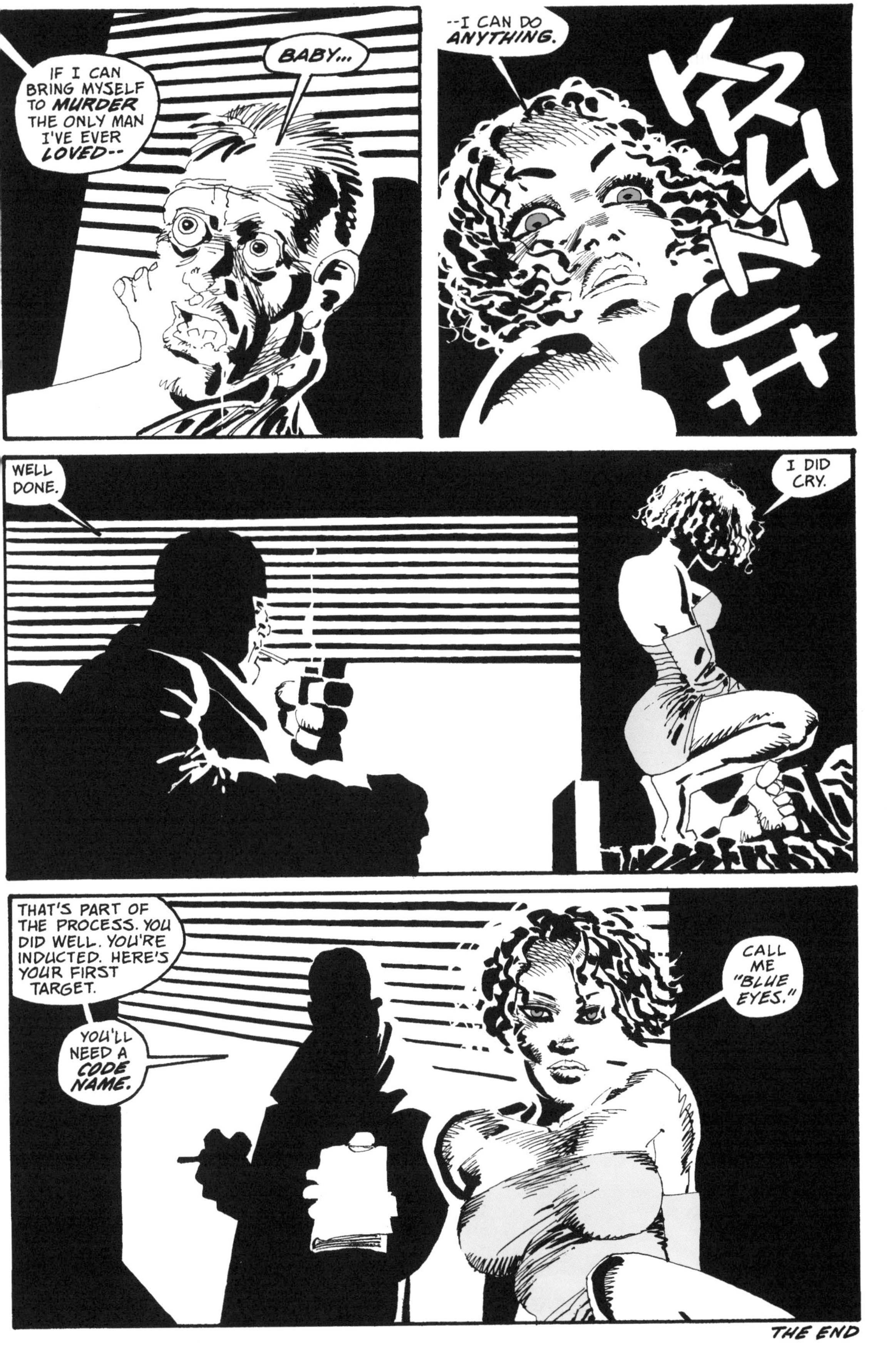
IF I CAN BRING MYSELF TO MURDER THE ONLY MAN I'VE EVER LOVED--
BABY...
--I CAN DO ANYTHING.
KRUNCH
WELL DONE.
I DID CRY.
THAT'S PART OF THE PROCESS. YOU DID WELL. YOU'RE INDUCTED. HERE'S YOUR FIRST TARGET.
YOU'LL NEED A CODE NAME.
CALL ME "BLUE EYES."

THE END

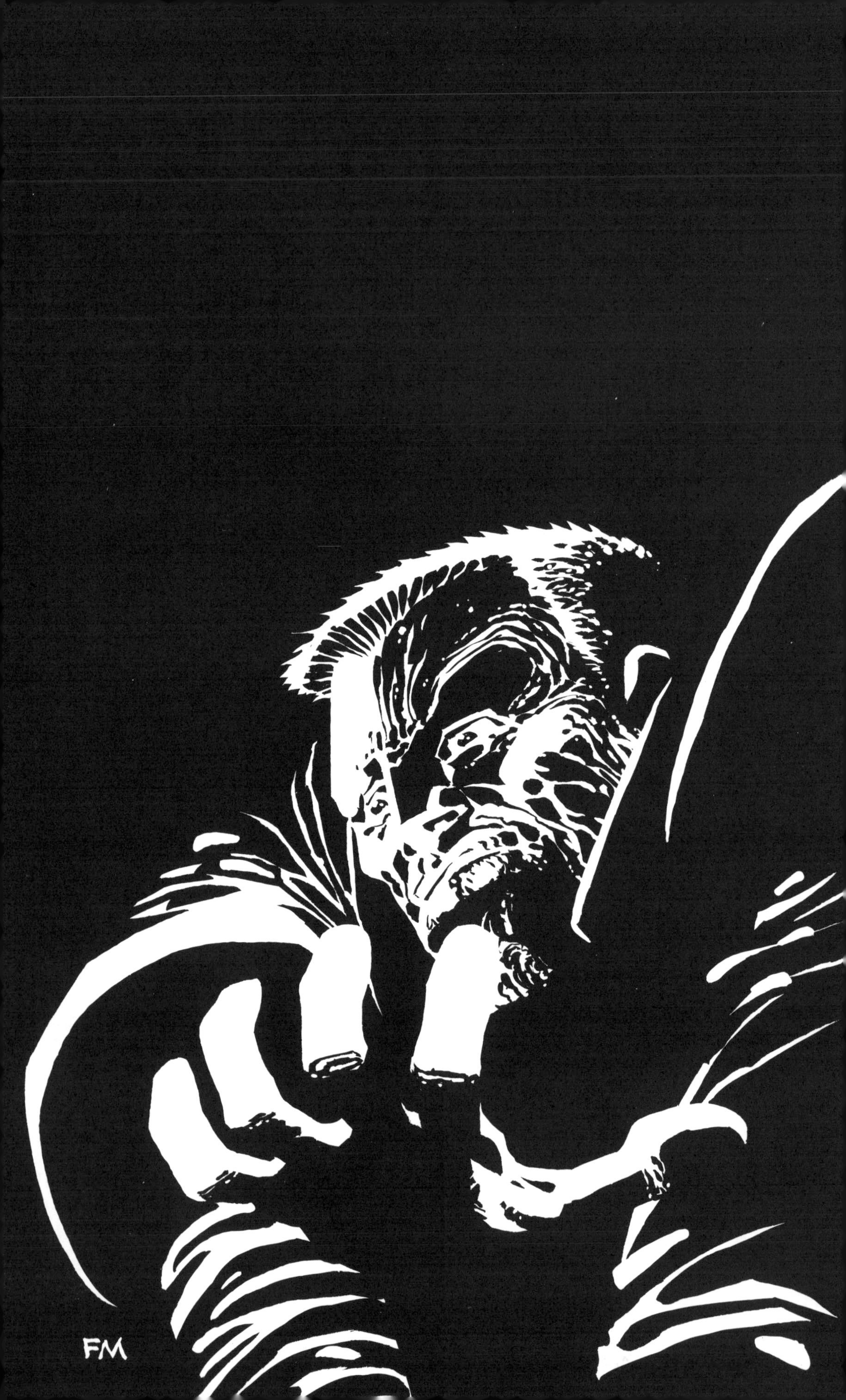
FM

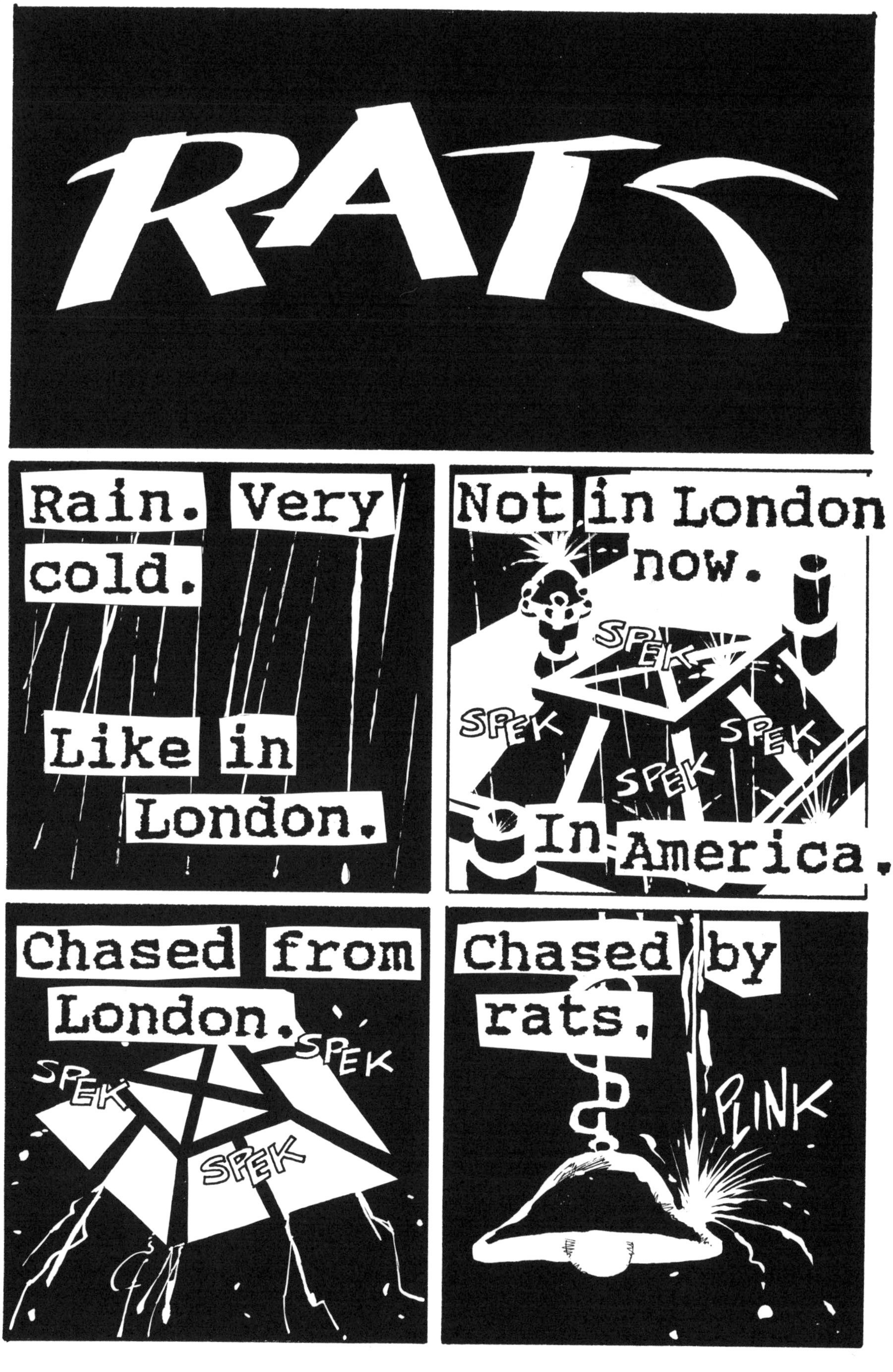
RATS
Rain. Very cold.
Like in London.
Not in London now.
SPEK
SPEK
SPEK
SPEK
In America.
Chased from London.
SPEK
SPEK
SPEK
Chased by rats.
PLINK

Always cold in London.
Always rains.
KREEK
SPUKK
Rain. Very cold.
Bad on arthritis.
KREEK
Worst in wrists.
KREEK
PO

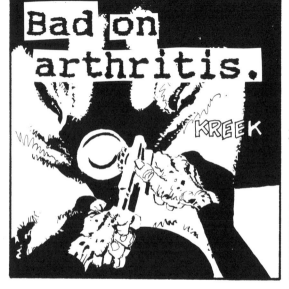

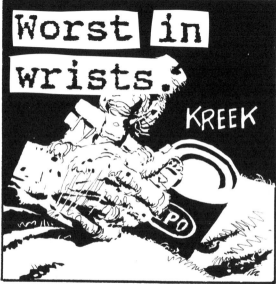

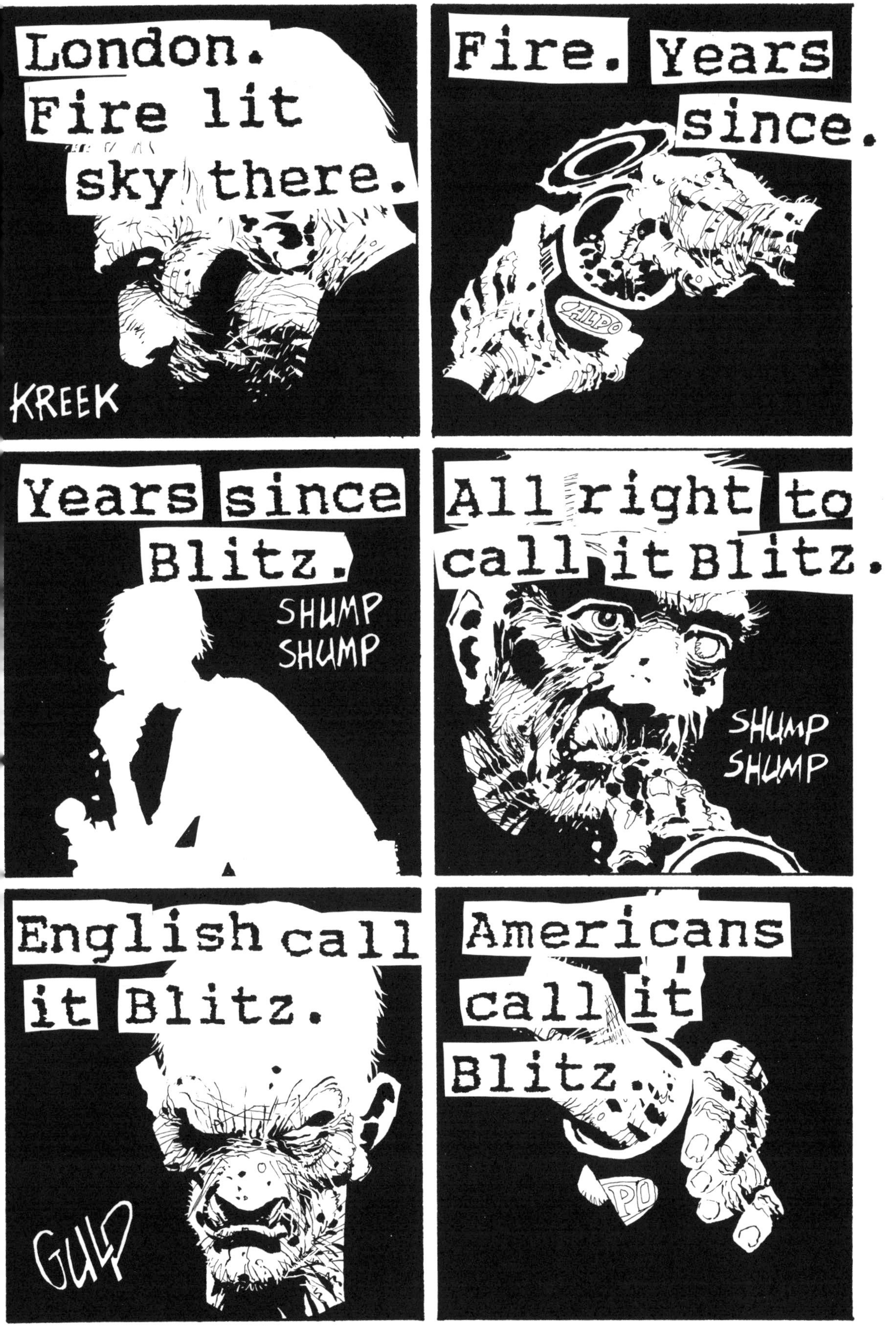

London. Fire lit sky there.
KREEK
Fire. Years since.
CALDO
Years since Blitz.
SHUMP SHUMP
All right to call it Blitz.
SHUMP SHUMP
English call it Blitz.
GULP
Americans call it Blitz.
PO

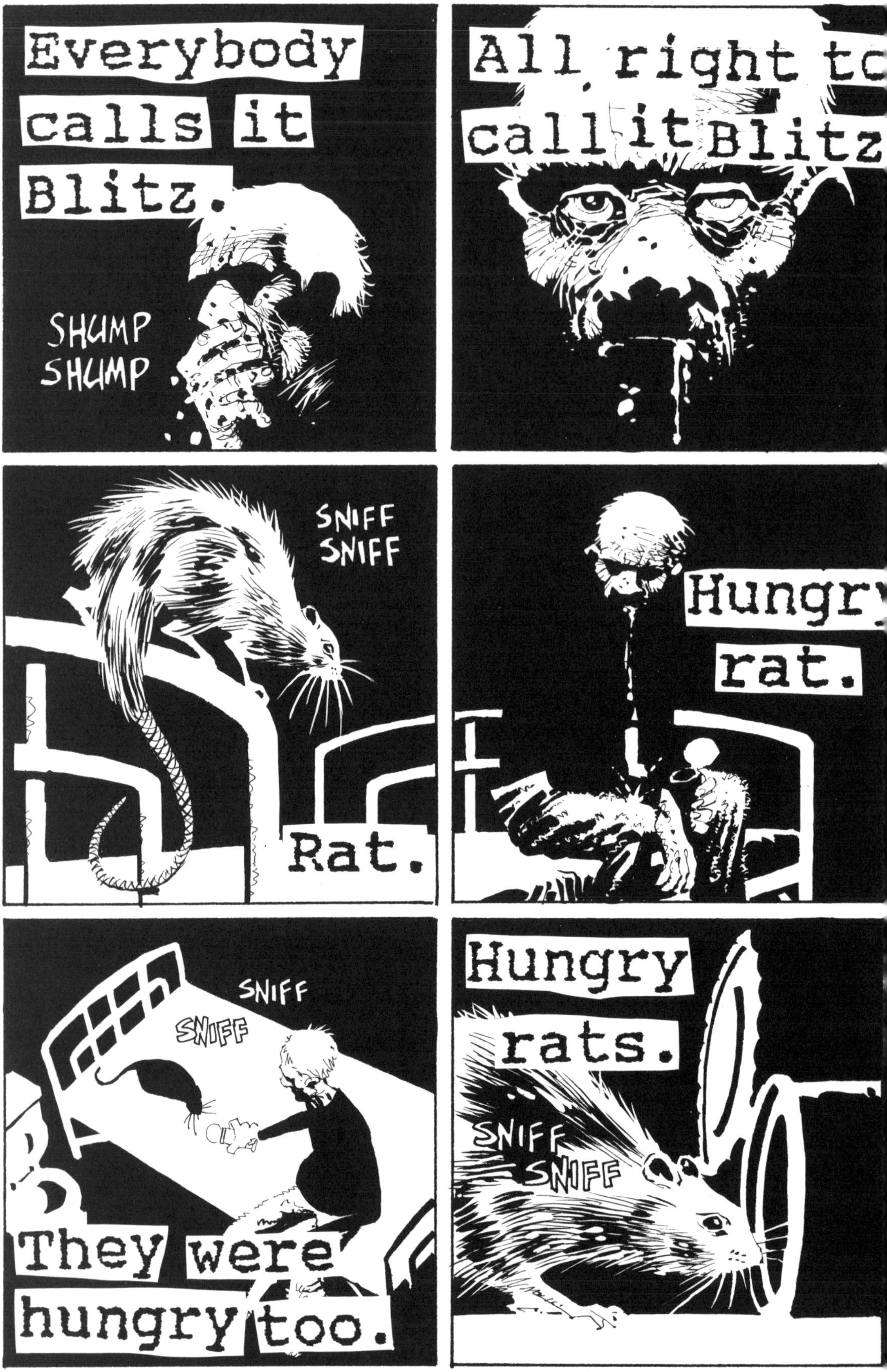

Everybody calls it Blitz.
SHUMP SHUMP
All right to call it Blitz
SNIFF SNIFF
Rat.
Hungry rat.
SNIFF
SNIFF
They were hungry too.
Hungry rats.
SNIFF SNIFF

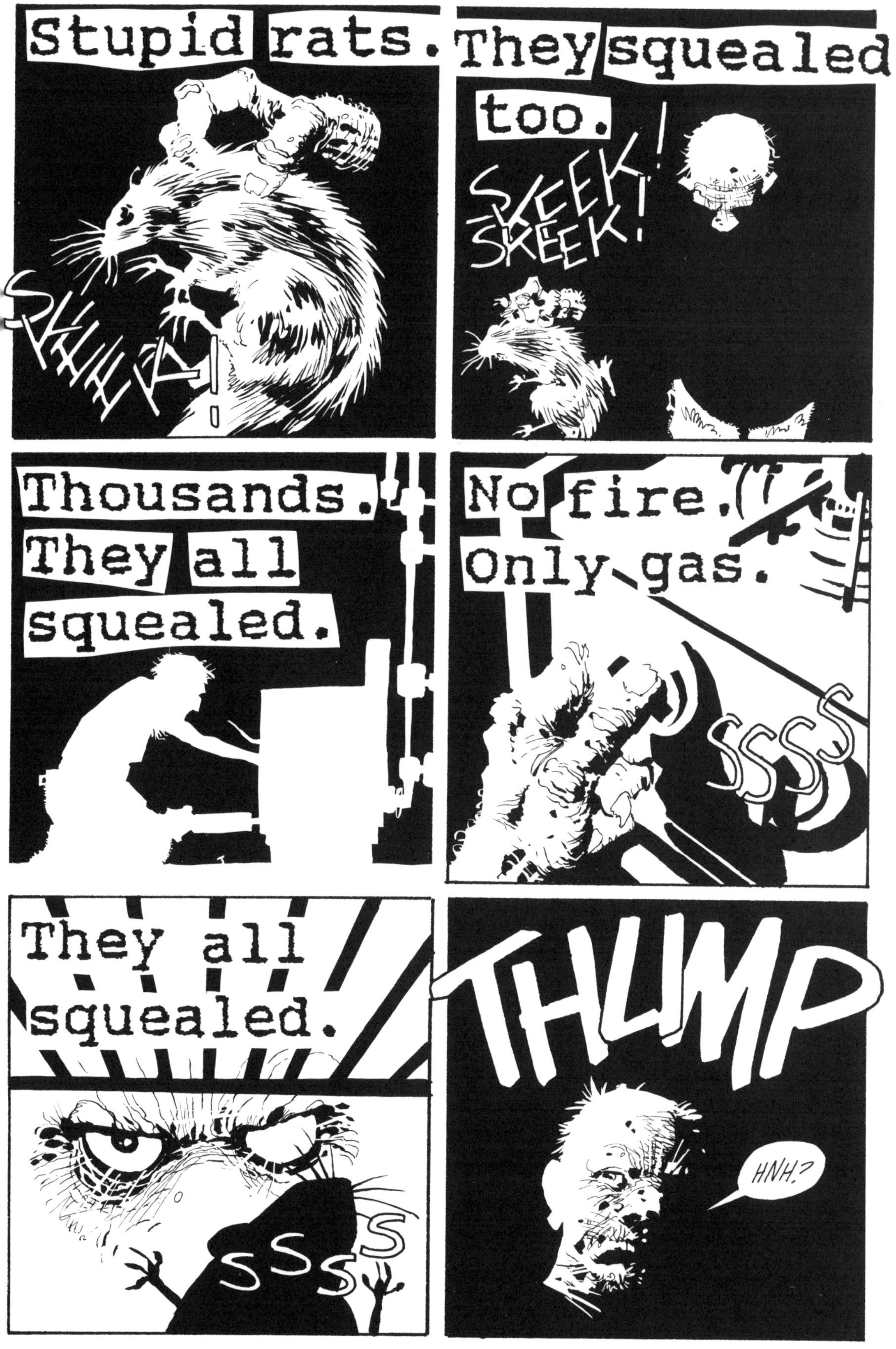

Stupid rats.
SKWEEK!
They squealed too.
SKEEK! SKEEK!
Thousands. They all squealed.
No fire. Only gas.
SSSS
They all squealed.
SSSS
THUMP
HNH?

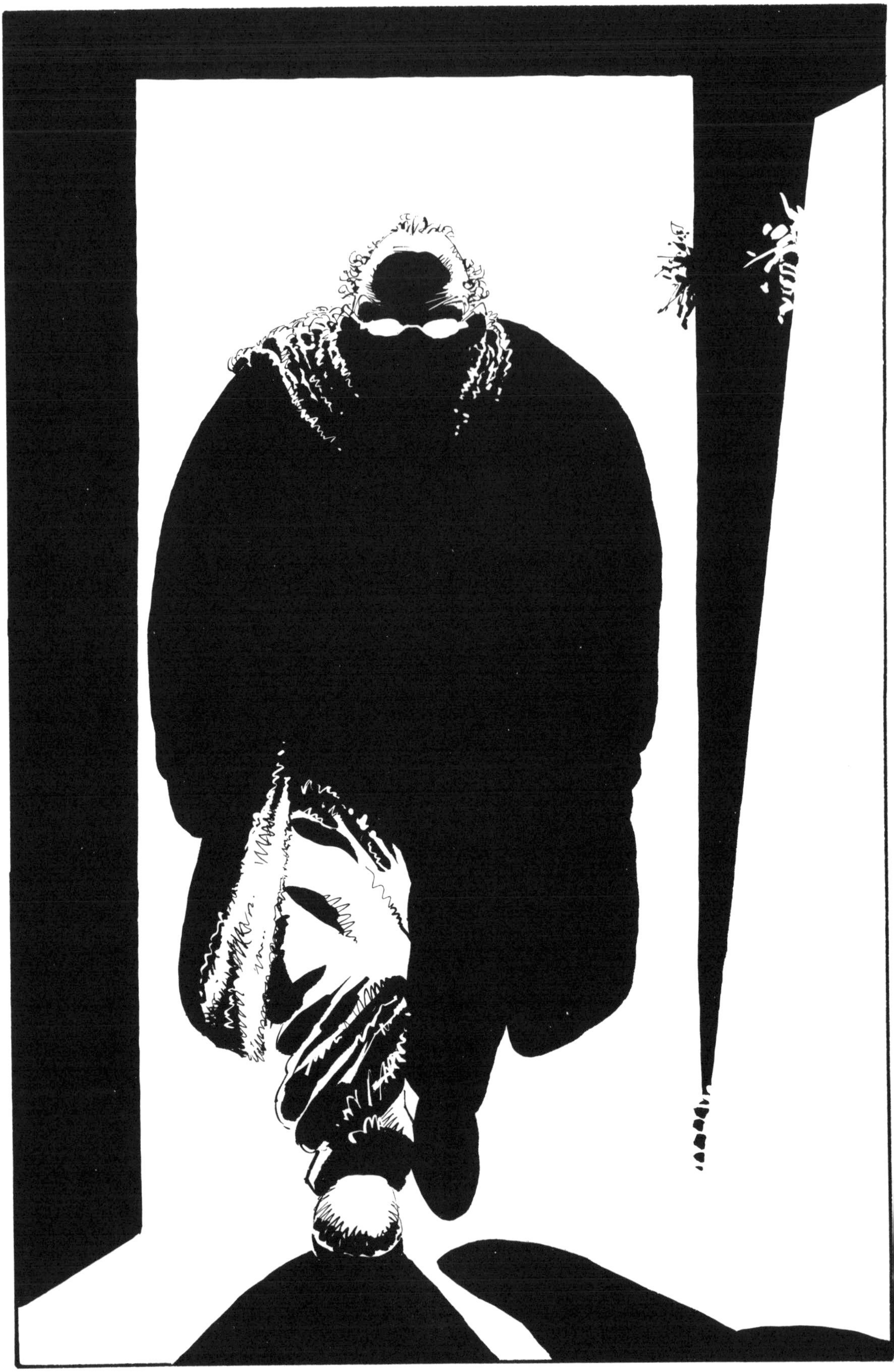

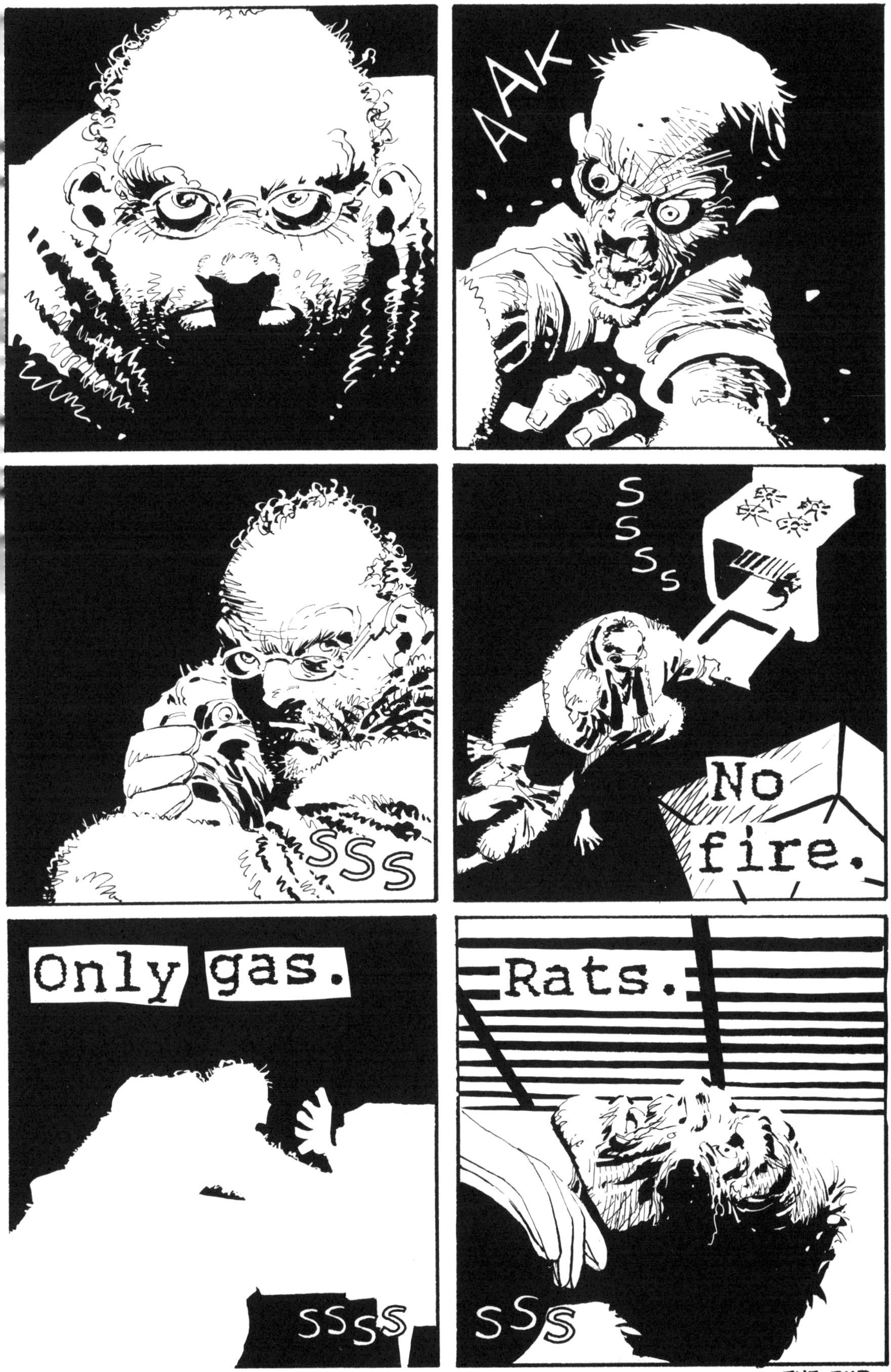
AAK
SSSs
SSSs
No fire.
Only gas.
SSSS
Rats.
SSS

THE END

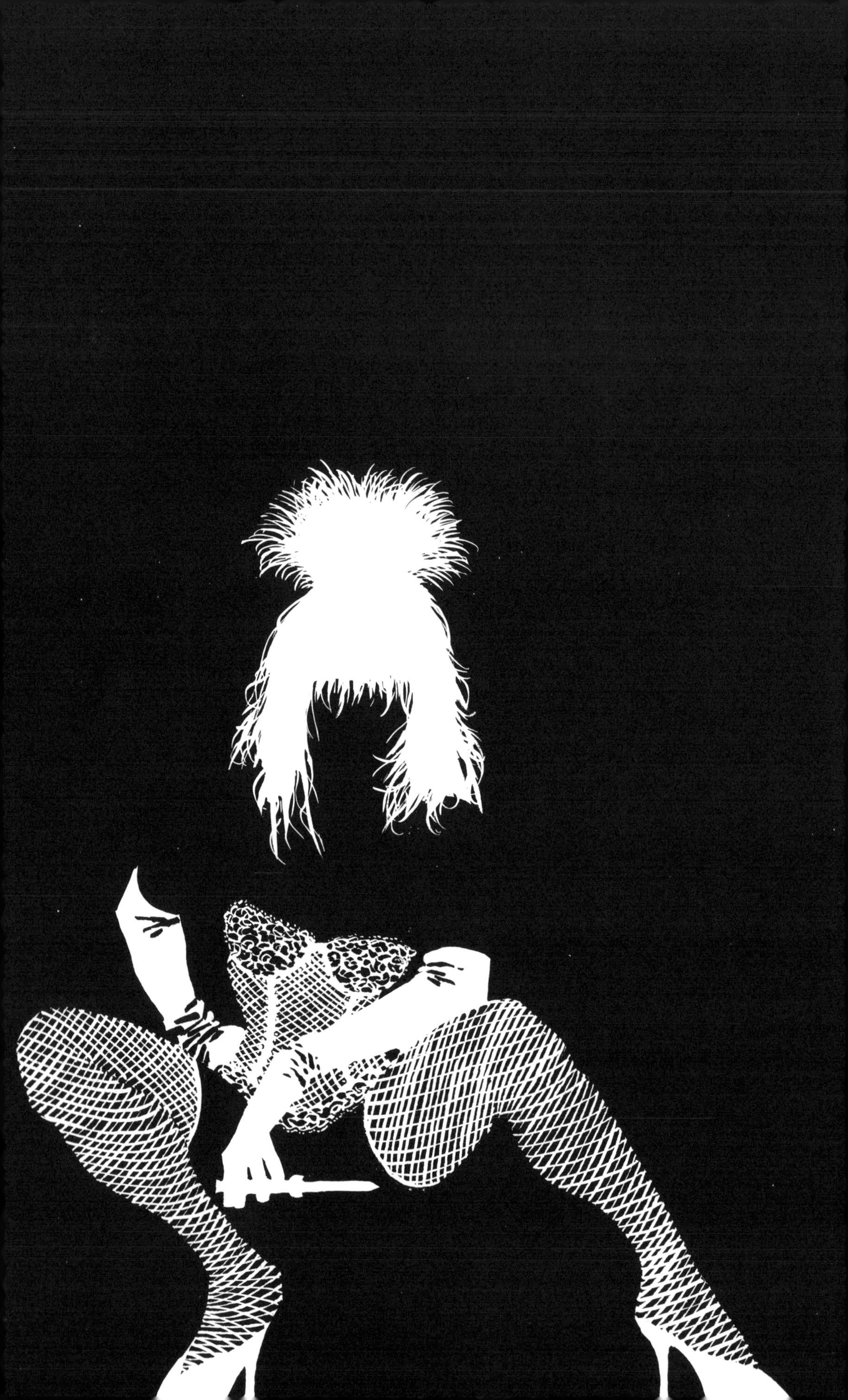

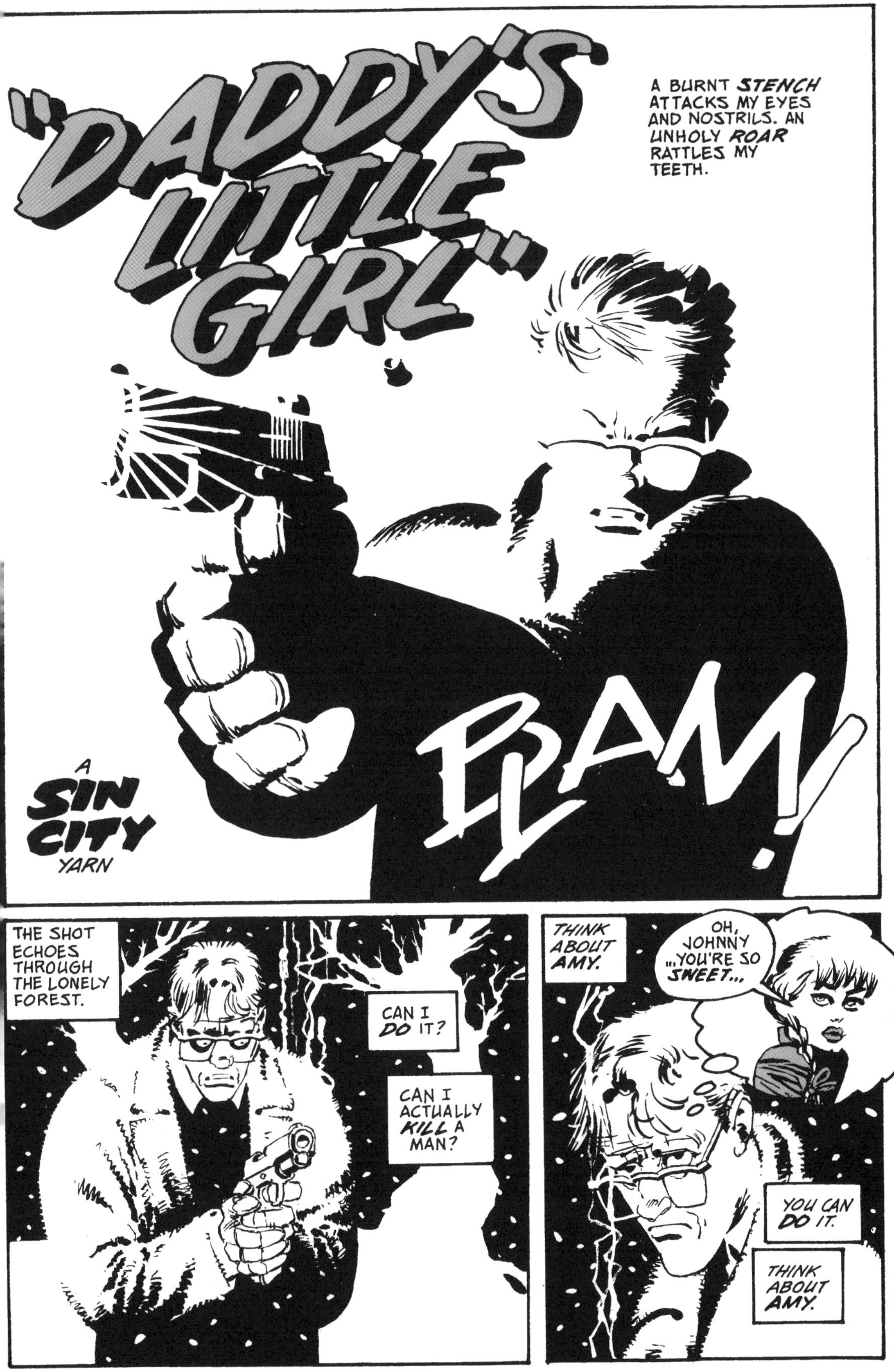
"DADDY'S LITTLE GIRL"
A BURNT STENCH ATTACKS MY EYES AND NOSTRILS. AN UNHOLY ROAR RATTLES MY TEETH.
BLAM!
A SIN CITY YARN
THE SHOT ECHOES THROUGH THE LONELY FOREST.
CAN I DO IT?
CAN I ACTUALLY KILL A MAN?
THINK ABOUT AMY.
OH, JOHNNY ...YOU'RE SO SWEET...
YOU CAN DO IT.
THINK ABOUT AMY.

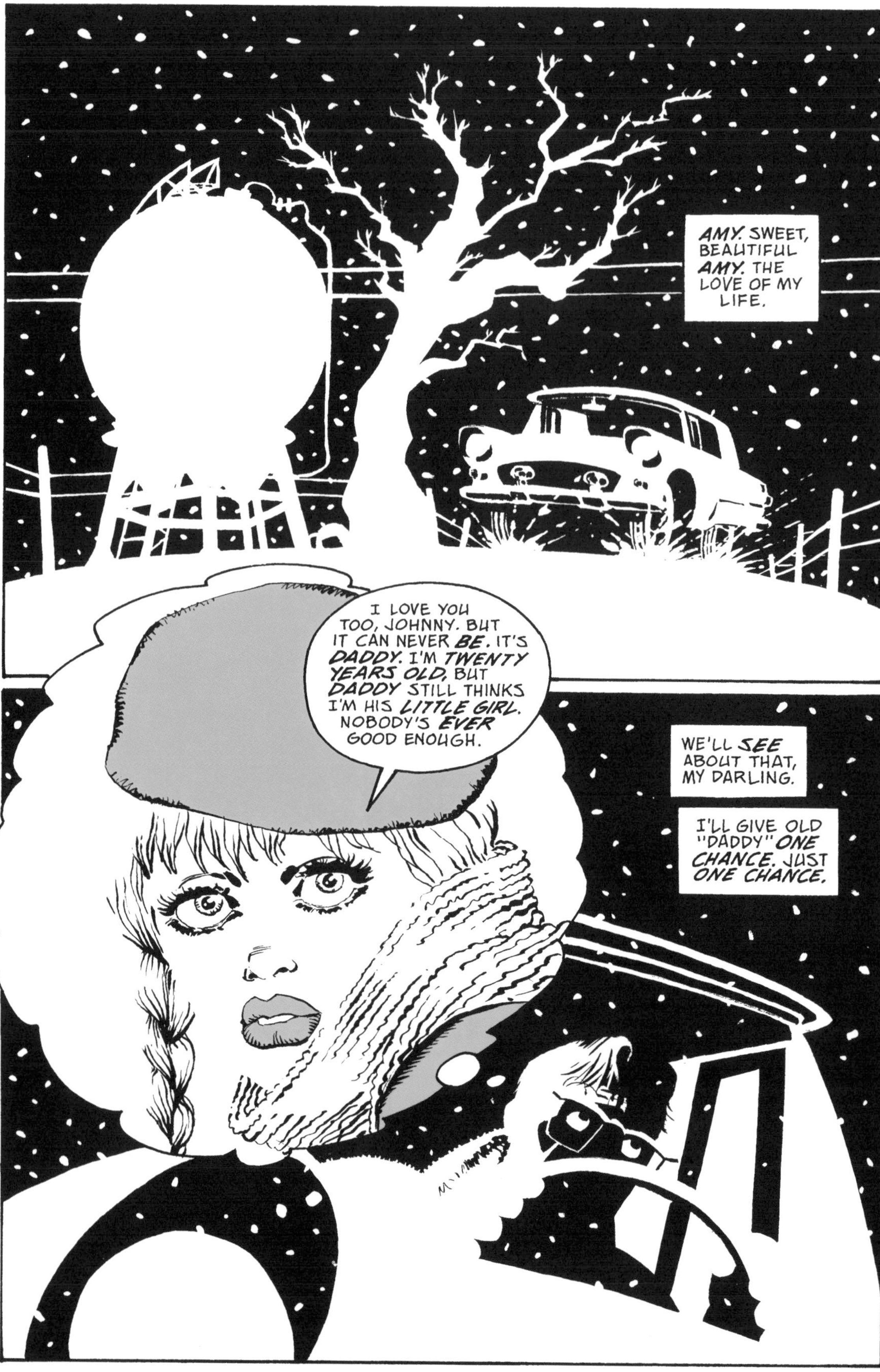
AMY. SWEET, BEAUTIFUL AMY. THE LOVE OF MY LIFE.
I LOVE YOU TOO, JOHNNY. BUT IT CAN NEVER BE. IT'S DADDY. I'M TWENTY YEARS OLD, BUT DADDY STILL THINKS I'M HIS LITTLE GIRL. NOBODY'S EVER GOOD ENOUGH.
WE'LL SEE ABOUT THAT, MY DARLING.
I'LL GIVE OLD "DADDY" ONE CHANCE. JUST ONE CHANCE.

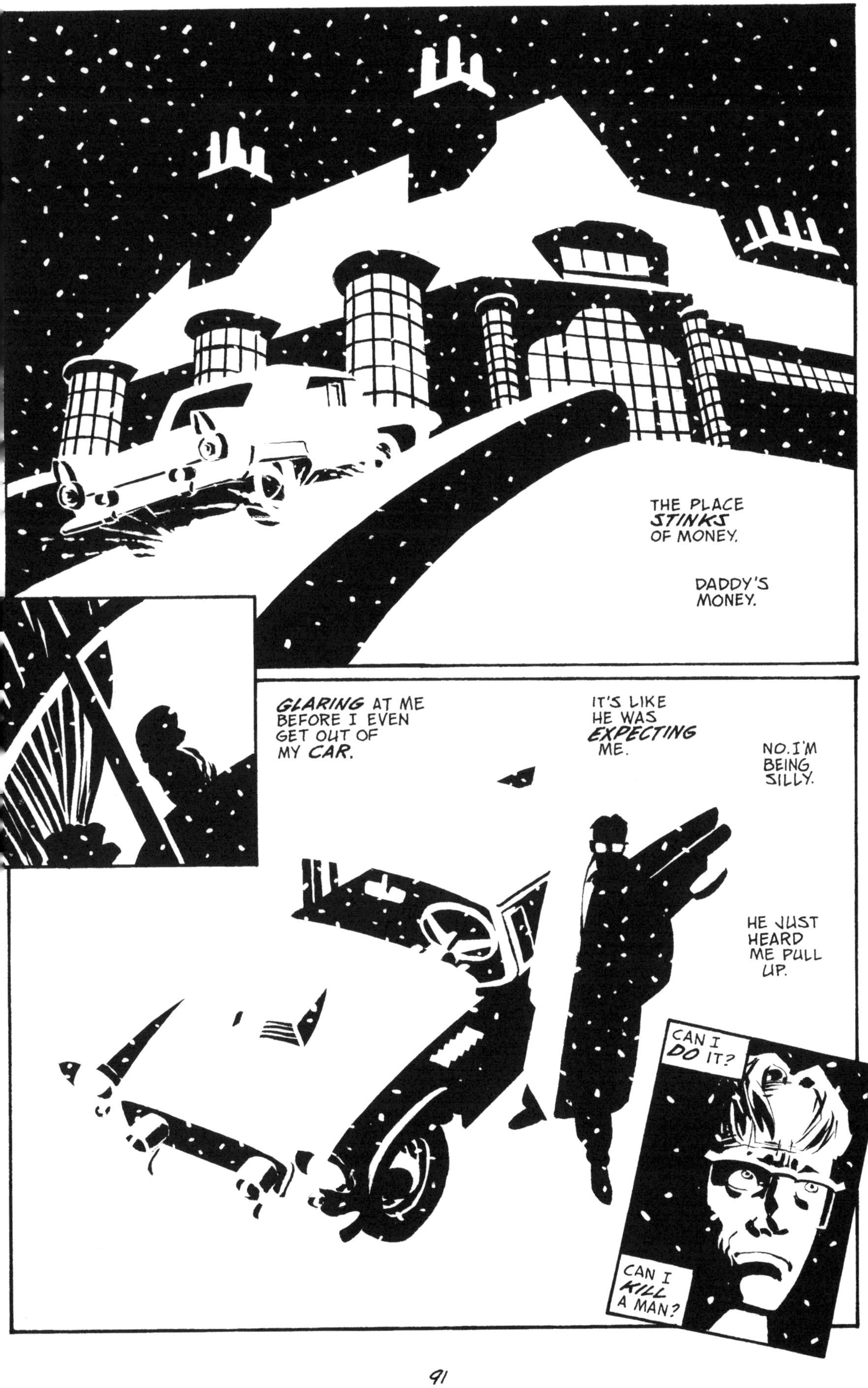
THE PLACE STINKS OF MONEY.
DADDY'S MONEY.
GLARING AT ME BEFORE I EVEN GET OUT OF MY CAR.
IT'S LIKE HE WAS EXPECTING ME.
NO. I'M BEING SILLY.
HE JUST HEARD ME PULL UP.
CAN I DO IT?
CAN I KILL A MAN?

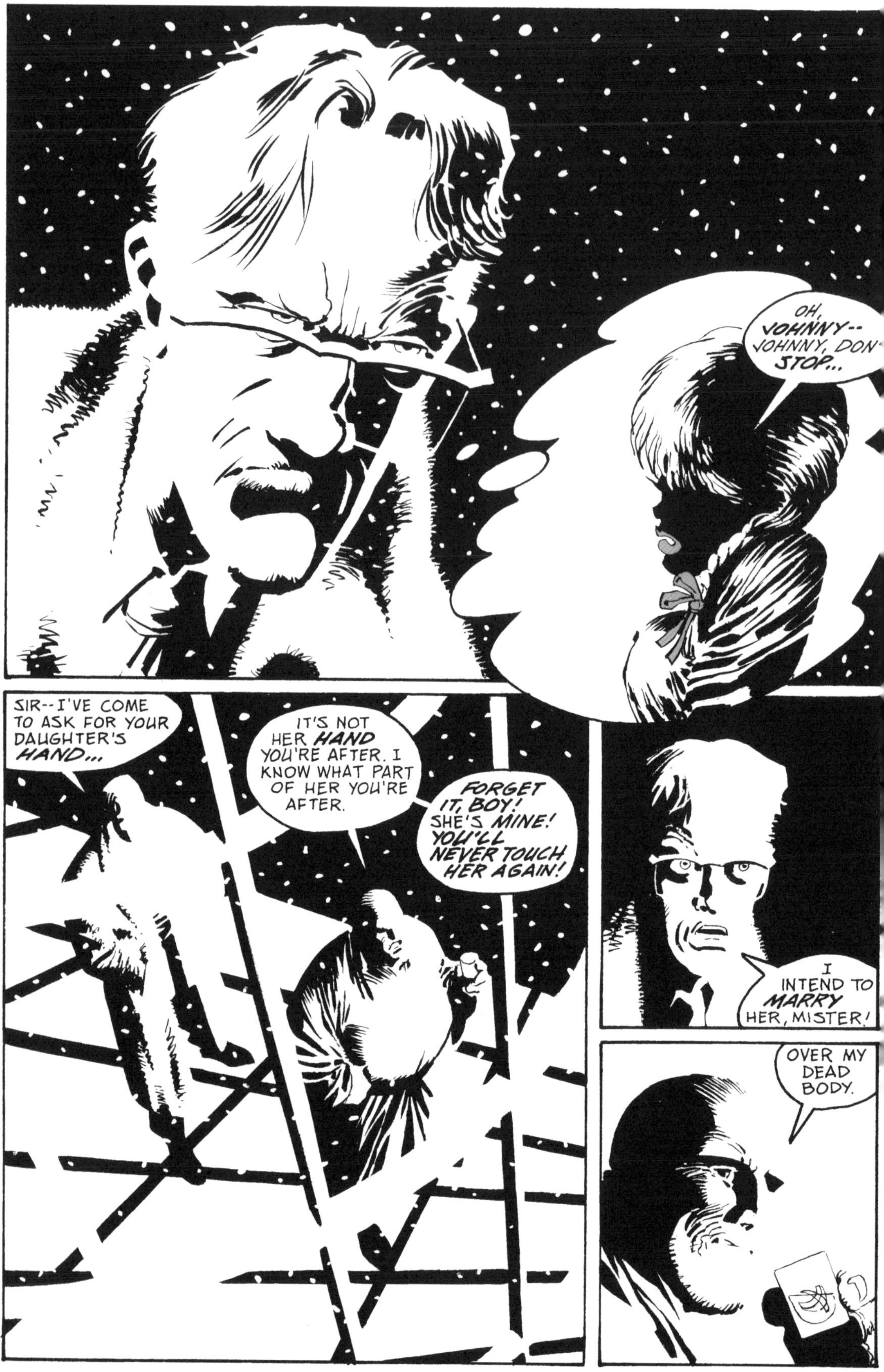

OH, JOHNNY-- JOHNNY, DON' STOP...
SIR--I'VE COME TO ASK FOR YOUR DAUGHTER'S HAND...
IT'S NOT HER HAND YOU'RE AFTER. I KNOW WHAT PART OF HER YOU'RE AFTER.
FORGET IT, BOY! SHE'S MINE! YOU'LL NEVER TOUCH HER AGAIN!
I INTEND TO MARRY HER, MISTER!
OVER MY DEAD BODY.

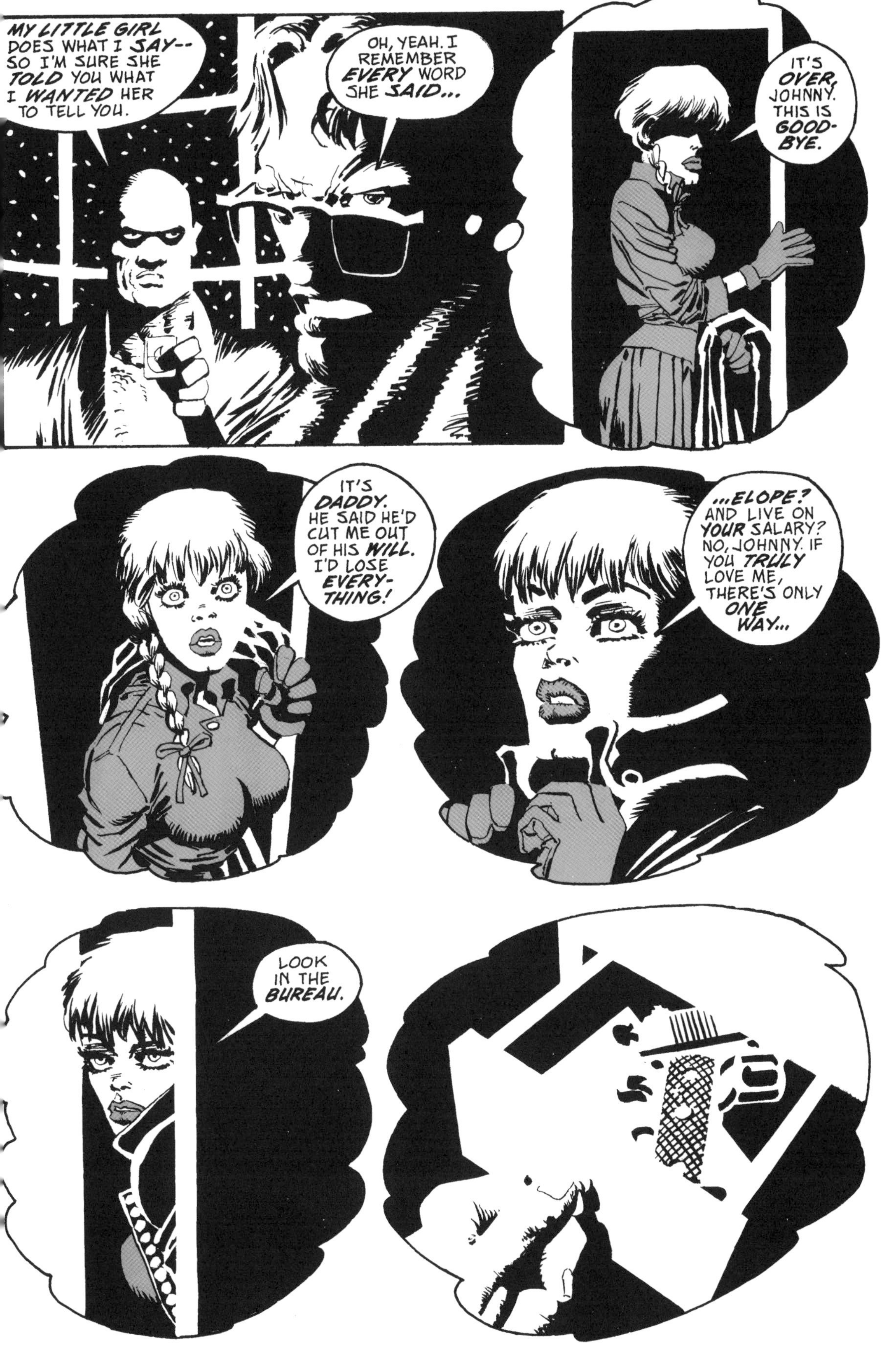
MY LITTLE GIRL DOES WHAT I SAY-- SO I'M SURE SHE TOLD YOU WHAT I WANTED HER TO TELL YOU.
OH, YEAH. I REMEMBER EVERY WORD SHE SAID...
IT'S OVER, JOHNNY. THIS IS GOOD-BYE.
IT'S DADDY. HE SAID HE'D CUT ME OUT OF HIS WILL. I'D LOSE EVERY-THING!
...ELOPE? AND LIVE ON YOUR SALARY? NO, JOHNNY. IF YOU TRULY LOVE ME, THERE'S ONLY ONE WAY...
LOOK IN THE BUREAU.

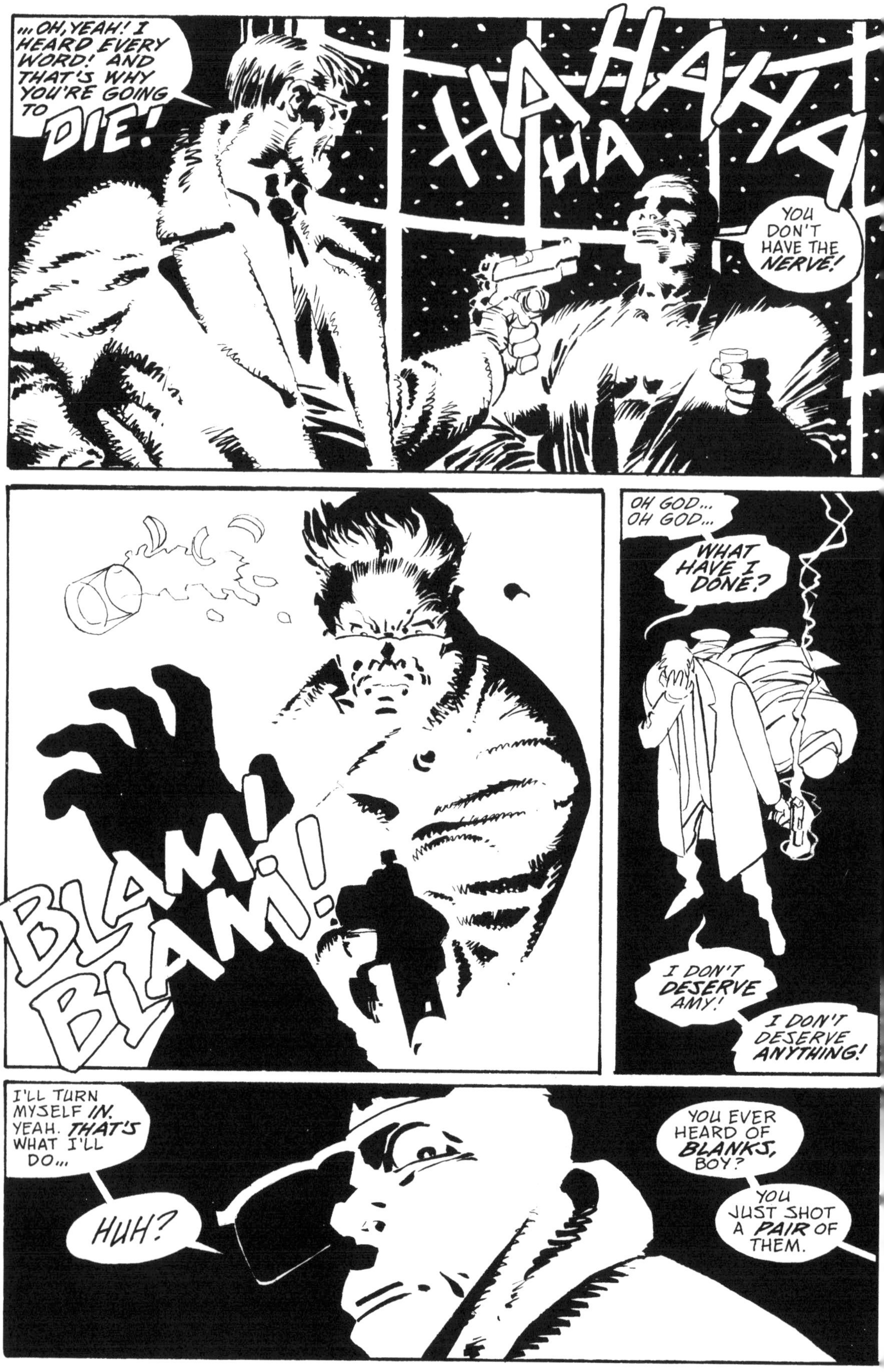

...OH, YEAH! I HEARD EVERY WORD! AND THAT'S WHY YOU'RE GOING TO DIE!
HA HA HA HA
YOU DON'T HAVE THE NERVE!
BLAM! BLAM!
OH GOD... OH GOD...
WHAT HAVE I DONE?
I DON'T DESERVE AMY!
I DON'T DESERVE ANYTHING!
I'LL TURN MYSELF IN. YEAH. THAT'S WHAT I'LL DO...
YOU EVER HEARD OF BLANKS, BOY?
YOU JUST SHOT A PAIR OF THEM.
HUH?

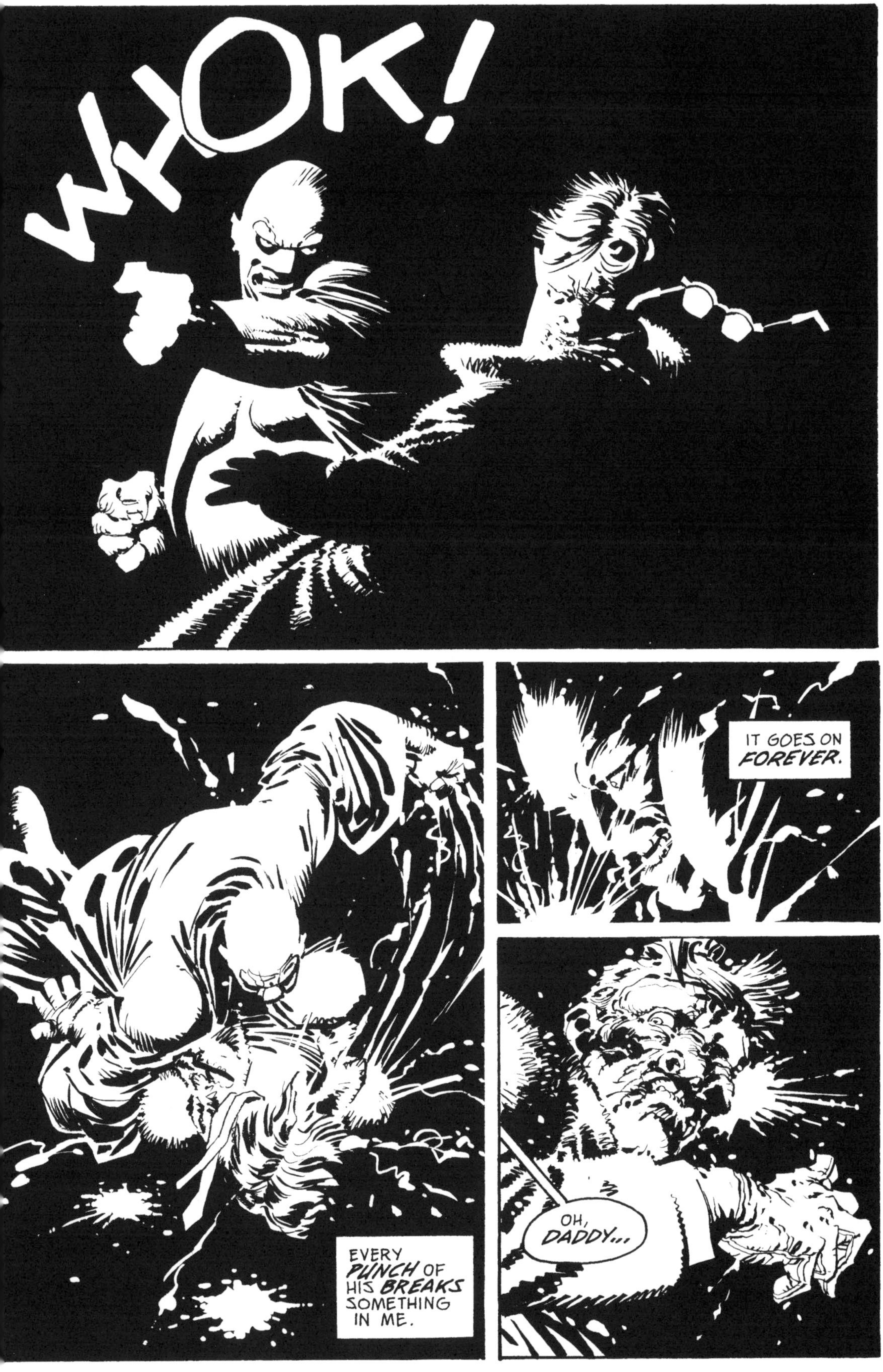
WHOK!
EVERY PUNCH OF HIS BREAKS SOMETHING IN ME.
IT GOES ON FOREVER.
OH, DADDY...

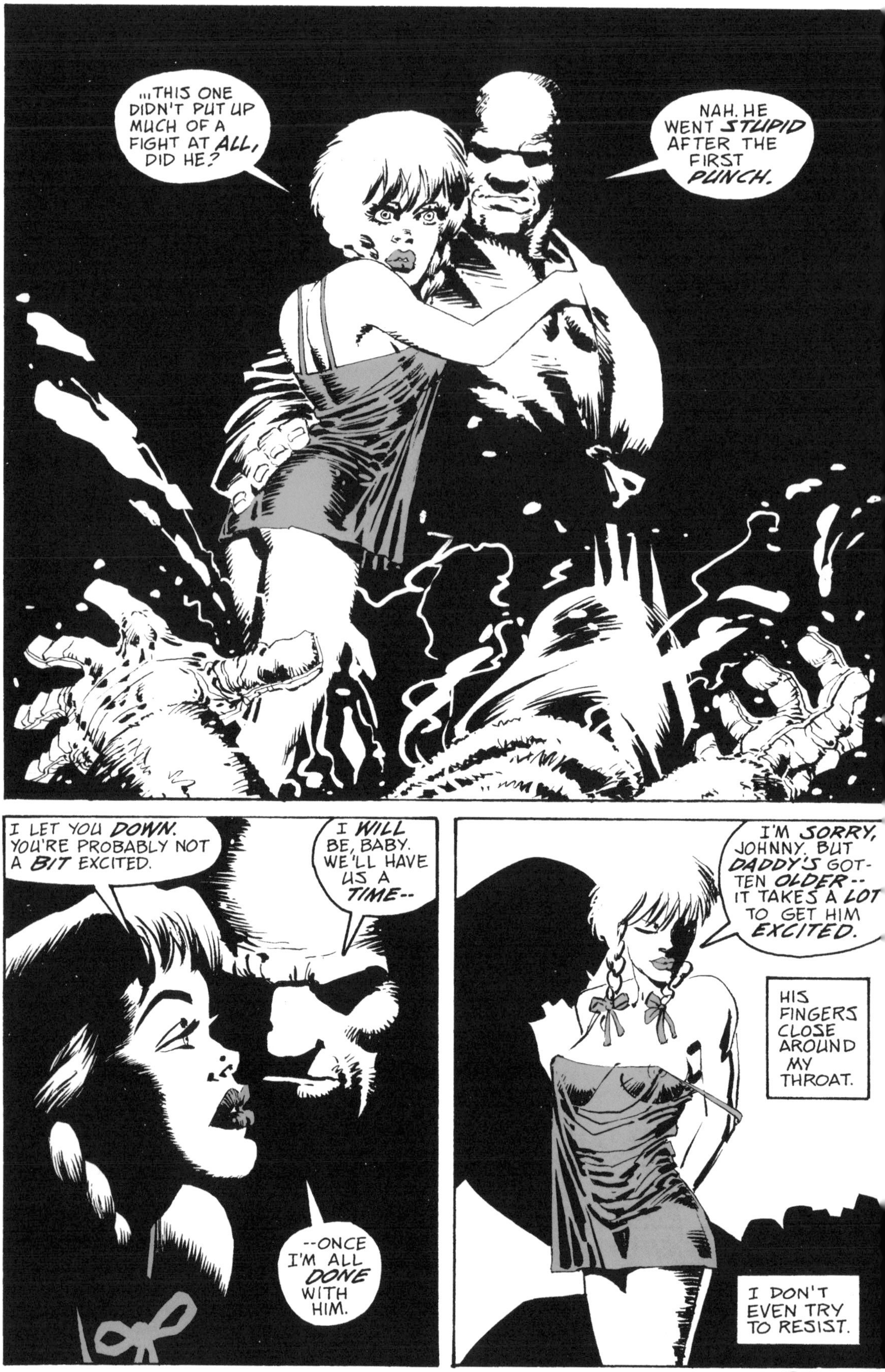
...THIS ONE DIDN'T PUT UP MUCH OF A FIGHT AT ALL, DID HE?
NAH. HE WENT STUPID AFTER THE FIRST PUNCH.
I LET YOU DOWN. YOU'RE PROBABLY NOT A BIT EXCITED.
I WILL BE, BABY. WE'LL HAVE US A TIME--
--ONCE I'M ALL DONE WITH HIM.
I'M SORRY, JOHNNY, BUT DADDY'S GOTTEN OLDER-- IT TAKES A LOT TO GET HIM EXCITED.
HIS FINGERS CLOSE AROUND MY THROAT.
I DON'T EVEN TRY TO RESIST.

THE END

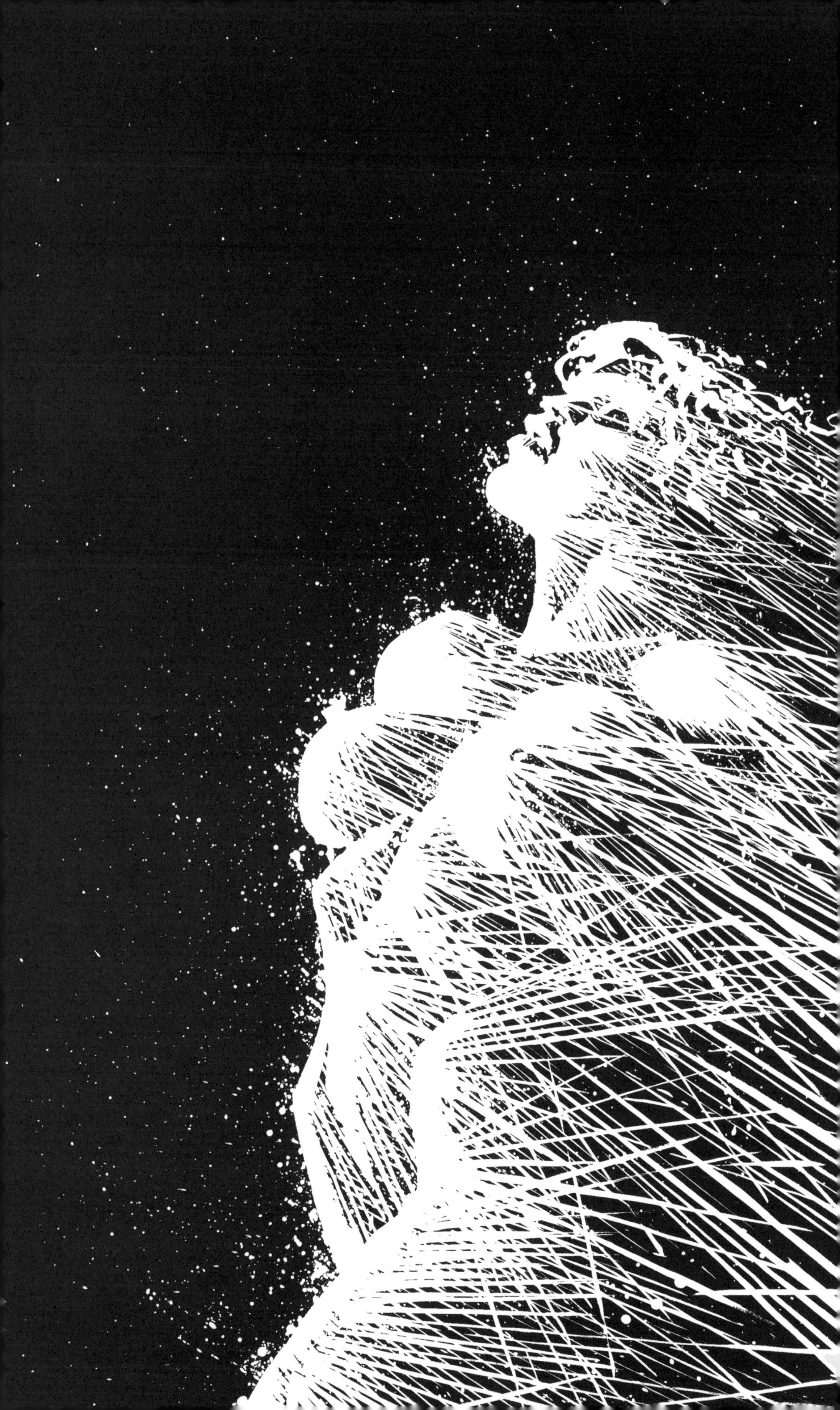

WRONG TURN

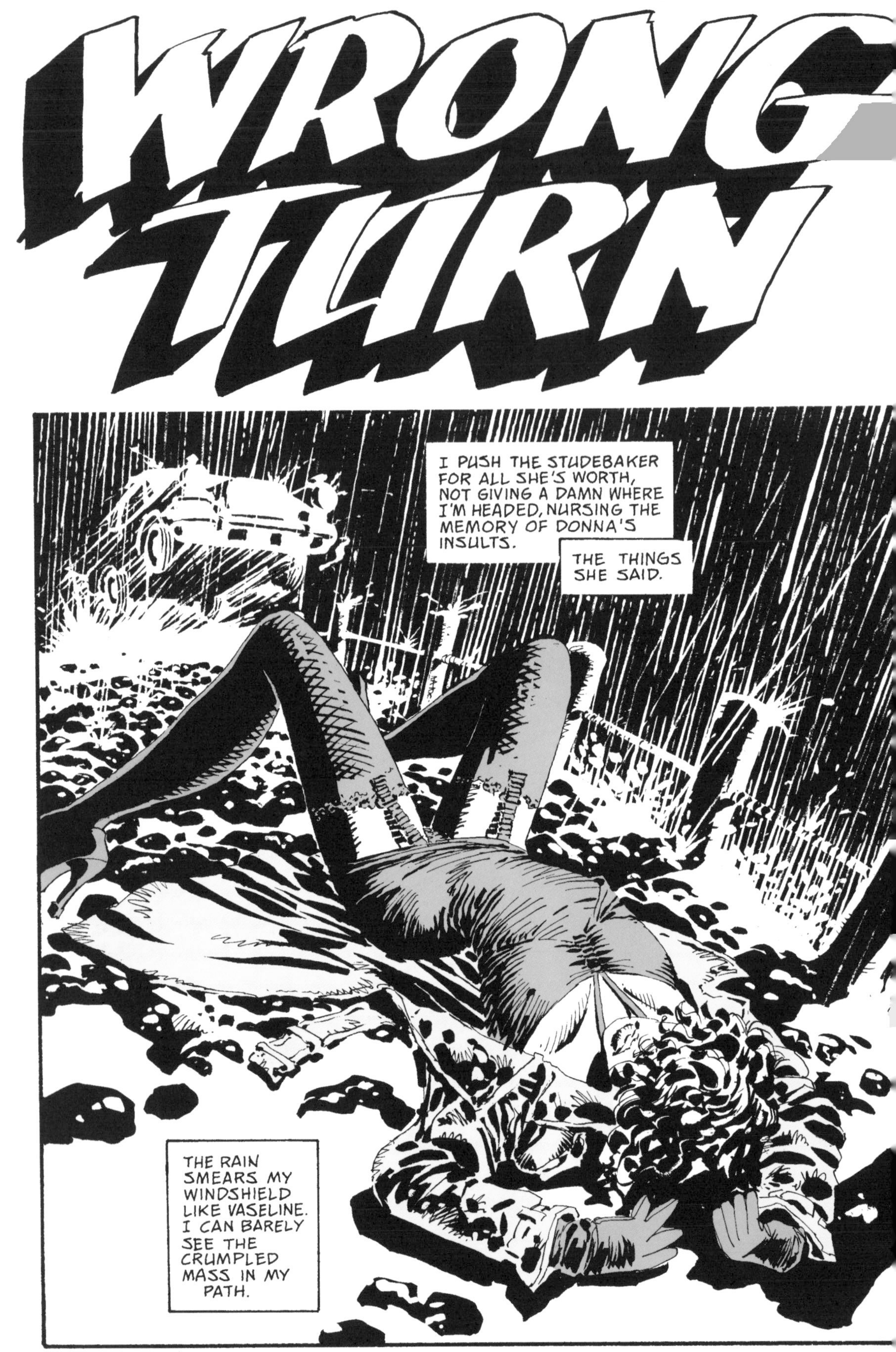

I PUSH THE STUDEBAKER FOR ALL SHE'S WORTH, NOT GIVING A DAMN WHERE I'M HEADED, NURSING THE MEMORY OF DONNA'S INSULTS.
THE THINGS SHE SAID.
THE RAIN SMEARS MY WINDSHIELD LIKE VASELINE. I CAN BARELY SEE THE CRUMPLED MASS IN MY PATH.

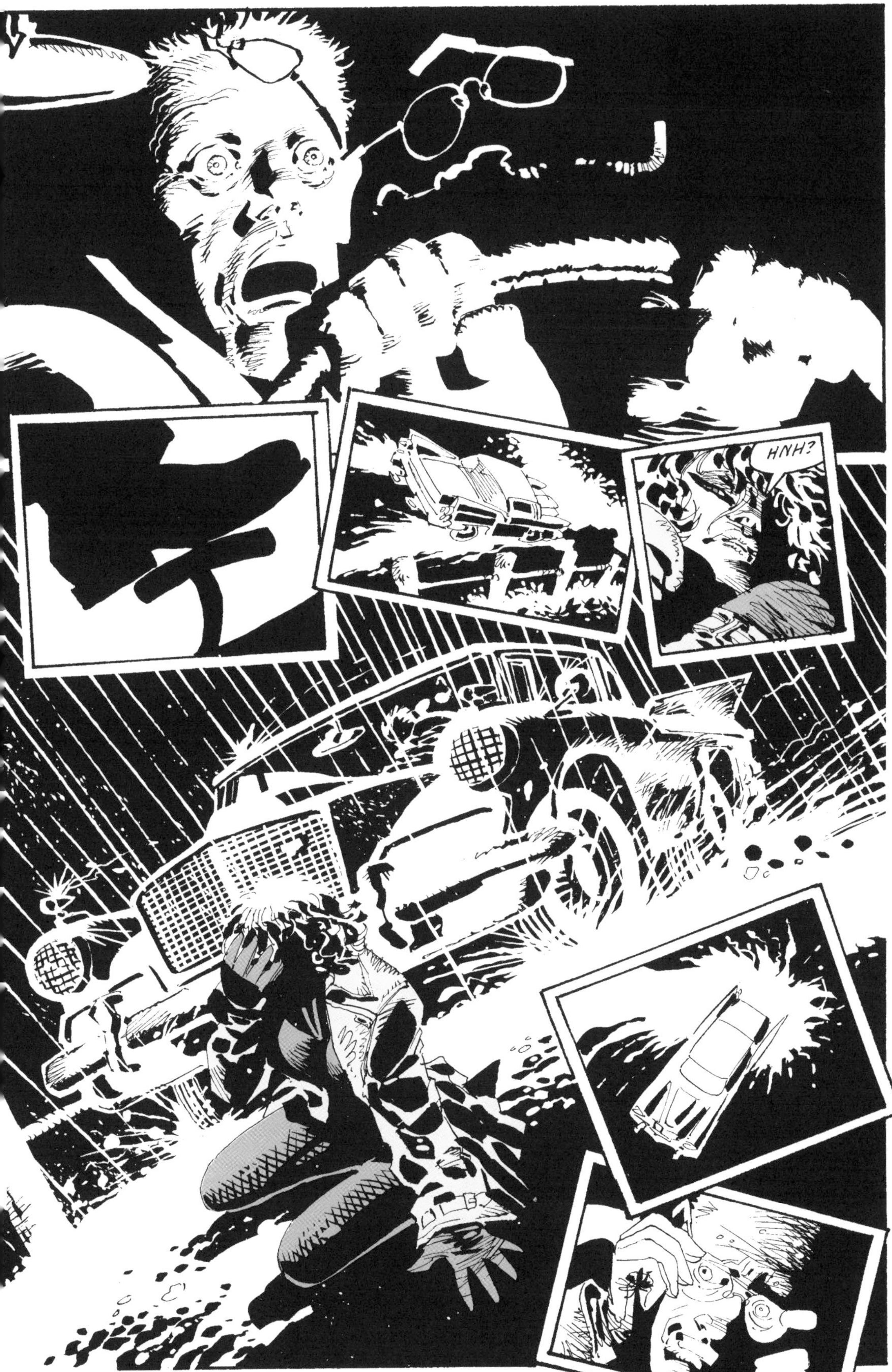
HNH?

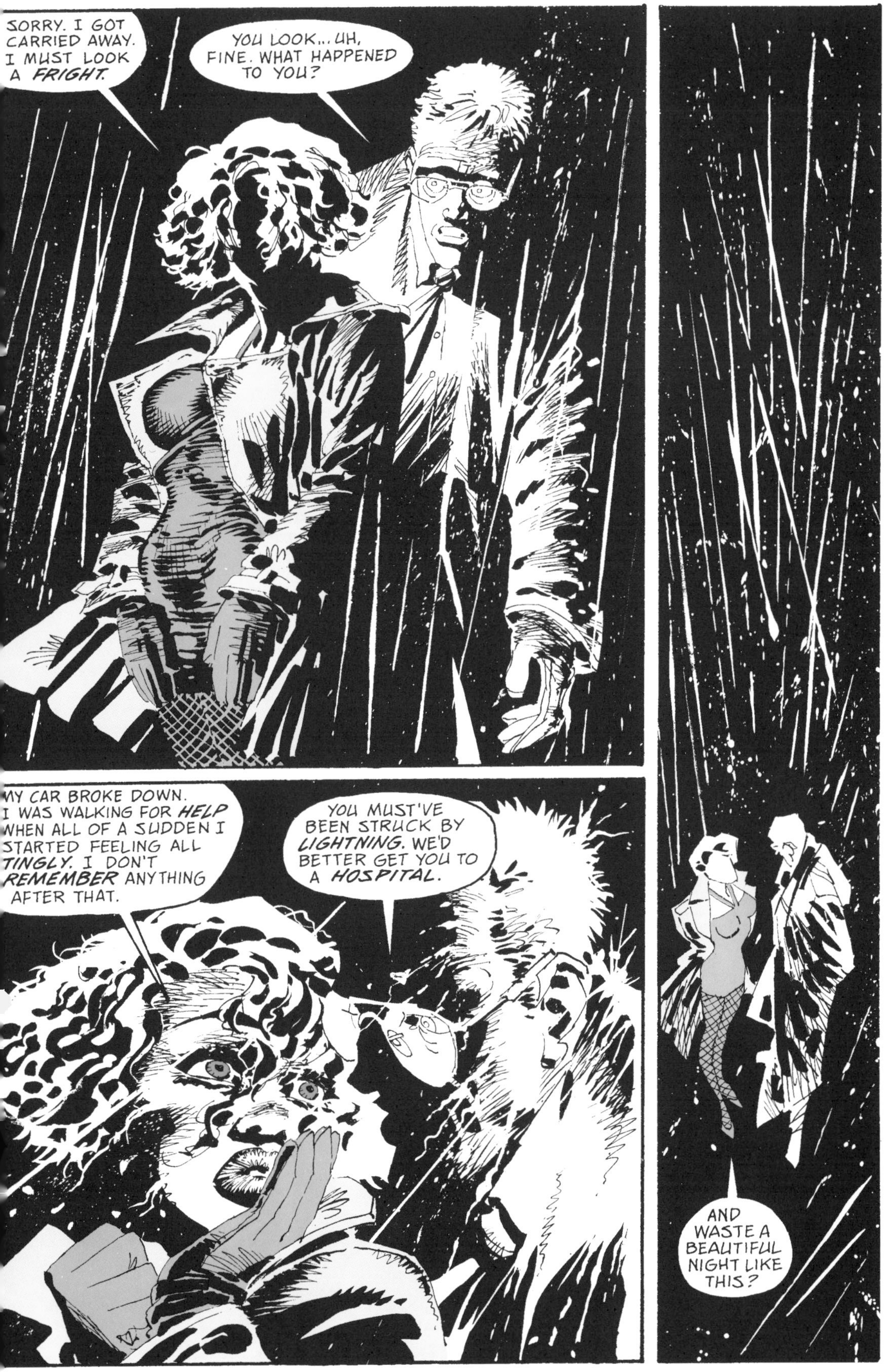
SORRY. I GOT CARRIED AWAY. I MUST LOOK A *FRIGHT.*
YOU LOOK... UH, FINE. WHAT HAPPENED TO YOU?
MY CAR BROKE DOWN. I WAS WALKING FOR *HELP* WHEN ALL OF A SUDDEN I STARTED FEELING ALL *TINGLY.* I DON'T *REMEMBER* ANYTHING AFTER THAT.
YOU MUST'VE BEEN STRUCK BY *LIGHTNING.* WE'D BETTER GET YOU TO A *HOSPITAL.*
AND WASTE A BEAUTIFUL NIGHT LIKE THIS?

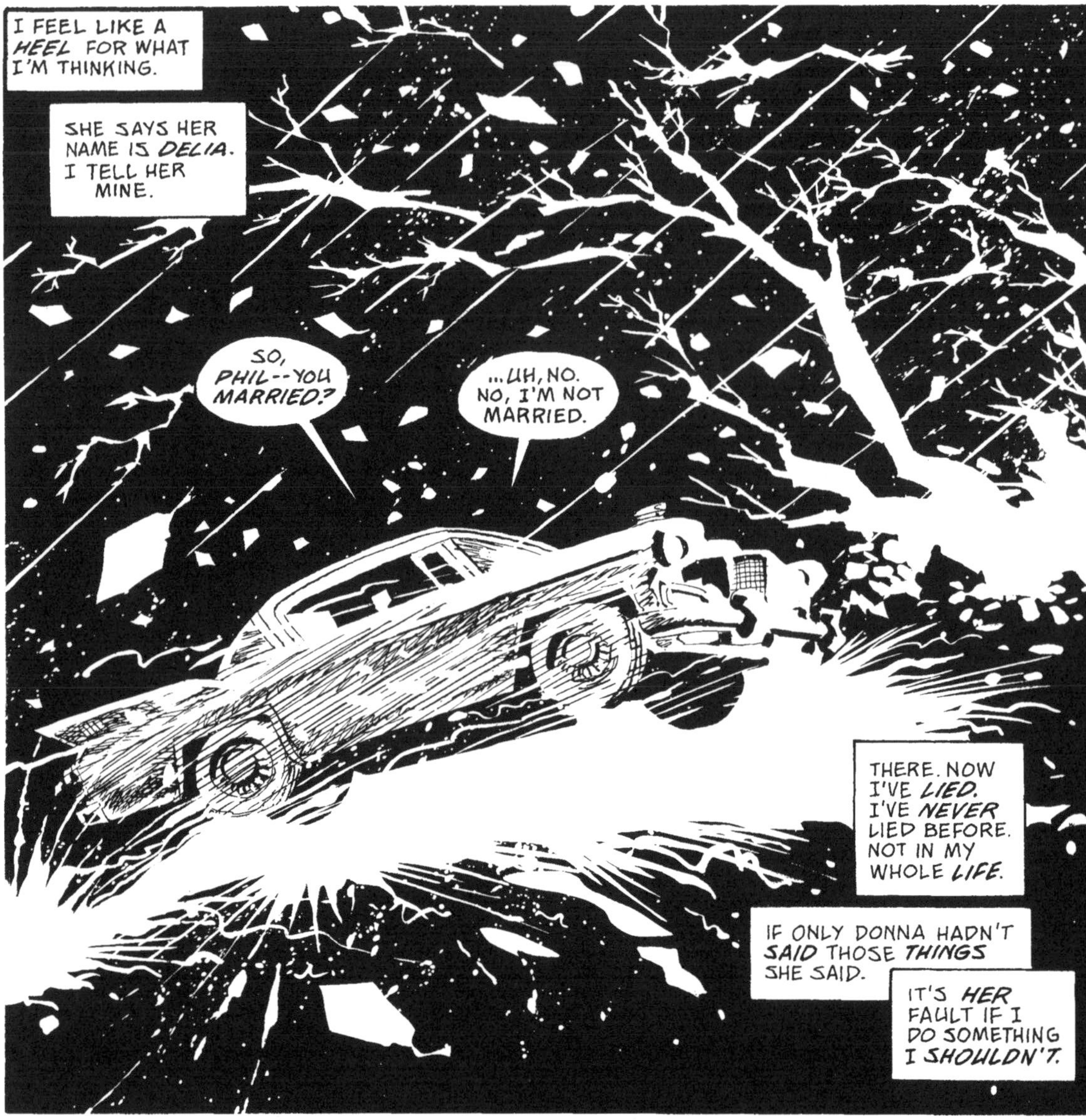
I FEEL LIKE A HEEL FOR WHAT I'M THINKING.
SHE SAYS HER NAME IS DELIA. I TELL HER MINE.
SO, PHIL--YOU MARRIED?
...UH, NO. NO, I'M NOT MARRIED.
THERE. NOW I'VE LIED. I'VE NEVER LIED BEFORE. NOT IN MY WHOLE LIFE.
IF ONLY DONNA HADN'T SAID THOSE THINGS SHE SAID.
IT'S HER FAULT IF I DO SOMETHING I SHOULDN'T.

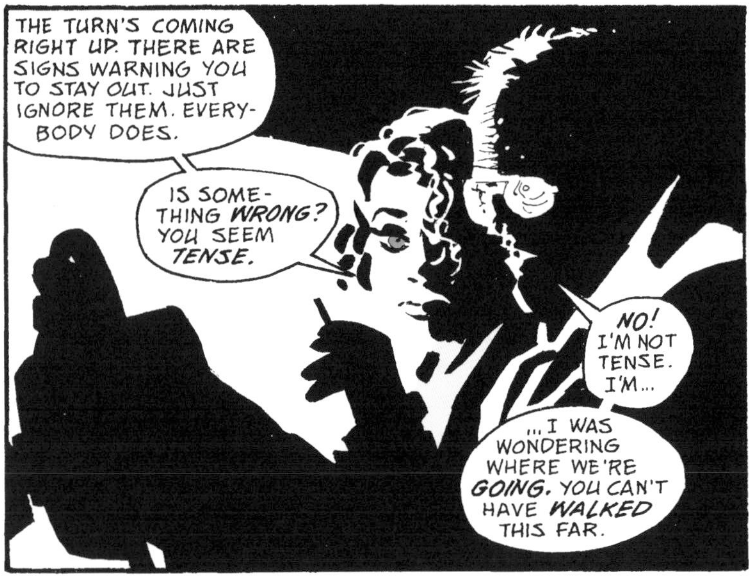
THE TURN'S COMING RIGHT UP. THERE ARE SIGNS WARNING YOU TO STAY OUT. JUST IGNORE THEM. EVERY-BODY DOES.
IS SOME-THING WRONG? YOU SEEM TENSE.
NO! I'M NOT TENSE. I'M...
...I WAS WONDERING WHERE WE'RE GOING. YOU CAN'T HAVE WALKED THIS FAR.

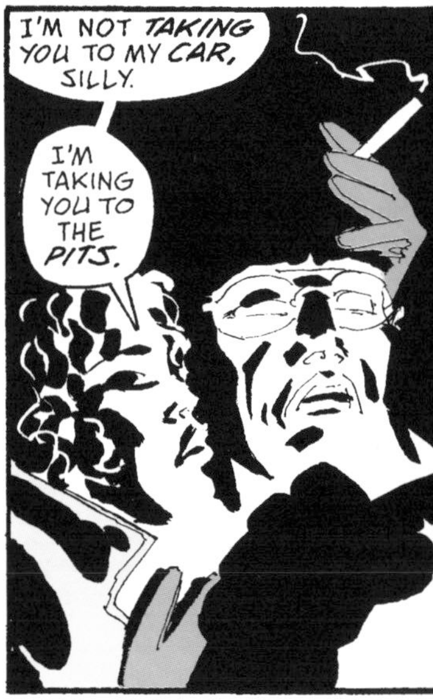
I'M NOT TAKING YOU TO MY CAR, SILLY.
I'M TAKING YOU TO THE PITS.

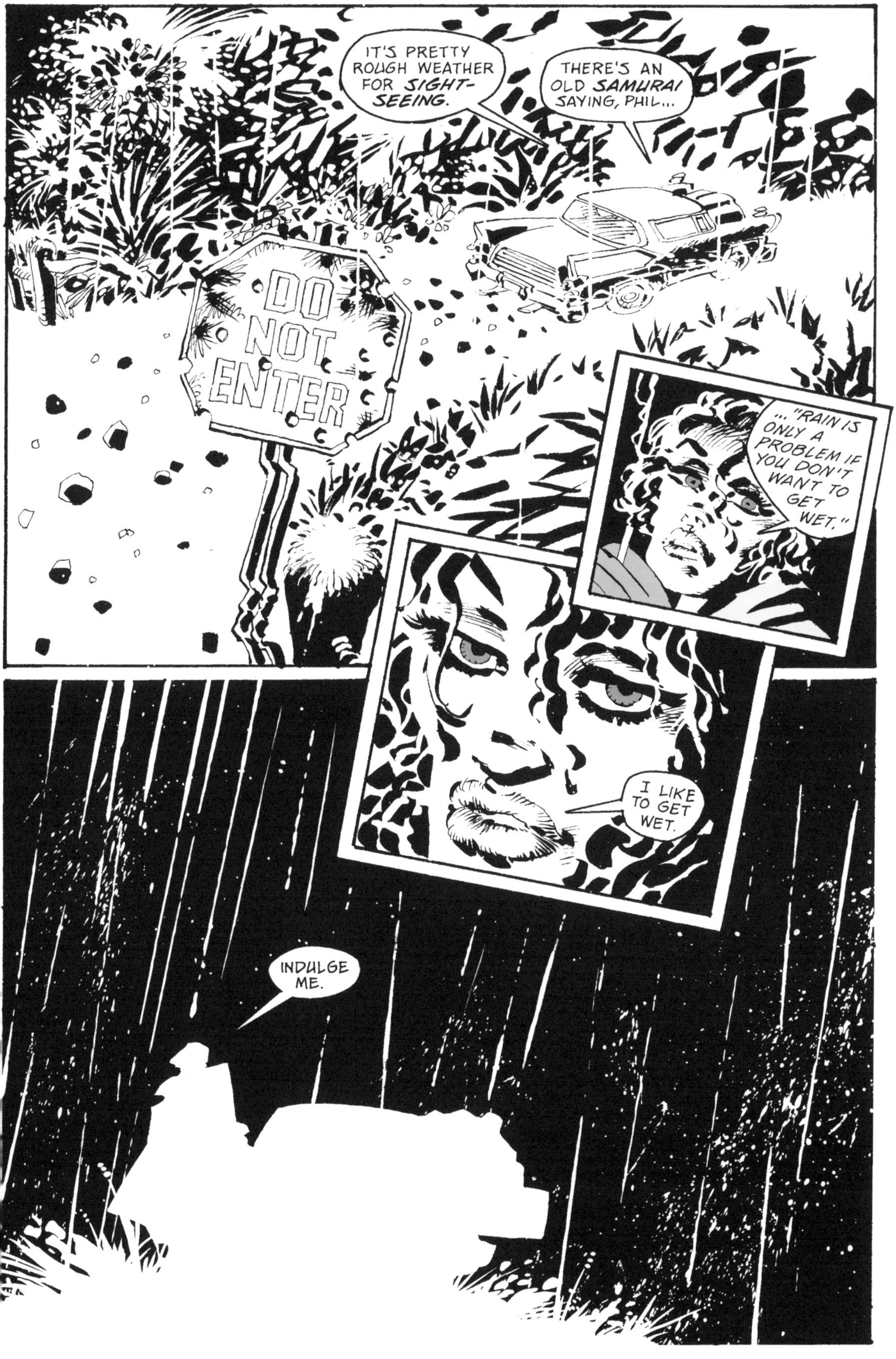
IT'S PRETTY ROUGH WEATHER FOR SIGHT-SEEING.
THERE'S AN OLD SAMURAI SAYING, PHIL...
DO NOT ENTER
..."RAIN IS ONLY A PROBLEM IF YOU DON'T WANT TO GET WET."
I LIKE TO GET WET.
INDULGE ME.

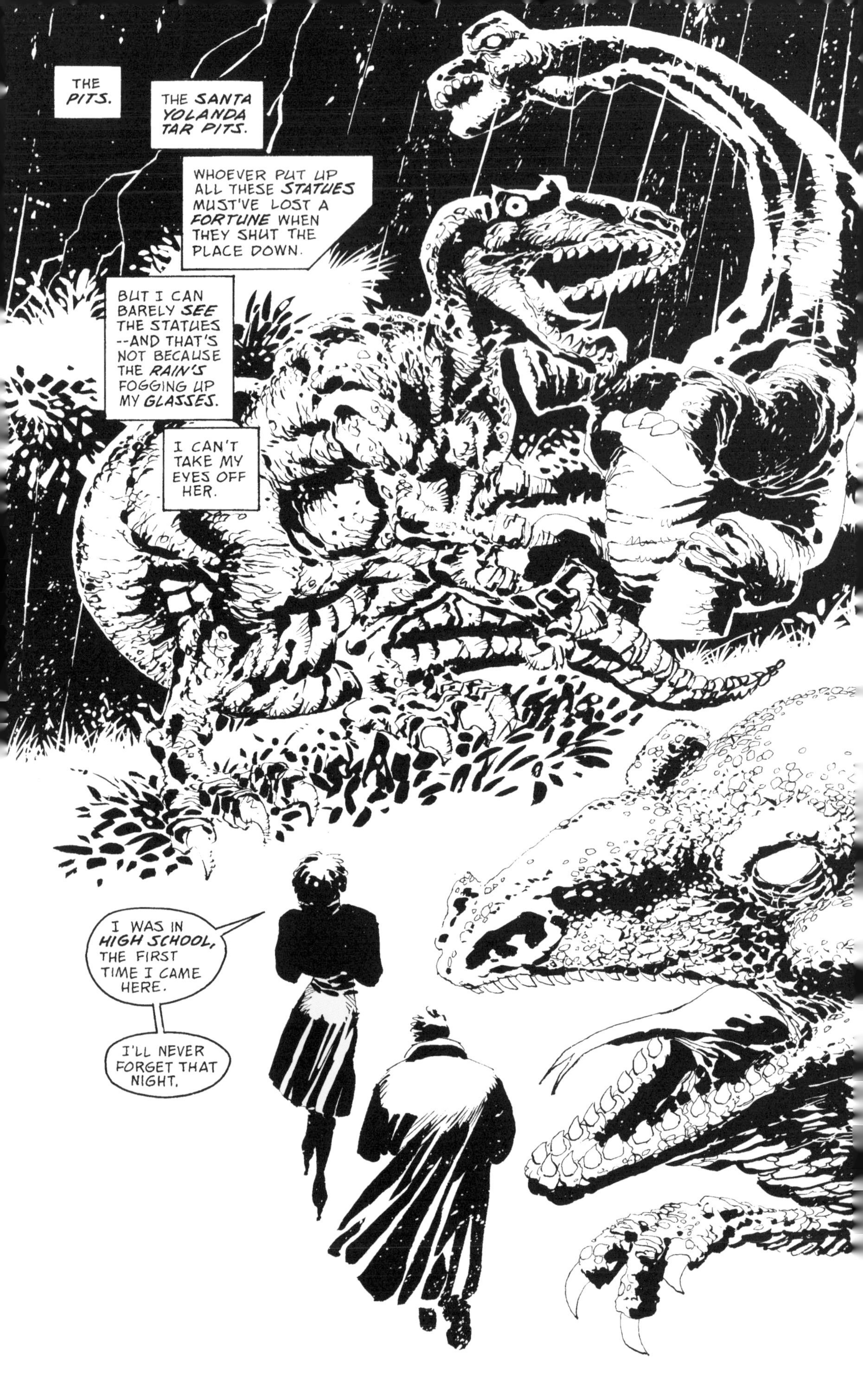
THE PITS.
THE SANTA YOLANDA TAR PITS.
WHOEVER PUT UP ALL THESE STATUES MUST'VE LOST A FORTUNE WHEN THEY SHUT THE PLACE DOWN.
BUT I CAN BARELY SEE THE STATUES --AND THAT'S NOT BECAUSE THE RAIN'S FOGGING UP MY GLASSES.
I CAN'T TAKE MY EYES OFF HER.
I WAS IN HIGH SCHOOL, THE FIRST TIME I CAME HERE.
I'LL NEVER FORGET THAT NIGHT.

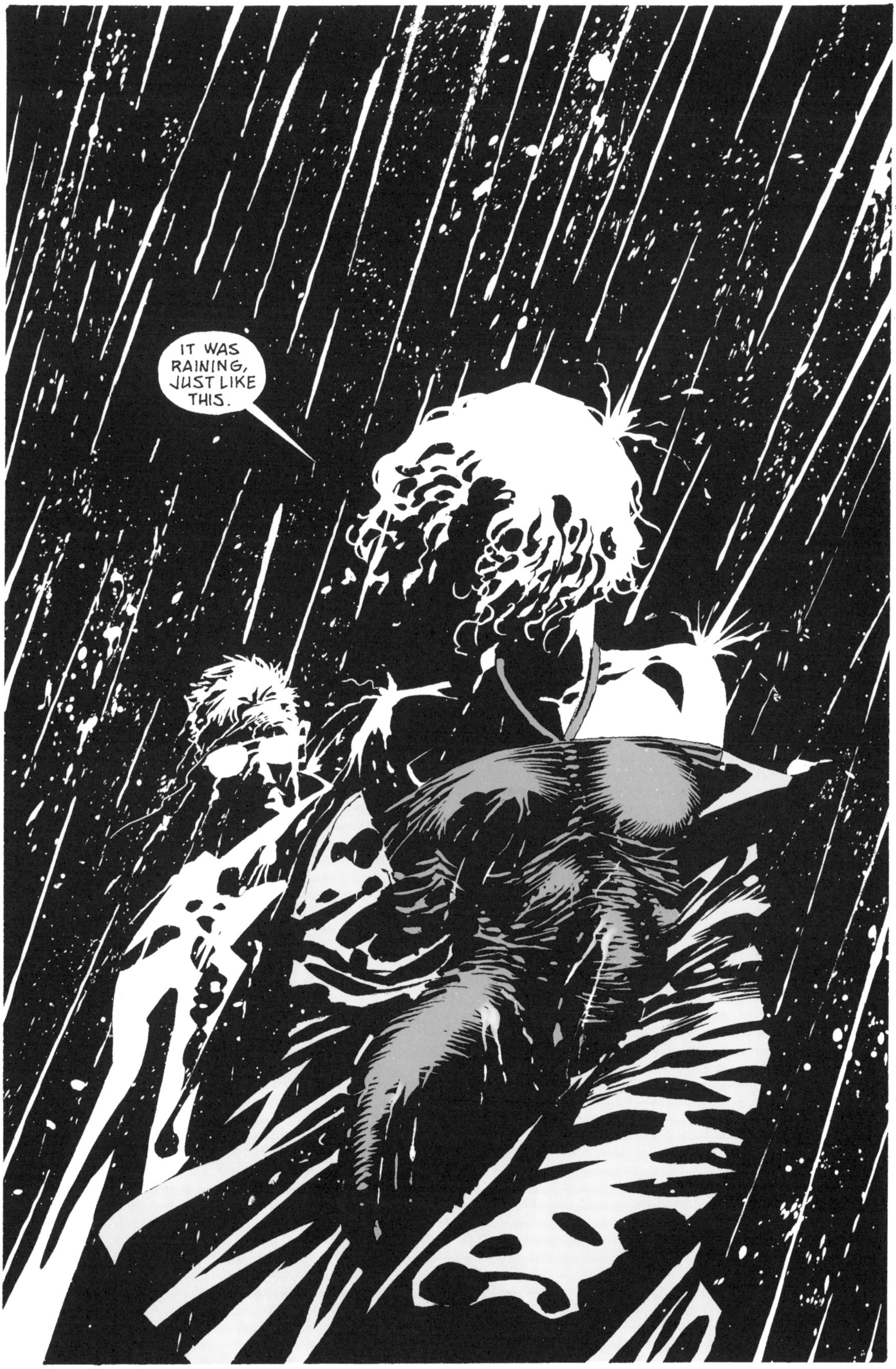
IT WAS RAINING, JUST LIKE THIS.

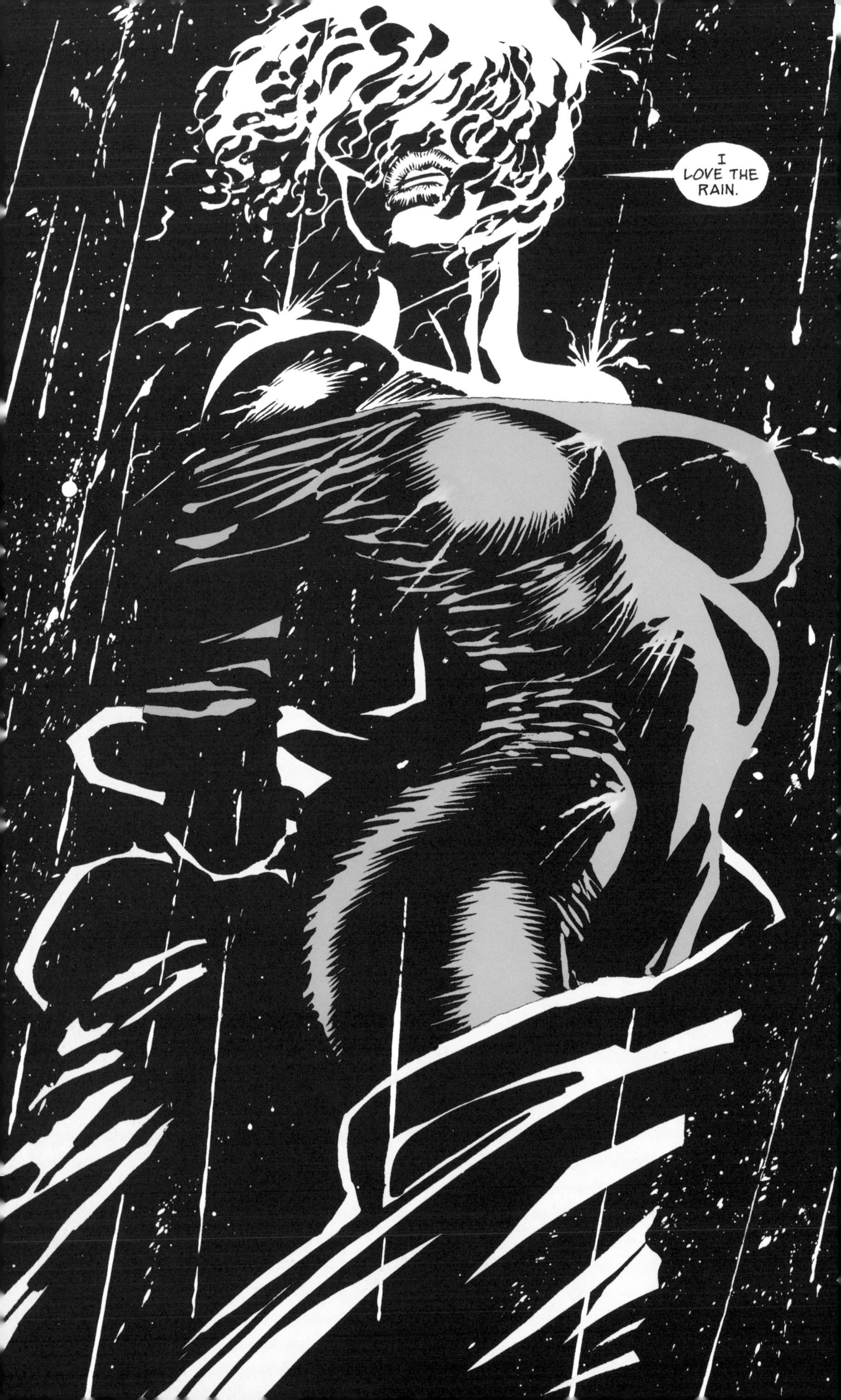
I LOVE THE RAIN.

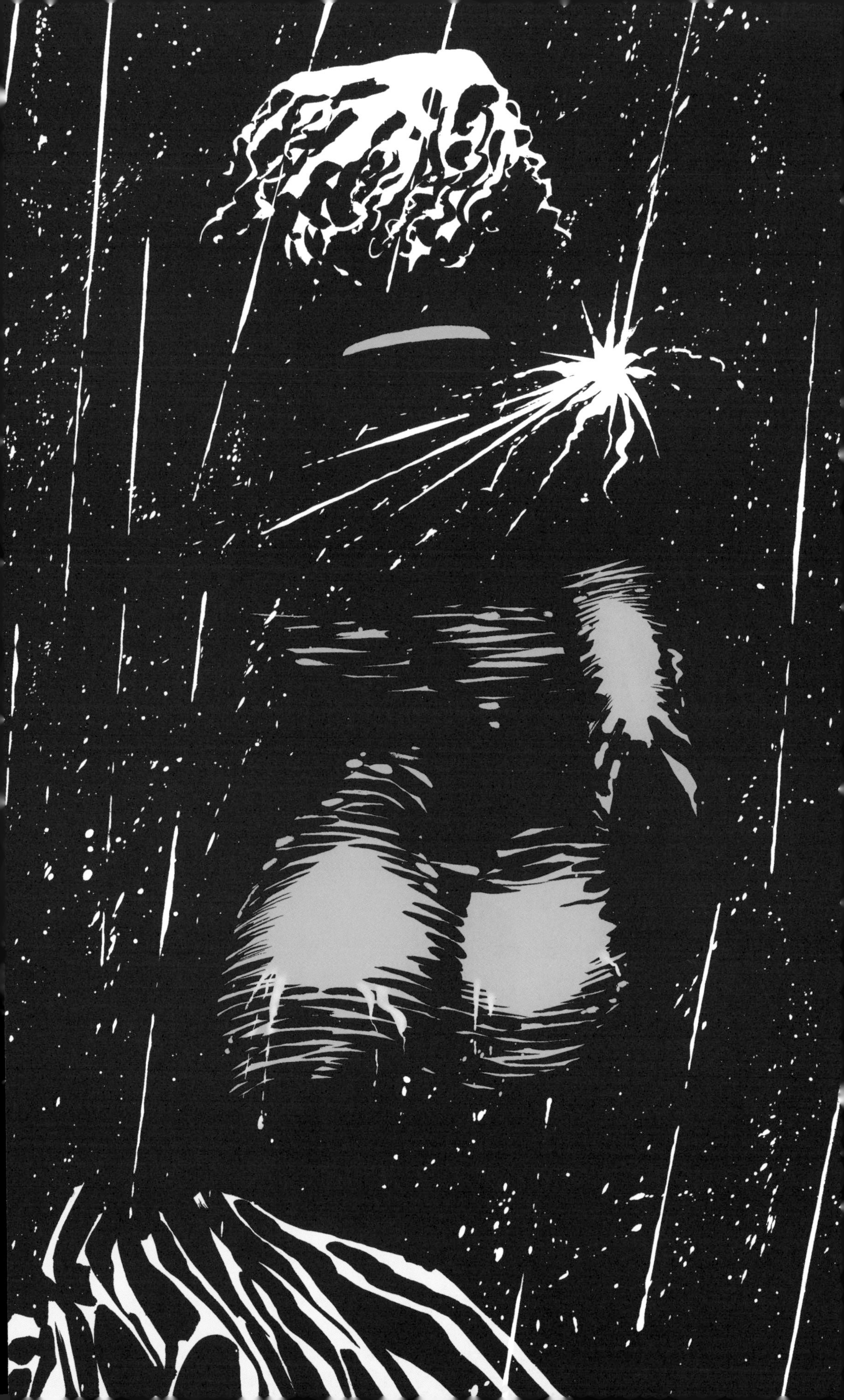

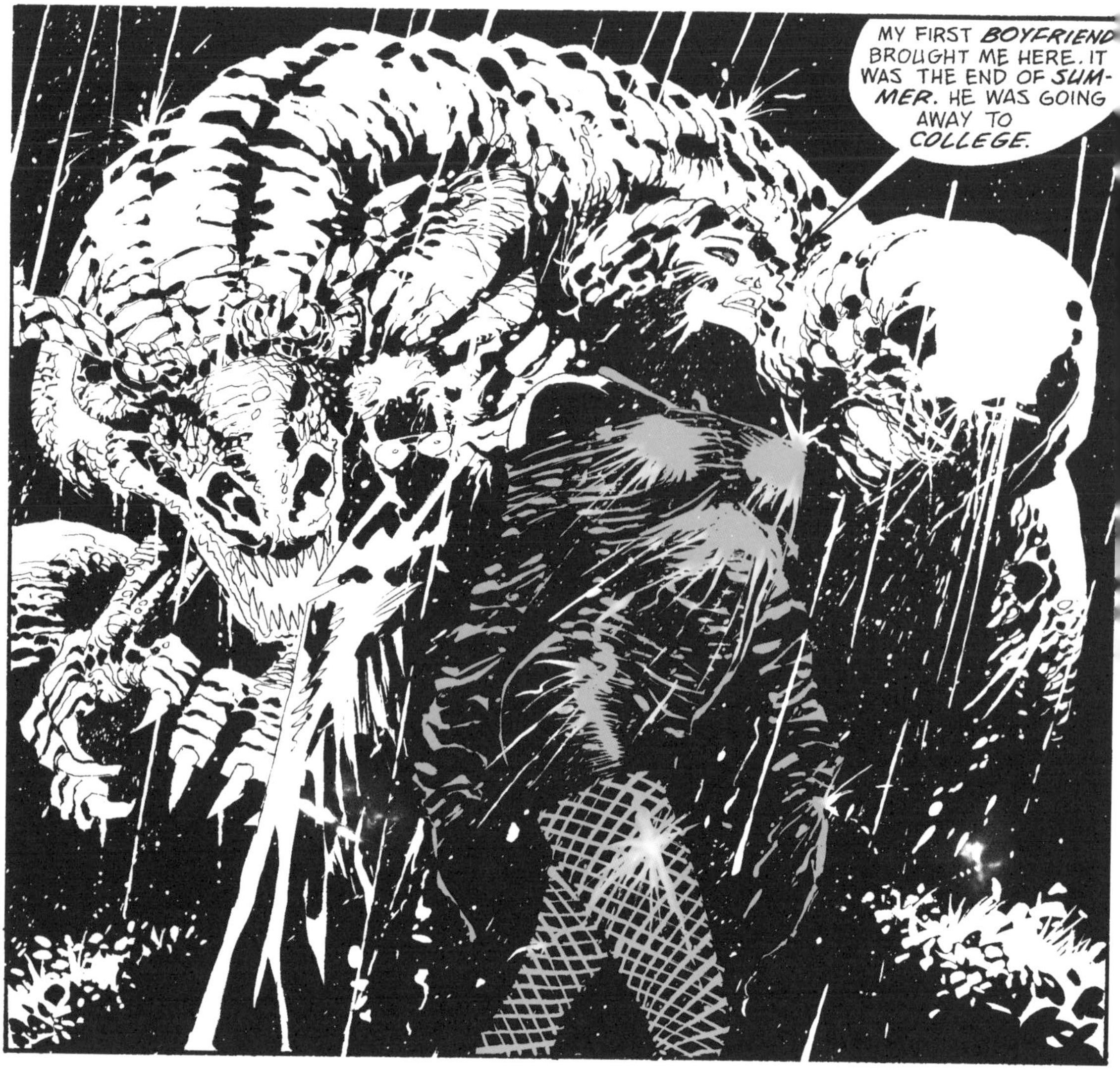
MY FIRST BOYFRIEND BROUGHT ME HERE. IT WAS THE END OF SUMMER. HE WAS GOING AWAY TO COLLEGE.

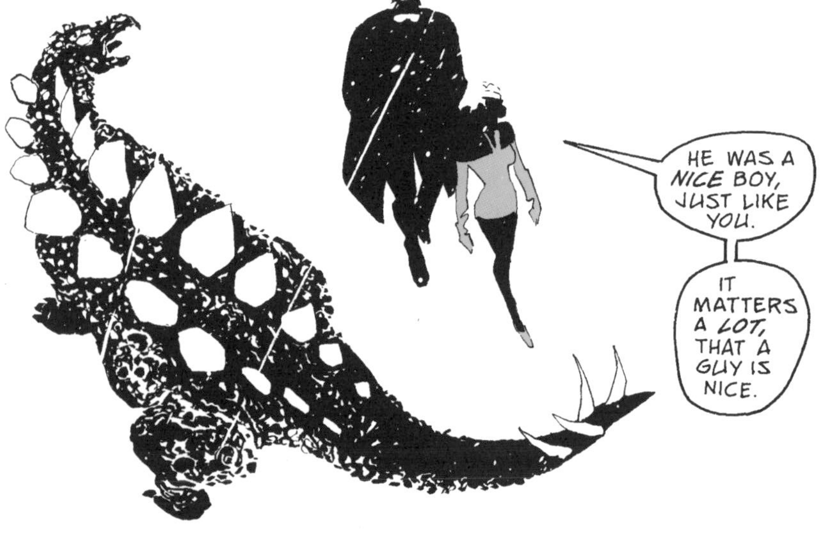
HE WAS A NICE BOY, JUST LIKE YOU.
IT MATTERS A LOT, THAT A GUY IS NICE.

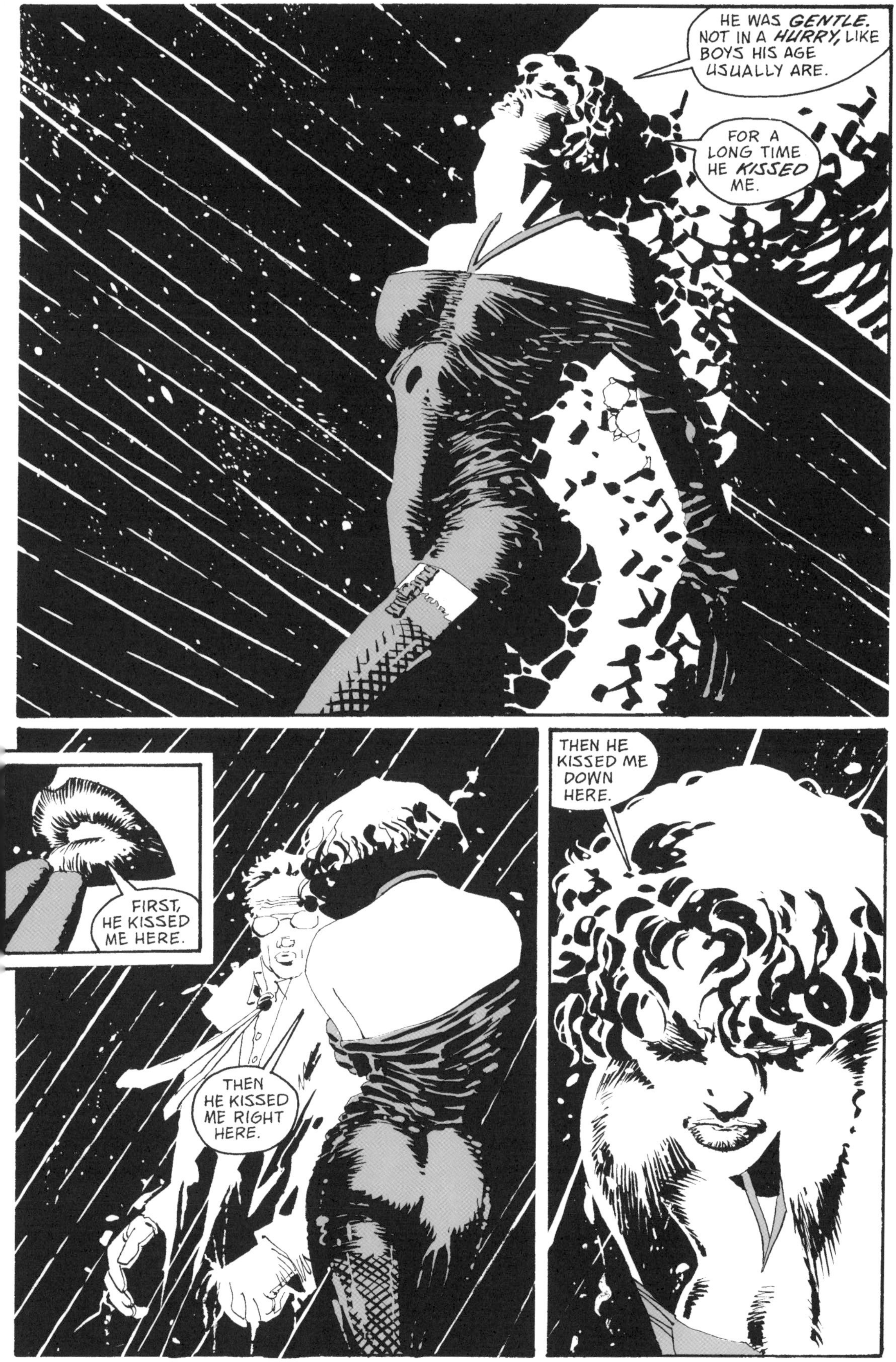
HE WAS GENTLE. NOT IN A HURRY, LIKE BOYS HIS AGE USUALLY ARE.
FOR A LONG TIME HE KISSED ME.
FIRST, HE KISSED ME HERE.
THEN HE KISSED ME RIGHT HERE.
THEN HE KISSED ME DOWN HERE.

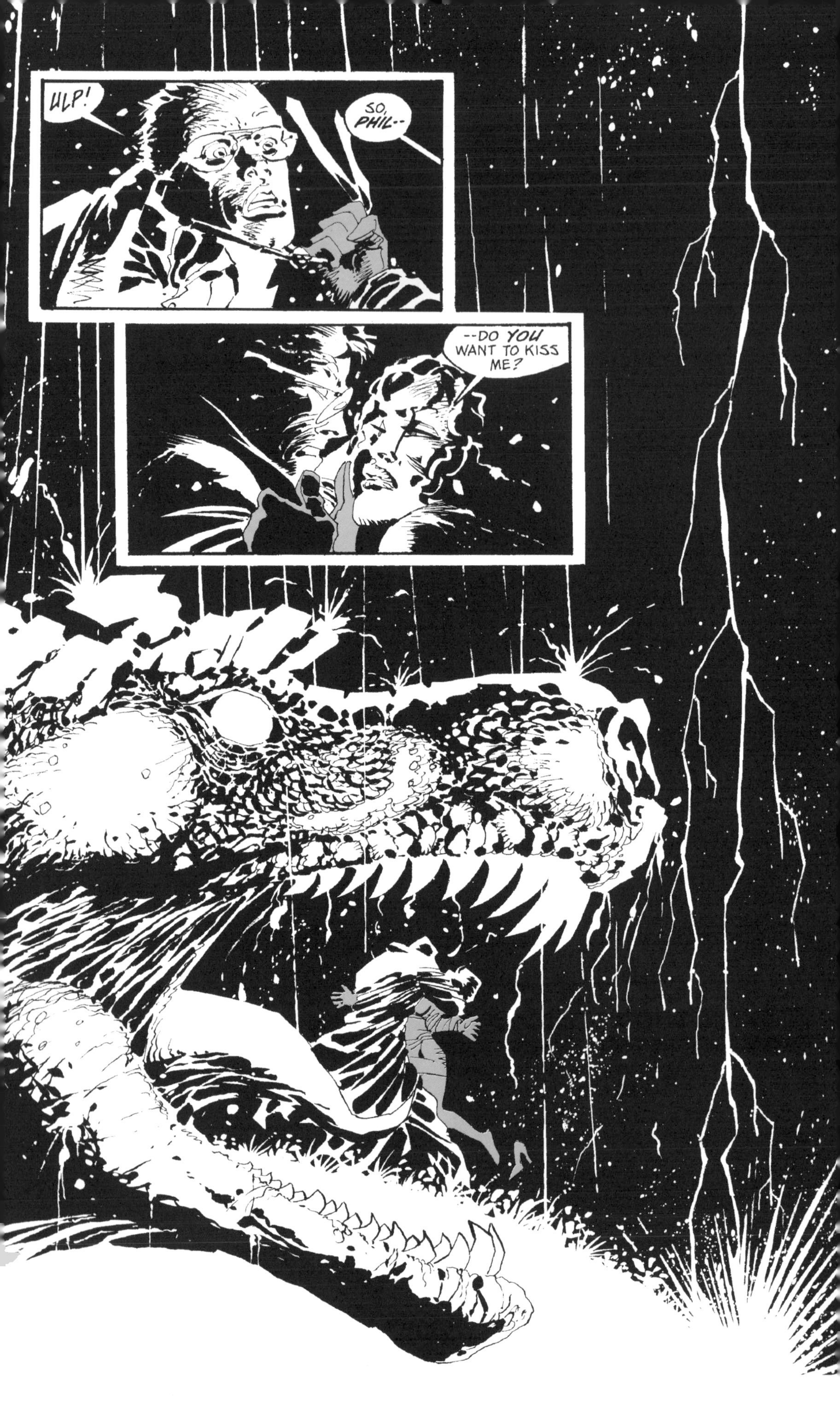
ULP!
SO, PHIL--
--DO YOU WANT TO KISS ME?

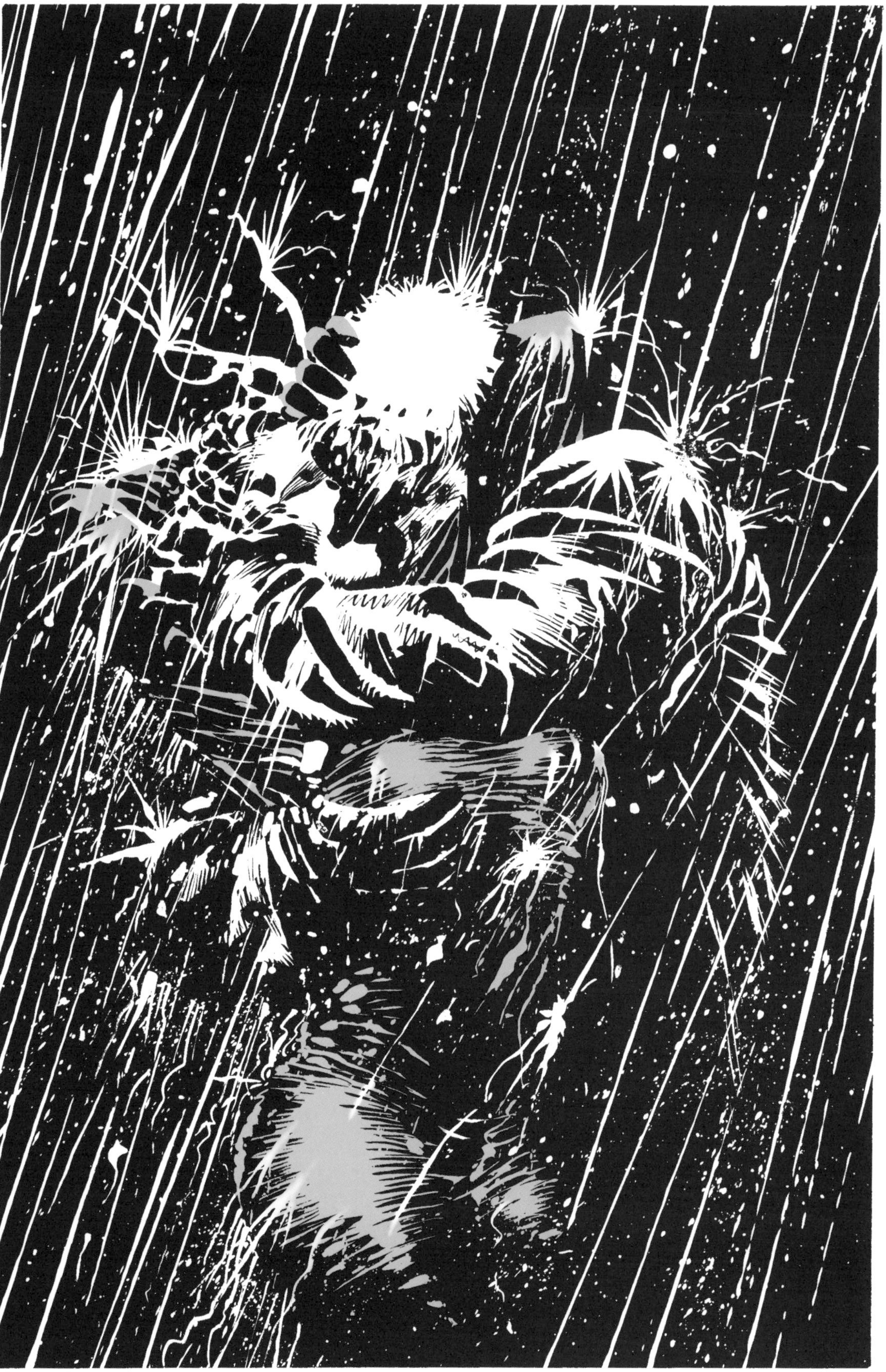

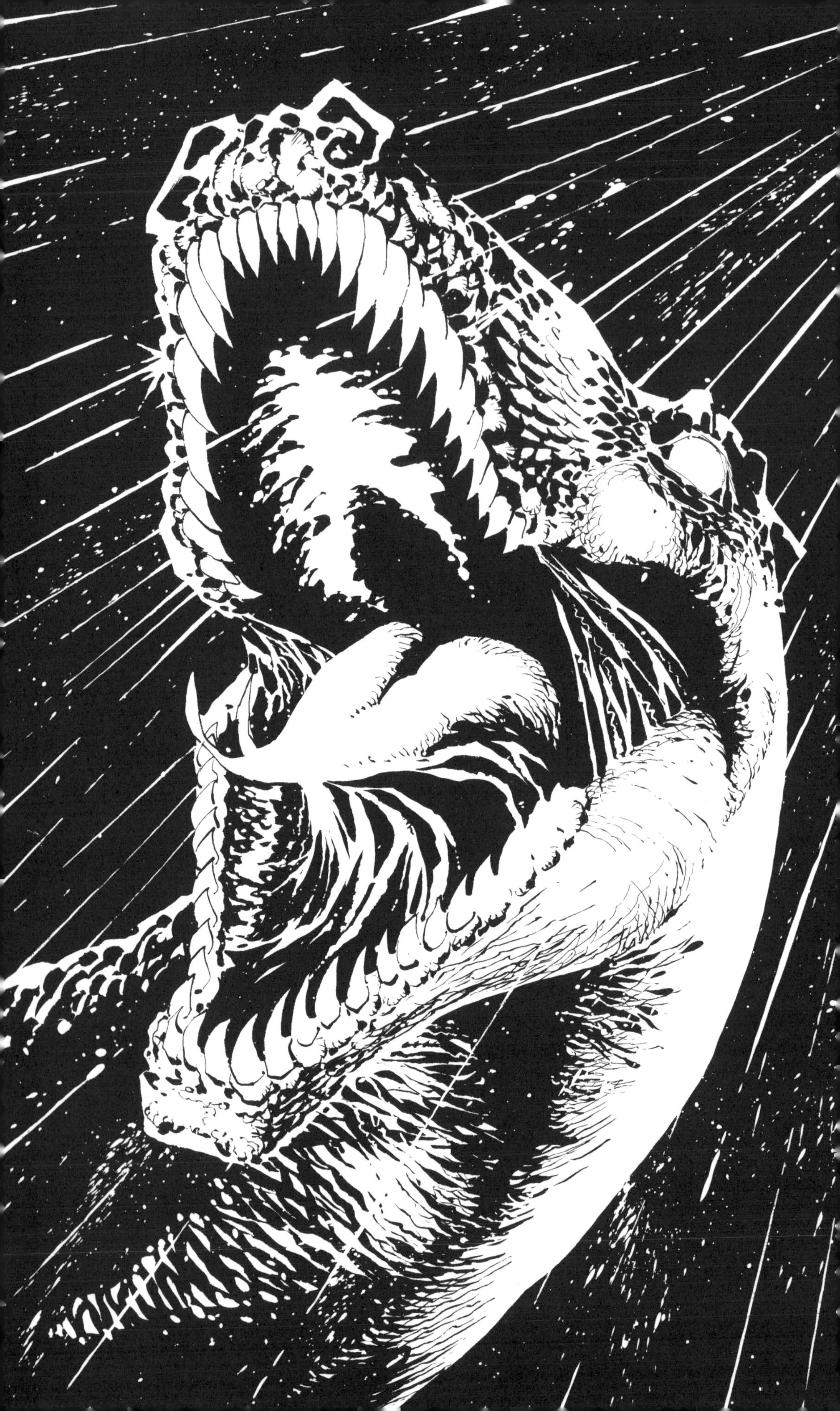

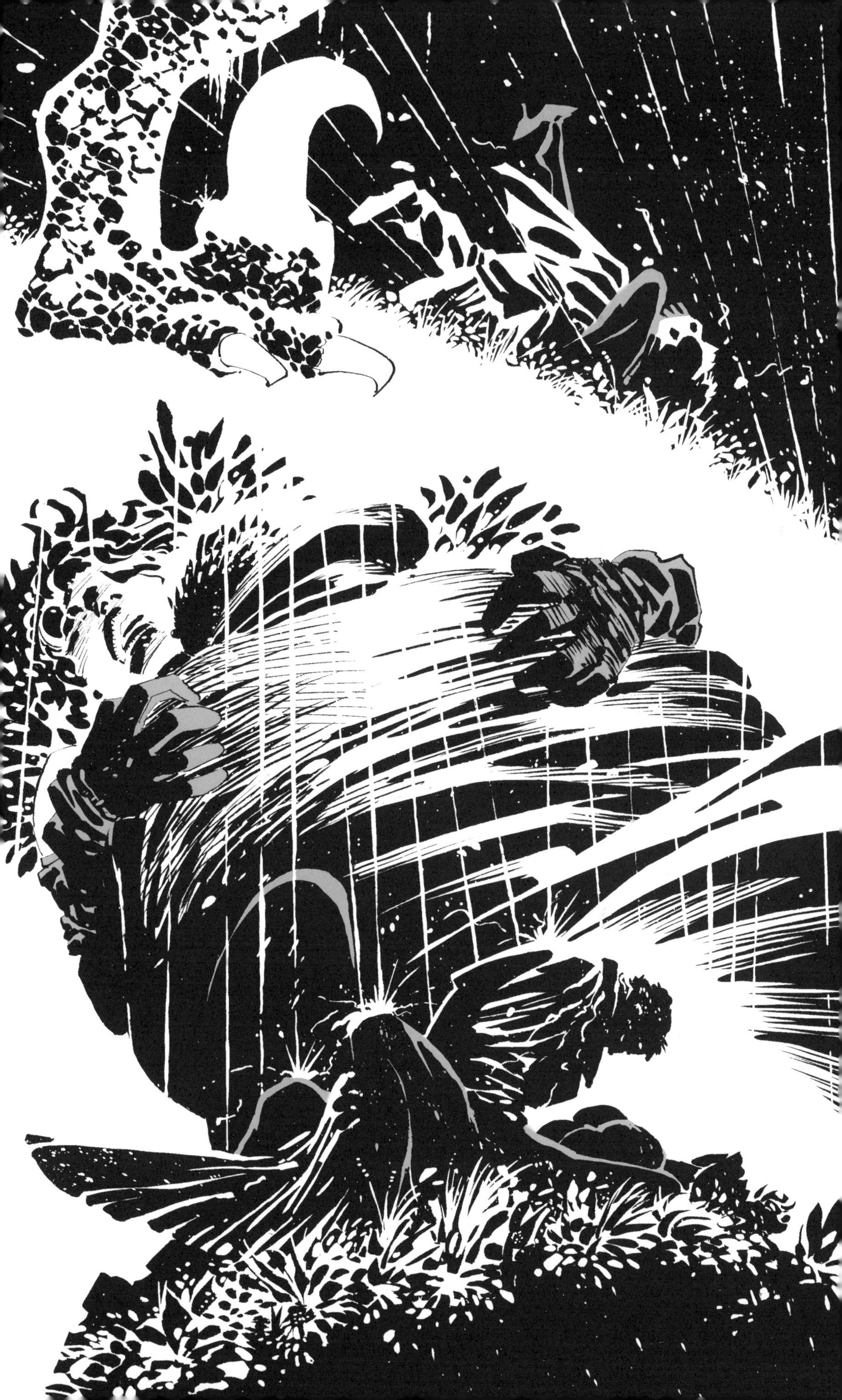

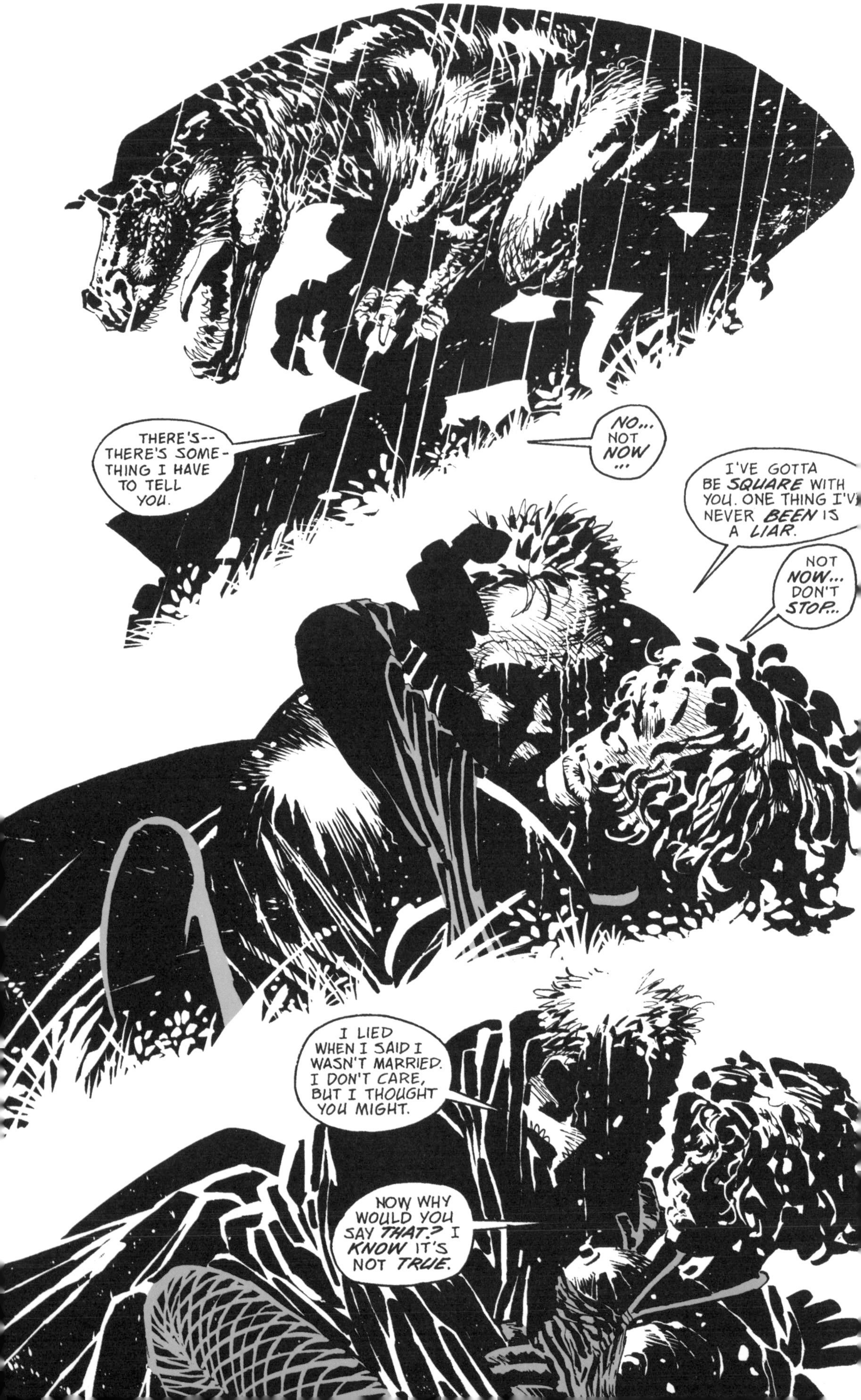
THERE'S-- THERE'S SOMETHING I HAVE TO TELL YOU.
NO... NOT NOW...
I'VE GOTTA BE SQUARE WITH YOU. ONE THING I'VE NEVER BEEN IS A LIAR.
NOT NOW... DON'T STOP...
I LIED WHEN I SAID I WASN'T MARRIED. I DON'T CARE, BUT I THOUGHT YOU MIGHT.
NOW WHY WOULD YOU SAY THAT? I KNOW IT'S NOT TRUE.

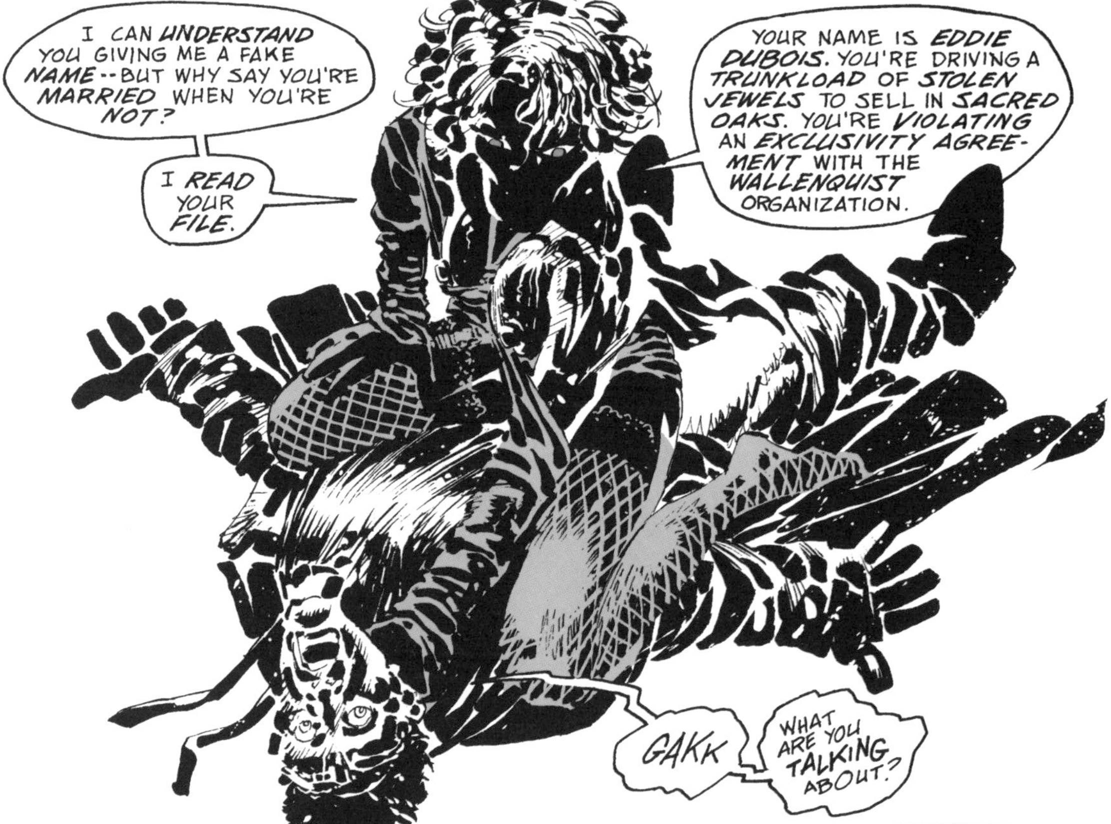
I CAN UNDERSTAND YOU GIVING ME A FAKE NAME--BUT WHY SAY YOU'RE MARRIED WHEN YOU'RE NOT?
I READ YOUR FILE.
YOUR NAME IS EDDIE DUBOIS. YOU'RE DRIVING A TRUNKLOAD OF STOLEN JEWELS TO SELL IN SACRED OAKS. YOU'RE VIOLATING AN EXCLUSIVITY AGREE-MENT WITH THE WALLENQUIST ORGANIZATION.
GAKK
WHAT ARE YOU TALKING ABOUT?

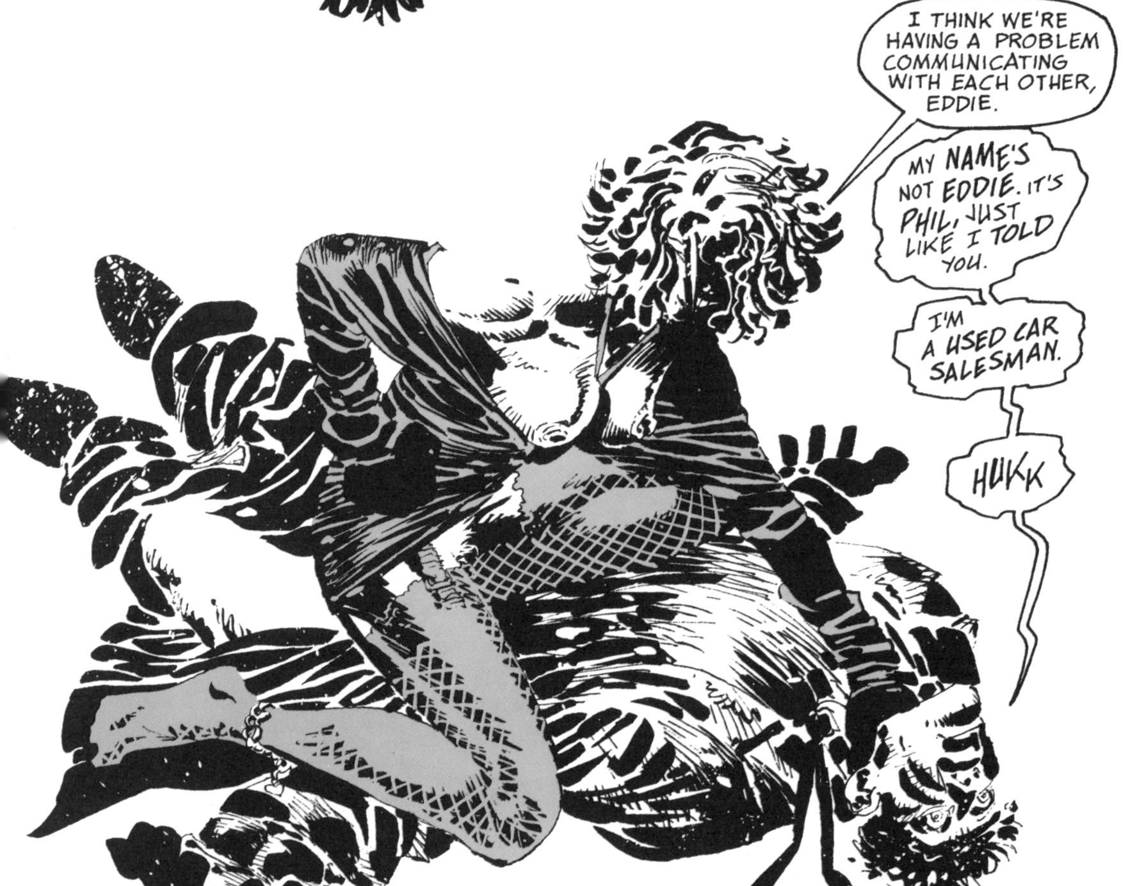
I THINK WE'RE HAVING A PROBLEM COMMUNICATING WITH EACH OTHER, EDDIE.
MY NAME'S NOT EDDIE. IT'S PHIL, JUST LIKE I TOLD YOU.
I'M A USED CAR SALESMAN.
HUKK

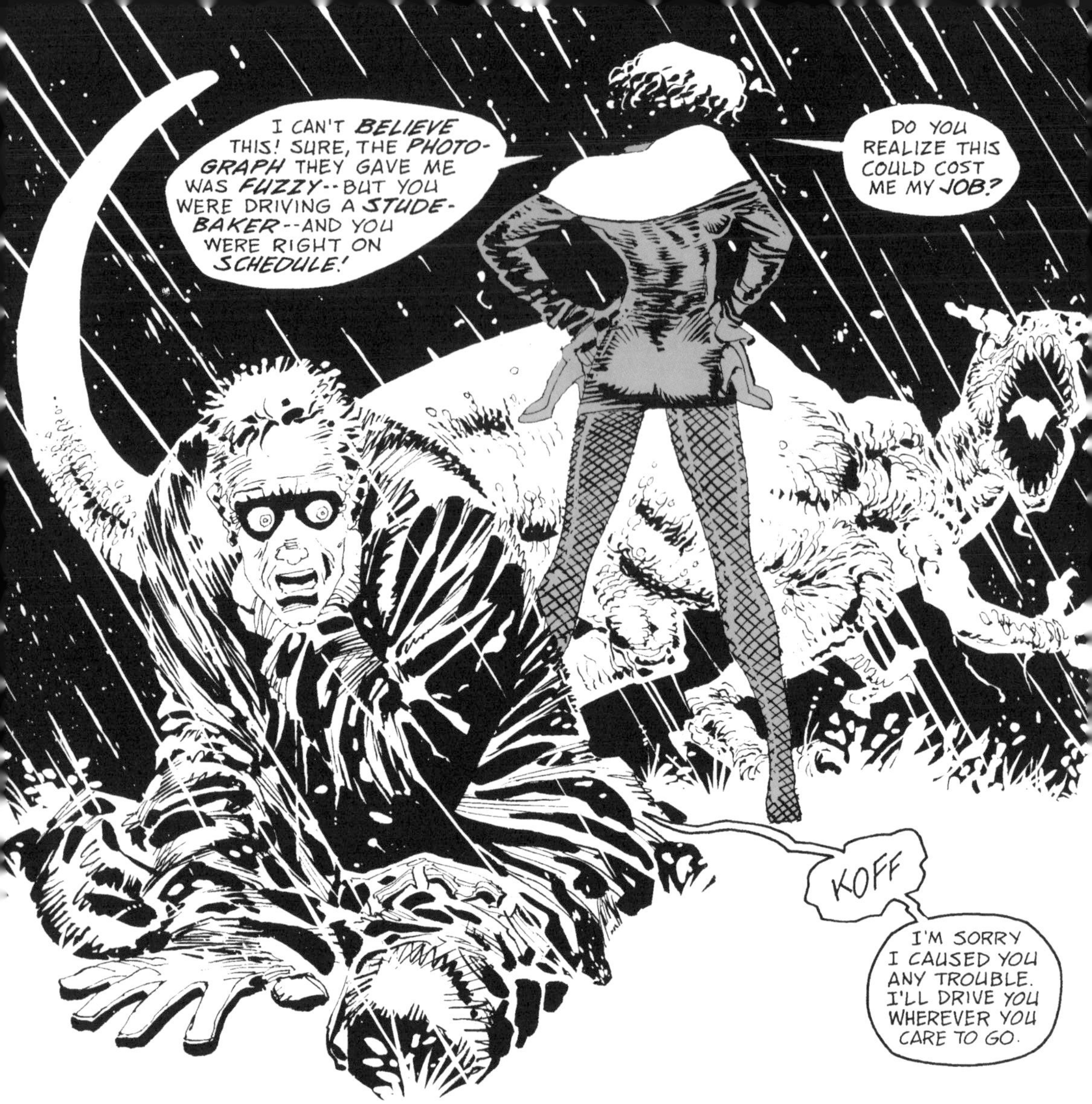
I CAN'T BELIEVE THIS! SURE, THE PHOTOGRAPH THEY GAVE ME WAS FUZZY--BUT YOU WERE DRIVING A STUDEBAKER--AND YOU WERE RIGHT ON SCHEDULE!
DO YOU REALIZE THIS COULD COST ME MY JOB?
KOFF
I'M SORRY I CAUSED YOU ANY TROUBLE. I'LL DRIVE YOU WHEREVER YOU CARE TO GO.

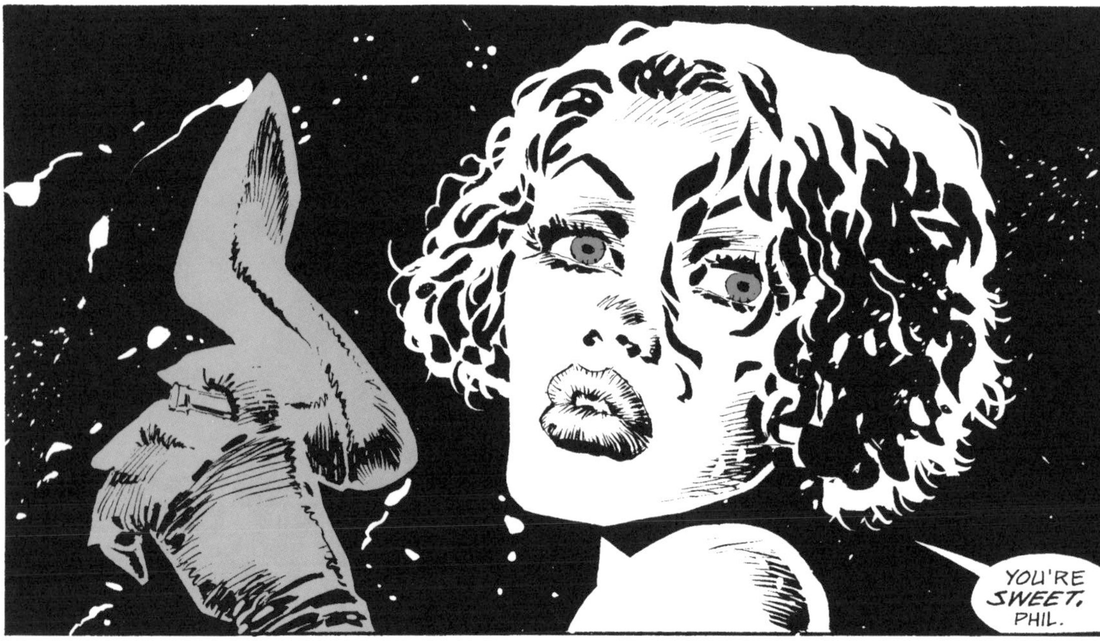
YOU'RE SWEET. PHIL.

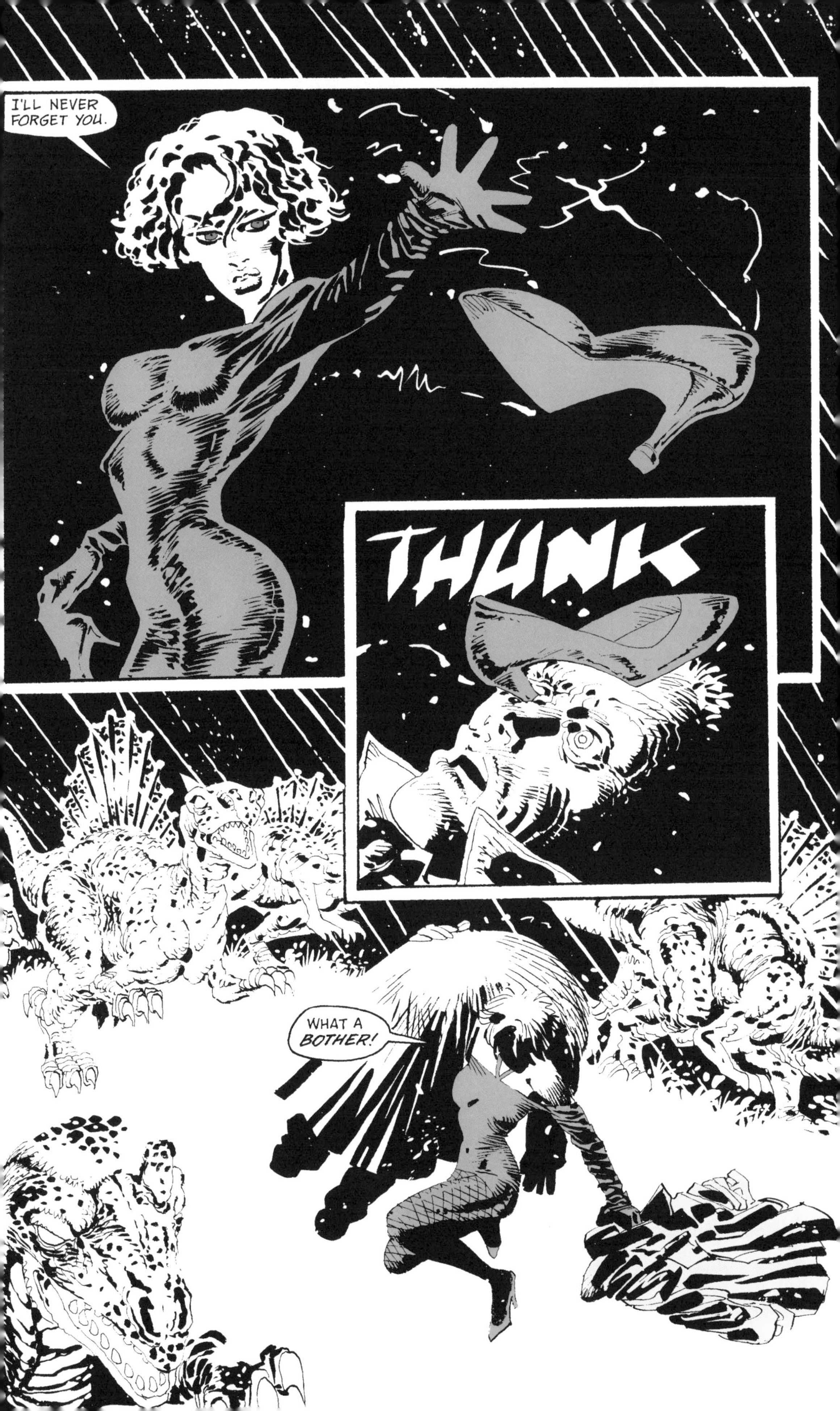
I'LL NEVER FORGET YOU.
THUNK
WHAT A BOTHER!

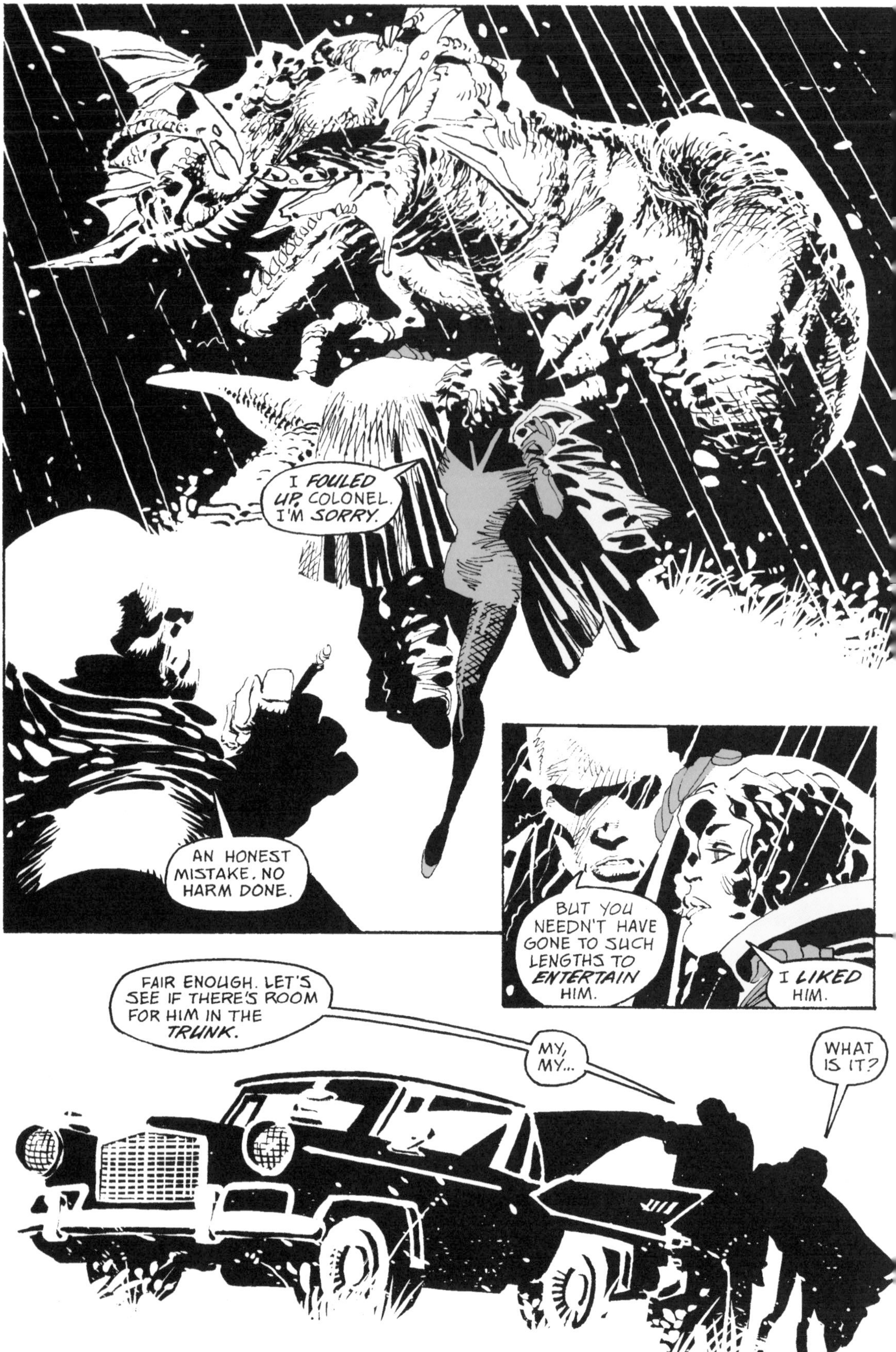
I FOULED UP, COLONEL. I'M SORRY.
AN HONEST MISTAKE. NO HARM DONE.
BUT YOU NEEDN'T HAVE GONE TO SUCH LENGTHS TO ENTERTAIN HIM.
I LIKED HIM.
FAIR ENOUGH. LET'S SEE IF THERE'S ROOM FOR HIM IN THE TRUNK.
MY, MY...
WHAT IS IT?

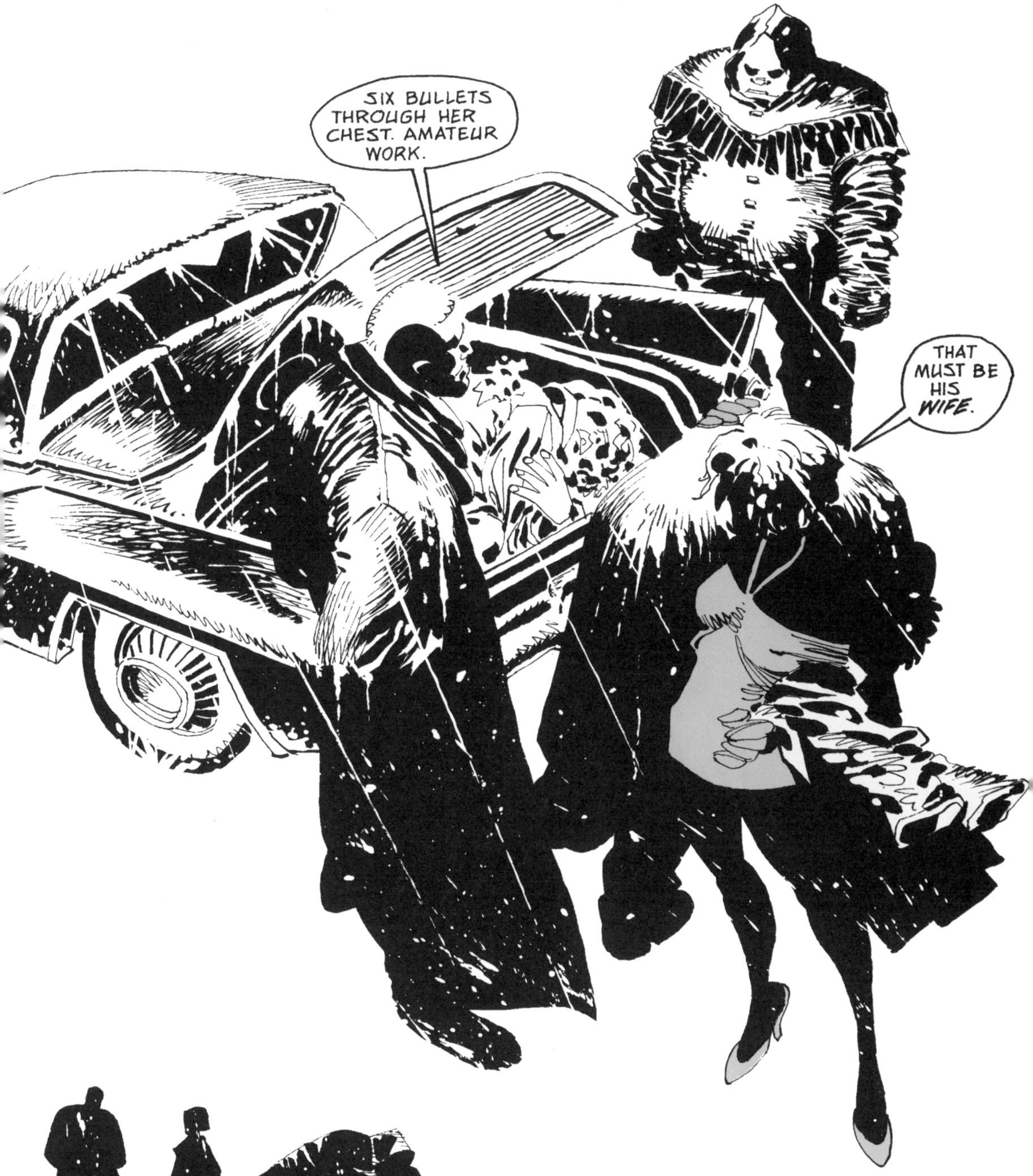
SIX BULLETS THROUGH HER CHEST. AMATEUR WORK.
THAT MUST BE HIS *WIFE*.

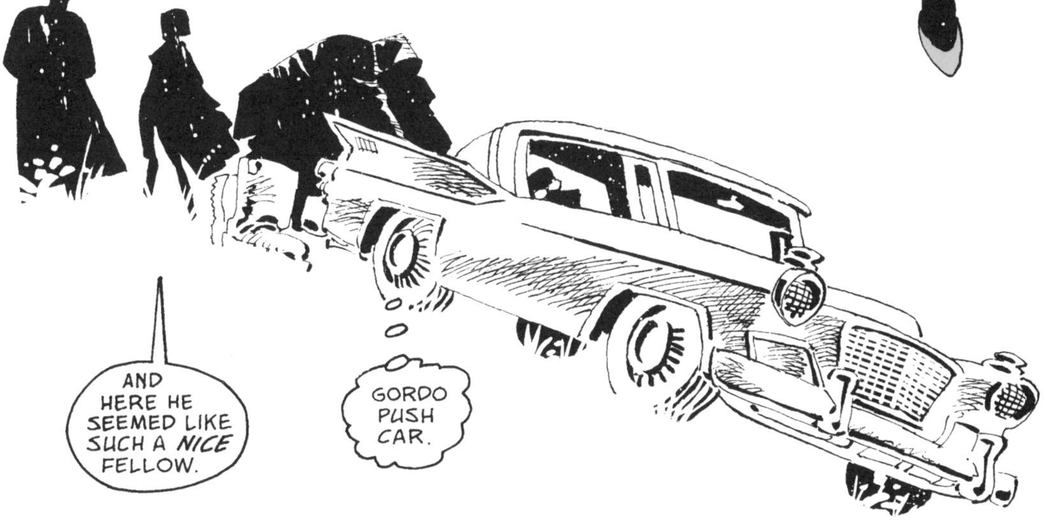
AND HERE HE SEEMED LIKE SUCH A *NICE* FELLOW.
GORDO PUSH CAR.

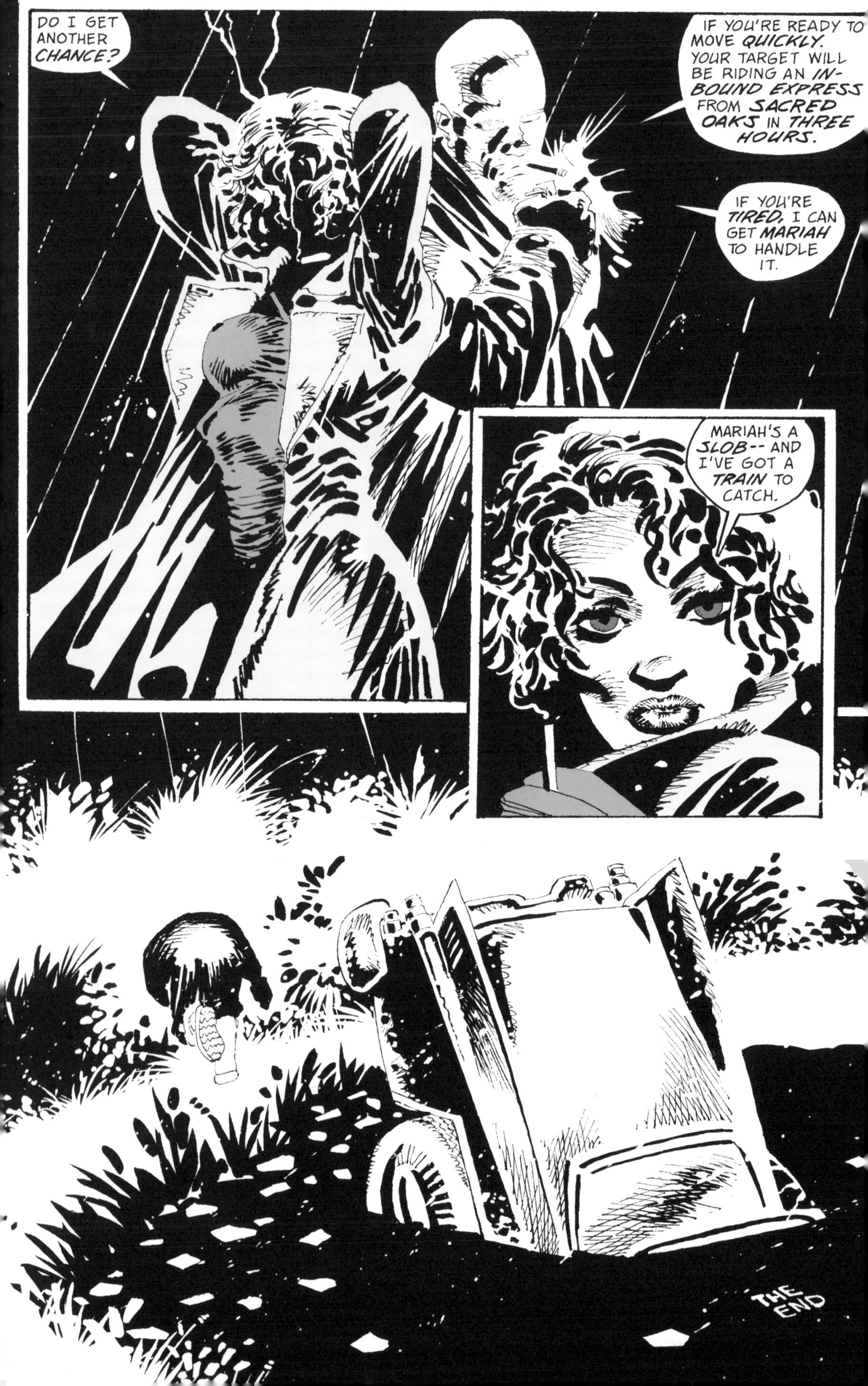
DO I GET ANOTHER CHANCE?
IF YOU'RE READY TO MOVE QUICKLY. YOUR TARGET WILL BE RIDING AN IN-BOUND EXPRESS FROM SACRED OAKS IN THREE HOURS.
IF YOU'RE TIRED, I CAN GET MARIAH TO HANDLE IT.
MARIAH'S A SLOB-- AND I'VE GOT A TRAIN TO CATCH.
THE END

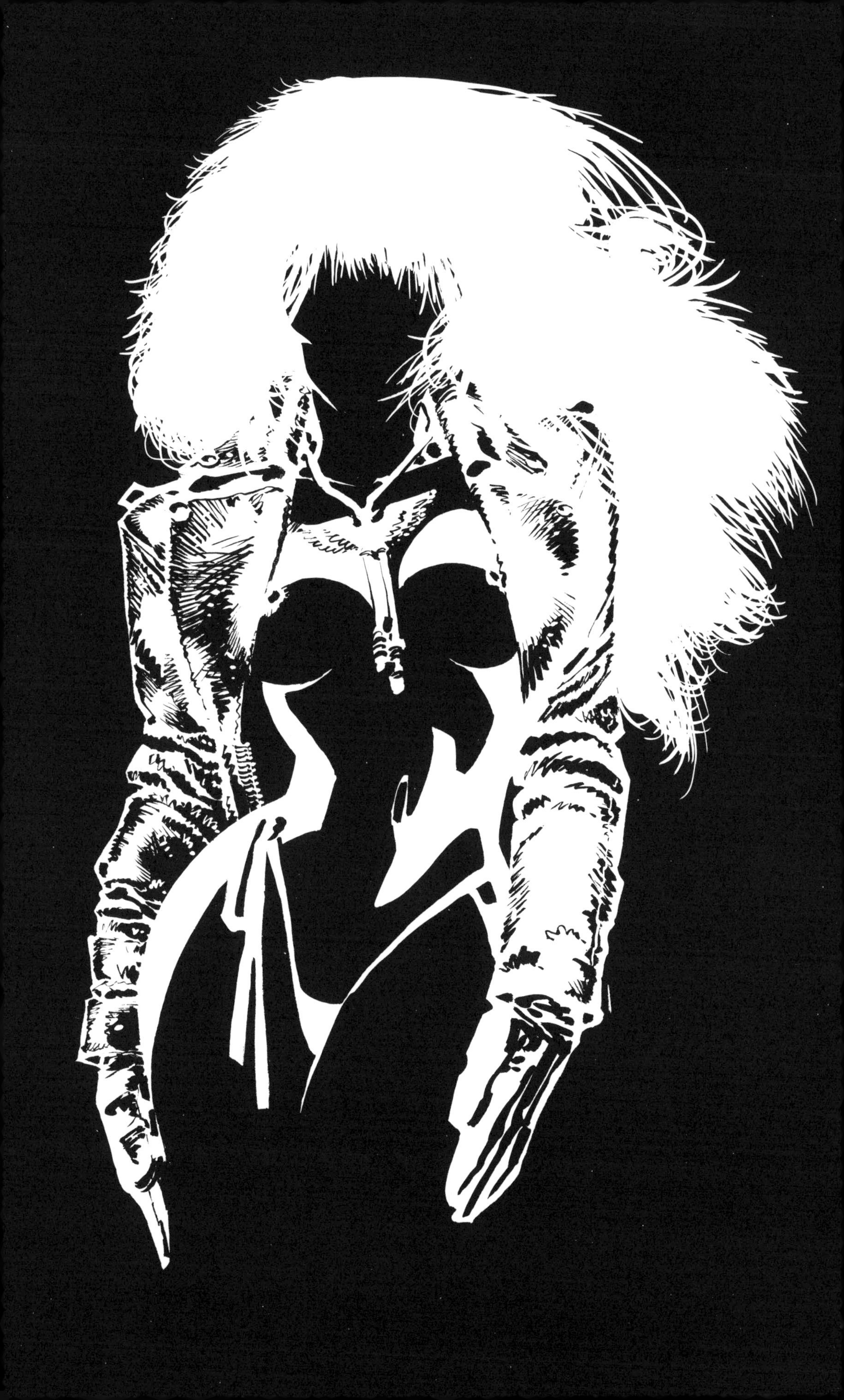

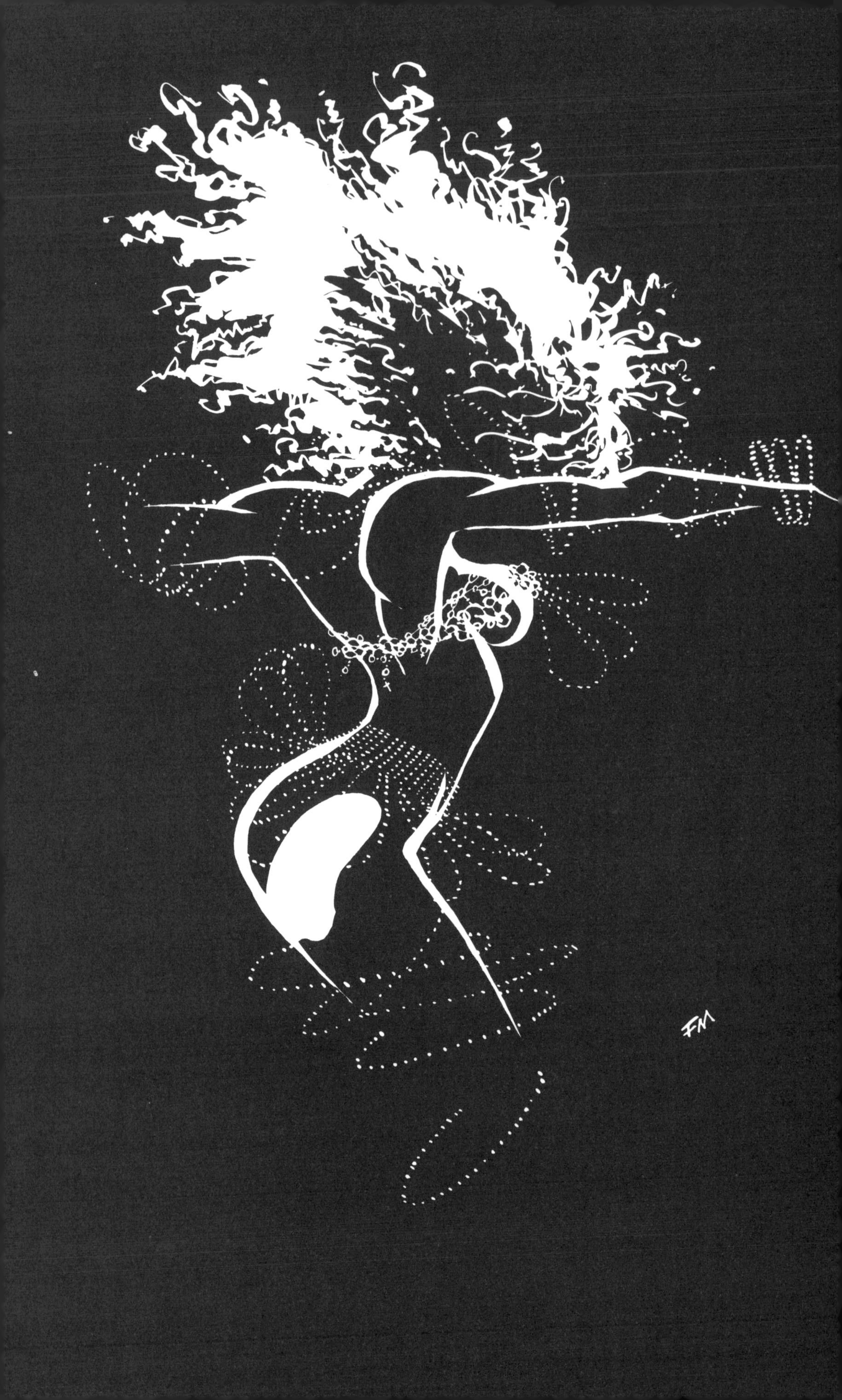
FM

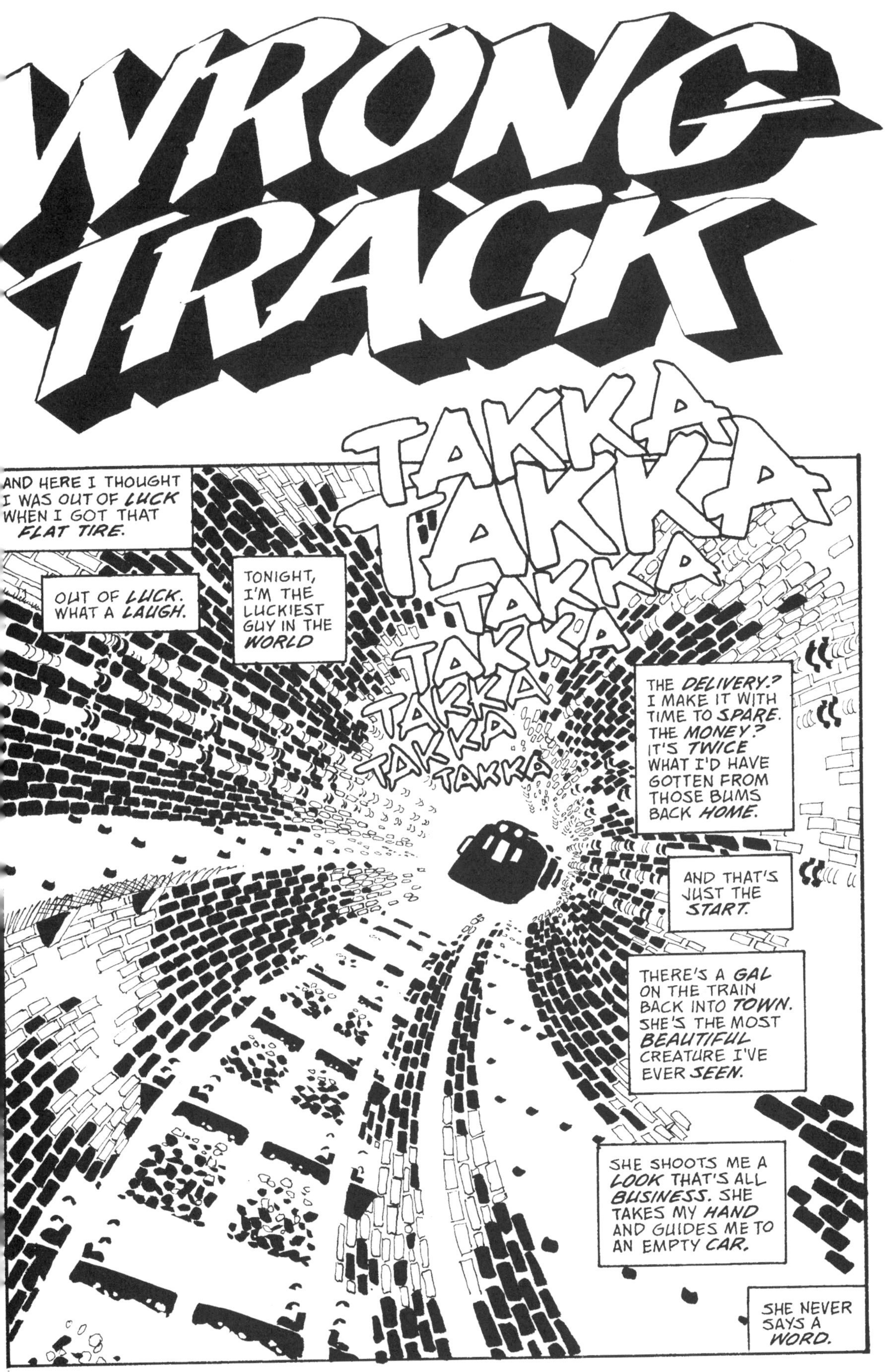
WRONG TRACK
TAKKA TAKKA TAKKA TAKKA TAKKA TAKKA TAKKA
AND HERE I THOUGHT I WAS OUT OF LUCK WHEN I GOT THAT FLAT TIRE.
OUT OF LUCK. WHAT A LAUGH.
TONIGHT, I'M THE LUCKIEST GUY IN THE WORLD
THE DELIVERY? I MAKE IT WITH TIME TO SPARE. THE MONEY? IT'S TWICE WHAT I'D HAVE GOTTEN FROM THOSE BUMS BACK HOME.
AND THAT'S JUST THE START.
THERE'S A GAL ON THE TRAIN BACK INTO TOWN. SHE'S THE MOST BEAUTIFUL CREATURE I'VE EVER SEEN.
SHE SHOOTS ME A LOOK THAT'S ALL BUSINESS. SHE TAKES MY HAND AND GUIDES ME TO AN EMPTY CAR.
SHE NEVER SAYS A WORD.

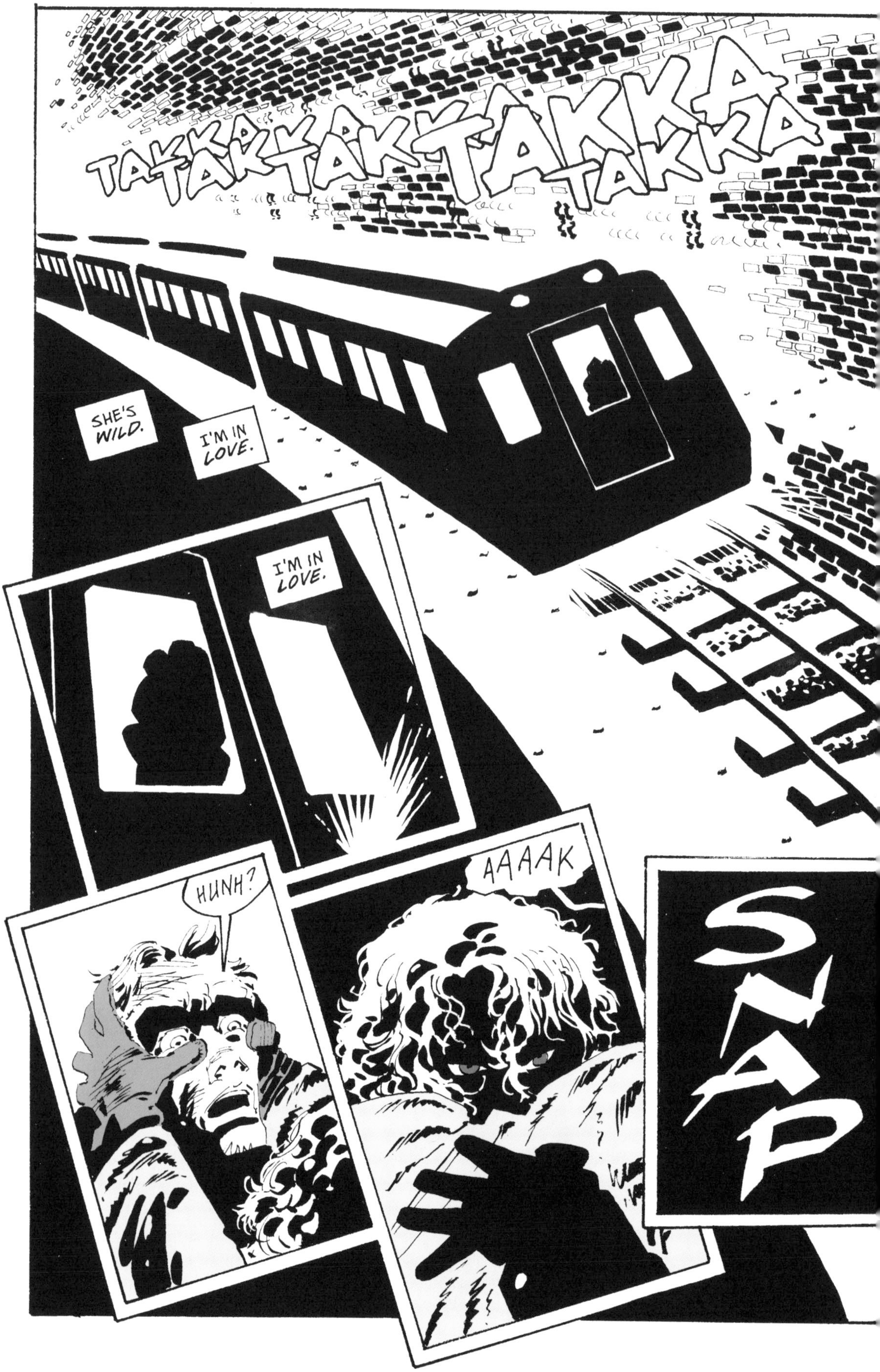
TAKKA TAKKA TAKKA TAKKA
SHE'S WILD.
I'M IN LOVE.
I'M IN LOVE.
HUNH?
AAAAK
SNAP

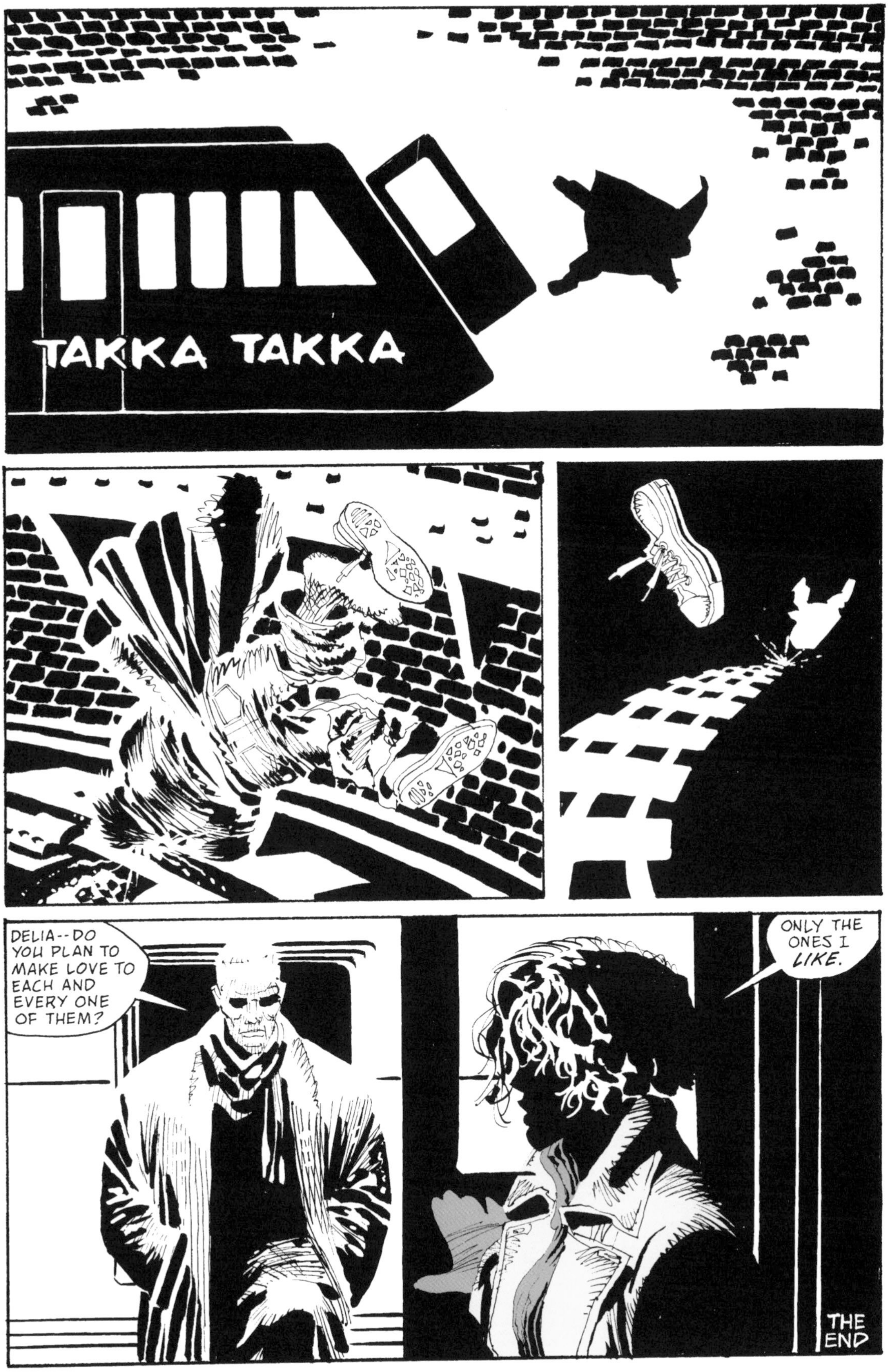
TAKKA TAKKA
DELIA--DO YOU PLAN TO MAKE LOVE TO EACH AND EVERY ONE OF THEM?
ONLY THE ONES I *LIKE*.
THE END

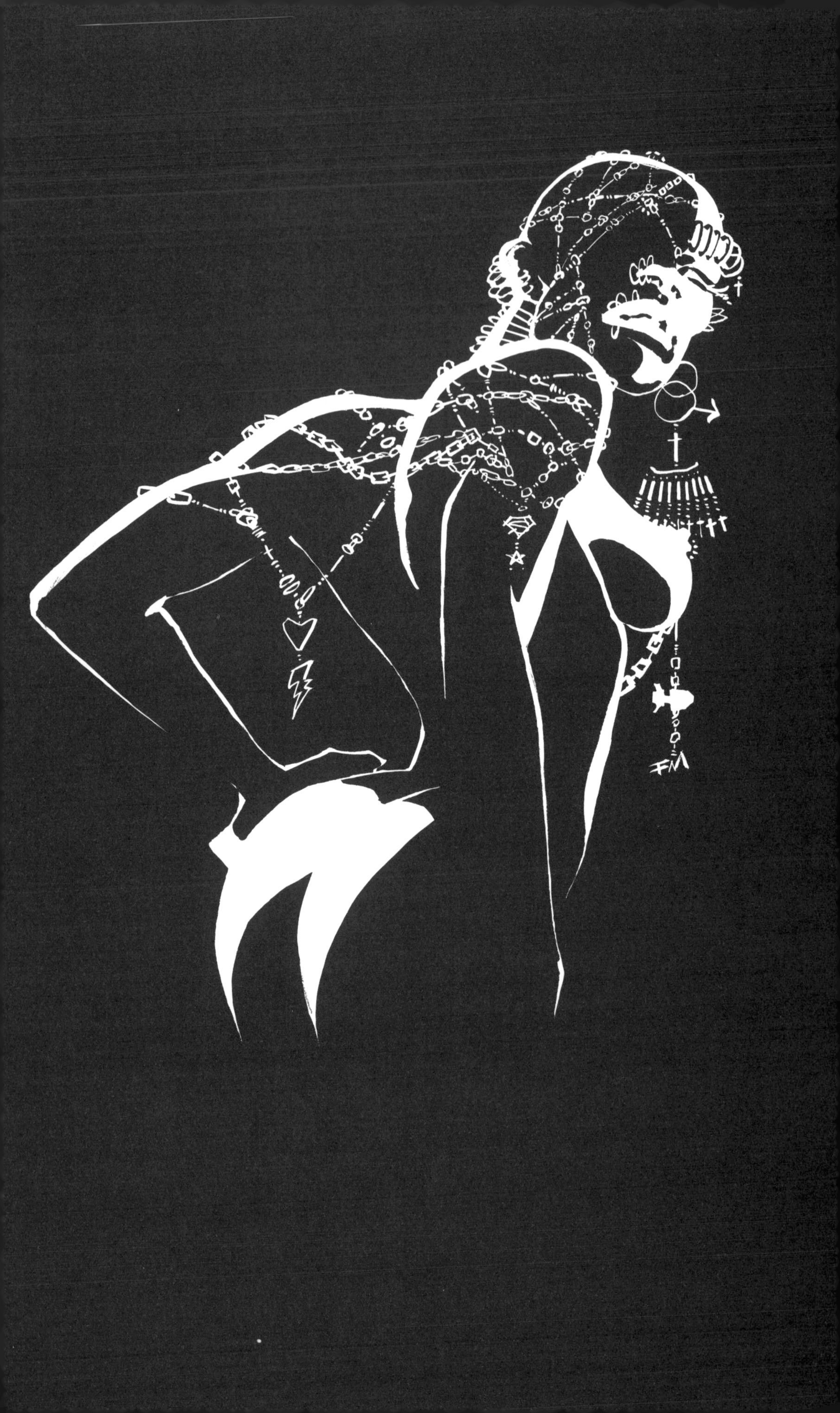
FM

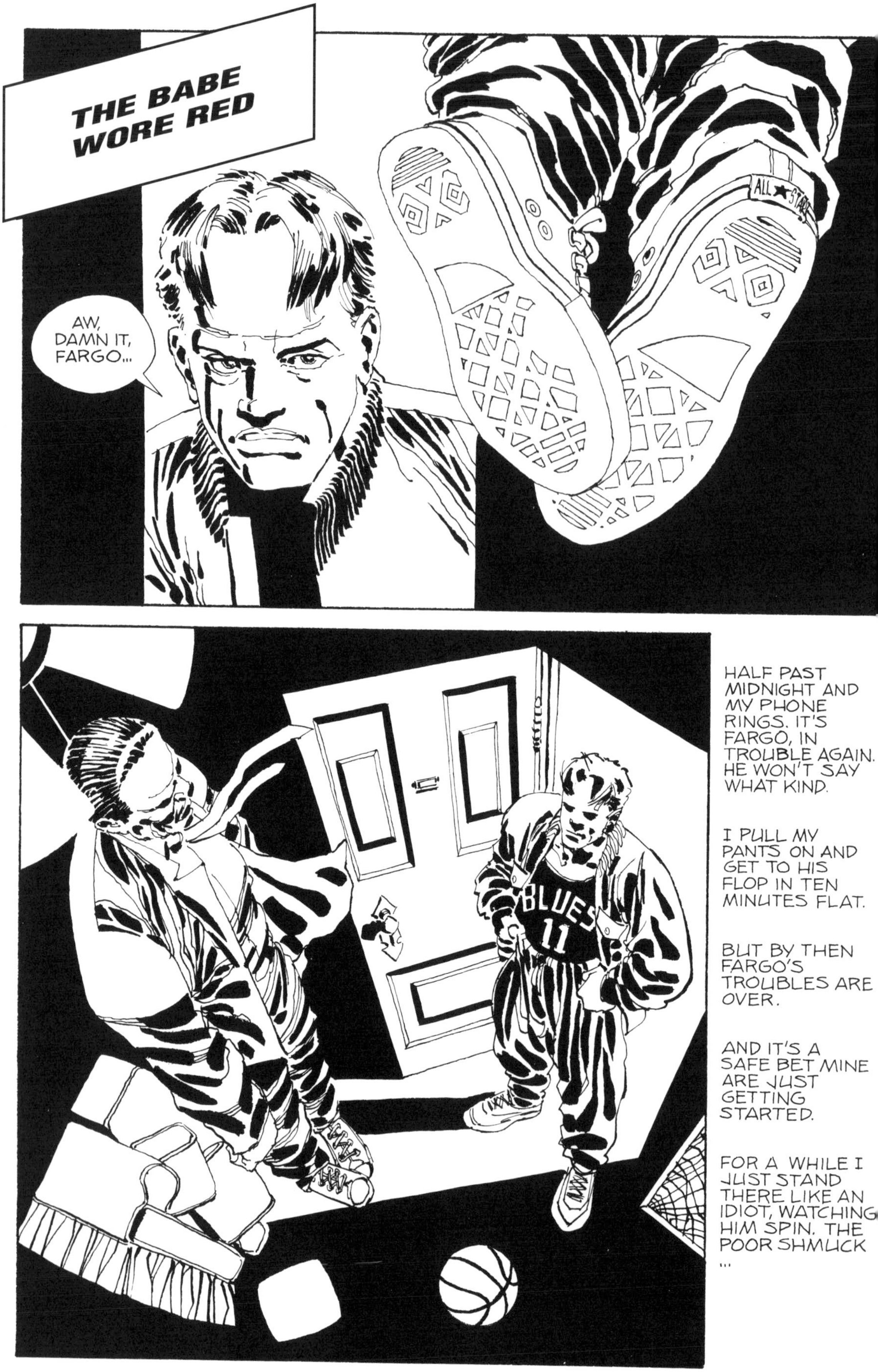
THE BABE WORE RED
AW, DAMN IT, FARGO...
HALF PAST MIDNIGHT AND MY PHONE RINGS. IT'S FARGO, IN TROUBLE AGAIN. HE WON'T SAY WHAT KIND.
I PULL MY PANTS ON AND GET TO HIS FLOP IN TEN MINUTES FLAT.
BUT BY THEN FARGO'S TROUBLES ARE OVER.
AND IT'S A SAFE BET MINE ARE JUST GETTING STARTED.
FOR A WHILE I JUST STAND THERE LIKE AN IDIOT, WATCHING HIM SPIN. THE POOR SHMUCK ...
BLUES 11

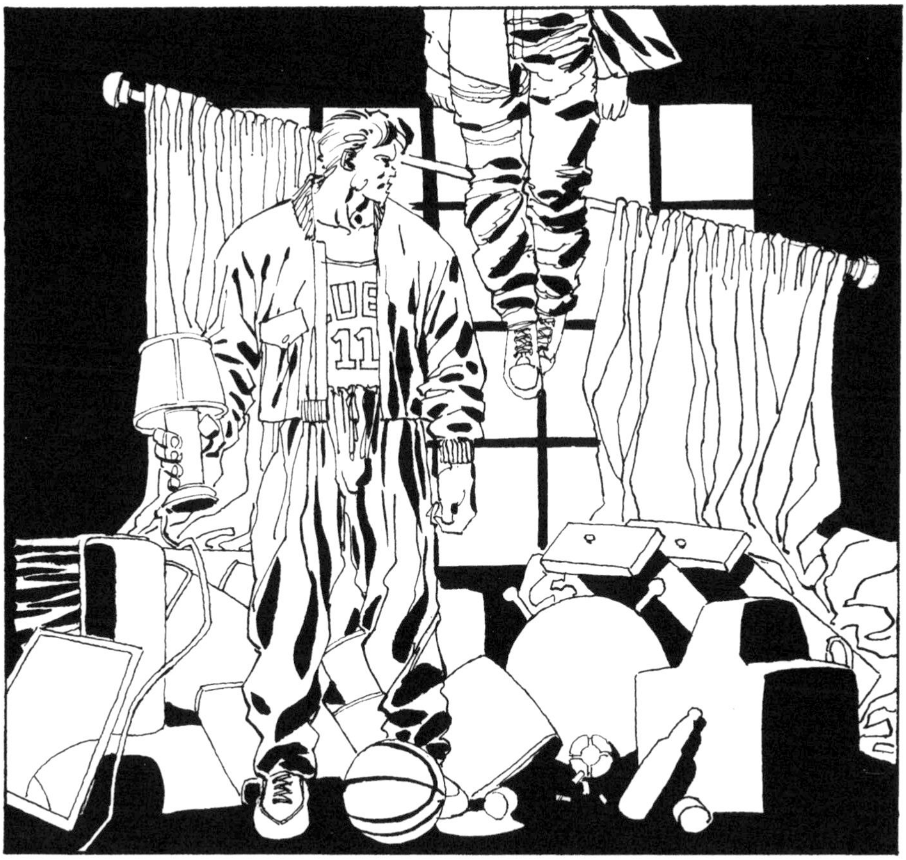

... HE WAS BOUND TO END UP LIKE THIS, NO MATTER HOW HARD HE TRIED.

AND HE TRIED DAMN HARD. HE'D BEEN CLEAN FOR THREE YEARS, AND HE DIDN'T SOUND LIKE HE WAS ON ANYTHING WHEN HE CALLED ME.

WERE YOU DEALING AGAIN, OLD BUDDY? WERE YOU DUMB ENOUGH TO CROSS THE BIG BOYS?

OR IS THIS SOME OLD, DIRTY BUSINESS? DID THE PAST CATCH UP WITH YOU?

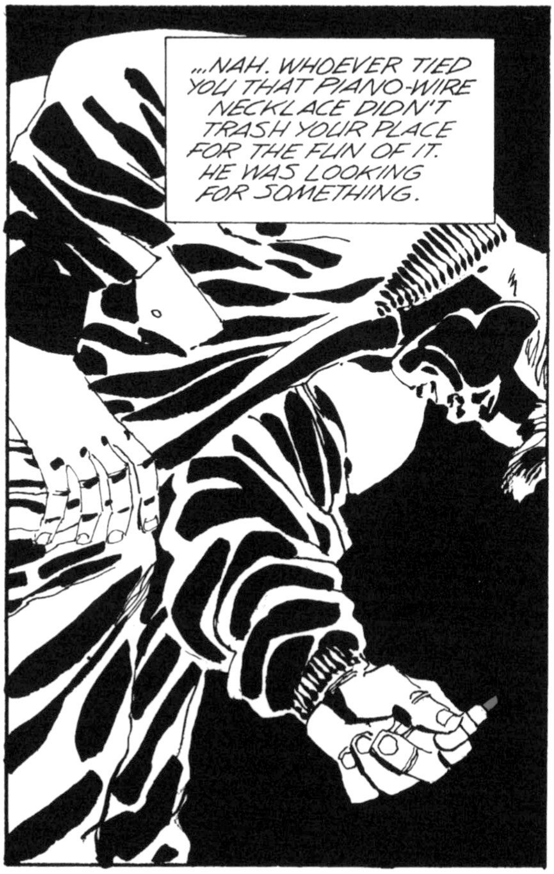
...NAH. WHOEVER TIED YOU THAT PIANO-WIRE NECKLACE DIDN'T TRASH YOUR PLACE FOR THE FUN OF IT. HE WAS LOOKING FOR SOMETHING.

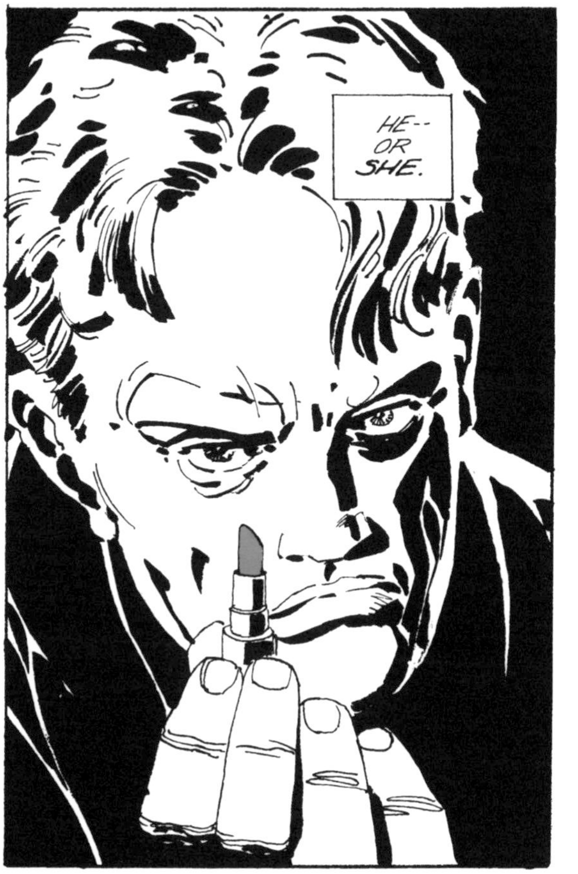
HE-- OR SHE.

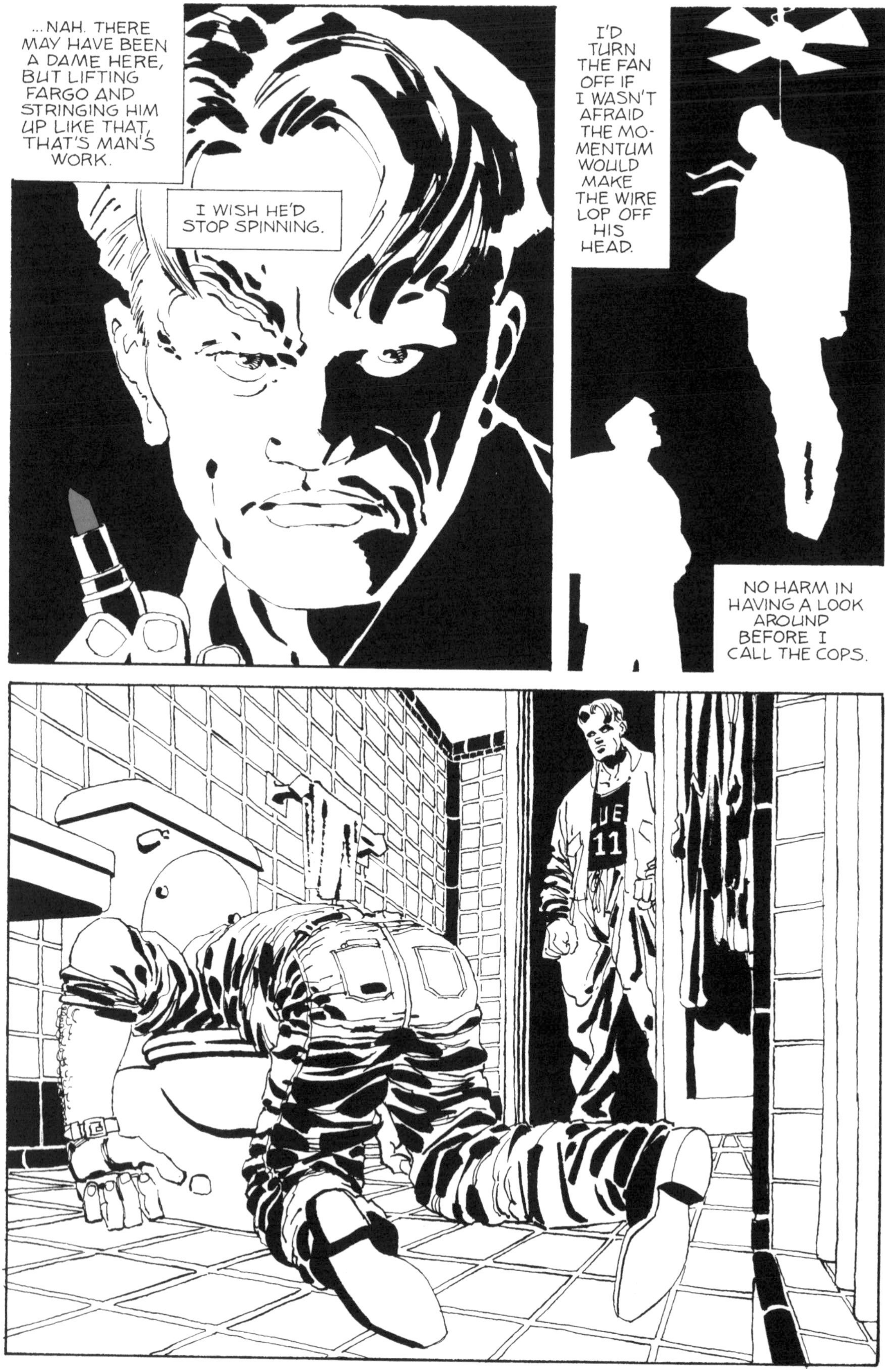
...NAH. THERE MAY HAVE BEEN A DAME HERE, BUT LIFTING FARGO AND STRINGING HIM UP LIKE THAT, THAT'S MAN'S WORK.
I WISH HE'D STOP SPINNING.
I'D TURN THE FAN OFF IF I WASN'T AFRAID THE MO-MENTUM WOULD MAKE THE WIRE LOP OFF HIS HEAD.
NO HARM IN HAVING A LOOK AROUND BEFORE I CALL THE COPS.

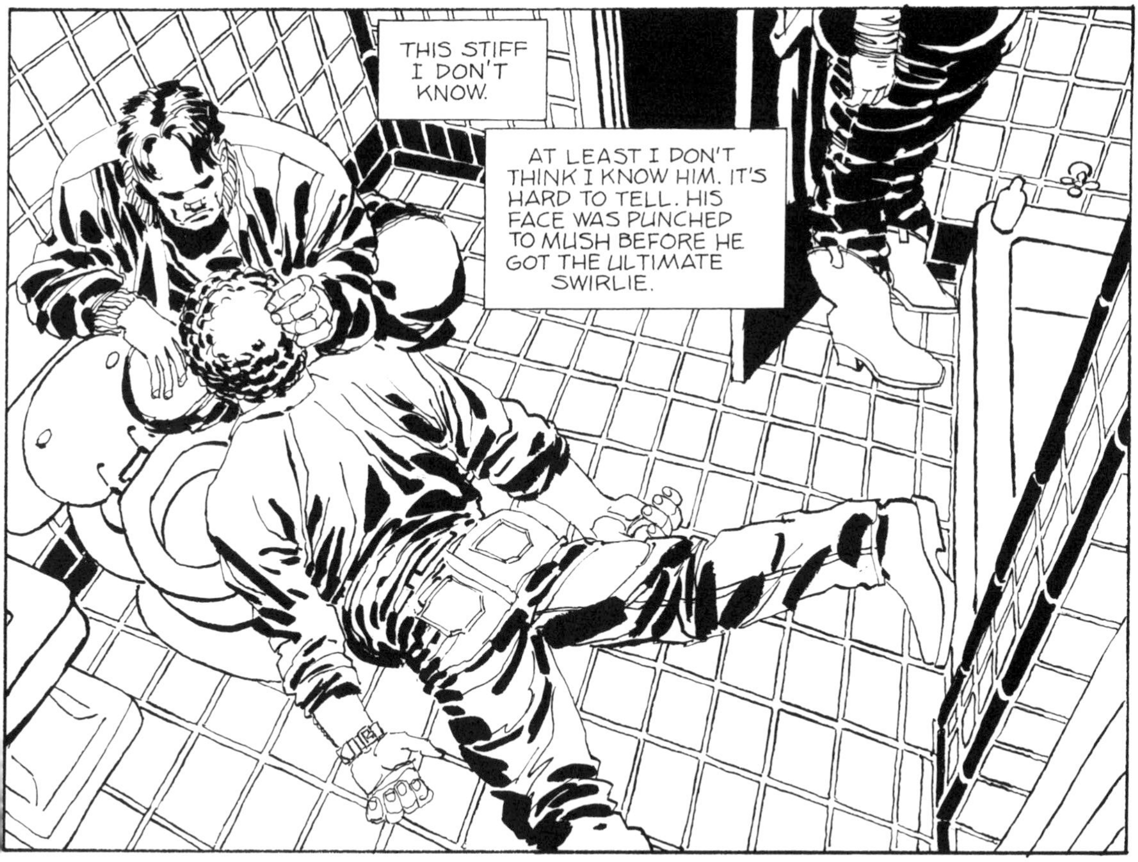
THIS STIFF I DON'T KNOW.
AT LEAST I DON'T THINK I KNOW HIM. IT'S HARD TO TELL. HIS FACE WAS PUNCHED TO MUSH BEFORE HE GOT THE ULTIMATE SWIRLIE.

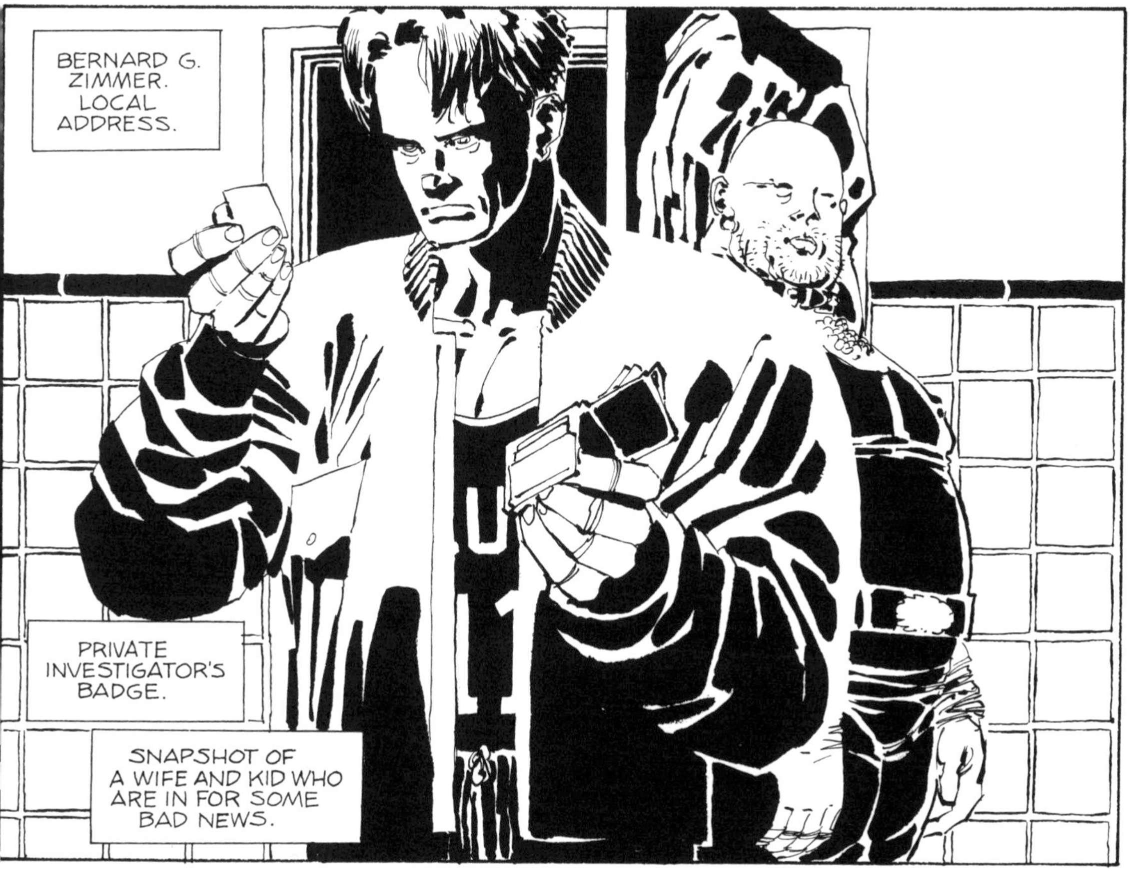
BERNARD G. ZIMMER. LOCAL ADDRESS.
PRIVATE INVESTIGATOR'S BADGE.
SNAPSHOT OF A WIFE AND KID WHO ARE IN FOR SOME BAD NEWS.

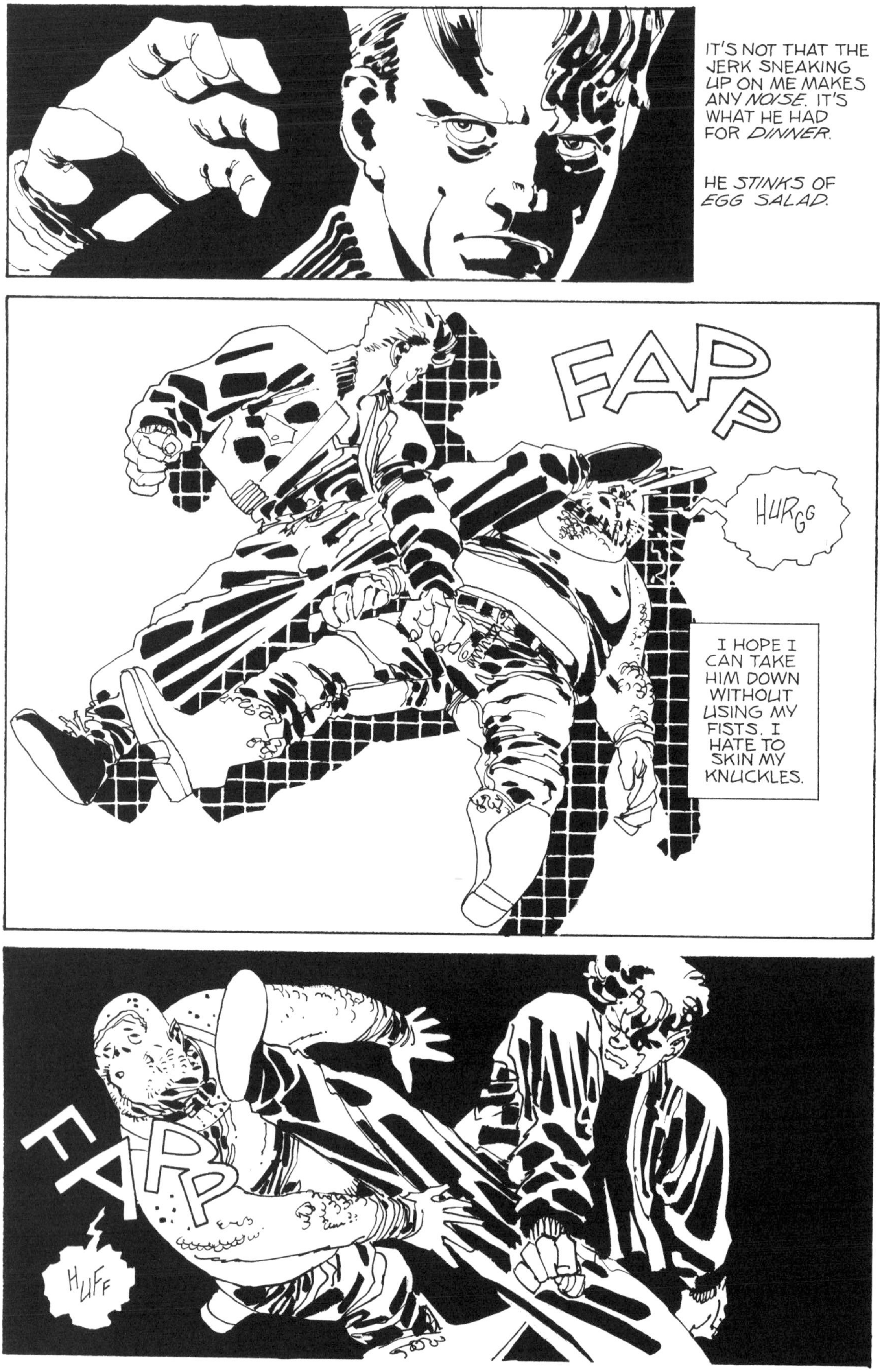
IT'S NOT THAT THE JERK SNEAKING UP ON ME MAKES ANY *NOISE*. IT'S WHAT HE HAD FOR *DINNER*.
HE *STINKS* OF *EGG SALAD*.
FAPP
HURGG
I HOPE I CAN TAKE HIM DOWN WITHOUT USING MY FISTS. I HATE TO SKIN MY KNUCKLES.
FAPP
HUFF

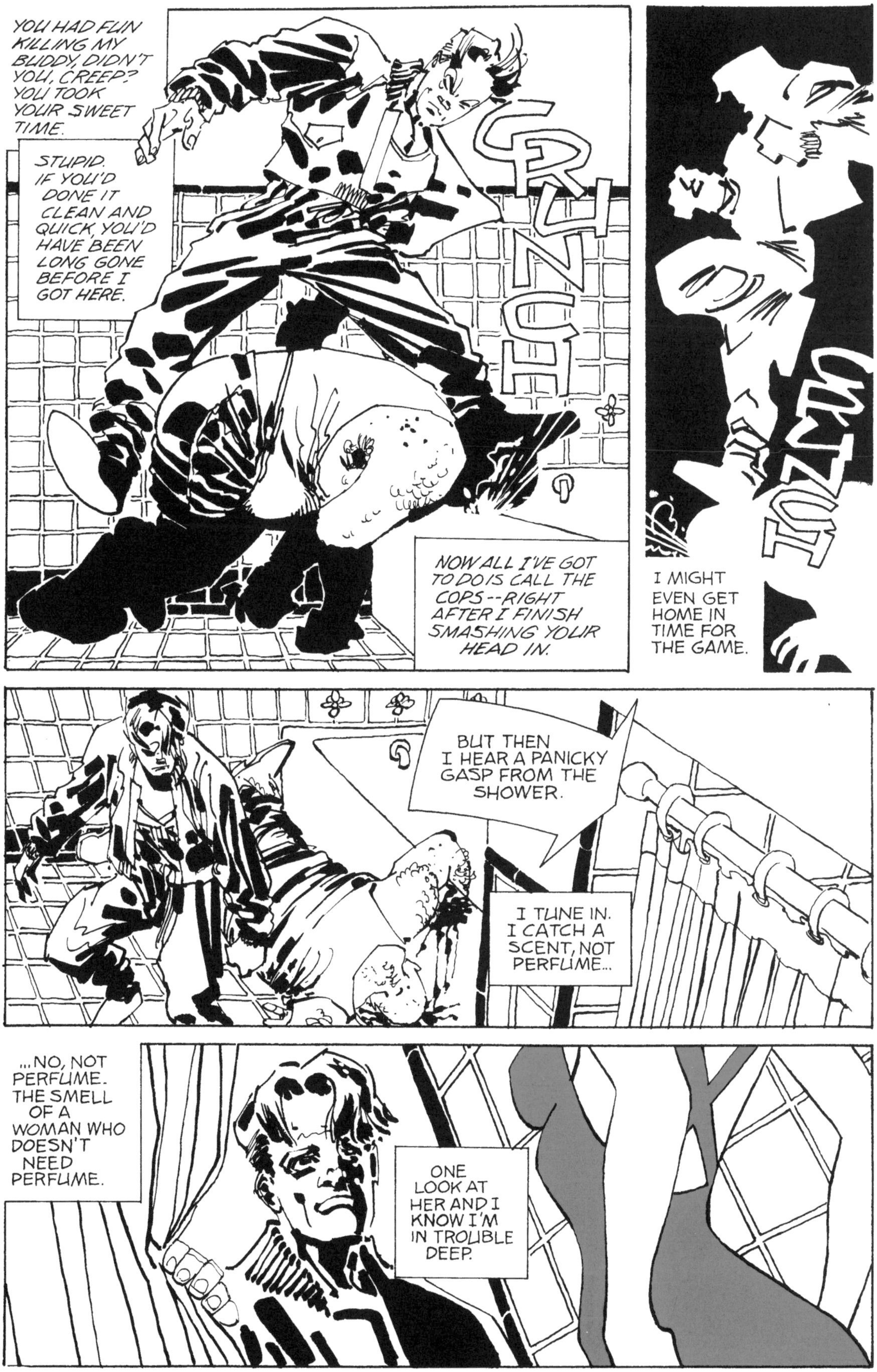

YOU HAD FUN KILLING MY BUDDY, DIDN'T YOU, CREEP? YOU TOOK YOUR SWEET TIME.
STUPID. IF YOU'D DONE IT CLEAN AND QUICK, YOU'D HAVE BEEN LONG GONE BEFORE I GOT HERE.
CRUNCH
NOW ALL I'VE GOT TO DO IS CALL THE COPS--RIGHT AFTER I FINISH SMASHING YOUR HEAD IN.
CRUNCH
I MIGHT EVEN GET HOME IN TIME FOR THE GAME.
BUT THEN I HEAR A PANICKY GASP FROM THE SHOWER.
I TUNE IN. I CATCH A SCENT, NOT PERFUME...
...NO, NOT PERFUME. THE SMELL OF A WOMAN WHO DOESN'T NEED PERFUME.
ONE LOOK AT HER AND I KNOW I'M IN TROUBLE DEEP.

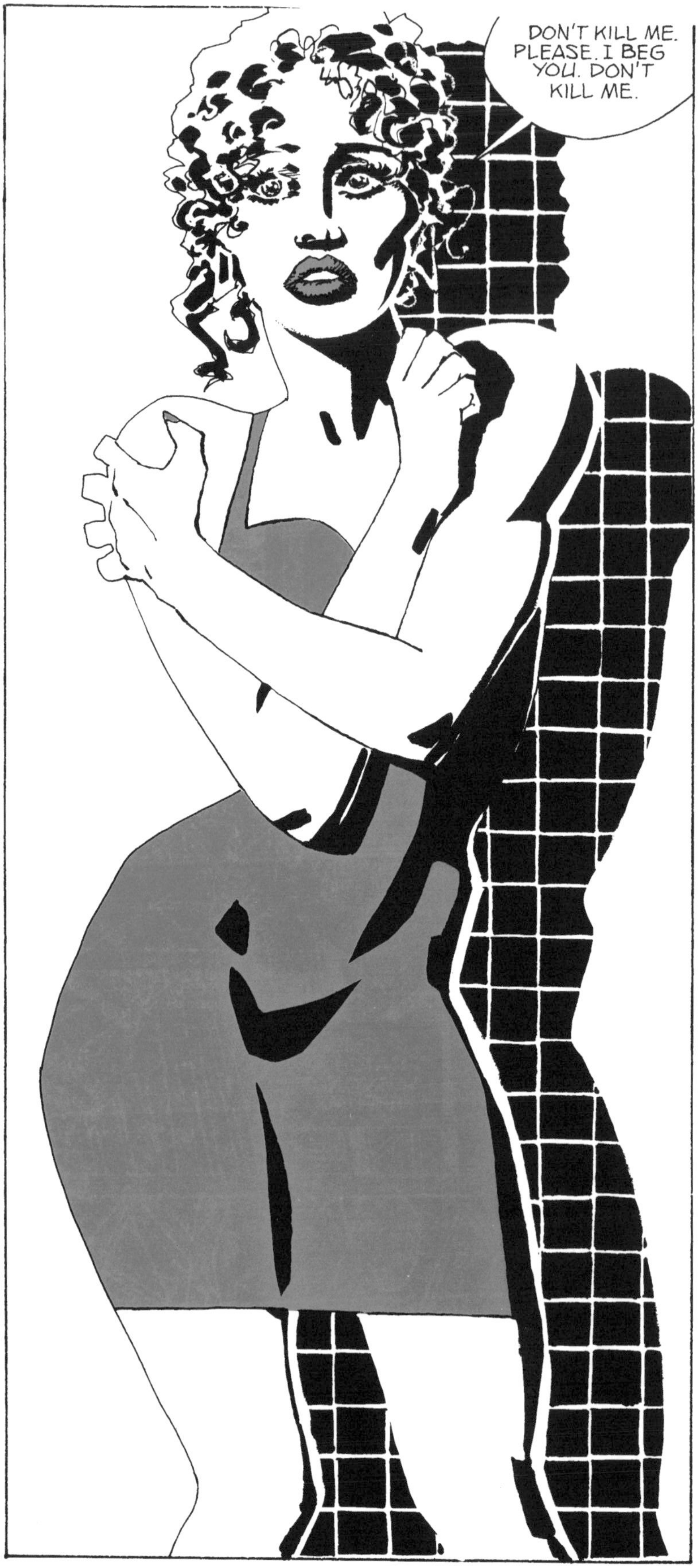
DON'T KILL ME. PLEASE. I BEG YOU. DON'T KILL ME.

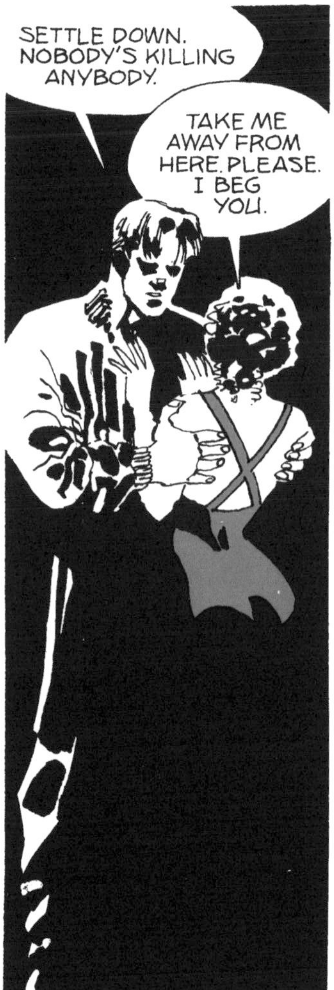
SETTLE DOWN. NOBODY'S KILLING ANYBODY.
TAKE ME AWAY FROM HERE. PLEASE. I BEG YOU.

WHAT IS IT ABOUT SOME WOMEN? THE ONE-IN-A-MILLION KIND, WHO MAKE YOUR HEAD GO LIGHT AND YOUR MOUTH GO DRY AND YOUR HEART CLIMB UP YOUR THROAT? IT'S NOT JUST THEIR LOOKS. IT'S SOMETHING ELSE-- SOMETHING YOU CAN FEEL FROM ACROSS THE ROOM.

WHATEVER IT IS, THIS BABE HAS IT IN SPADES.

BE CAREFUL, THE **SMART** PART OF ME SAYS. *BE DAMN CAREFUL.* **REMEMBER** *THAT OLD ENEMY. HOW SHE SMILED AND TOLD YOU THAT SEX ALWAYS MAKES YOU STUPID.*

SHE WAS RIGHT.

BE CAREFUL.

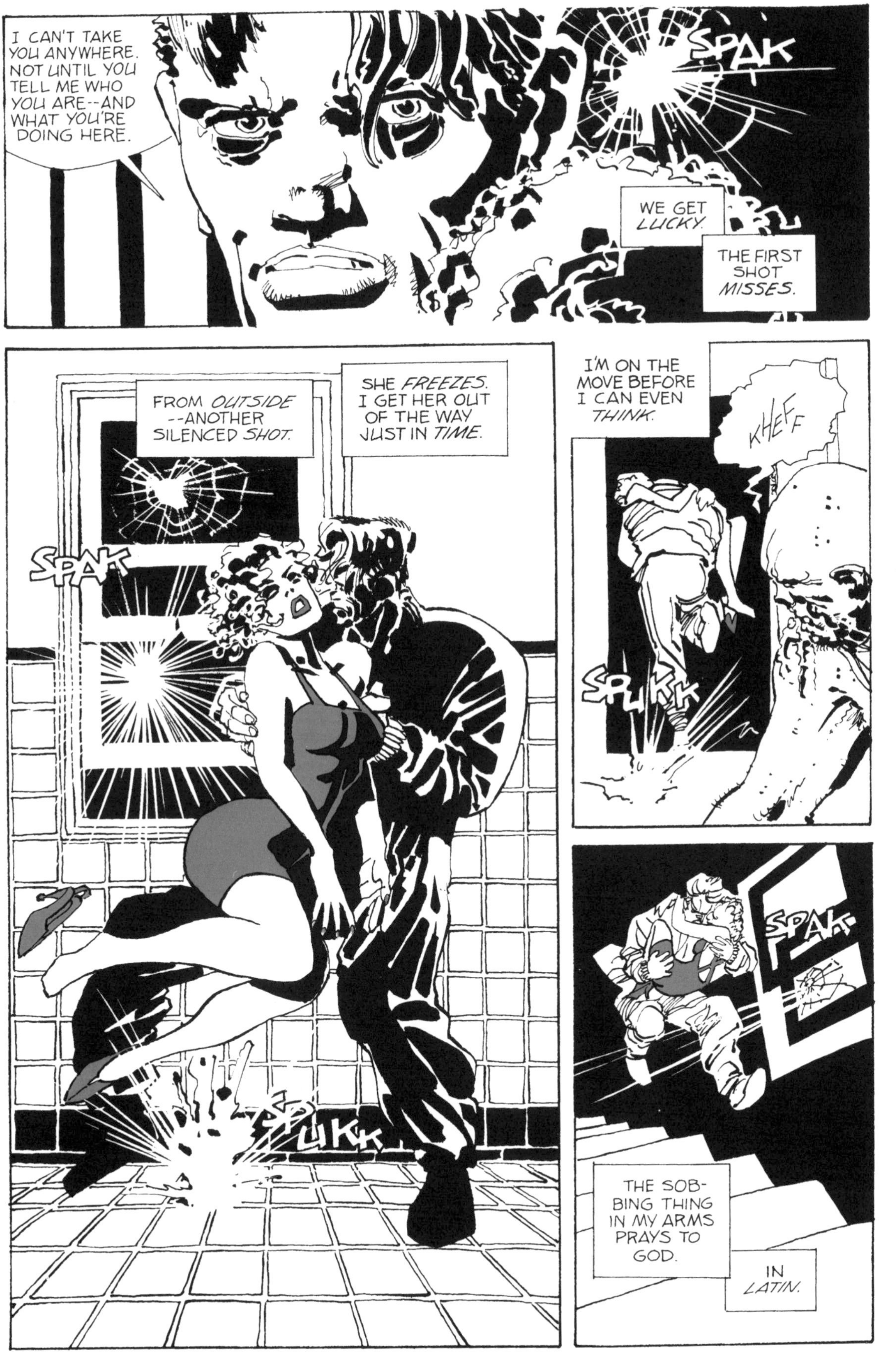
I CAN'T TAKE YOU ANYWHERE. NOT UNTIL YOU TELL ME WHO YOU ARE--AND WHAT YOU'RE DOING HERE.
SPAK
WE GET LUCKY.
THE FIRST SHOT MISSES.
FROM OUTSIDE --ANOTHER SILENCED SHOT.
SHE FREEZES. I GET HER OUT OF THE WAY JUST IN TIME.
SPAK
SPUKK
I'M ON THE MOVE BEFORE I CAN EVEN THINK.
KHEFF
SPUKK
SPAK
THE SOBBING THING IN MY ARMS PRAYS TO GOD.
IN LATIN.

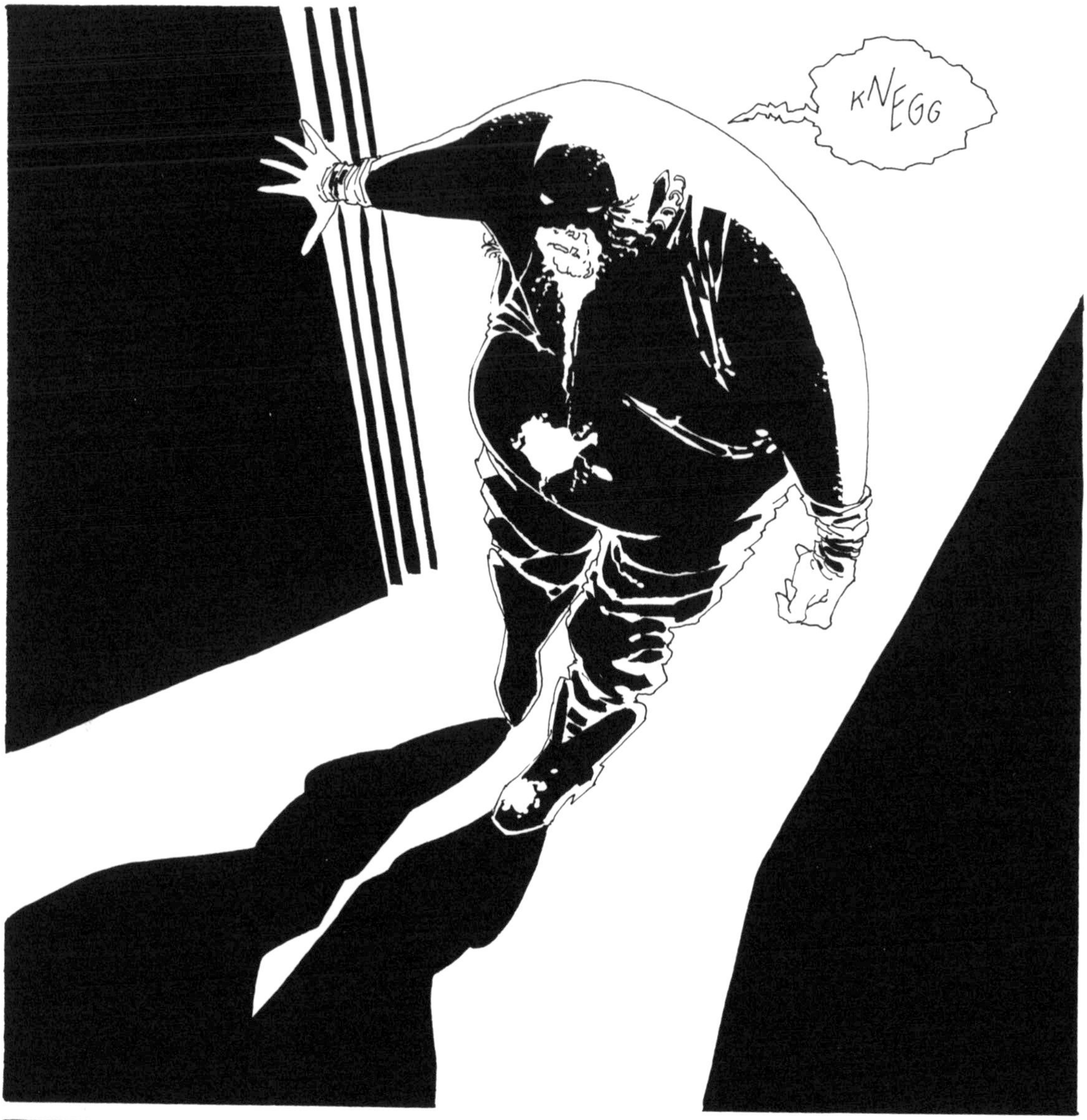
KNEGG

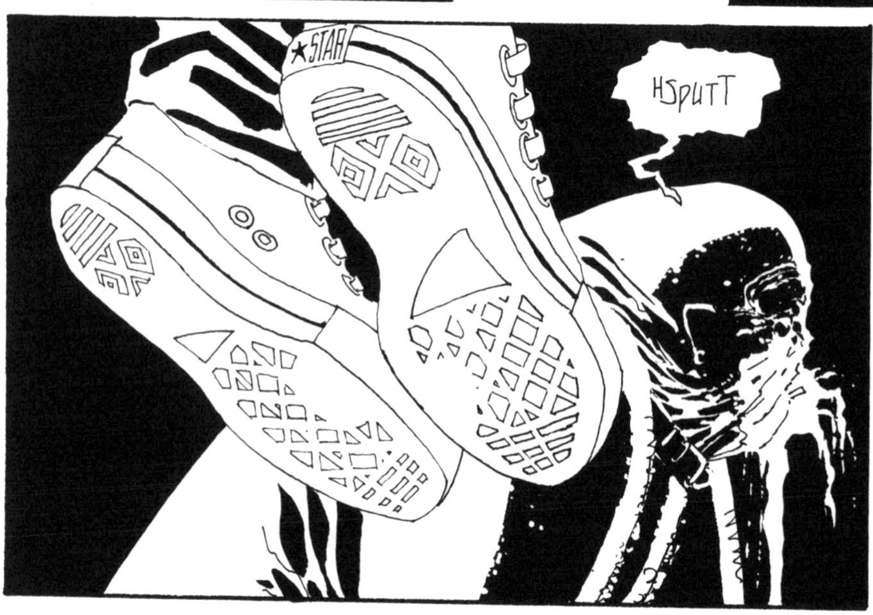
STAR
HSPUTT

I CAN'T STAND IT WHEN YOU GO TO ALL THE TROUBLE OF BREAKING A GUY'S FACE AND HE WON'T STAY DOWN LIKE HE OUGHT TO.

IF IT WEREN'T FOR HIS BUDDY WITH THE RIFLE, I'D TAKE THE TIME AND GO BACK UPSTAIRS AND DO SOMETHING PERMANENT TO THE SLOB.

HIS BUDDY WITH THE RIFLE--AND THE SCARED, SOFT DREAM OF A WOMAN WHO'S PRESSED AGAINST ME...

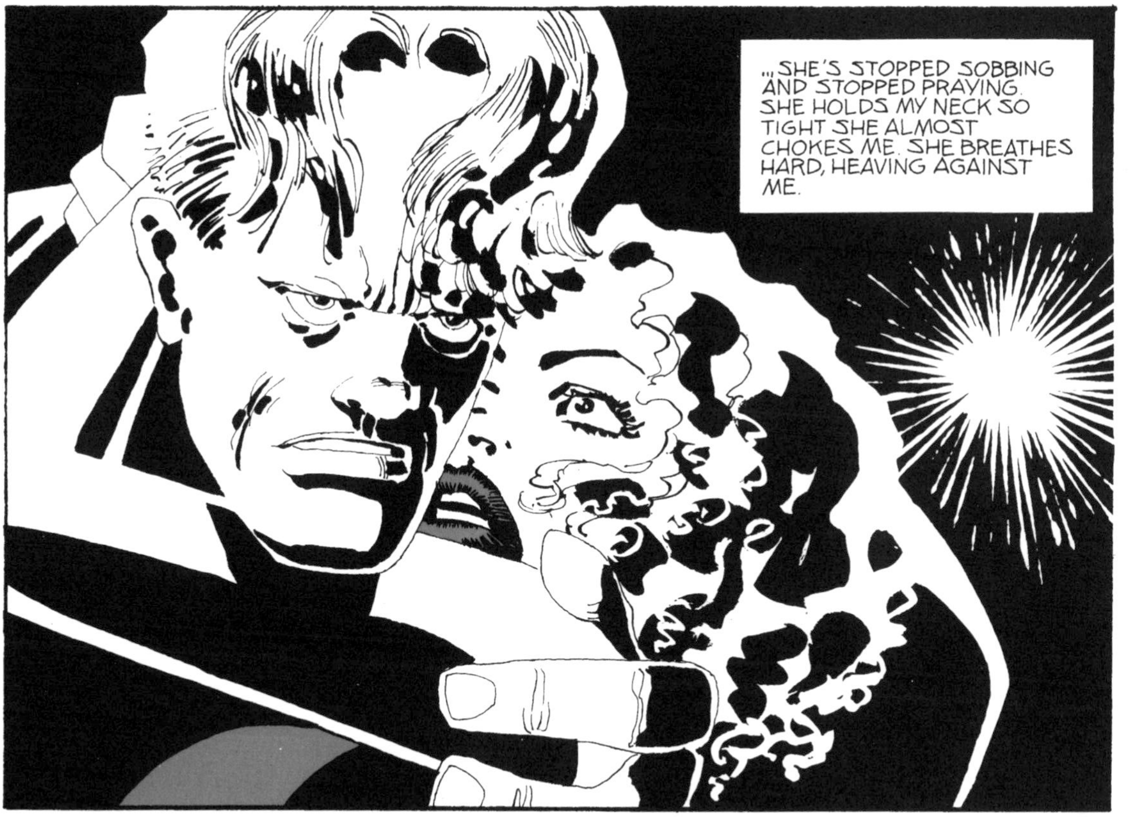
...SHE'S STOPPED SOBBING AND STOPPED PRAYING. SHE HOLDS MY NECK SO TIGHT SHE ALMOST CHOKES ME. SHE BREATHES HARD, HEAVING AGAINST ME.

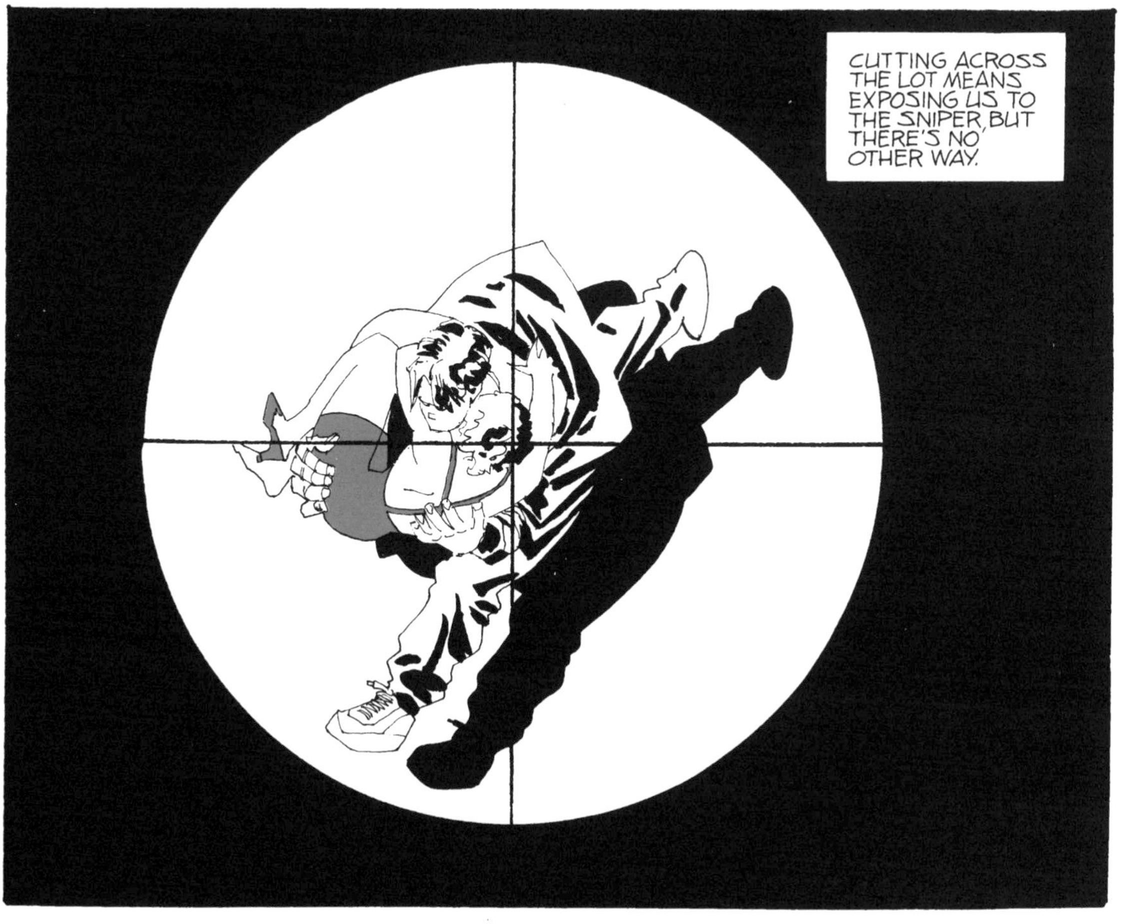
CUTTING ACROSS THE LOT MEANS EXPOSING US TO THE SNIPER, BUT THERE'S NO OTHER WAY.

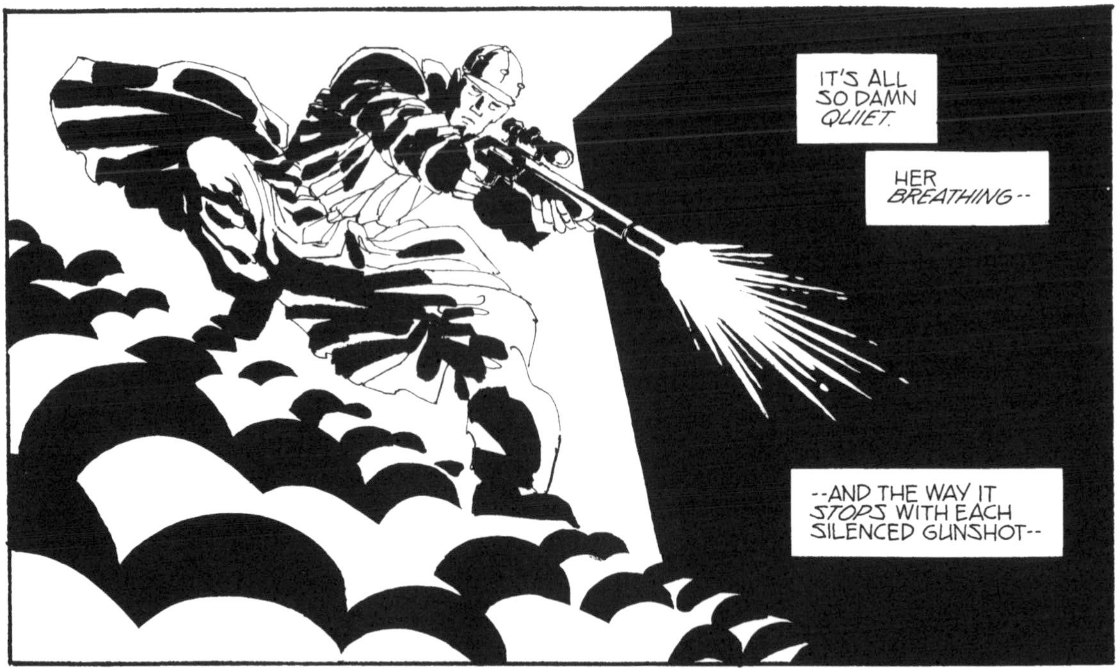
IT'S ALL SO DAMN *QUIET.*
HER *BREATHING*--
--AND THE WAY IT *STOPS* WITH EACH SILENCED GUNSHOT--

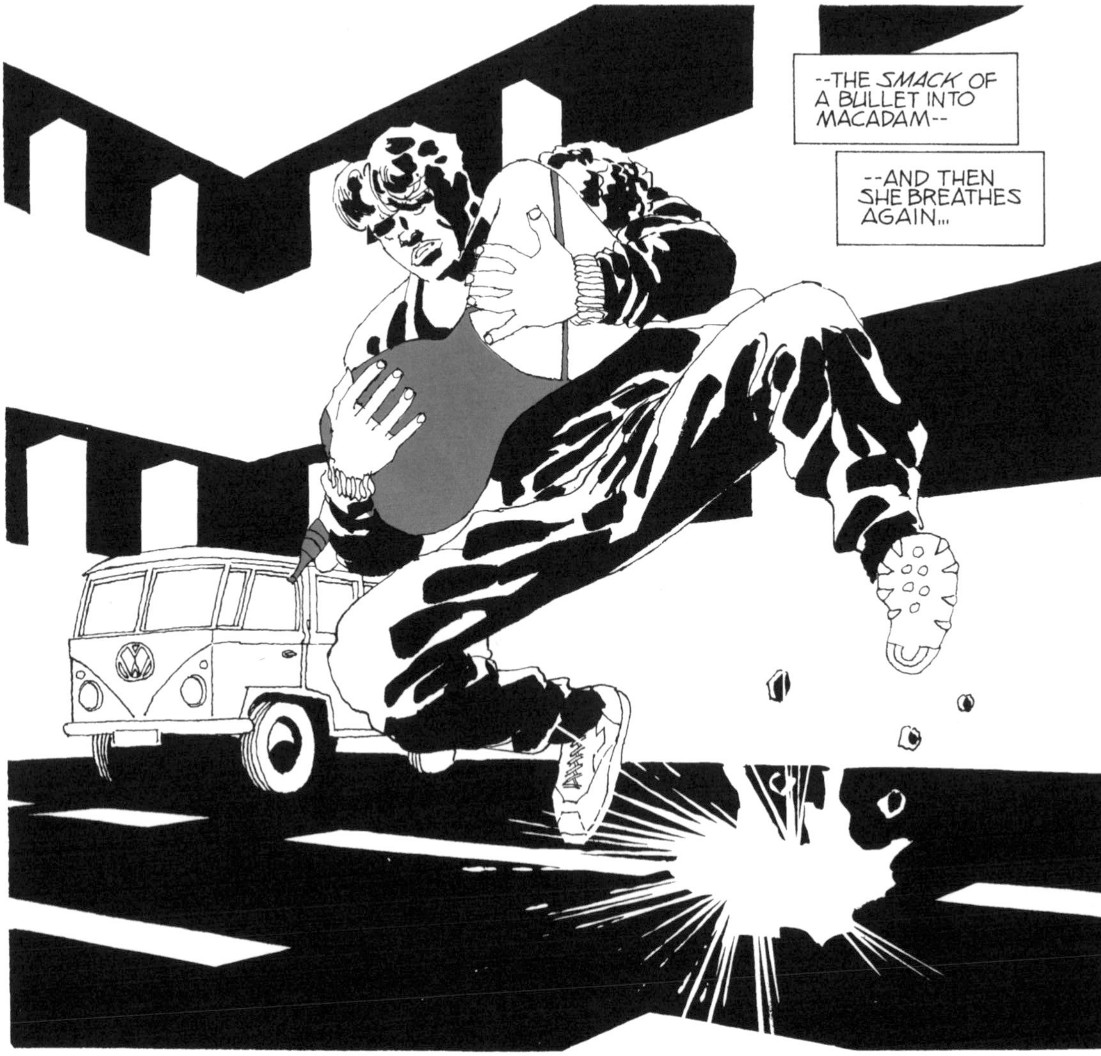
--THE *SMACK* OF A BULLET INTO MACADAM--
--AND THEN SHE BREATHES AGAIN...

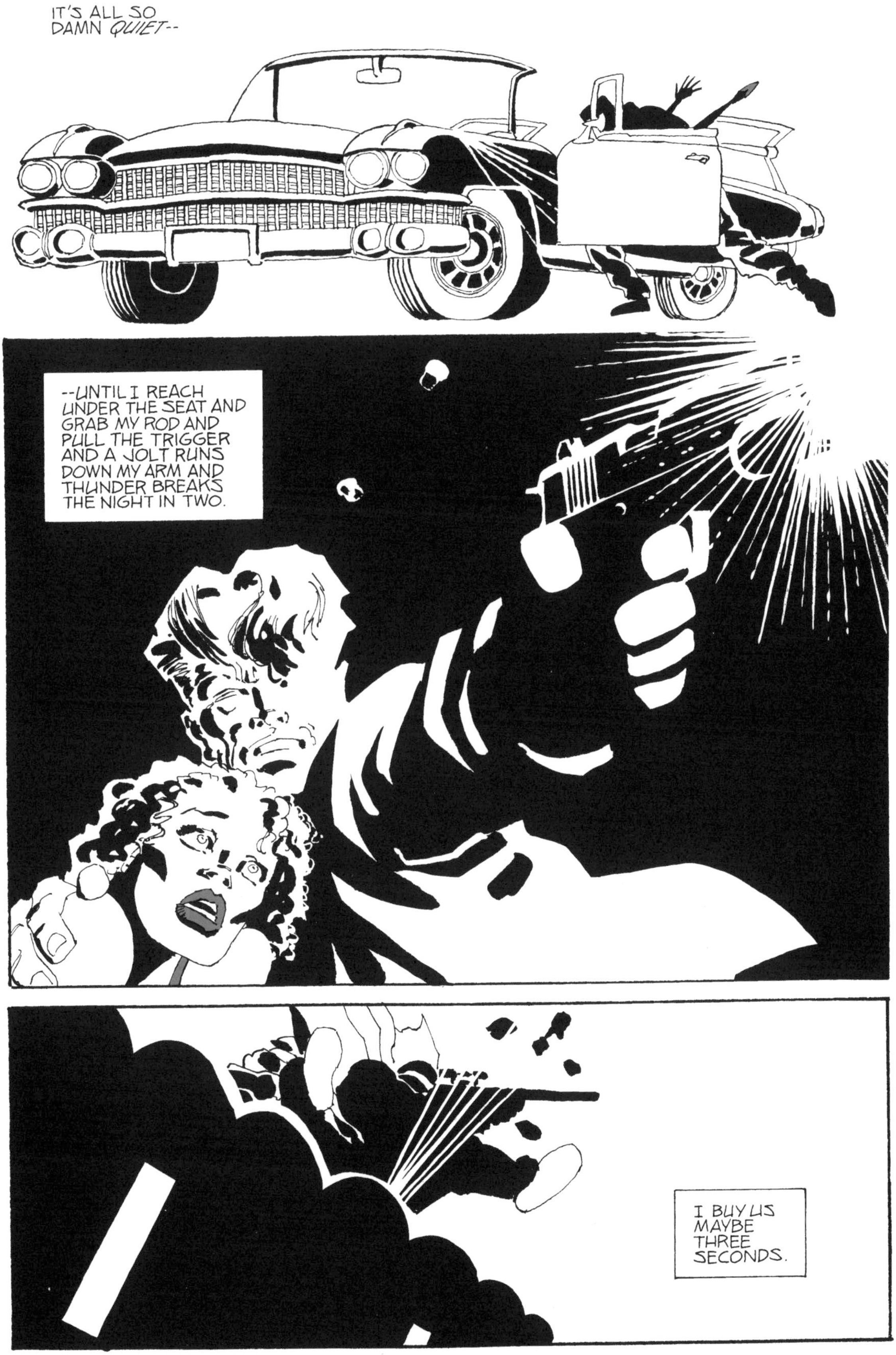
IT'S ALL SO DAMN *QUIET*--
--UNTIL I REACH UNDER THE SEAT AND GRAB MY ROD AND PULL THE TRIGGER AND A JOLT RUNS DOWN MY ARM AND THUNDER BREAKS THE NIGHT IN TWO.
I BUY US MAYBE THREE SECONDS.

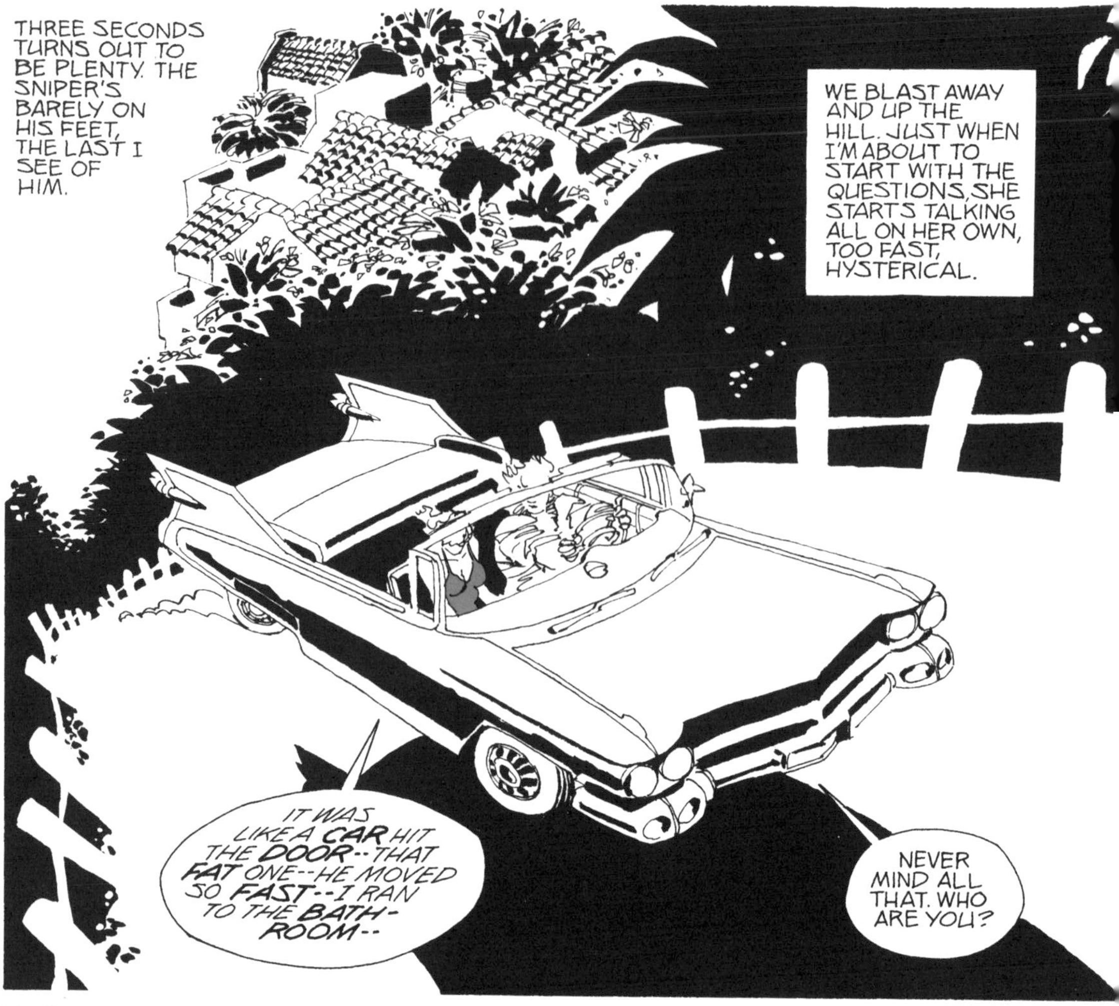
THREE SECONDS TURNS OUT TO BE PLENTY. THE SNIPER'S BARELY ON HIS FEET, THE LAST I SEE OF HIM.
WE BLAST AWAY AND UP THE HILL. JUST WHEN I'M ABOUT TO START WITH THE QUESTIONS, SHE STARTS TALKING ALL ON HER OWN, TOO FAST, HYSTERICAL.
IT WAS LIKE A CAR HIT THE DOOR--THAT FAT ONE--HE MOVED SO FAST--I RAN TO THE BATH-ROOM--
NEVER MIND ALL THAT. WHO ARE YOU?

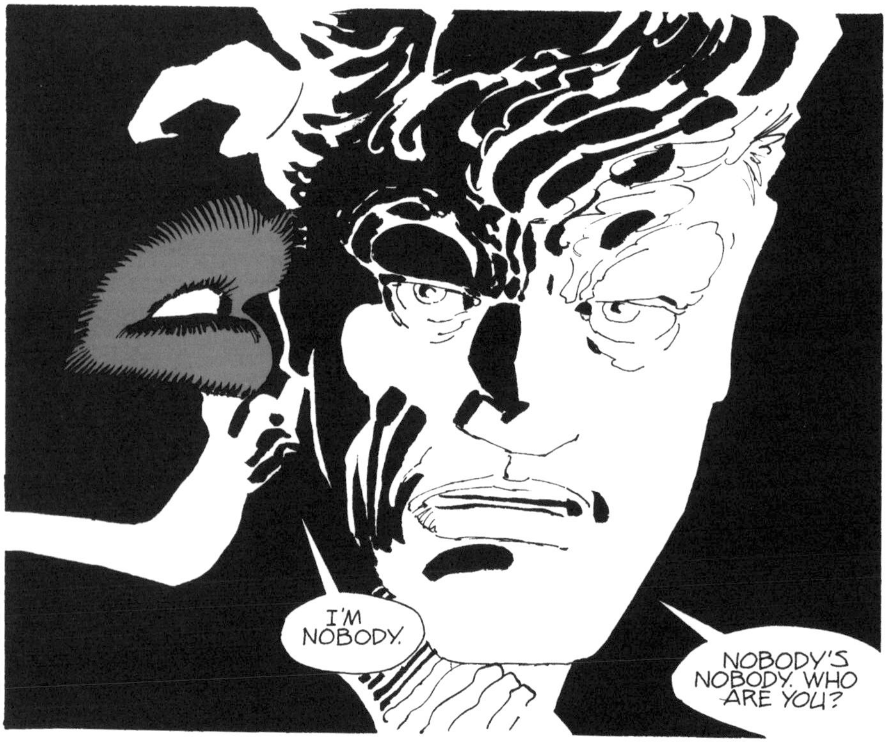
I'M NOBODY.
NOBODY'S NOBODY. WHO ARE YOU?

I LOOK BACK AT THE ROAD EVERY ONCE IN A WHILE. OFTEN ENOUGH TO KEEP FROM DRIVING INTO THE GUARD RAILS. IT'S HARD TO TAKE MY EYES OFF HER.

SHE TAKES THE BETTER PART OF A MINUTE TO COME UP WITH AN ANSWER FOR ME.

"MARY," SHE SAYS WITH A WEIRD CHUCKLE. *"MY NAME IS MARY."*

MARY.

AT LEAST SHE'S GOT A *NAME*...

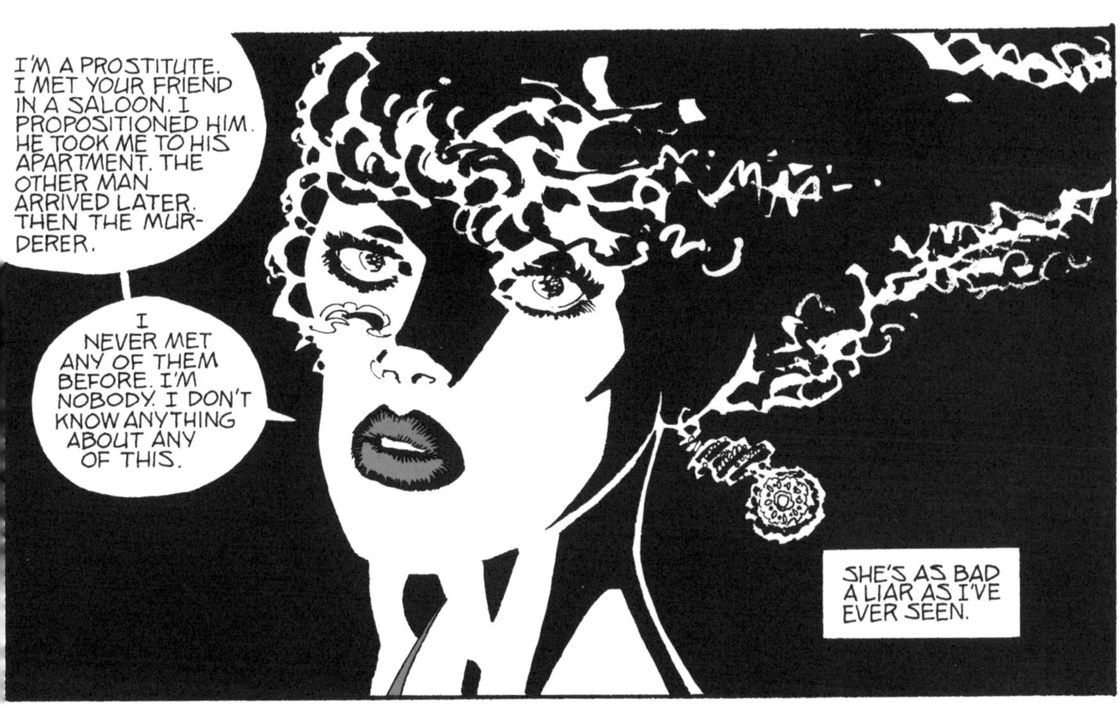
I'M A PROSTITUTE. I MET YOUR FRIEND IN A SALOON. I PROPOSITIONED HIM. HE TOOK ME TO HIS APARTMENT. THE OTHER MAN ARRIVED LATER. THEN THE MUR-DERER.
I NEVER MET ANY OF THEM BEFORE. I'M NOBODY. I DON'T KNOW ANYTHING ABOUT ANY OF THIS.
SHE'S AS BAD A LIAR AS I'VE EVER SEEN.

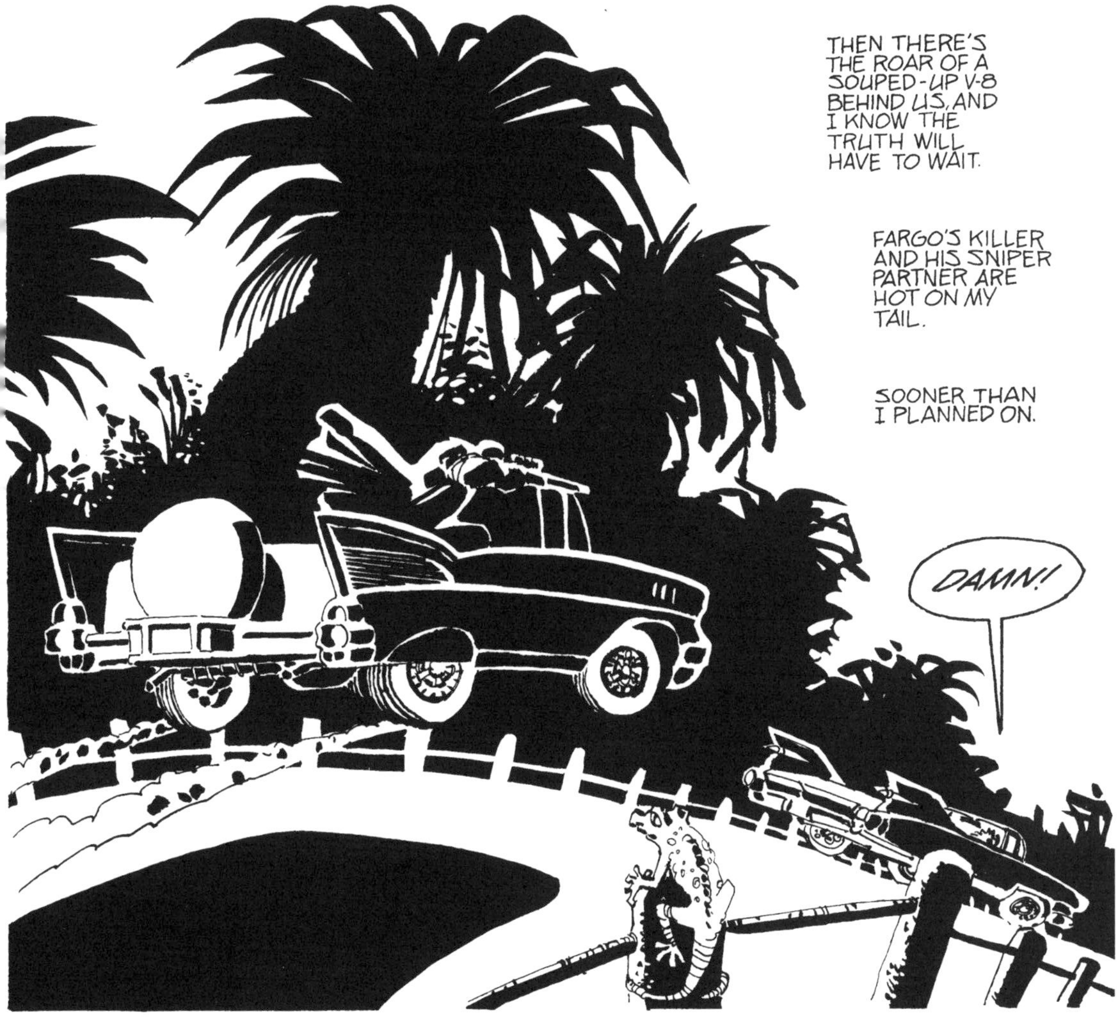
THEN THERE'S THE ROAR OF A SOUPED-UP V-8 BEHIND US, AND I KNOW THE TRUTH WILL HAVE TO WAIT.
FARGO'S KILLER AND HIS SNIPER PARTNER ARE HOT ON MY TAIL.
SOONER THAN I PLANNED ON.
DAMN!

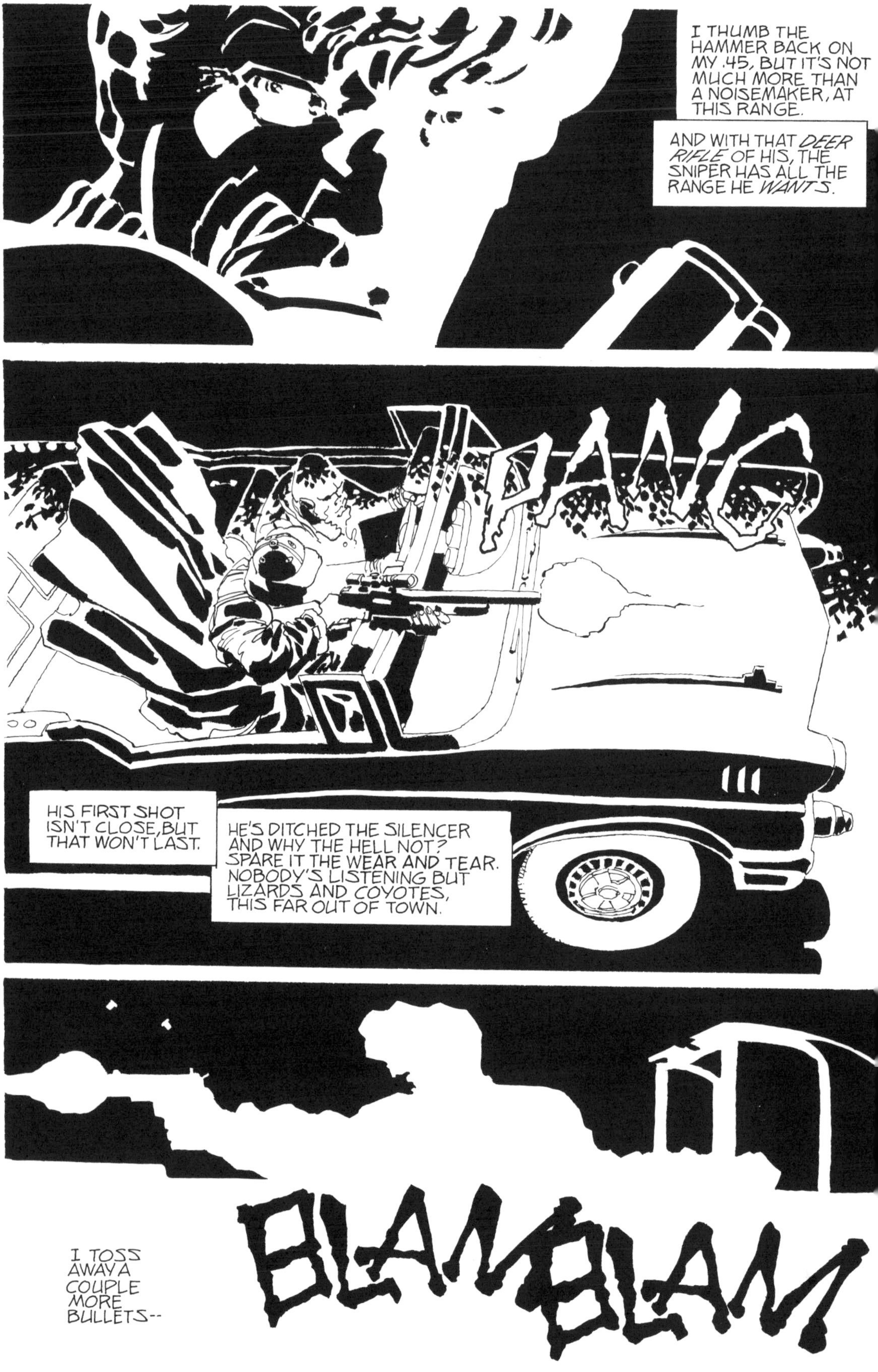
I THUMB THE HAMMER BACK ON MY .45, BUT IT'S NOT MUCH MORE THAN A NOISEMAKER, AT THIS RANGE.
AND WITH THAT *DEER RIFLE* OF HIS, THE SNIPER HAS ALL THE RANGE HE *WANTS*.
PANG
HIS FIRST SHOT ISN'T CLOSE, BUT THAT WON'T LAST.
HE'S DITCHED THE SILENCER AND WHY THE HELL NOT? SPARE IT THE WEAR AND TEAR. NOBODY'S LISTENING BUT LIZARDS AND COYOTES, THIS FAR OUT OF TOWN.
I TOSS AWAY A COUPLE MORE BULLETS--
BLAM BLAM

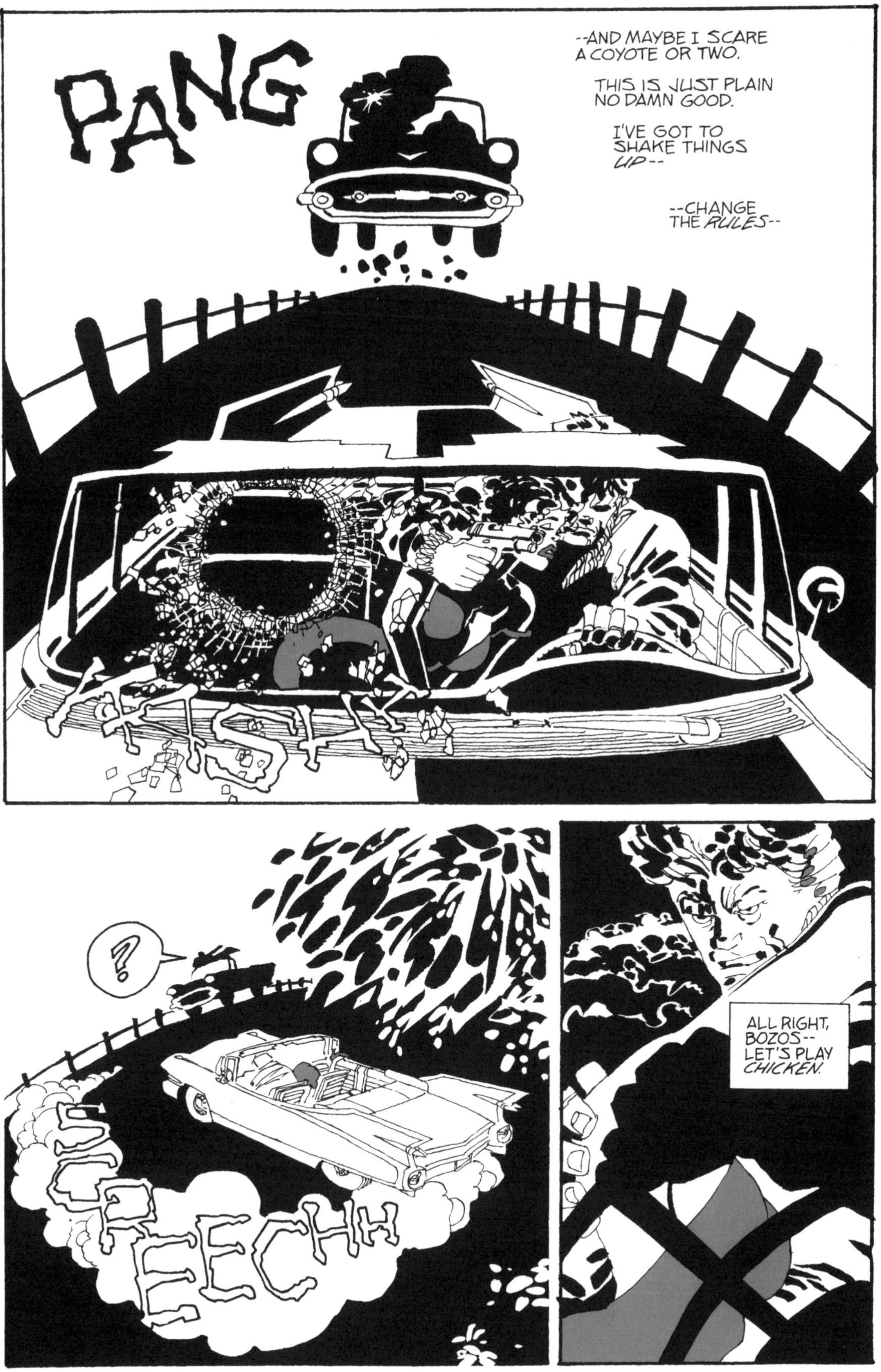
PANG
--AND MAYBE I SCARE A COYOTE OR TWO.
THIS IS JUST PLAIN NO DAMN GOOD.
I'VE GOT TO SHAKE THINGS *UP*--
--CHANGE THE *RULES*--
?
ALL RIGHT, BOZOS-- LET'S PLAY *CHICKEN.*

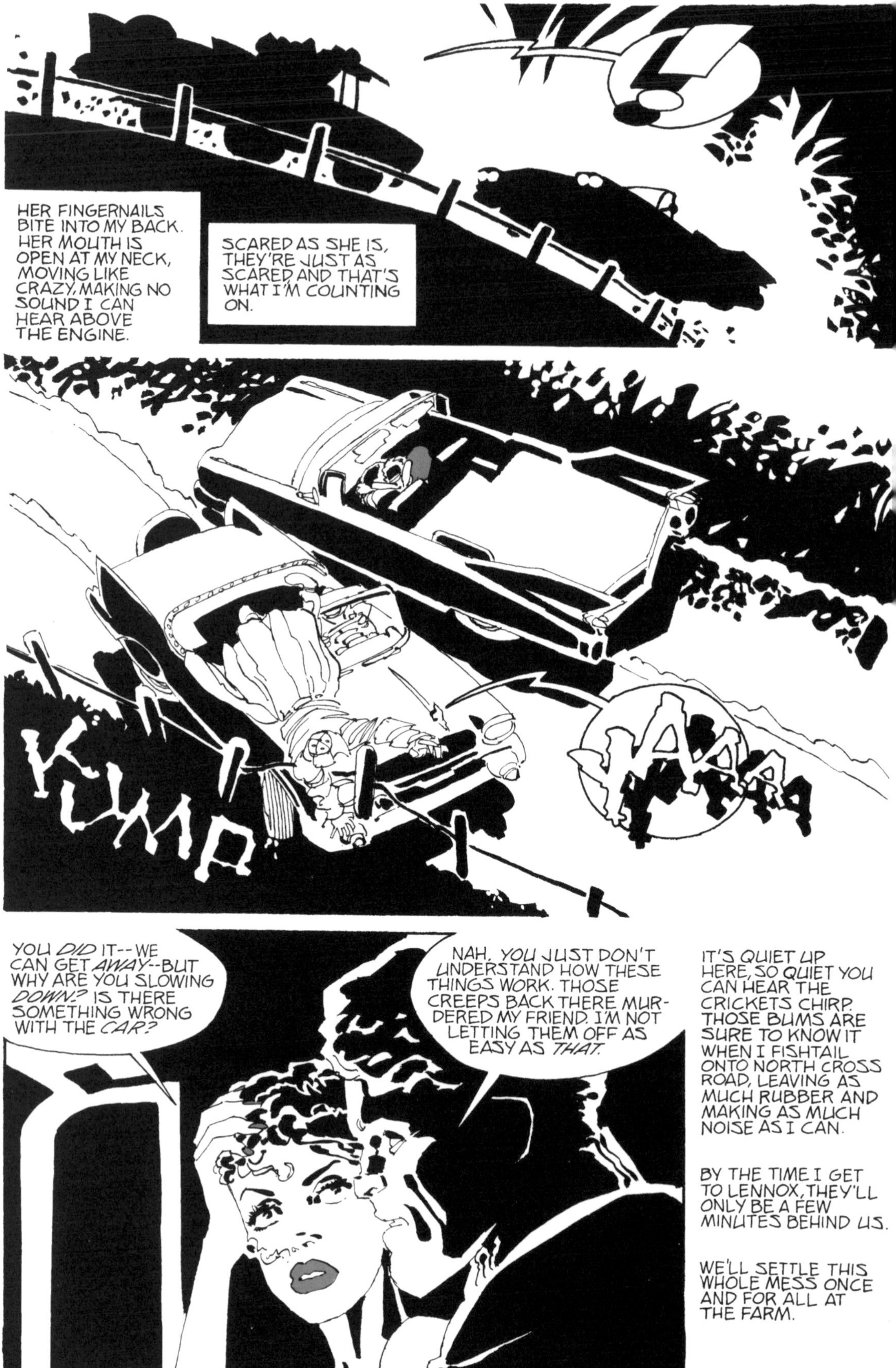
HER FINGERNAILS BITE INTO MY BACK. HER MOUTH IS OPEN AT MY NECK, MOVING LIKE CRAZY, MAKING NO SOUND I CAN HEAR ABOVE THE ENGINE.
SCARED AS SHE IS, THEY'RE JUST AS SCARED AND THAT'S WHAT I'M COUNTING ON.
YOU *DID* IT--WE CAN GET *AWAY*--BUT WHY ARE YOU SLOWING *DOWN?* IS THERE SOMETHING WRONG WITH THE *CAR?*
NAH. *YOU* JUST DON'T UNDERSTAND HOW THESE THINGS WORK. THOSE CREEPS BACK THERE MURDERED MY FRIEND. I'M NOT LETTING THEM OFF AS EASY AS *THAT.*
IT'S QUIET UP HERE, SO QUIET YOU CAN HEAR THE CRICKETS CHIRP. THOSE BUMS ARE SURE TO KNOW IT WHEN I FISHTAIL ONTO NORTH CROSS ROAD, LEAVING AS MUCH RUBBER AND MAKING AS MUCH NOISE AS I CAN.
BY THE TIME I GET TO LENNOX, THEY'LL ONLY BE A FEW MINUTES BEHIND US.
WE'LL SETTLE THIS WHOLE MESS ONCE AND FOR ALL AT THE FARM.

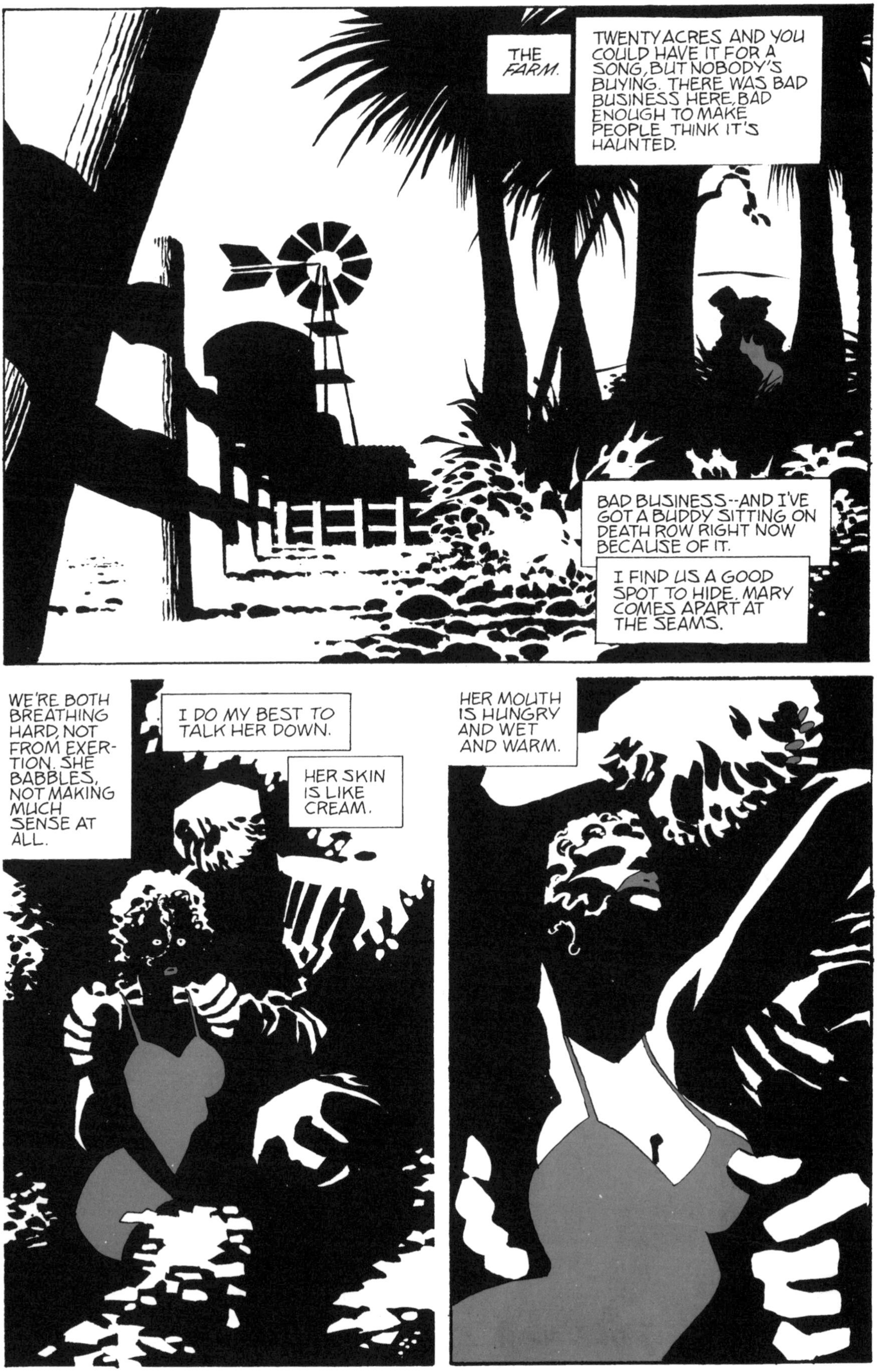
THE FARM.
TWENTY ACRES AND YOU COULD HAVE IT FOR A SONG, BUT NOBODY'S BUYING. THERE WAS BAD BUSINESS HERE, BAD ENOUGH TO MAKE PEOPLE THINK IT'S HAUNTED.
BAD BUSINESS--AND I'VE GOT A BUDDY SITTING ON DEATH ROW RIGHT NOW BECAUSE OF IT.
I FIND US A GOOD SPOT TO HIDE. MARY COMES APART AT THE SEAMS.
WE'RE BOTH BREATHING HARD, NOT FROM EXERTION. SHE BABBLES, NOT MAKING MUCH SENSE AT ALL.
I DO MY BEST TO TALK HER DOWN.
HER SKIN IS LIKE CREAM.
HER MOUTH IS HUNGRY AND WET AND WARM.

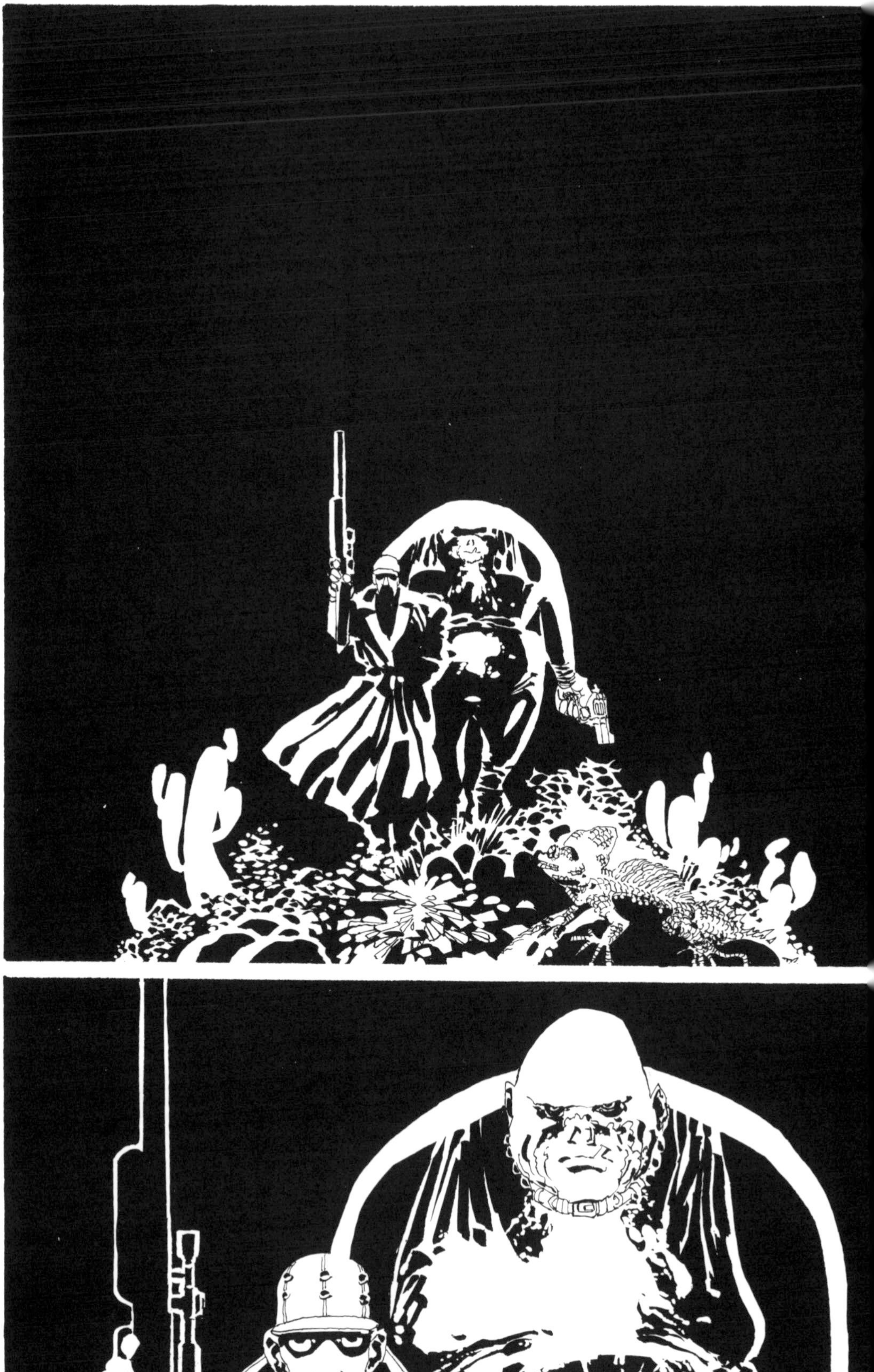

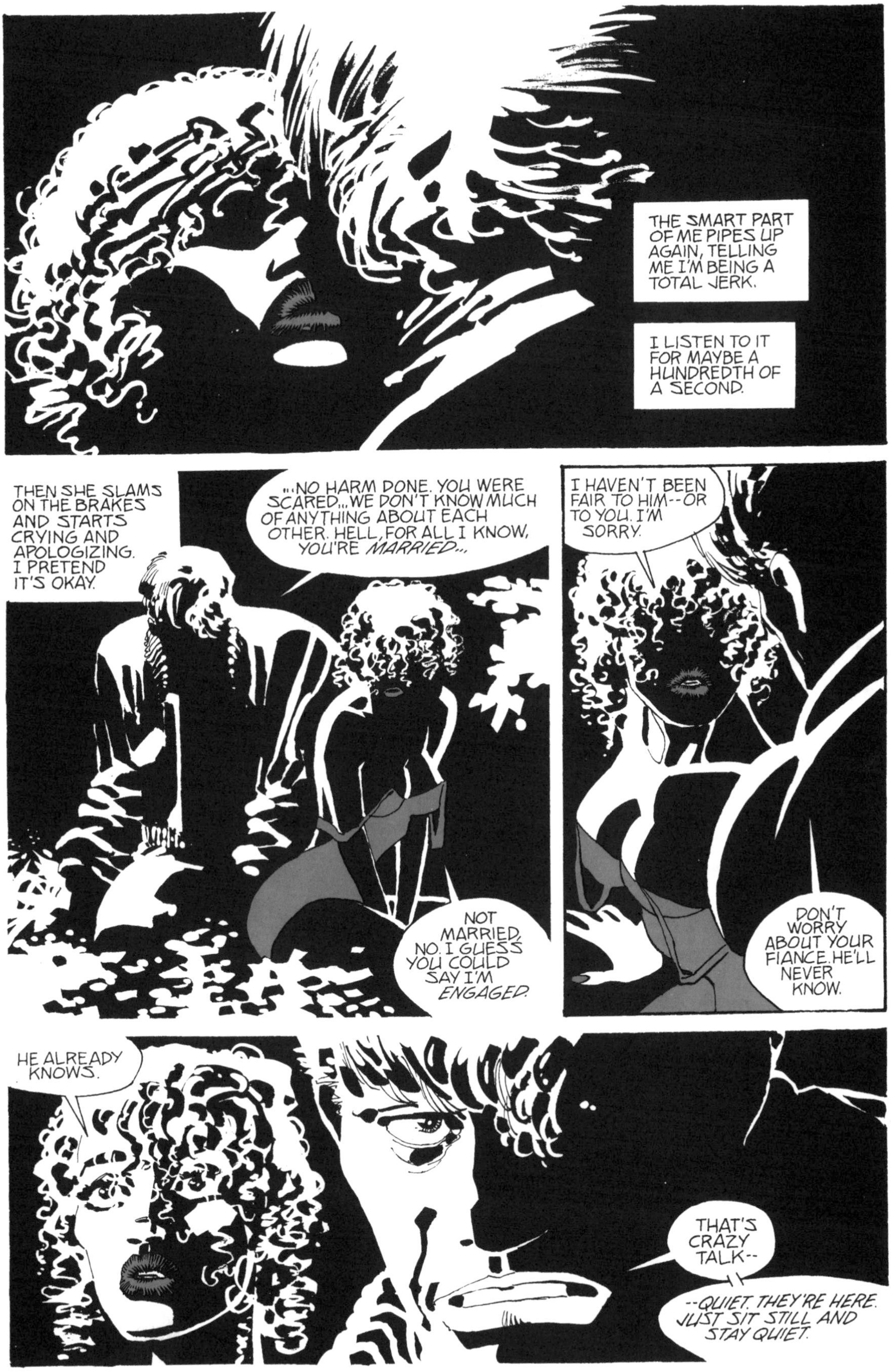

THE SMART PART OF ME PIPES UP AGAIN, TELLING ME I'M BEING A TOTAL JERK.
I LISTEN TO IT FOR MAYBE A HUNDREDTH OF A SECOND.
THEN SHE SLAMS ON THE BRAKES AND STARTS CRYING AND APOLOGIZING. I PRETEND IT'S OKAY.
...NO HARM DONE. YOU WERE SCARED... WE DON'T KNOW MUCH OF ANYTHING ABOUT EACH OTHER. HELL, FOR ALL I KNOW, YOU'RE *MARRIED*...
NOT MARRIED, NO. I GUESS YOU COULD SAY I'M *ENGAGED*.
I HAVEN'T BEEN FAIR TO HIM--OR TO YOU. I'M SORRY.
DON'T WORRY ABOUT YOUR FIANCE. HE'LL NEVER KNOW.
HE ALREADY KNOWS.
THAT'S CRAZY TALK--
--QUIET. THEY'RE HERE. JUST SIT STILL AND STAY QUIET.

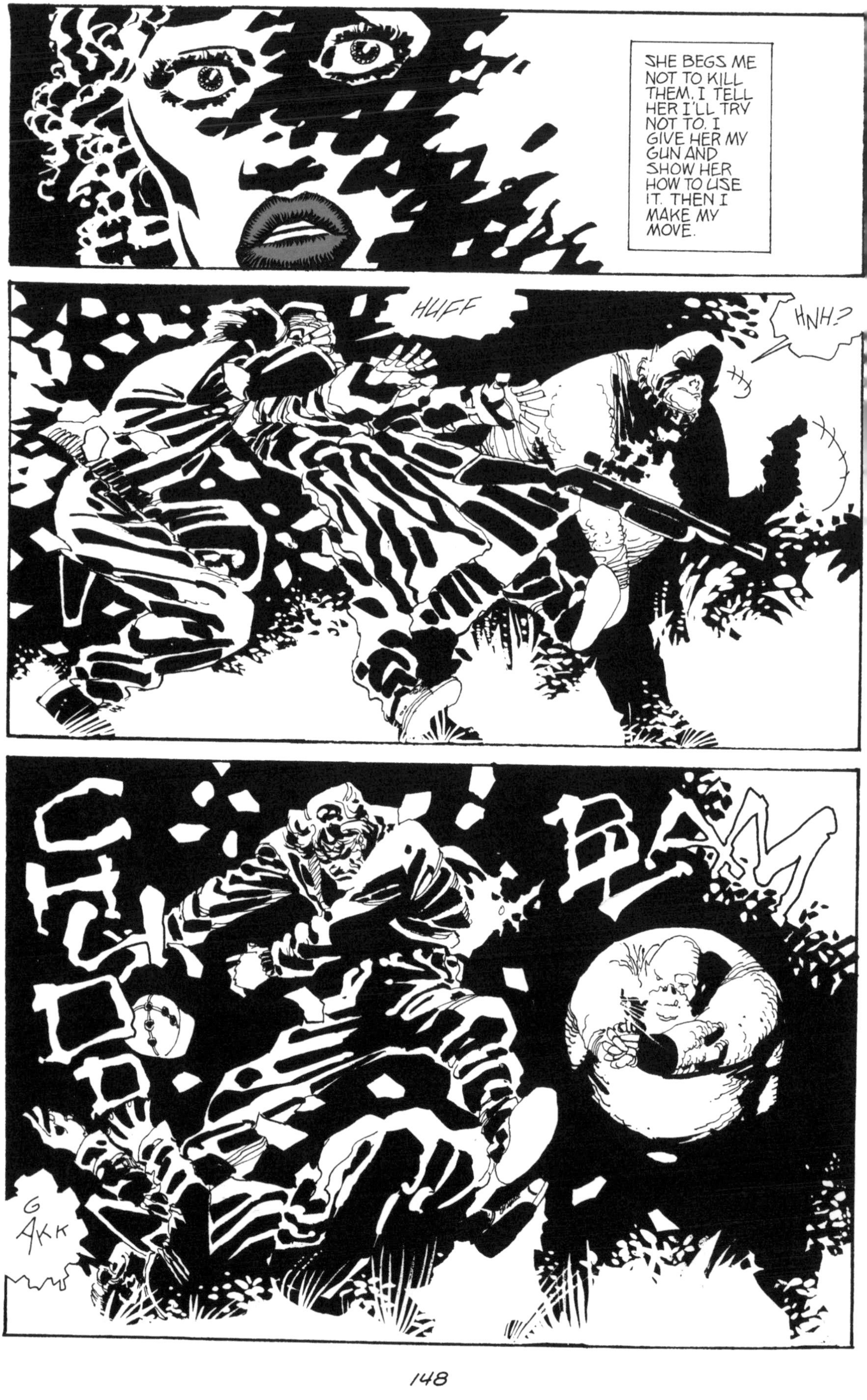
SHE BEGS ME NOT TO KILL THEM. I TELL HER I'LL TRY NOT TO. I GIVE HER MY GUN AND SHOW HER HOW TO USE IT. THEN I MAKE MY MOVE.
HUFF
HNH?
BAM
G AKK

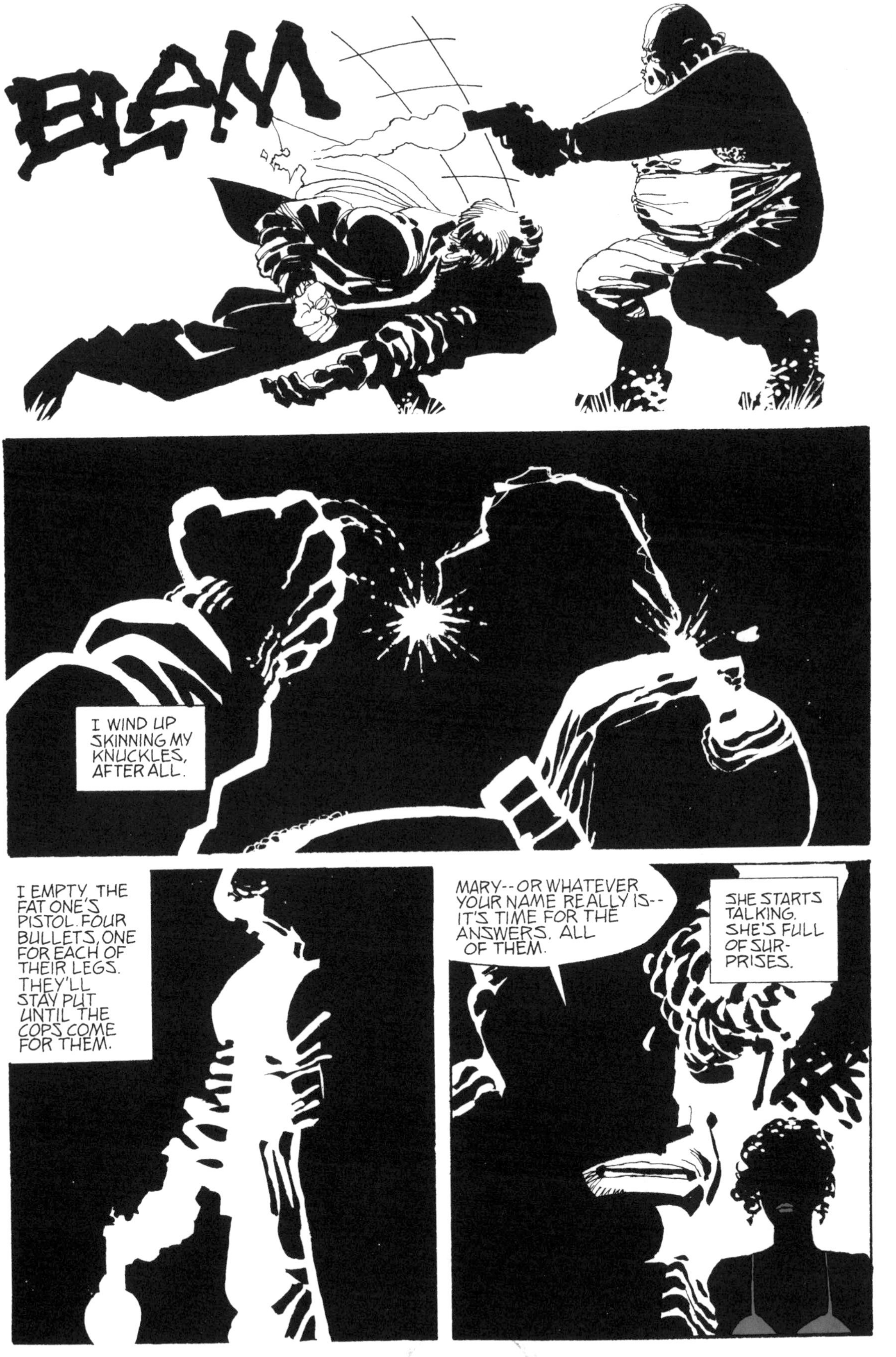
BLAM
I WIND UP SKINNING MY KNUCKLES, AFTER ALL.
I EMPTY THE FAT ONE'S PISTOL. FOUR BULLETS, ONE FOR EACH OF THEIR LEGS. THEY'LL STAY PUT UNTIL THE COPS COME FOR THEM.
MARY--OR WHATEVER YOUR NAME REALLY IS--IT'S TIME FOR THE ANSWERS. ALL OF THEM.
SHE STARTS TALKING. SHE'S FULL OF SURPRISES.

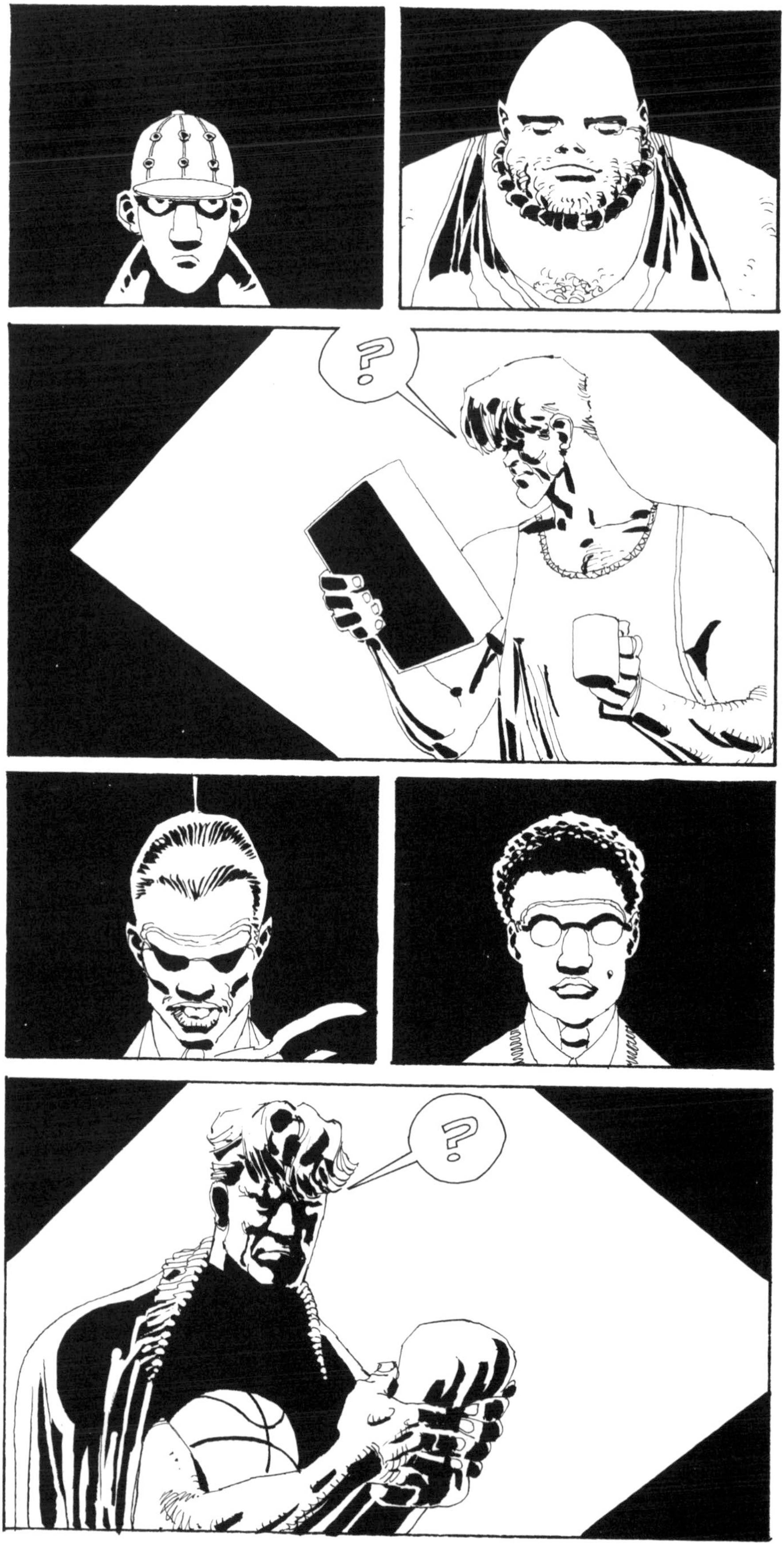

?
?

THE *ANSWERS.* SOME OF THEM COME WITH THE MORNING *PAPER.*

THE GOONS TURN OUT TO BE *DOUGLAS KLUMP* AND *BURT SHLUBB,* A PAIR OF LOW-RENT *HIT MEN* WHO GO BY THE NAMES OF *"FAT MAN AND LITTLE BOY."*

I'M ON MY SECOND CUP OF COFFEE WHEN A *PACKAGE* ARRIVES. BEING OFFICIALLY *DEAD,* I'M ALWAYS SURPRISED WHEN I GET *MAIL.*

FARGO SHIPPED IT OFF TO ME BEFORE THEY GOT TO HIM. IT'S *EVIDENCE.*

MY OLD PAL WAS WORKING WITH PRIVATE EYE *BERNARD ZIMMER*--

--ON A *DRUG TRAFFICKING EXPOSE* THAT SENDS *SHIVERS* DOWN THE SPINES OF THE *MAYOR* AND THE *DISTRICT ATTORNEY* AND SENDS BOSS *WALLENQUIST'S* LIEUTENANTS SCRAMBLING TO FIND SOMEBODY TO PIN IT ON.

A FEW DAYS LATER I'M JUST BACK FROM A DECENT WORKOUT AND I FIND *ANOTHER* PACKAGE.

FROM *MARY,* THIS TIME.

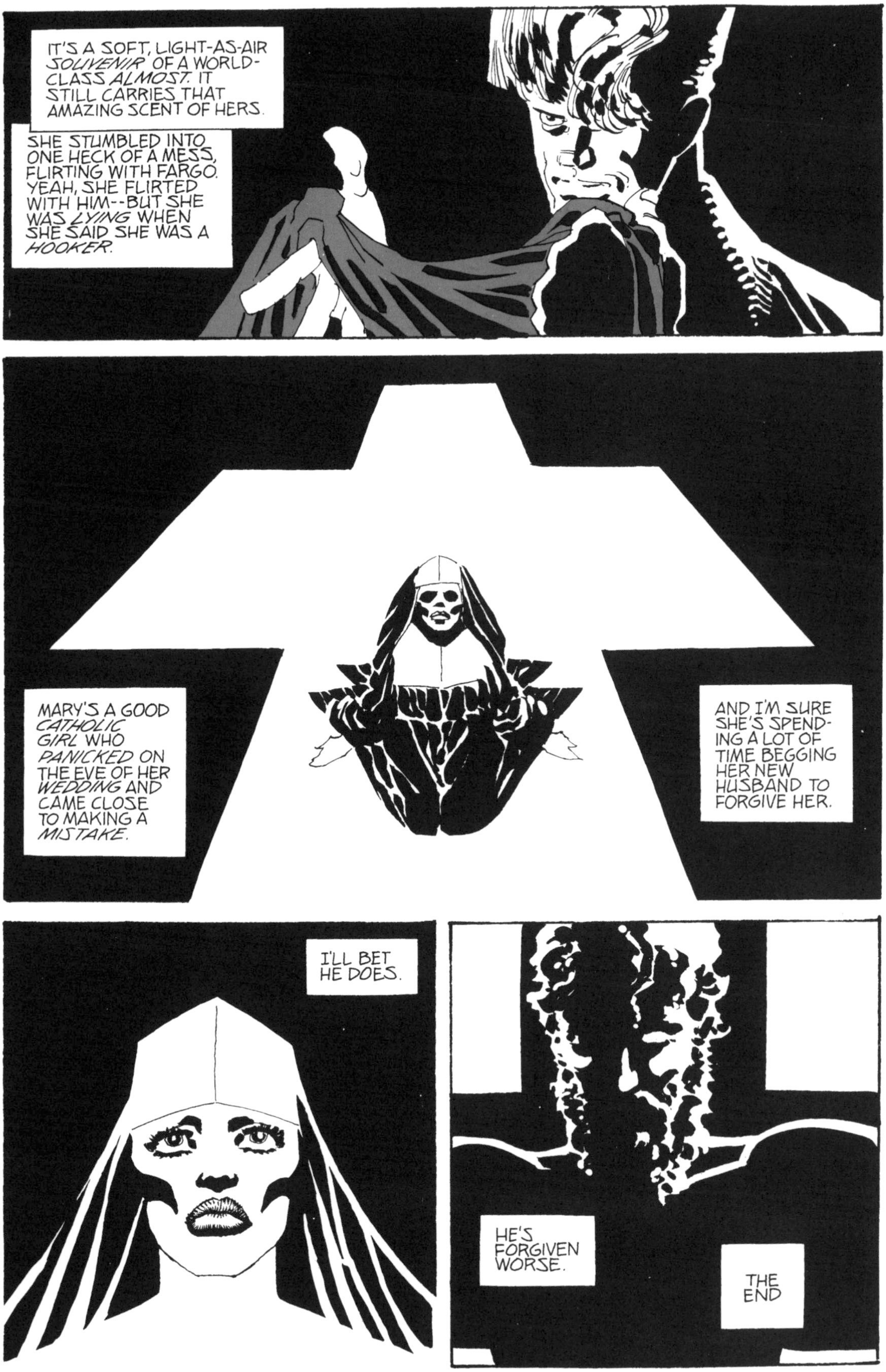
IT'S A SOFT, LIGHT-AS-AIR SOUVENIR OF A WORLD-CLASS ALMOST. IT STILL CARRIES THAT AMAZING SCENT OF HERS.
SHE STUMBLED INTO ONE HECK OF A MESS, FLIRTING WITH FARGO. YEAH, SHE FLIRTED WITH HIM--BUT SHE WAS LYING WHEN SHE SAID SHE WAS A HOOKER.
MARY'S A GOOD CATHOLIC GIRL WHO PANICKED ON THE EVE OF HER WEDDING AND CAME CLOSE TO MAKING A MISTAKE.
AND I'M SURE SHE'S SPENDING A LOT OF TIME BEGGING HER NEW HUSBAND TO FORGIVE HER.
I'LL BET HE DOES.
HE'S FORGIVEN WORSE.
THE END

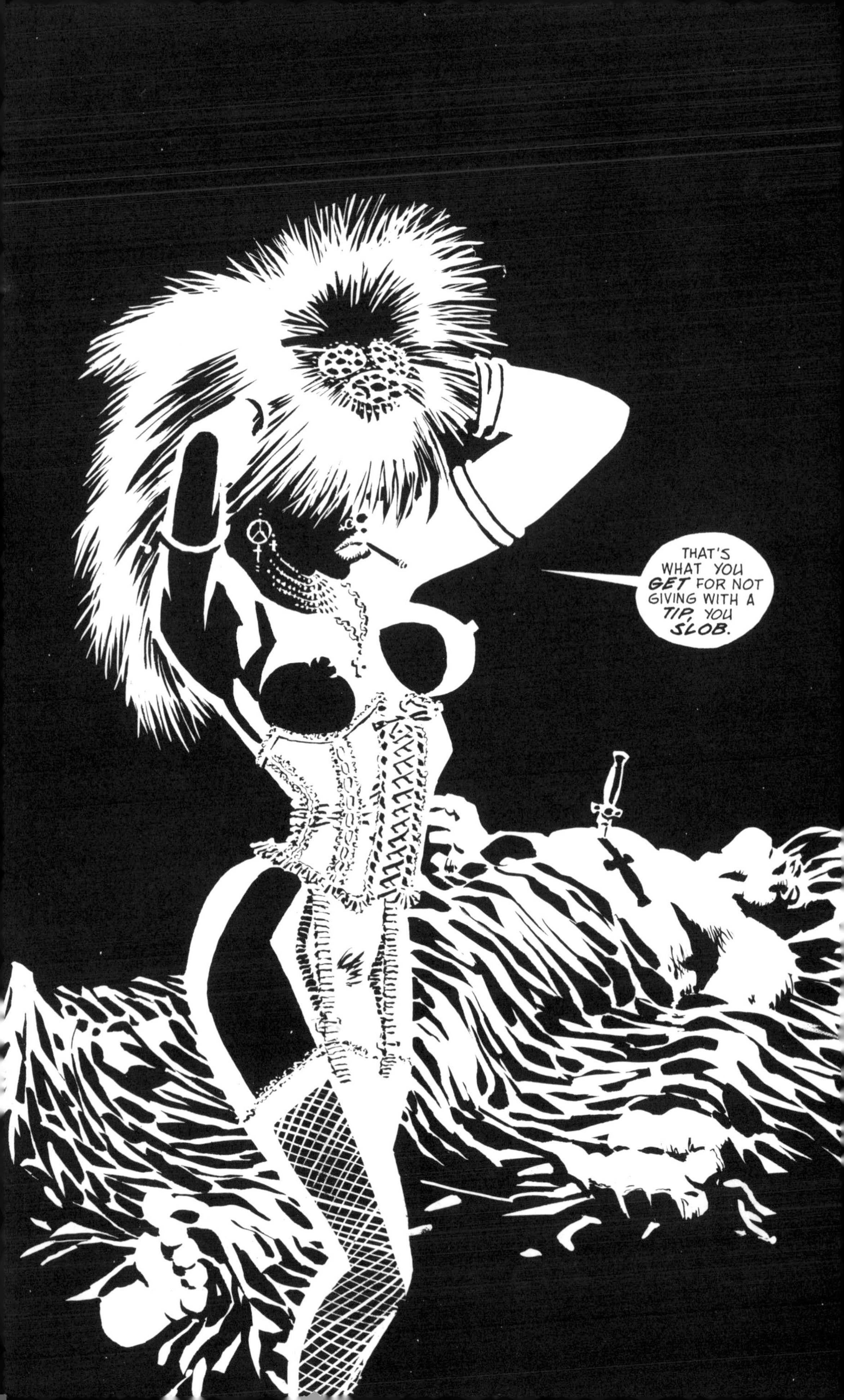
THAT'S WHAT YOU GET FOR NOT GIVING WITH A TIP, YOU SLOB.

COVER GALLERY

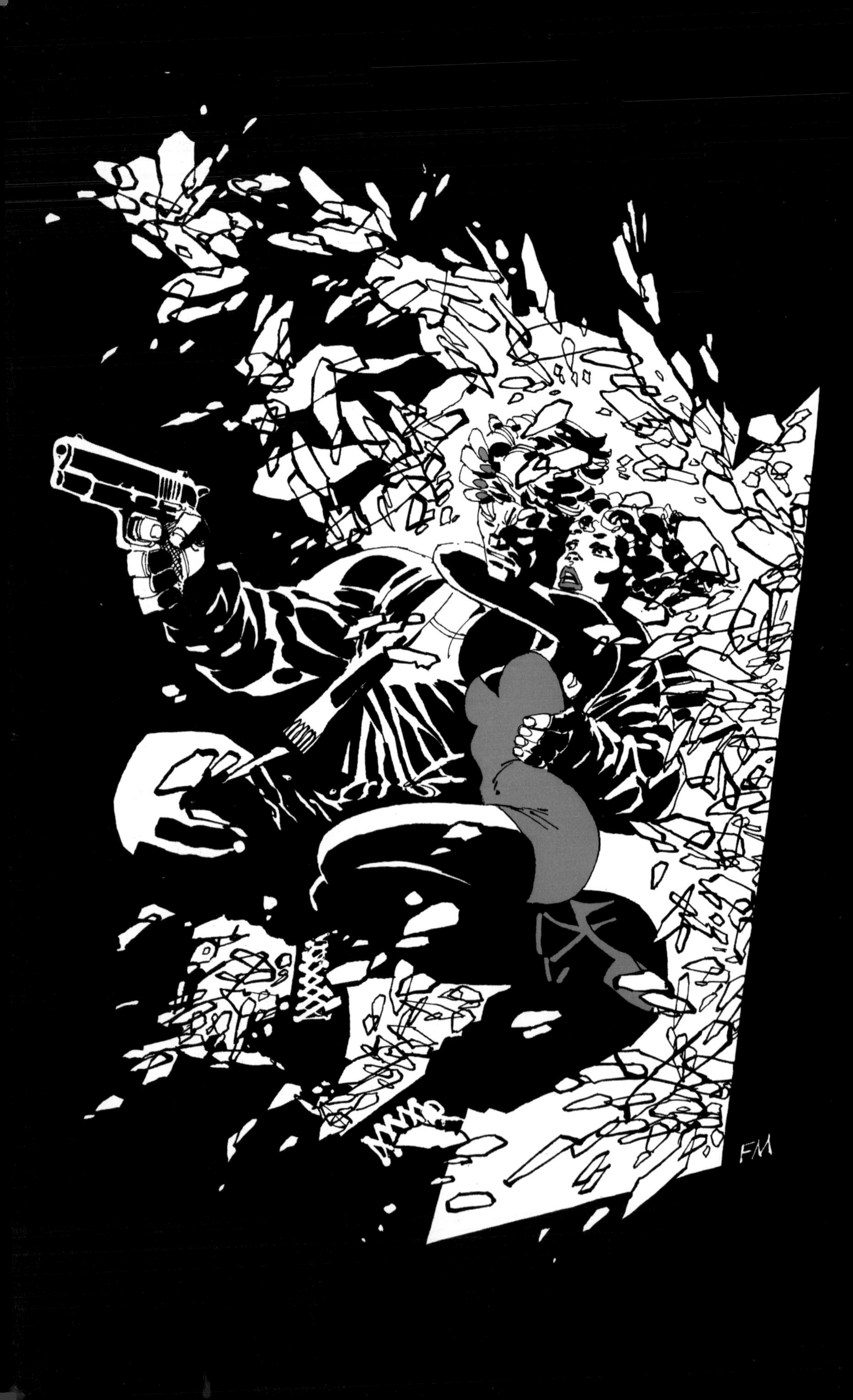

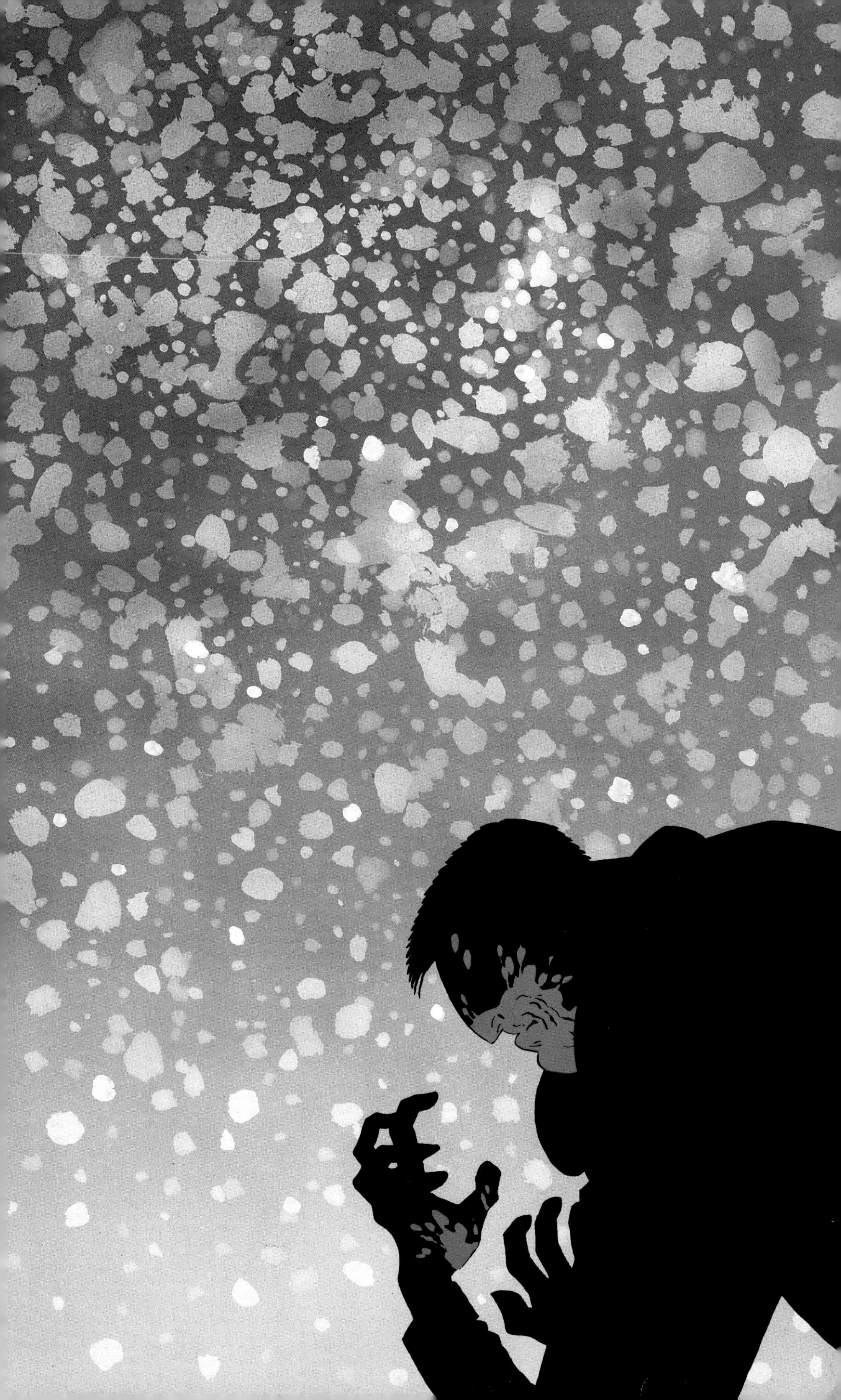

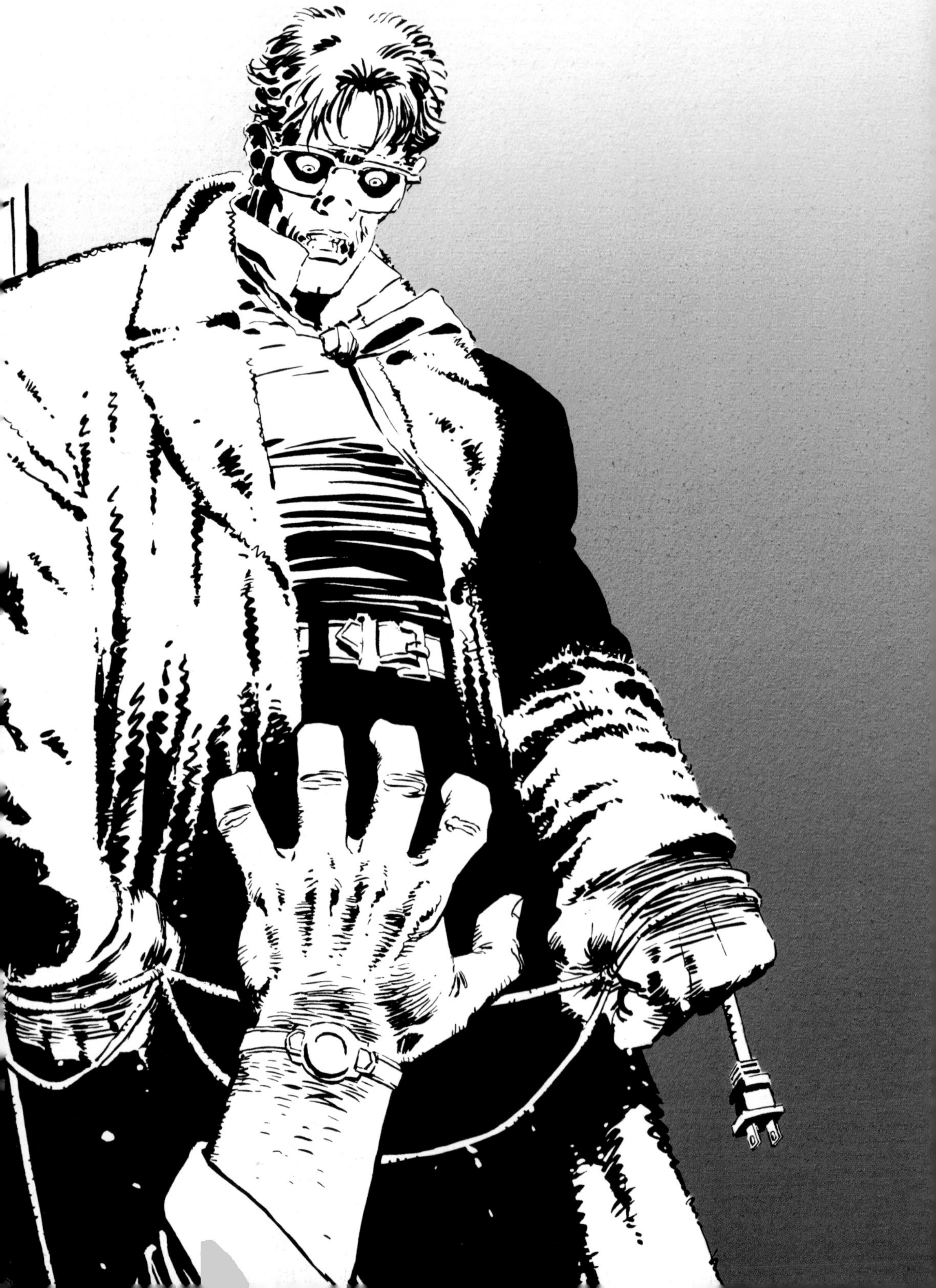

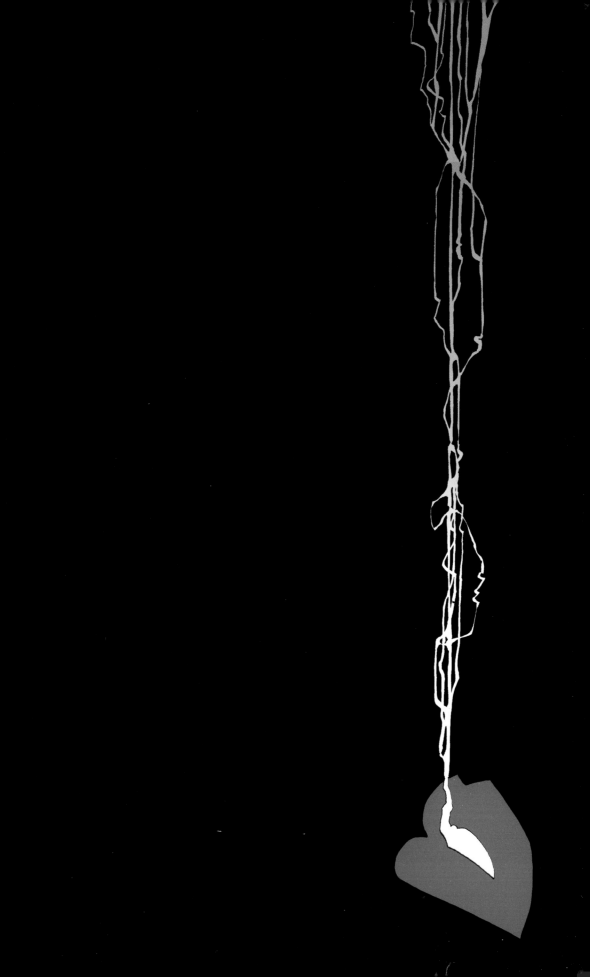

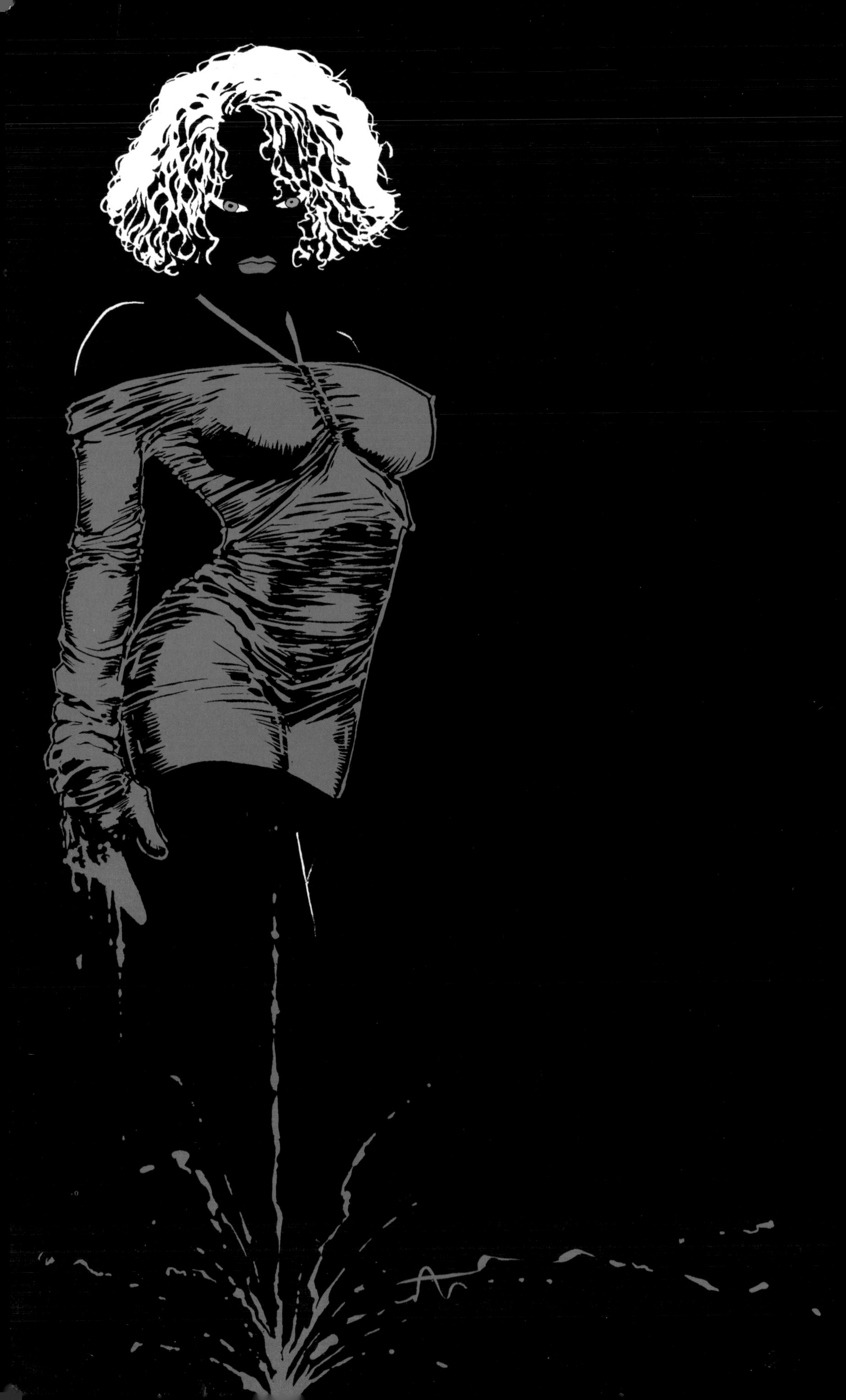

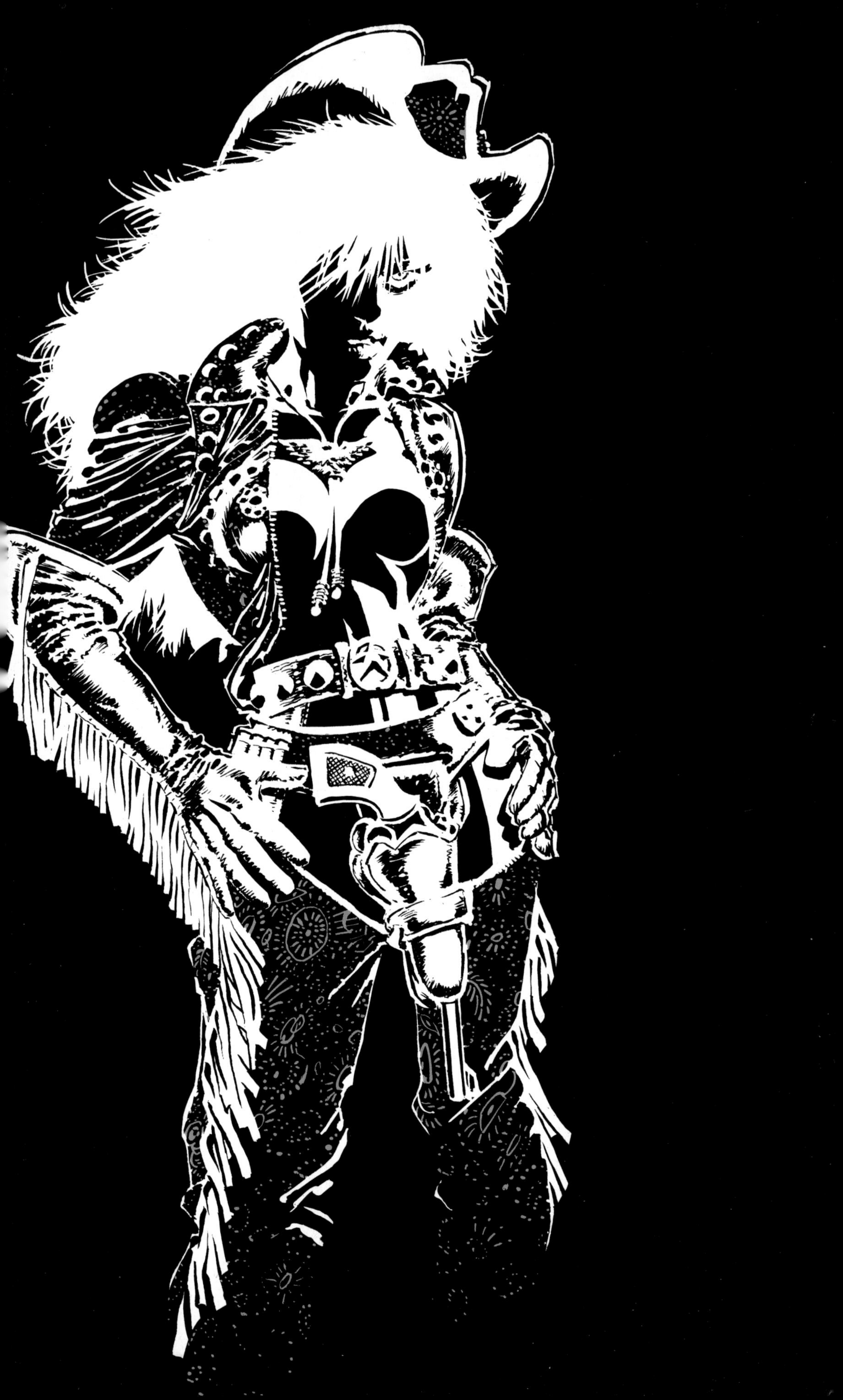

YARNS FROM SIN CITY